THE MOON THAT FELL FROM HEAVEN

N.L. HOLMES

The Moon That Fell from Heaven

Red Adept Publishing, LLC

104 Bugenfield Court

Garner, NC 27529

https://RedAdeptPublishing.com/

For my husband

Chapter 1

Ehli-nikkalu told herself she had many reasons to be proud and happy. She was a princess—in fact, the eldest princess, the Great Lady—of mighty Hatti Land. As of seven years ago, she had been the king's wife of the rich little maritime state of Ugarit, her father's vassal. She was thirty-five years old and healthy. And yet, frankly, she was miserable.

Every time she thought about her lot, she wanted to gnash her teeth. Even though she had been educated to sit on the throne beside her husband and help him formulate policies, she had been reduced to ceremonial roles. *That's what a Hittite princess is trained to do—be a coruler.* Who knew if she might not find herself *tawananna* or whatever the local equivalent was in the country where she married? And maybe someday she, Ehli-nikkalu, would be elevated to that role in Ugarit. But for now, her mother-in-law held the post, and Sharryelli was only three years older than Ehli-nikkalu herself. It would be a race to see who died first. Sharryelli would delight in living to a doddering old age just to thwart the ambitions of her son's wife.

More galling still, Ehli-nikkalu's husband, King Niqmaddu, held her in contempt despite her higher rank. He had left word—sent a slave to tell her, if you please—that he was coming to talk to her, and so she had to wait, as if every word from his mouth were a priceless gem. Her face blazed with fury and humiliation at the thought of him. *He complains that I've borne him no children, but how many times has he deigned to grace my bed, the hypocritical snake?*

She fought down her anger. It wouldn't do to let Niqmaddu know how much his disdain ate into her equanimity. Ehli-nikkalu prided herself on her self-control. Her father was famous for never breaking his calm, and she was determined to follow his example. To do otherwise would be to surrender, to submit to her husband's superiority. And he was not superior, by all the gods.

The door clicked, and she looked up at the panel as it opened quickly, without a "May I?" or an "Are you decent?" It was the king.

They faced each other, and the hostility filled the air like smoke from tinder that had caught—not yet a blaze but smoldering. She backed against the heavy table, as if to find a defensible position, and lifted her nose slightly. *The armor of dignity.* The king said nothing, just stood there with his swaggering good looks, and the corner of his mouth began to curl, a caustic smile. His black eyes seemed to penetrate her. He knew exactly what she was thinking, she suspected—it cost her considerable effort not to snarl "What do you want?"—and he, too, had his pose of supremacy to maintain. Ehli-nikkalu found her face growing hotter and hotter.

Still biting her tongue, she forced herself to bow, infusing it with as much sarcasm as a humble gesture could bear.

"Well. We're in a respectful mood this evening, are we?" Niqmaddu asked, approaching. But then he passed by her without a look, as if she didn't exist, and took up a seat in the heavy carved chair. He leaned back and stretched out his legs. "I have something to tell you, and I didn't want anyone else to hear me."

"You do me too much honor, my lord."

The king smiled coldly. "Your father's emissary is making a visit in a few weeks, and I just wanted to make it clear that you need to be a loyal queen of Ugarit. No telling tales, no whining about how everybody is cruel to you. Understood?"

"Perfectly," she said. "I lie."

Niqmaddu's eyes narrowed, and he said pointedly, "But no one *is* cruel to you, you know. It's all a story you've told yourself to feel above us. Have I ever struck you? Are you lacking for clothes or jewels or food? No." He tilted his head as if to consider her from another angle. "Have I ever called you barren in public?"

She clenched her fists in the folds of her skirts, the better to control some menacing gesture she might regret. "It's my understanding that a woman cannot conceive without the intervention of a man, my lord. Since you so rarely condescend to visit my bed, it isn't much wonder that I haven't given you an heir."

Niqmaddu laughed. "I guess I must admit my capacity for self-sacrifice has its limits. Couching with you, my dear, has all the charm of tupping a hedgehog. You are very sharp—and I don't just mean your tongue."

Ehli-nikkalu expelled a carefully controlled breath through her nose. She knew she wasn't beautiful. She was tall and thin and angular, with a long, equine face—very much her father's daughter. It was a measure of her husband's shallowness that he hurled this at her so often. *So that he can blame me for his lack of a first-rank son.* So that, perhaps, he could express his contempt for his suzerain, the Great King of Hatti, through her own pierced self-confidence.

"Well, that's neither here nor there. We don't have to love each other. Fortunately, I have another wife if I want children. Pu-haddu has provided me with the heir you seem unable to manage, even if her rank is lower than yours. But then, whose rank *isn't* lower than yours, the Great Lady, with her ancient birth and imperial aura? I just want you to understand that if you enter the emissary's presence, you will mind your manners, or there will be consequences." He fixed her with a frigid smile that had in it much menace.

"I will behave myself with appropriate dignity," she said through clenched teeth. "I suppose you will inform him of all the disloyal overtures you're making toward Mizri."

Suddenly his cool facade dropped away, and he sprang to his feet with a snarl. "What would you know about my policies? All you do is sew." He seemed to recover his aplomb and said more calmly, "You have a reputation for being overzealous, my queen. Who is going to believe yet another of your wild-eyed accusations? Can you offer any evidence? I think not."

She smirked at him, letting him wonder what evidence she could offer. His discomfiture pleased her. It was so rare that she could ruffle his air of indifference. Niqmaddu strode past her to the door, and she noticed a small clay tablet had dropped from his sash into the cushioned seat of his chair.

She dragged her eyes away from it, burying her face in a deep bow. "I thank my lord husband for his gracious visit."

He shot her a dark look and let himself out the door. Ehli-nikkalu listened until his footsteps died away through the outer chamber and down the corridor. Then, much as she wanted to scream and slam something breakable to the floor, she tiptoed to the chair and, heart pounding, lifted the tablet.

It was in Akkadian, she saw, the formal diplomatic language that united every kingdom. *Something to or from a foreigner, then. Not just a billet-doux.*

Although Ehli-nikkalu had a degree of literacy in the simplified script of Ugarit, this was written in a system that required a lifetime to learn and was hence inaccessible to all but a small class of professional scribes. She pressed the tablet to her heart and stared into space, thinking hard. *Who can I find to translate it? Who can I trust?* Her secretary might or might not be sober at this hour, but at least she felt he was loyal.

"Pidaya," she called to her handmaid, who was spinning in the antechamber. "Go find Hattatamu. I need to see him immediately, even if he's drunk."

The slave nodded and backed from the room, and Ehli-nikkalu heard her rapid footsteps fade away. The queen turned on her heel and began to pace up and down, her nerves so taut she was almost twitching. What did this letter mean? It might be nothing, or it might be the evidence she needed to prove her husband was betraying Hatti Land behind everyone's back.

Finally, she sank into her chair and spread her hands on her thighs. It seemed an age later that a knock on the door proclaimed the presence of Hattatamu. As she had feared, he was unsteady on his feet, but at least he could stand. *The poor fellow,* she thought. *Nobody else would keep him in their service. And where would a man his age go then to find work?* But it made her correspondence trying.

"My lady wishes to dictate something?" the secretary asked in a thick-tongued slur.

An attempt at a bow ended in a stumble, and the queen herded him to a chair in front of her big table, setting a damp, blank tablet and a stylus before him. He reeked of wine and sweat. He had stopped taking care of himself again, she observed with pity.

"Read this letter to me, Hattatamu, and keep your voice down."

Having squinted at the tablet then adjusted its distance from his eyes, he started to read aloud words that meant nothing to her. He looked up apologetically. "It's in Akkadian."

"I know. I know. Translate it. Can't you do that?" Ehli-nikkalu's flesh seemed to crawl with urgency. She could have shaken the secretary in frustration.

"In response to your inquiry," he began, stammering though an experienced translator for all that. "We will ready the ships and meet you at Gubla by the end of the month, as we decided before. See to it that the soldiers you promised are here by New Year's Day. The Great King's viceroy will be presiding, and that would be an appropriate time to seize the port, while everyone is in the courtyard for the ceremonies. Your master will find he has many loyal subjects already in the city, for the king of Hatti's exactions fall heavily on our people, especially the merchants who form our ruling class. Don't correspond again unless it is necessary. Niqmaddu son of Ibi-ranu." Hattatamu looked up at her, his red-rimmed eyes bleary. "The king's seal is set at the end, my lady."

The hair stood up on Ehli-nikkalu's neck. This was more than proof—it was damnation. "My father must know of this at once!" she murmured in a voice trembling with excitement. "Niqmaddu is getting ready to sell the city to Mizri! Who else would be strong enough to stand up to us like that?"

She advanced on her secretary and seized him by the shoulders. "You must write a letter to my father then take it and *this vile thing* to Rab-ilu."

Rab-ilu was an emissary, the only man in the chancery she was sure she could trust. He was incorruptible—he alone among the lords of Ugarit who groveled before the king and his mother.

"Yes, my lady," Hattatamu said uncertainly, fumbling in his sash for his writing tools.

Ehli-nikkalu pushed them toward him over the tabletop. Wine fumes enveloped her. She held her breath until she had withdrawn from his proximity, and it was all she could do not to make a sour expression.

"Take dictation, Hattatamu: 'My Sun and Father, I greet you and pray that all is well with you and our land. Alas, all is not well in Ugarit. The king has made concrete overtures to Mizri to overthrow your rule—'" She paused. *How to make this pressing?* "'With violence. I attach for you the very letter which Niqmaddu intended to send to his collaborators across the border. May it please you to act swiftly and forcefully, my dear father. Your Loving Daughter' and so forth. Do you have all that?"

Hattatamu, who seemed to be rubbing out and rewriting quite a lot, his mouth hanging open, finally looked up from the tablet and replied, "Yes, my lady."

She thrust at him the tablet the king had left behind, and when he seemed at a loss for what to do with it, she stuffed the two patties of clay into his sash. "Be careful with this. It's still damp, and you don't want to rub anything off. Take them to Rab-ilu. You know where he lives."

He nodded, struggling for the words to answer.

"Then go. Go. Waste no time. We must have this on the road to Hatti before the king realizes he's lost it." Ehli-nikkalu watched him get unsteadily to his feet, and fear and irritation got the better of her control. "By all the gods, Hattatamu. What use are you, you hopeless drunk? After all I've done for you," she cried in exasperation. Then she made her tone milder. "Can you walk? Can you perhaps run? This is urgent. Urgent."

He bowed, one hand steadying himself against the table, and departed with a suspiciously careful tread. As he passed into the darkness of the vestibule, Ehli-nikkalu clutched her head, half mad with frustration. The handmaids, whom she had banished to the outer chamber with their spinning, looked up, curious, but she hastily closed the door in their faces. They were all meddlers and, no doubt, spies for Sharryelli.

Crackling with nerves, the queen parted the shutters and stared out the window into the night garden, where a full moon was rising over the wing of the palace opposite, bathing it in a bleached brightness. Good. Hattatamu needed all the light he could get. *The wretched creature,* she thought, fighting off hopelessness. *Please to the gods he can make it to Rab-ilu's house without falling down drunk in the street somewhere.* How infuriating to have to lean on such a frail reed for a matter of such importance. But that was her life. Niqmaddu could say it was all in her mind, but she had been surrounded by disloyal bearers of tales until there was no one left for her to confide in but these incompetents. She was isolated, alone. *And that,* she pronounced bitterly, *is cruelty.*

All at once, she saw Hattatamu's unsteady silhouette tottering through the garden on the way to the service exit. Except there was no exit from the garden other than the two that led back into the palace. *Dear gods, he's taken a wrong turn. This will cost him precious time.*

The shadows of palm fronds danced on the path until even she might have stumbled, unsure of what was darkness and what was a rut. Then another man's shadowy form stepped out before the secretary. They seemed to exchange some words. She heard a peal of deep laughter. *Oh, no. It's Shipti-ba'al, the king's brother-in-law.* She saw Shipti-ba'al gesture widely then poke a finger at Hattatamu's chest. *What are they talking about? I hope Hattatamu has the judgment to keep quiet about his mission.* Her stomach clenched with sudden anxiety. *Don't let Shipti-ba'al invite Hattatamu for a drink somewhere.*

But after a moment, the two figures separated. Shipti-ba'al moved off toward the interior of the palace, while Hattatamu was soon lost in the shadow of the garden wall. He would have to enter through the garden kiosk then follow the service passage to the gate. Ehli-nikkalu murmured a prayer. If the secretary didn't get through to Rab-ilu with her message and Niqmaddu found out what she was up to, her life would become even more of a misery.

A faint sound of a gate being unbarred reached her through the hush of the night air. Then silence. Hattatamu had at least made his way out into the street. The letters were on their way.

Amaya was combing out her hair, preparing for bed, when she heard a knock at the door. Since her mother's death, she had become the mistress of the house for her father and little brother and sister. It was her duty to greet and offer hospitality to any who might visit, no matter the hour.

The knock came again, louder and more insistent. Footsteps thudded from the back of the house, marking the approach of Karranu, the steward. Amaya hastily knotted her hair into a braid and pinned her cap back on. She needed to see to this. Karranu would have to ask her what to do anyway. Having just arrived after a grueling two weeks on the road, Papa was asleep and not to be disturbed.

Amaya slipped on her shoes and descended the stairs as quietly as possible. Karranu, an oil lamp in his hand, was standing in the open doorway, his broad back to her. "Do you know what time it is, man?" he said to whoever stood in the street outside, his voice sharp with annoyance and still pasty with sleep. "Give me the letters, and I'll pass them to Lord Rab-ilu in the morning."

"Who is it, Karranu?" Amaya called.

The steward turned to her, exasperated. "It's some fellow who says he's the queen's secretary. He says he has a message that has to go off to Hatti tonight. Frankly, I think he's just having drunken delusions, my lady."

Amaya swept him aside. A heavy middle-aged man with red cheeks stood swaying in the dark shadow of the house against the moonlit brightness of the wall across the street. "Enter our house, friend. Can I offer you some... some dates?" She had a feeling he didn't need anything else to drink. Turning to the slave, she said quietly, "That's all, Karranu. I can take care of this."

Something in Amaya wondered if it were proper for an eighteen-year-old girl to receive an unknown man at night like this, but she had the duties of an adult now. And this fellow didn't seem like he was in much shape for aggression. She seated him and brought a dish of dates. *If I were a good hostess, I'd wake one of the girls and have her wash his feet.* But she really just wanted him to conclude his business and go so she could get back to bed.

She seated herself across the table from him. "Now, tell me who you are and what brings you here at such an hour."

"I am the young queen's secretary, my lady," he said, extending toward her two clay tablets he produced from his belt with a trembling hand. "She has an urgent letter for the Great King in Hattusha. It has to get out tonight." As if he realized she might not trust that he was who he said he was, the man pointed to a bar of raised images at the end of one of the documents. "See? There's Lady Ehli-nikkalu's seal."

Amaya stared at him in disbelief. "Tonight? There's no way my father can take it tonight. He's just returned from the northern frontier and needs to sleep first. Don't worry. I'll see to it that he delivers this as soon as he recovers from the journey." She rose.

But the man, looking panicked, reached out a hand to hold her back. "Oh, my lady, the queen says it's urgent. It has to go out right away, before the king realizes he lost it."

What's this all about? Amaya asked herself, uneasy. She stood in perplexed silence for a moment, staring at the two tablets and wondering what she should do. *Mother, what would you do if* you *were you receiving this man?* "Very well. Wait here, and I'll see if my father wants to talk to you."

She turned and made her way up the stairs, again on tiptoe so as not to waken the children. She hesitated before her father's door. The corridor was faintly lit from the full moon shining through the open door of her own room, and her hands looked as white as bone. She knocked.

At first there was silence, then a growl that might have been "Who's there?"

"Father," she whispered. "There's a man here to see you from the queen. He has a message to go to the Great King."

After a moment, Rab-ilu opened the door and stared blearily down at his daughter, still half-asleep. His hair stood out in all directions. "Have him leave the message. I'll take it in the next few days."

"He says it's urgent, that it has to go out tonight—"

"Tonight?" he cried then lowered his voice. "What sort of message is this?"

"He said it has to be en route before the king finds out he's lost it." Amaya felt almost ashamed of herself, rousing her weary father for such a lunatic mission. But he could make his own judgment.

With a sigh, he ushered her ahead of him and started down the stairs in his bare feet. By the light of the guttering lamp, he saw the secretary slumped over on the table, asleep. "Just what I'd like to be doing," Rab-ilu commented dryly.

Amaya's father reached out a hand to the fresher of the two tablets and drew it toward the light to read. His face grew grave. He took up the second tablet and, a moment later, heaved a reluctant sigh. "He's right. These must go now."

"Right now? Oh, Father, how can you? You just got back and haven't had even a night's sleep." Amaya put a hand against his chest as if to stop him physically.

"I can sleep somewhere on the way, my love, but these letters must be out of Ugarit by daybreak." Rab-ilu turned and pounded up the stairs, where he left her in the hallway as he disappeared into his room.

Amaya was so disappointed she felt tears prickle in her nose. For her father's sake, she didn't want him to go so soon—but also for her own. It was lonely work being a parent and a householder all by herself when she was scarcely more than a girl. She and the children hadn't seen him for weeks, and now, without so much as a day with the family, he was off once more for over a month. Hattusha, their suzerain's capital, was weeks away.

Don't go, she pleaded silently. *Please don't leave us again.*

But Rab-ilu reappeared in the doorway, dressed, a sword at his hip and his traveling basket in hand. He put his arm around her shoulders and bent to give her a quick kiss. Then, as if he, too, realized how long it might be before he saw his daughter again, he took her in his arms and held her tightly against his chest for a moment. "I'm sorry, little girl," he whispered. "Tell the children where I've gone. I don't know what I'd do without you."

She dashed away her tears and tried bravely to smile. "I'll take care of everything until you're home, Father. The slaves are getting to the point where they'll actually obey me."

He clattered down the stairs to find the queen's secretary snoring on his arms folded over the table. "Come on, old man. Time for you to go home." Rab-ilu lifted him to his feet and helped him on his unsteady and uncomprehending way to the entrance. Amaya threw open the door, and her father pushed the secretary gently out into the street. "Go home and sleep this off, Hattatamu."

Turning back to his daughter, he said, "Be brave, Amaya. I love you." Then he was gone into the night, heading for the stable and his chariot, and Amaya was left staring at the empty doorway and the small orange glow of the lamp's flame on the pavement.

Author Note: Ugarit, a vassal state of Hatti, should be proud to have a Hittite princess. But not so. A queen who doesn't bear an heir is a liability. Ehli-nikkalu is a real person, as are the other major characters in this book, which takes place in Syria in 1213 BCE.

Niqmaddu is the grandson of the assassinated king Ammishtamru from The Queen's Dog. *He did flirt with Egyptian overlordship.*

Chapter 2

Eventually, she closed and barred the panel. She was fully awake now, but there wasn't enough oil left in the lamp to finish out the night with her spinning, so she drifted up the stairs, still populated as they were with the memory of her father's hurried footsteps. The children were sleeping. She felt her way toward her room through the dark corridor and gave a smothered yip of pain as she stepped on something hard. Amaya knelt and groped around until she found the offending object. It was her father's seal stone, a small roller of hard agate carved with his name and some images of gods, threaded on a leather cord.

She clapped a hand to her mouth in horror. "This must have fallen from his sash," she murmured. But he would need it; it was proof of his identity. *What if they won't even let him into the Hittite capital without it?*

Mother, what should I do? She stood frozen in indecision for a moment then galloped back downstairs. "Karranu!" she called aloud, hoping fervently he hadn't fallen asleep again.

In a moment, the steward emerged from the slave quarters, rubbing his eyes. He was half standing on top of his shoes, which had doubled over at the heel in his haste to slide them on. "What is it, mistress?"

"I must take Father his seal," she said, trying to control the anxiety in her voice. "Come with me."

"Now?" He scratched his face dubiously.

Amaya's voice was sharp with fear. "Yes, now. Are you going to obey me or not?"

He muttered something that seemed to be "Yes, mistress" and slipped the shoes up over his heels.

Amaya grabbed the lamp, and the two of them hurled themselves out the door into the silent street.

"Which way did the master go, do you know?" Karranu whispered.

"He must have headed for the east gate, which leads to the road north. If we hurry and take back alleys, we may be able to catch him before he's left the city. They'll have to unbar for him, and he may not even be able to get out without his seal." Amaya walked as fast as she could until she was breathless, but even so, the blocks seemed to pass at a dream's resinous pace. *We'll never get to him in time. Dear Yarikh, the traveler, help me. Help me.*

Above them, Yarikh, the moon, burned with a cold, fierce light that set their shadows skittering across every intersection until they plunged back into the darkness of the crowded houses. The tiny flame of the lamp guttered and died, but it hadn't helped them anyway. Amaya dropped it in the street, where it smashed upon the paving stones with a sound like an explosion in the cricket-laced silence of the summer night. She cringed. Everything seemed somehow ominous to her. The girl pulled Karranu down a small alley that she thought would cut some time off their journey, but it was completely dark. She felt garbage squish and slide beneath her feet.

At last, the houses fell back, and the alley opened out into a square that she recognized. *The gate isn't far away. We have to hurry.* In fact, she could already hear the approaching clop of horses and a rumble of wheels over the pavement. At this hour, it was only likely to be her father. She began to run, Karranu at her back, heaving with exhaustion. *So close. Can I intercept him? Can I make myself heard over the noise of the chariot?* She saw ahead in the brightly lit plaza the car and horses, her father's back erect, his head alert. The team moved at a trot, which was all Rab-ilu would have dared within the city walls, no doubt. *We can catch him.*

She had opened her mouth to call out when two dark figures darted from the shadows and rushed toward her father. One of the men seized the horses' bridles, and the other leaped upon the box of the chariot. A third appeared alongside them and cut the reins.

"What's going on?" she stammered breathlessly. "What's happening?"

She was too surprised to react. It was like a nightmare, where she wanted to run but her legs wouldn't move. At her side, Karranu goggled, equally helpless.

At last, she lurched toward the chariot and screamed, "Father! Father!"

Rab-ilu looked around as the attacker wrestled him backward. "Amaya!" he cried in horror. "Run!"

The plunging horses and the dark-clad figures struggling in the setting moonlight had the flat, jerky look of leather stick-puppets. Her father writhed to free his arms, managing to get his sword out of its sheath. But the man who had cut the reins jumped into the box. Amaya saw his arm pump forward and back and the flash of metal. Rab-ilu arched then sagged to the floor, his sword dropping from his grasp. With a clang, it hit the pavement. Her father shot her one last beseeching look, his eyes glittering in the moonlight. "Run, my love..." he gasped, clinging to the rail of the box. Then the third man dragged him from the box into the street, where the other two fell on him brutally.

Amaya gave out a high-pitched, inarticulate noise of terror and denial. The men turned as one to fix their gazes on her and the petrified steward. Then they ran toward her. She spun and took off like a frightened rabbit into the darkness.

Through the night-veiled backstreets she pounded, Karranu thudding at her heels. She could hear his breaths dragging desperately in his throat. Yet the assassins were not far behind and were fast closing the distance. She dodged suddenly down a side street, hoping they wouldn't notice she had turned. But a quick glance over her shoulder revealed the shadow pursuers still in her wake.

Amaya was reaching her limit, her heart hammering, her breath rasping in her chest. The men were getting closer and closer, their feet thudding tirelessly. Her own footsteps began to drag until she feared she would stumble and fall.

A scream made her turn. The men had reached Karranu. With a whimper, he sank into the street, a knife projecting from his back. *This is the end.* Amaya gasped silently. But faithful Karranu had fallen across the alley and dragged down one of his attackers as he went, and it cost her pursuers a moment's delay to pull out the blade and haul him aside.

By that time, she had whipped around a corner, and she began to pound desperately on a door. Almost immediately, the door swung open a space. Amaya hurled herself into the dark interior, and the door shut behind her.

She stood there on her trembling legs, leaning against the wall, panting, her heart throbbing in her throat, too relieved to wonder where she was.

Outside the door, muffled by the heavy wood, she heard men's voices. "Where'd the little vixen go?"

"She's probably a witch. She just vanished."

But a third man with a better-educated voice said dryly, "She slid into one of these houses, you fools. Start knocking on the doors."

Amaya cringed against the plaster wall, expecting the worst. She heard the dreaded knock, and from the darkness of the room stepped an older woman, her hair in a tousled braid. She shot the girl a sharp look, and Amaya realized she must have been standing there all along. The woman opened the panel and set her hands on her broad hips.

"We're chasing a thief, a young girl who stole something valuable from me," said the man with the cultured accent.

"What? Your virginity?" The woman's voice was tart and brooked no nonsense. "Go home, where you belong at such an hour, and leave honest folks to sleep in peace."

The man insisted, "So you haven't seen a girl?"

"Why, yes, I've seen a few in my day. Not tonight, though."

She made as if to close the door, but Amaya, with wide, fearful eyes, saw a foot thrust into the opening. She flattened herself even farther against the wall, willing herself to be a part of the chilly plastered stone. But she was flesh and blood. If the man looked in, he would certainly perceive her there, a cubit or so from the open doorway.

"You're sure? She disappeared right around here."

"Unless you think you might have mistaken me for a thieving girl, then no. None here. Now shoo." And she slammed the door shut and barred it.

Amaya dared to breathe at last. "Thank you, mistress," she murmured in a shaking voice.

Her rescuer turned to her. "So, what did you really do that had them on your heels?"

Amaya realized that somewhere in the house a lamp was lit, and it was far from pitch-black as her eyes grew accustomed to the moonless interior. Her rescuer was a big woman, well into middle age, with a round, lumpy face like a slab of flatbread.

Amaya said, "I saw them kill my father."

Ili-milku had often reflected on the burdens of being chief scribe during the five years he had held that office, but the one he had never thought to include was the "bringer of bad news"—and in this case, the very worst kind of news. He stood in the young queen's vestibule, rehearsing in his head the various ways he might present the sad tidings, but there seemed to be no way to slide it down gently. "Your courier has been murdered," he said aloud, just to test the sound of it. And at that very moment, the inner door opened, and Lady Ehli-nikkalu stepped into the room. Ili-milku dropped into a bow, his face burning.

The queen hurtled toward him, her long face sharpened with horror. "What did you just say?"

The chief scribe sighed. That was not quite the way he had planned to break the news. "My lady, I fear to tell you that Lord Rabilu, your courier, was murdered last night. His body was found in the street near the east gate."

Wide-eyed, she clapped her hands to her mouth as if to repress a shriek. "May the thousand gods defend us! Were his documents still upon him? Oh, please, let that be the case."

"His diplomatic pouch was certainly there. His basket of personal goods was there, but no one found any documents, I fear." Ili-milku cleared his throat uncomfortably. "Was he carrying something sensitive?"

"Oh, all you gods!" Ehli-nikkalu howled, raising her fisted hands to the sky. "I'm ruined!" She spun away and took several staggering paces as if she didn't know where to turn or what to do.

Ili-milku knew nothing about what was going through the queen's mind, but the contents of her heart were only too legible. She was terrified. He said with reluctance, "There's more, I'm afraid. Your secretary has died too. He was identified by your seal, and I could confirm it was indeed Hattatamu. Both in one night."

Ehli-nikkalu sank into a chair, her face in her hands.

Ili-milku didn't know what to do for her. He couldn't very well put an arm around her—she had a reputation as a hard and imperious woman. Many of his people were afraid of her. But those who worked more closely with the younger queen, like Rab-ilu and Hattatamu, had always praised her fairness—and kindness, even. *Who else would have continued to employ the poor old drunken scribe?* Ili-milku had been urged more than once to let him go from the chancery—the man was so useless. But the queen had kept him on, fearing that he would fall into beggary otherwise.

Finally, Lady Ehli-nikkalu raised her face, stretched and pallid but dry-eyed. "Can I trust you, Ili-milku? Will you promise me that not a word of what I'm about to say will pass your lips? Because if you tell anyone, my life is as good as over."

The chief scribe swallowed with difficulty. "I... I suppose. If it's disloyal to the king, I—"

"It's the king who is disloyal!" she hissed. Her hands clenched tautly, and she half rose from her seat with nerves. "He's plotting to turn the city over to Mizri at sword point. Rab-ilu was carrying the very letter Niqmaddu wrote to his confederates, Ili-milku. It would have implicated him hopelessly. I was sending it to my father, and he would have had the viceroy send troops. Niqmaddu might even have been deposed." She drew a heavy, unsteady breath. "But now..."

If Ili-milku had had any hair to speak of, it would have been standing on end. *The king? Such treachery?* Although, as chief scribe, Ili-milku knew well that there was a party eager to break with Hatti Land and ally themselves to Mizri. "I... I don't know what to say. Is there anything I can do, my lady? Notify the viceroy?"

The queen's eyes grew suddenly wider, as if in hope, and she surged to her feet. "The emissary! My father's emissary is coming!" She laughed out loud in relief. "I can tell him what is happening, although we no longer have any proof. They'll believe me. I'm the Great Lady of Hatti, after all—the emperor's eldest daughter."

Ili-milku let out a big breath through his pursed lips. "I'm glad my lady finds some way around this dreadful loss."

Ehli-nikkalu looked down, calm but sad. "The really dreadful part, of course, is not my loss but the bereavement of the men's families. I understand Rab-ilu's wife just died not long ago. His poor children."

"Yes, his clan has had its share of sorrows. A few years back, his brother's family died in a terrible fire."

The queen's eyebrows knitted in compassion. "And I was feeling sorry for myself." She gave a rueful laugh. "Even if the king puts me to death, the rebellion will be stopped. Niqmaddu will receive what he deserves as a traitor to his overlord. That would be worth dying for."

Ili-milku saw the expression of cold hatred on her face and realized what he had never seen before—the deadly enmity between the king and his wife. He shuddered.

"Is there anything else I should know, Ili-milku? Have the bodies been taken back to the families for burial?"

"Yes, my lady. The chancery has concluded its involvement. It's up to their next of kin now. Except," he added, "we'll need to find you a new secretary."

The queen said, "Please. Someone discreet." Then she sniffed ironically. "Although it may not matter now. I'll probably be dead."

Oh dear, thought Ili-milku. *I don't want to get involved in politics. I may have incriminated myself just by coming here.* "If that's all then, my lady...?"

She smiled grimly. "Thank you for telling me this, Ili-milku. Find me a secretary, and you'll have discharged your duties."

He bowed his way out, past the curious eyes of the queen's ladies. As he made his way down the corridor that led to the chancery, his sense of prudence kept telling him he had made a terrible mistake by talking personally to Lady Ehli-nikkalu. If she was in such bad odor with her husband as to fear being executed, her very touch was poison. Ili-milku sighed. He had no ambition; he hadn't wanted to become chief scribe. He had spent a happy thirty-five years at the big writing table in the chancery with never a longing to hobnob with the powerful. He longed for the safe life of a rank-and-file scribe once more—although it hadn't proved safe for Hattatamu—and the leisure to work on his poems, to enjoy the presence of his family, the friendship of his colleagues. *May the will of the gods be done...*

E hli-nikkalu had just sat down to a solitary lunch in her chamber when the door slammed back against the wall, and the king strode in, steaming with anger that was almost visible. She looked up, her heart pounding, and forced upon herself the respectful gesture of rising.

"Where is it?" Niqmaddu demanded, stalking straight up to her and staring at her fiercely.

"Where is what?" It was all she could do not to recoil from his proximity in distaste. She was taller than he was and used her height to create a wall of offended dignity between them.

"That letter I left in here. Don't tell me you don't know what I mean."

She lifted an eyebrow. "At risk of seeming disobedient, no, I don't know what you mean." But she did. He had come for the record of his betrayal. *Yet if it was taken from Rab-ilu, why would Niqmaddu be looking for it here?*

"When I was in here yesterday, I had a letter on me. Last night it wasn't there. I want it now." The king's handsome face was crimson with rage—and perhaps fear. He thrust out a peremptory hand.

Ehli-nikkalu shrugged. Despite the pounding of her heart, she feigned indifference. "I'm not charged with keeping up with my lord husband's lost objects. Perhaps you left it somewhere else."

"This is the only place it could be." He rushed to the bed, threw off the covers, and upended the mattress. With a growl of frustration, he began peering into every vessel, every jewel box, throwing them to the floor. He rifled through her clothes chest, leaving the room strewn with her dresses. At last he stood, red-faced and panting, glaring at the queen with a wild and desperate light in his eye. "Give it back, you skinny turd."

"I don't ha—" she began.

But her husband hurled himself at her and grabbed her arm with a grip like the jaws of a savage predator. "Give. It. Back."

She tried to pry his hand away, but Niqmaddu double-handed his grip and wrenched her arm up behind her back. An involuntary cry of pain escaped her. "I don't have it, by all the gods. Wouldn't you have found it if it were here? You didn't leave it here at all."

With a growl of frustration, he let go and pushed her away. She staggered backward, nearly falling over the overturned chest in the middle of the floor. "I'll find it. You can be sure. And if it turns out you're hiding it, you'll pay. Do you understand? Great Lady or not."

Ehli-nikkalu managed to put on an uncaring face, but she was more afraid than rebellious at that point. Niqmaddu, for all his verbal cruelties, had never used physical violence on her before. Somehow his show of bodily domination over his wife scared her in a way that all the bitter dialogues between them never had. As his social superior, she could hold her own verbally, despite—something he was fond of mocking—her accent. But she could never defend herself against his blows. And what was coming was no doubt far worse than blows.

Radiating fury, the king stalked to the door and tore it open, then slammed it viciously against the wall. An ewer tottered and fell to the floor. Niqmaddu's footsteps stomped through the vestibule, where the wide-eyed handmaids doubled in bows, then Ehli-nikkalu closed the door behind him and the curious girls and leaned against it, limp. She slowly rubbed her bruised forearm and waited for her heartbeat to calm. The room was utterly silent; only the razz of cicadas from the garden provided a kind of background noise, inaudible in its familiarity.

"What just happened?" she asked herself in a kind of daze. *If Niqmaddu is looking for his letter here, that means one of two things. Either they didn't find it on Rab-ilu, or it wasn't the king at all who sent the assassins. Had someone else been trying to find the damning missive before the king? Someone loyal to my father, their suzerain?* But the fact that Hattatamu had been killed at the same time—the only other witness to the letter's incriminating contents—suggested that it wasn't a loyalist. *Will I be the next target? If I can convince the king that I haven't seen the letter, maybe my life expectancy will increase.* But she had a feeling that would be a difficult prayer to fulfill.

Ehli-nikkalu scrubbed her face with her hands. She should let the handmaids come in and clean up the room, which lay wrecked about her in mute testimony to the king's desperation. But she didn't trust any of them. There were too many reasons to suspect that they had reported on her to Sharryelli.

*A*uthor Note: The *"maryannu" class to which Amaya belongs is composed of rich merchants, shippers, and landowners who rule the maritime kingdom of Ugarit under its king.*

Excavations in Ugarit (modern Ras Shamra—Latakia, Syria) have given us a pretty good idea of how the palace looked. The kingdom was unknown, except by name, until 1929, when it was rediscovered.

Chapter 3

Her heart numb, Amaya had washed and laid out her father's body on the table, draped in black cloth—the second time she had prepared a parent for burial in a matter of months. The tears had yet to flow as she knew they would; she was cocooned in a kind of protective disbelief, busy enough not to have to think much. Her only adult sister was married and lived in Geru province, far to the north, and the other two were only children, so all the duties of survival fell on her. She wasn't even sure Anani-nikkalu would be able to get back in time for the obsequies. In this weather, the corpse wouldn't last long. The thought of her father's strong, handsome body putrefying—the body which had been such a comfort and bulwark for the children so many times—brought a prickling to her nose. Something in her wouldn't accept that such a thing as his death had happened. As an emissary, he was frequently gone. How often had they waited for his return over the years, her mother, brave even in the last stages of her illness, still visibly longing for the love of her life to come back. But he would never come back to them from this journey. *Father was only thirty-seven. It isn't just, Lord Ilu. How could you let this happen to your servant?*

Dully, she arranged the branches of pungent basil around him, straightened up, and turned away, eager to have something else in her eye than the still effigy that was her father. Admittedly, he looked peaceful, no sign on his face of the terror that must have enveloped him at the end. The wounds were in back, and nothing showed of violence.

Amaya shook out the bloodied garments she had cut off Rabilu and prepared them for the slaves to burn. As she lifted the tunic, something clacked against the edge of his traveling chest, on which she had stacked them. She felt the hem, which seemed to be weighted.

What is this? she thought curiously.

Turning the hem inside out, she noticed with surprise that there was a kind of pouch designed into the edge of the garment and closed with lace, a sort of secret purse.

"What's that?" Amaya asked. With tingling fingers, she unlaced the pouch and spread the opening to extract the contents—two clay tablets, written on with tiny wedge-shaped tracks that meant nothing to Amaya but which were important to someone, it seemed. *Why would they be concealed like this otherwise?* In fact, one of these must be the letter that was so urgent her father had had to rush out in the middle of the night to deliver it.

What should I do, Mother? She stared around the dimly lit room as if to discern her mother standing protectively beside her and decided, *I should give them back to whoever sent them. They won't even know that the letters haven't been delivered unless they've heard about Father. And then they'll be worried about what happened to them.*

But who sent them? That drunken man was the younger queen's secretary, she knew. Last night she had spoken to him for the first time, but his face was familiar. To the queen, then.

Amaya left the children in the care of the slaves and slipped out into the street without even cleaning herself up. She was in mourning; it was normal that she should look disheveled. Over her arm was a small basket in which she had concealed the letters. Everyone knew where the palace was—it dominated the city's highest point, and only the towers of the temples could rival it in visibility. Dry-mouthed with nerves but determined, she set off toward the upper city in the bright sun of late morning.

What a morning, thought the queen, already exhausted. *I'm afraid to ask what can possibly happen next.* No doubt the king's men appearing at the door to drag her away to the executioner. She was so convinced of this likelihood that when a knock sounded on the inner door of her apartment, she flinched, and her heart picked up its pace. Ehli-nikkalu jumped up and stood, back to the table, her hands steadying herself against its edge. "Come in."

It was one of her handmaids, who bowed with every appearance of respect, although the queen seriously doubted that it was genuine. "A girl has asked to see you, my lady. She wouldn't say who she is. Are you willing to admit her?"

"A girl?" That didn't sound dangerous. Ehli-nikkalu's curiosity was aroused. "Send her in."

A moment later, a young woman in her late adolescence appeared in the doorway, a small basket over her arm. She made a deep court bow that spoke of good breeding. Someone of the *maryannu* class, then. Her husband or father must be attached to the palace.

Ehli-nikkalu said kindly, "What brings you here, my girl?"

"My name is Amaya, my lady. I'm the daughter of your courier, Rab-ilu."

Oh, the poor child. "Does the family want me to attend the funeral?" the queen asked, a little uneasy. She had been debating between her respect for the late emissary and the dangerous appearance of seeming to be involved in his death, if only because she had sent him on the fatal mission. *What might Sharryelli and her son make of that admission of complicity?*

"If my lady wishes to, we would be honored. But I've come about something else," said Amaya.

The queen looked her up and down. She was a slim, beautiful girl with a heart-shaped face and the most enormous black-lashed eyes the queen had seen, even in this country of fine dark eyes. They were bare of any cosmetics, and the disheveled hair and dress she wore, with its ripped neck, was eloquent of her state of mourning.

"Have a seat, my dear. And forgive me for not offering you my condolences immediately." Ehli-nikkalu led her to a stool and brushed off the broken pieces of pottery she had overlooked after the king's departure. She took her place in her own carved chair and drew her skirts about her. Except in official appearances, she refused to wear the local tunic and preferred the heavy gathered skirt of her homeland. It gave her the illusion of hips. "Now, how can I help you?"

Amaya proffered the basket and drew aside the napkin that covered its contents. Within lay a pair of clay tablets of different sizes and slightly different colors.

Ehli-nikkalu almost leaped from her chair. "What are these?" Although she thought she knew, recognizing them from the evening before. One of them had been written right in this room.

"I found these sewn into the hem of my father's tunic, my lady. When... when I removed them to wash his body." The girl lowered her eyes for a moment, her lip trembling. But she looked up once more, hanging onto her composure with admirable strength. "I knew they were letters you had given him to deliver, and since... since they couldn't be delivered, I thought you'd want them back."

Ehli-nikkalu stared, her jaw hanging open. Whoever had killed Rab-ilu hadn't found and taken them after all. They hadn't been in the diplomatic pouch or traveling chest that Ili-milku had discovered empty. She reached out a hand, almost in disbelief. The gods were surely looking out for her. Lady Nikkal had been gazing down in the moonlight with her husband, Arma, the moon, and protected her daughter with a motherly gesture.

Thank you, queen of the night.

"Oh, thank you, Amaya. You did just the right thing." She lifted the tablets from the basket and held them to her heart. "I'll give them to my father's emissary when he comes." *But where can I hide them until he's here? What if Niqmaddu is so convinced I have the letters that he comes back and searches again?* She gnawed her lip in indecision.

"There's... there's something else, my lady," the girl said shyly. "I saw the men kill my father."

Ehli-nikkalu's head jerked up, and she gaped at Amaya. "You saw them? Would you recognize them?"

"Probably not by sight—they were mostly silhouetted. But I would recognize their voices. Especially one. He seemed to be upper-class, well educated. I think he's someone who has been to our house to talk to Father in the past."

The queen absorbed this news with a fluttering in the stomach. Perhaps she could actually determine who had done this terrible deed, who wanted to stop her letter at any cost. To be sure, Niqmaddu was almost certainly behind it—or his mother—but it would be good to know who in their services was so ruthless as to kill an innocent man.

Then another thought struck her. "Did the men know you saw them, my dear?"

Amaya looked something between ashamed and fearful. Her hands were twisted tensely into her skirt. "Yes, my lady. I cried out, 'Father,' and they came after me. I escaped by dodging into someone's house."

So the assassins knew exactly who she was. She was still in danger, a witness who had to be eliminated. "We must hide you," the queen said earnestly. "But where? Do you have any relatives?"

"My uncle lives in the city, but I don't think he wants to see any of us. My sister is married in Geru province."

"Oh, dear. There's all sorts of trouble with those awful outlaws up there—the Umman-manda, or whatever they call themselves. That might not be a good choice."

The girl looked so uncertain, her black eyes so huge and lost, that Ehli-nikkalu's heart was wrung. *She may be an adult in age, but she's an orphan.* The queen remembered how her own mother's death had hit her at much the same age; she had felt like a little child all over again. She rose, extended a hand, and smoothed back the girl's tousled hair. "Listen, Amaya. How would you like to stay here at the palace? I can protect you. You can be my lady-in-waiting—the only one I can trust."

"But what about the twins? They're just eight..."

"Bring them too." Ehli-nikkalu felt herself growing excited as the idea revealed itself. It would be like those long-ago days in the royal nursery, where she had been a virtual little mother to her sisters and brothers. How she had loved the children and longed for the day when she would have her own. "We can make them pages or something."

Her brows wrinkling uneasily, the girl said, "This is a lot to ask, my lady. We don't want to be a burden to you."

"Not at all, my dear. I feel responsible for your father's death. And I desperately need someone in my household I can trust not to spy on me." She took Amaya by the shoulders and looked her in the eye. "Those men know where you live if they know you're Rab-ilu's daughter. Neither you nor the children will ever be safe there, and it seems risky to try to get to Geru at the moment. Later, when things are better on the roads, you're free to leave whenever you like."

"Very well. I'll get the twins and pack our bags and be back around sundown, if that pleases my lady." The girl bobbed a brief bow and darted away through the vestibule full of gawking handmaids.

The chamberlain had just brought Ehli-nikkalu's lunch, and she seated herself at the table for yet another solitary meal. The presence of the handmaids made her so uncomfortable that she forbade them all but the most essential entry to her chamber. She was strangely excited at the thought that Amaya would be returning that evening with her little brother and sister. To be sure, she did have a sense of guilt about Rab-ilu's death—or at least, responsibility for it—but even more, she wanted the girl's companionship. She had liked Amaya. Had liked her simplicity and bravery, her good manners and the way she spoke respectfully without seeming cowed. Rab-ilu's daughter was about the age her own eldest daughter might have been, if she'd had one, if she'd married at the normal age—if she hadn't been wed to an arrogant jackal who wanted to punish her for not being the vapid, decorative princess of his dreams. *Let him console himself with his fecund little concubine.*

A knock at the door made her look up from her roast quail. Fearing it was her husband, she licked the gravy from her lips and rose, putting on a dignified and imperturbable look of cool hostility. But it wasn't her husband; it was his mother.

Sharryelli approached with her dimpled smile. Soft and plumpish, she was barely more than Ehli-nikkalu's age and pretty in an undistinguished way. While Ehli-nikkalu refused to dissemble her mistrust of her mother-in-law, the latter veiled every unkindness with a sweet, rosy-cheeked affability that drove the younger queen wild. If there was one thing Ehli-nikkalu abhorred, it was sanctimony.

"Oh, I do apologize if I've interrupted your meal, dear. I've actually come on Niqmaddu's behalf. He wondered if you ever found that letter he left in here." Sharryelli smiled brightly and patted her daughter-in-law's shoulder in a familiar way.

Ehli-nikkalu stiffened. With cold, barest courtesy, she said, "No. He never left it here, or he would have found it this morning when he completely overturned my whole apartment."

"Oh, did he? How like a man." Sharryelli clucked her tongue disapprovingly. "You think you've brought your sons up to be gentlemen, but they're just brutish rascals underneath."

More brutish than you know, thought the younger queen, still feeling the bruises on her arm. *Or maybe you know very well.* "Then I suppose that was all you wanted to see me about? When is my father's emissary coming?"

"Not for weeks yet. You'll know before he gets here, of course. Why? Was there something in particular you wanted to say to him?"

"I was just curious."

Sharryelli turned to go then spun back and said in a deeply sympathetic voice, "Oh, I forgot to offer my condolences, my dear. I hear your courier and your secretary both died last night. Were they involved in an accident together, do you know?"

Ehli-nikkalu gave a sarcastic snort. "Yes. They both fell on a knife, and probably the same one."

"How dreadful." Sharryelli shivered and turned again toward the door. Over her shoulder, she called, "Don't hesitate if you need anything. We can find you a new secretary."

I wager you can, all right. One who would report to you every word I wrote. Ehli-nikkalu waited until the door had closed behind her mother-in-law, then she spat, "You dishonest bitch."

The queen sank into her chair and pushed away her plate, having lost every sliver of her appetite. *I've got to find a place to hide those letters until our emissary comes.*

Ehli-nikkalu spent the afternoon in solitary spinning, unwilling to sit with those handmaids for hours of hypocritical pleasantries. She counted the moments until Amaya and the children would come.

Rab-ilu's funeral was over. It had already become a blur of well-meaning friends and neighbors hovering around, wailing and keening, offering their condolences, praising the man her father had been. Amaya's sister hadn't had time to get down to the capital from the north. She, herself, unsupported by anyone, had sat in frozen, dry-eyed pain during the prayers and sacrifices, comforting the children, whose loss was beginning to sink in. Then they had lowered the shrouded body of her father into the family crypt beside her mother and sealed the tomb. It seemed as if an eon had passed since the nighttime mission had awakened Amaya from her innocence and pitched her into this state of numbness—between her mother's death followed shortly by her father's, the last month had brought more loss than she could deal with.

After the mourners had left, the girl roamed the house like a heavyhearted ghost. It all looked the same—the plastered walls with their red dado, the cedar-beamed ceilings darkened with generations of smoke and the exhalations of the living—but it wasn't. It was a soulless husk with its master and its mistress gone. Home no longer. The slaves tiptoed around her as if she were, perhaps, invisible.

At last Lady Shapshu, the sun, began her descent behind the whitewashed walls of the city, and cicadas gave way to the gentler music of crickets. Cautioning the servants to tell no one where she could be found, she bundled up the children and a basket of their clothes and prepared to slip out into the street, when Yanakh hung back and whined unhappily, "I want to take my toys."

"You can't," said his twin. "Amaya said. We can't carry anything else."

Amaya controlled her impatience with difficulty. "We have to go now. We can't wait for you to run back in and get things. The queen will see to it you have new toys."

"But I don't want to go," he said sullenly, dodging back into the doorway. "I want my old toys that Mama and Papa gave me."

His elder sister gritted her teeth with impatience and nerves. She didn't want to frighten the children by speaking too much about the stakes of their being found, but Yanakh's badly timed stubbornness was more than she could take. He could be fearfully immature sometimes.

"If they find us, they'll kill us, Yanakh. We have to go *right now*, before they find out where we're heading," she hissed. "Right now." She took him by the arm and pulled him after her.

He only half resisted while little Ba'aluya muttered something dire about boys.

Her heart pounding, Amaya led the way up the narrow streets in the deepening gloom. Here and there, a bar of orange light through the crack of the shutters revealed where some family was dining inside. Others were eating on their roof terraces, with laughter and clinking of dishes. It was still bright up there on the second or third floor—happy, safe, and normal—even while purple darkness had begun to swallow up the features of the neighborhood below. Amaya hadn't even thought to bring a lamp.

Occasionally, she heard footsteps on the paving stones and froze, her arms outspread to defend the children. But it was just someone making their way home after a day's work, and they spared scarcely a glance for the three furtive travelers. The young people trudged up the steep approach to the palace, whose massive whitewashed walls seemed to glow in the twilight, where they found the service gate at which the queen had told them to knock. A soldier standing at the door in the deep-red uniform of the palace guard admitted them, saying the queen was expecting their arrival.

And just within stood the queen herself, a tall stork of a woman. Her long face lit up with delight at the sight of the three children of Rab-ilu. She laid a finger over her lips and led them silently around the unroofed corridor that ringed what seemed to be a garden with trees, the whole surrounded by the wings of the building. It was getting quite dark, and while they could hear the clean-up crew in the kitchens, nobody seemed to be in the vicinity.

Yanakh started to say something—no doubt to complain that he hadn't been able to bring his ball and knucklebones—but Ba'aluya shushed him urgently. And together they tiptoed in silence upstairs and down the hall to the queen's apartment. The only person they saw was a buxom young woman swaying along in the other direction, who exchanged a hostile look with Lady Ehli-nikkalu and turned her head to follow them with curious eyes as they passed.

The queen threw open the door of her vestibule and hustled the three inside. "Here we are at last," she said. "I want as few people as possible to know you're here because, if questions start, someone's bound to discover who you are."

"Who was the pretty lady? She knows," said Yanakh, who had kept quiet as long as he could.

Amaya saw how the queen's nostrils grew white and tense.

"That's Pu-haddu, the king's favorite concubine. The mother of the crown prince." But Lady Ehli-nikkalu rallied and smiled. "Let's put your things away. I've sent away the night maids. Let them find out tomorrow I've hired some new staff." She grinned conspiratorially.

The queen had cleared a little storage chamber with a small window to be their sleeping quarters and had some camp beds set up. She showed the way in with a lamp, which she set in the windowsill. "It's not much, but it will do until we can get you to your sister's house."

Yanakh said petulantly, "I don't see why Uncle won't take us so we don't have to go all the way up to Auntie. I have friends here."

"Well, so do I," his twin informed him, her small fists on her hips. "We have to get out of the city because those men who killed Papa will be after Amaya."

"And Amaya says it's time for the younger members of the family to go to bed," Amaya said firmly.

She helped the twins slip into their night tunics and turned down their covers. Their night prayers for Rab-ilu were so poignant Amaya wasn't sure she could bear it without falling apart, and it was with relief that she kissed them good night and slipped from the room.

The queen watched her emerge, such happiness in her face that it was almost embarrassing, as if Amaya had seen something a little too intimate. "They're lovely children," Ehli-nikkalu said quietly. "It's so sad to think they're orphans."

Amaya nodded, her throat beginning to knot.

"Tell me, my dear. Why doesn't your uncle want you? It's clearly his duty to take in the family of his brother." The two women seated themselves on a pair of beautifully carved stools.

"That's another sad story, my lady. Five years or so ago, my father's twin brother was gone one evening, and when he came back, he found the house on fire and his wife and children trapped inside. He ran in to save them, but he couldn't get through, and he was burned so badly that he lost his hand along with his family. That was the end of his military career. He's been a strange, bitter person ever since." Amaya lowered her eyes and added in a trembling voice, "I think he can't bear to see children when his own are dead, or perhaps he feels he can't take the responsibility again."

The queen gazed at her in compassion. "But surely having a family again would take him out of himself. Don't you think? Give him someone to love?"

"I don't know, my lady. My father said Uncle Teshamanu was a gambler and was always short of money. Perhaps he feels he can't afford us."

Ehli-nikkalu shook her head pensively. "How very different the two men are—your father was so upstanding. And you said they were twins?"

Amaya managed a laugh. "Yes. But Yanakh and Ba'aluya couldn't be more different either."

They chatted for a while. It was clear to Amaya that the queen was lonely and eager to talk, but despite the girl's goodwill, she could hardly keep a yawn stifled.

At last, Lady Ehli-nikkalu rose and said kindly, "You need to sleep, my dear. It's been a long and terrible day." She leaned over to the girl and kissed her on the forehead. "You're safe now."

Amaya returned to the little room, where the children lay sleeping. The lamp still burned in the windowsill. *Only a day has passed,* she marveled. *This time last night, Father was still alive. And a month before that, Mother was, too, and we hadn't a care in the world.* All that happiness had been so fragile all along—one little breath from the gods and it had all fallen apart as quickly as dandelion fluff. And suddenly, the grief she had been keeping at bay for the twins' sake flooded over her like a winter storm, and she cried as if her broken heart might empty itself from her very body.

A*uthor Note: Aristocrats in Ugarit (including the kings) are often buried in family crypts right under the house.*

Chapter 4

Ehli-nikkalu had taken a long time to fall asleep the previous night, her wakefulness whetted by both anxiety and exhilaration. She and Amaya had had the first honest human conversation the queen could remember enjoying in the seven years since she had come to this kingdom. But neither she nor the girl were altogether safe yet. Swinging her feet to the floor, she felt the weighted hem of her shift, where she had sewed the incriminating letters—Rab-ilu's ruse had worked before, so she would employ it again. Surely Niqmaddu wouldn't dare to tear her very clothes from her in search. It was only for a few weeks, anyway, until her father's emissary came and she could unburden herself of the proof of her husband's disloyalty.

"Amaya," she called softly, so as not to wake the children. "I need your services. I have things to do today." She felt a stab of pity. She had heard the weeping last evening and knew the girl must have had a poor night's sleep, but activity was probably the best cure.

After a brief delay, Amaya emerged from the little room and closed the door quietly behind her. Her eyes were swollen and her cheeks pale, but she managed a brave smile. "I'm ready, my lady. Show me what you want me to do."

Ehli-nikkalu showed the girl where the clothes were kept and the toilet articles, and Amaya helped her to dress in her heavy skirt and linen blouse and an appropriate amount of jewelry. Then Ehli-nikkalu sat on a stool while her new lady-in-waiting began the arduous job of brushing her mistress's thick, bushy hair.

"I'm sure the other girls have already reported your presence to Sharryelli and the king," the queen said after Amaya had positioned Ehli-nikkalu's cap and veil. "I worry about the children. It's going to be impossible to keep them penned up in this room." *And yet I never want them to leave*, she had to admit. Despite the tragedy that had brought it about, the last day had been the happiest she could remember since her marriage. It was certainly the least boring. "We'll have to see about some toys for them."

About midmorning, when the twins were playing on the loggia and Amaya had joined them, there came a knock at the door, and the queen's chamberlain appeared. She saw the surreptitious glance of curiosity he shot around the room.

"My lady, the chief scribe is here to see you."

Ehli-nikkalu put on her cool, imperious face and tone. "Send him in." *Sharryelli's spies, all of them.*

But her disdain lifted as Ili-milku toddled into the room. He was a round little man in his fifties, mostly bald on top, with protruding eyes that crinkled with good humor. She hadn't had much contact with him until yesterday, but he seemed to her a genuine kind of person.

He bowed respectfully. "My lady charged me with finding her a new secretary, and I have a candidate, if he meets with your approval. A man named Teshamanu." Ili-milku lowered his eyes momentarily. "He's a prickly sort of person, but his family's impeccably loyal to Our Sun—he's the twin brother of your late courier, in fact."

Ehli-nikkalu widened her eyes in astonishment. "I know about him," she blurted.

"Don't believe everything you hear, my lady," said Ili-milku. "He had a rather wild youth, but he's been very steady in the last few years. I... I suppose you've heard about the tragedy with his family?"

"I have." Her thoughts were whirring. "I thought he was a soldier."

"He was, but after the loss of his hand, he turned to a scribal career. There aren't many honorable options for the *maryannu* class, you know. I can recommend his skill. And he certainly won't bother you with chitchat."

My, my, thought the queen. *I wonder how Amaya will feel about this. Maybe if the man sees his nieces and nephew, he'll agree to take them on.* Perhaps she owed them this, even if Teshamanu was a complete curmudgeon. "Very well, Ili-milku. Bring the fellow whenever you like. I need to start my correspondence again."

She started to dismiss him, but then she held out a hand. "Wait. There's something I want to show you." The queen stooped and fiddled with the hem of her under shift while Ili-milku discreetly turned his eyes aside. Then she rose and handed him the two small tablets. "Read these. They weren't found after all."

He stared at the king's letter for a moment, his lips moving as he read. Then he looked up at her, his popping brown eyes round. "My lady, I thought you said the king was selling the kingdom to Mizri."

"Well, he is. Don't you see that?" the queen cried, exasperated.

"But it doesn't mention Mizri anywhere here."

"Who else could it be? No one else is powerful enough to challenge my father."

Ili-milku stammered, "But they've been our allies for over a generation. What motive would they have for provoking a war by breaking the treaty—poaching one of Our Sun's vassals?"

"How should I know?" She felt the heat mount to her face and said a little wildly, "Maybe they just want to weaken the grain supply route. You know, Hatti Land is in a terrible famine. If Mizri doesn't sell us grain, and Ugarit doesn't ship it, the kingdom will starve."

Ili-milku looked reluctantly skeptical. "They'd lose a pretty substantial income if the shipments stopped."

"What, then? What's this letter about?" Frustration was driving her almost to anger. She shook the tablet at the chief scribe in accusation. "Who else would send soldiers? Who else would fancy itself a less onerous suzerain than Hatti Land?"

"I'm sure I don't know, my lady. And maybe it is Mizri. But you'll have a hard time proving that since it isn't mentioned in the letter."

Ehli-nikkalu spun away, her cheeks burning. *He's in Niqmaddu's pay too. Just like all of them. Nobody is honorable except the poor outcasts like Hattatamu and a few noble, old-fashioned souls like Rabilu.* She felt very alone and disappointed. For some reason, she had hoped this happy-looking little scholar would be in her camp. Drawing up to her full, imperious height, she said coldly, "I expected the chief scribe of the kingdom to show a little more loyalty to his overlord."

Ili-milku looked suddenly worried. He clasped his hands. "Oh, my lady, I'm totally loyal to Our Sun. Believe me. I'm just trying to be pragmatic. If this is all the proof you have of the king's machinations, then he may well be able to explain them away somehow. That's all I wanted to say."

"Well, the king seems more than a little worried at the thought that the letter has fallen into someone's hands. *He* must think it's incriminating."

"My lady is assuredly right," he said humbly.

Her hackles lowered hair by hair. "Well, then, we understand one another. My father's emissary will know what to make of this. And bring me the secretary when you get a chance."

Ili-milku bowed himself out, and still irritated, the queen parted the thin linen curtains that screened the loggia.

Amaya, who was sitting on the floor of the loggia with the two children, looked up. "Can I serve you, my lady?" She started to her feet, but Ehli-nikkalu gestured her down.

"Better to stay low so no one can see you from the garden." She stared out into the late-morning glare.

A palm whispered lazily in the slight breeze from the sea, but otherwise the garden was still, as if napping, radiating heat from its white gravel walks. The cicadas roared their late-summer song.

Suddenly, the queen drew back from the edge of the parapet. Two people were talking almost directly below her, in the slice of shade the residential wing of the palace cast at this hour. Sharryelli and Sharryelli's son-in-law, Shipti-ba'al. Shipti-ba'al was one of the city's richest merchants—richer than the king, rumor had it. So it was no surprise that the dowager had married her daughter to him, even though he was old enough to have been the girl's own father. Still, Ehli-nikkalu had to admit he was a handsome man with his slate-gray hair and long, deceptively good-humored dimples.

Deceptive because rumor also said that he was Sharryelli's henchman, arranging whatever ruthless things she needed arranged. *Was he behind the assassination of Rab-ilu? And if so, how did Sharryelli find out about the message the courier was taking to my father?* But then, Ehli-nikkalu remembered the last time she had seen the royal brother-in-law—right in that very garden—two nights before. He had been talking to Hattatamu, whose tongue was undoubtedly looser than it should have been under the effects of wine. She closed her eyes and blew out a huff of disgust.

It was impossible to hear the conversation under her feet because of the cicadas, so Ehli-nikkalu turned and went back inside her chamber, mortally tired of those four walls.

A week had passed, and while the pain of her father's loss had settled into a dull ache that she felt was bleeding her youth from her, Amaya was in other ways strangely happy. She and the children were virtually imprisoned in the queen's apartments, which meant the two women constantly had to be finding new and interesting games for the twins to play. And Lady Ehli-nikkalu, for all her severe appearance and the haughtiness with which she could interact with others, was a warm and attentive nursemaid. She seemed perfectly content sitting on the floor, sewing hand puppets or making cat's cradles with a bit of string while her spindle and distaff sat forgotten on top of the clothes chest.

"Amaya, dear," the queen said when the twins had finally scampered off to play a board game together. "We need to have some nice new clothes made for you. You must be tired of the same few dresses you brought with you."

"Whatever my lady wants," she replied humbly.

"Don't be too meek," Ehli-nikkalu said, a twinkle in her greenish eyes. "You're not my servant but a lady companion. What colors do you like? We'll have the dressmaker come. I'm sure she'll be delighted to make something other than these heavy skirts of mine."

"I can't believe you're so kind to us." Amaya looked up at the queen with deepest gratitude. She found her heart expanding with something close to love, although the two had not known each other for very long. "You don't owe us anything, and look at you—you've treated us like your own family."

Ehli-nikkalu dropped her eyes and said with a touch of sadness, "Perhaps I think of you as my family. I haven't seen them for seven years. I've had no one to love, no one to talk to..."

Amaya was afraid to think about what this meant about the relationship of the queen and her royal husband. He hadn't so much as paid her a visit in the week Amaya had spent in the royal quarters.

"Do you have brothers and sisters, my lady?"

"I do indeed. I'm the oldest of eight, then I have brothers and sisters by my father's other wives. Plus, all the cousins who were raised in the royal nursery. It was wonderful. I was like a little mother to them. It gave me great joy." The queen's plain face was transfigured with the sweetness of her memories. "I thought that having children of my own would be the most wonderful thing upon the black earth. I wanted to become someone's queen and live with him as happily as my parents lived together and help him rule, just like my mother did, so I could do good things for everyone." Her happiness faded, and she added grimly, "The gods had other plans."

Amaya thought in silent compassion that the queen had found herself in a very miserable place. *Who could have imagined, with all her wealth and power, her imperial birth?* "Is your mother still alive, my lady?"

"No, alas. She died when I was about your age, Amaya. And she was my present age, I suppose. She was the most beautiful woman I've ever seen—and I say that not because she's dear to me. Everyone thought so." The queen smiled wryly. "Clearly, I didn't take after her. But she never made me feel I wasn't pretty."

Amaya said comfortingly, "But it's better to look like your father, my lady, because he's Our Sun. He's the most powerful man in the world."

"I love my father very much, although I didn't see much of him growing up. You can imagine how busy a Great King always is. I usually saw him in a procession or riding in from battle, all sweaty and dirty. But I remember once, when I was thirteen, he called me and my sisters into our mother's chamber and greeted us as his beautiful daughters." The queen's voice broke. "He caressed my hair and looked at me with such love and pride that I felt he could hardly bear it. He's a shy man. I don't think it comes easy for him to show what he feels." She lowered her face and tried to regain her control.

Amaya's heart was torn. Her father hadn't been shy, and he had showed his love for her all the time. But she knew that unspeakable tenderness that passed between parents and children without words. Her sorrow welled up like the blood in an old wound when one tore off the scab.

"When I came here, I pictured myself helping my father somehow. I would help steer the kingdom into the ways of loyalty and friendship with Hatti Land. I would let him know how things were going in ways that might not make it into official reports. I would provide heirs so that Hittite kings would sit upon the throne in Ugarit. But it was just a girlish dream." She looked up, mistress of herself once more, and Amaya was surprised at the depth of bitterness in her face. "Now, tell me about *your* mother and father. How many children are you?"

But before Amaya could speak, there was a knock on the door, and the chamberlain appeared in the opening. "My lady, the chief scribe and another man are here to see you."

The queen rose to her feet and said haughtily, "Show them in."

Ili-milku entered, with his toddling gait. Amaya knew him because he had sometimes visited her father to conduct business late in the evening. He bowed to the queen then saw the girl at her side. "Why, Amaya, my dear. My deepest condolences. Rab-ilu was a man admired and beloved by all of us. We will miss him greatly."

Then the man at his heels entered.

Amaya cried in surprise, "Uncle!" She ran toward him a little hesitantly. One never knew what to expect from Uncle Teshamanu; he might return her embrace, or he might turn a shoulder to her. In fact, he nodded, clearly embarrassed and no doubt surprised himself.

Ili-milku watched their awkward greeting from the corner of his eye. He said to the queen, "My lady, I have brought the man I recommend for your new secretary. Of course, you have a choice, but I can vouch for his skill and his—ahem—loyalty."

"Very well. Let me interview him."

Amaya watched with interest as her uncle stepped forward. For all that they were twins, he and Father didn't look much alike. They shared the same strongly arched nose and dark eyes, but Teshamanu had a broader face and—although he certainly wasn't fat—was shorter and broader in general.

In spite of herself, Amaya dropped her gaze to his left sleeve, which hung half empty. Poor Uncle. He had become so cold, so abrupt in the last few years. But although he had always seemed anx-

ious and preoccupied, she had the feeling this new, unpleasant manner was because he lived in his own world of sorrow and guilt so that
any word he was forced to waste on the living was an interruption of
his real business, which was to hate himself. And now, he shared with
the whole family the fresh grief of losing his brother.

The queen eyed him up and down appraisingly and said in her
chilly official voice, "So, Teshamanu, I understand you are a skillful
scribe. Are you prepared to write whatever I dictate without feeling
obliged to pass political judgment on it?"

"I am, my lady," he growled.

Ili-milku stood beside him, nodding encouragement.

"You share your family's loyalty to our rightful suzerain?"

"I do. I've shed blood for him."

Uncle had been in the chariot forces until he lost his hand. Now
of course, he couldn't hold a shield. She wondered if that was one
more source of bitterness.

The queen turned to her big table and picked up a moist, blank
tablet and stylus. "I'd like you to write down what I say."

He drew a stool up to the table and settled himself. Amaya saw
him tug down his empty sleeve, lean well over, and use the stump to
brace the tablet. It made her heart hurt for him.

"Dear Father, the man who is sitting on the throne of Ugarit is a
disloyal pig."

Teshamanu finished his writing almost as quickly as the queen
stopped speaking. He handed her the tablet without any expression.
Ili-milku, on the other hand, stared about uneasily, as if spies might
be under the bed.

The queen looked over his tablet with approval. "You write
Akkadian, too, I suppose?"

"Yes, my lady. Neshite too."

The queen's severe persona cracked for a moment, and she said,
pleased, "Ah. How is it a soldier is so practiced a scribe, Teshamanu?"

"My father trained me. He believed it was a source of shame to be unable to communicate with other kingdoms." Since it seemed clear his test was over, he rose from the table.

The queen dropped the incriminating tablet into an ewer of water that stood nearby. Soon it would be indecipherable mud. "Very well. You have the job. Report tomorrow morning."

He bowed silently and left with the chief scribe at his heels, but the queen called out, "Ili-milku, stay a moment. I want to talk to you."

Author Note: The Ugarites use phonetic characters from the writing of Mesopotamia to create an alphabet of thirty letters, well before the Phoenicians.

Ehli-nikkalu's mother is a Babylonian princess, as readers of The Sun in Twilight *will remember. Neshite is the language spoken by the Hittites, who inhabit what we call today Turkey.*

Chapter 5

He turned back and looked up questioningly. "How may I serve you, my queen?"

"Thank you for finding this man for me. He's very good—far faster and more accurate than Hattatamu."

Ili-milku beamed. "I think you'll find him to be more reliably sober, too, my lady."

"His manners are a little rough. But then, I know about his past."

Ili-milku's mobile face twisted in compassion, and he said quietly, "I think he needs this job, my lady. He apparently has quite a few debts. I suppose the long convalescence..."

"Has Rab-ilu left him nothing?"

Ili-milku glanced at Amaya. "I've been told our late friend has left his entire property to his children, my lady. The only way Teshamanu could gain access to it would be to marry Amaya here."

Amaya stared at Ehli-nikkalu, round eyed. No one had ever told her this. Perhaps it wasn't even a real possibility, but the very thought filled her with dismay. That would be the end of her dreams of a happy marriage like her parents'.

The queen said dryly, "Such a marriage doesn't seem like much of a treat for the girl. Teshamanu is, obviously, old enough to be her father—and not a very charming fellow. She deserves better than that."

Ili-milku nodded. "I agree. But he's legally their guardian, and he would be the one to make any decisions about her marriage."

"Isn't anyone going to ask what *I* want to do?" Amaya cried in spite of herself. Her cheeks had grown hot with anger. "If he won't even take us in when we're orphaned, why should I marry him to let him pay off his debts?"

"Exactly, my dear," said Ili-milku with a sigh. "But no one has ever said anything to make me think he's contemplating that. Perhaps it's never crossed his mind."

Now, however, the fear was implanted in Amaya's mind and had become yet another anxiety. If Teshamanu was working in the queen's apartment every day, he would see his niece constantly. Perhaps it was best if she left, despite her growing attachment to Lady Ehli-nikkalu. She fidgeted uneasily.

"If that's all, my lady..." The chief scribe looked up at the queen with his bulging brown eyes.

He struck Amaya as looking like a fat little boy with a beard. She had always rather liked him, even from afar.

"No, wait, Ili-milku. When is my father's emissary coming?"

The chief scribe looked stunned. "But, my lady—he's come and gone. He left yesterday."

The queen sprang from her chair, her eyes goggling, her face a furious crimson. "What?"

"I'm sorry, my dear lady. He's... he's come and gone. Did no one tell you?"

"No, no one told me. They said it would be weeks before he arrived." The queen gave a bitter little bark of laughter. "Does that surprise you?" She cast her eyes around the room and finally picked up the stylus from the table and hurled it to the floor with a rather unladylike curse. It bounced and rolled harmlessly away. Ehli-nikkalu stalked back and forth across the room with angry strides, her hands clenched at her sides, her veil rippling out behind her. "Those wretched criminals! They lied to me to see to it I couldn't get word to our emissary about their low acts of rebellion. Does this convince you at last, Ili-milku, that Niqmaddu was up to no good?"

The chief scribe looked sad and anxious, his bushy eyebrows wrinkled. "This should never have happened. You shouldn't be prevented access to your family."

The queen rounded on him, her voice still raised in anger. "Of course it shouldn't happen. And those many times I've tried to let someone know that I'm all but a prisoner here, they've pooh-poohed me and insinuated that I was just pathologically suspicious. If I try to send a letter now, what would you say are the chances that it will actually reach Hattusha?"

Ili-milku sighed. "Slim, my lady. Almost any messenger you send will be in the king's pay."

"Exactly." She turned to Amaya and said in a gentler anguish-filled voice, "Oh, my dear, I thought I was protecting you, but I've led you and the children right into the jackal's den."

"That's all right, my lady. You didn't mean to—your intentions were generous and kind. Perhaps we should all go up to our sister's. She's married to the governor of Geru province. It would be much easier for her to hide us there in the countryside." *And it would get us away from Uncle if he's really wanting to marry me for gold.*

"Perhaps if the governor is loyal to Our Sun, she has a point," the chief scribe said.

"Oh, he is," Amaya assured him. "Our father would never have blessed the marriage otherwise."

"Perhaps I should go too—surely I have some holdings in the north. It would certainly be easier to get a message out from there than from right under our monarch's noble nose." The queen's eyes were hard, her thin mouth sarcastic.

"And if you don't have accommodations, no doubt the governor's household would be happy to put you up." Ili-milku smiled now, looking delighted.

As for the queen, she seemed suddenly enthusiastic, full of ener-gy. "Let's do it! I swear I'll go mad if I have to stay cooped up in this apartment another instant."

But a shadow of sudden concern darkened the chief scribe's chubby face. "My lady, aren't the roads dangerous up there? The Um-man-manda have been active. We get reports all the time of caravans robbed, messengers killed. Should you risk this, do you think?"

Ehli-nikkalu turned a frosty expression to the man. "I'm not afraid of a gang of riffraff, Ili-milku. What are they? Runaway slaves and escaped petty criminals. We'll take soldiers—Niqmaddu will certainly agree to that. He'll be glad to have me far away." A wry little smile twitched her lips. "And if I don't go, I'll die of boredom any-way."

"Whatever seems best to my queen. I suppose Teshamanu will accompany you?"

A cold wave of disappointment sloshed over Amaya. *I should have thought of that.*

"Of course. I'll have quite a few letters to write." The queen smiled broadly. "Look up any holdings I have in Geru. There must be something."

Ili-milku took his leave, and Ehli-nikkalu turned to Amaya, ra-diant and lit by a kind of girlish mischief. "Oh, my dear, this will be such fun!"

Amaya's strained smile took on a genuine warmth. "The children will love it, my lady. It will be an adventure. I should write to my sis-ter, don't you think?"

"By all means. The twins'll be much happier with her—able to play outside without fear of being spotted. This is no life for a child. They're in prison here."

"Will... will you still want my services, my lady?" Amaya asked shyly.

Her heart full of sincere warmth, Ehli-nikkalu cried, "Oh, yes. Unless you want to live with your sister too. I understand if you do—she's your family, after all, and there's no better place to be than with one's family."

A sudden painful wave of longing broke over Ehli-nikkalu. *I'll never see them all again.* She would end her miserable days in exile, while those who loved her were far away. Only her grandmother wrote to her anyway, and rarely—Ehli-nikkalu understood why her father couldn't answer her personally—but Puduhepa spoke for the Great King and for all the brothers and sisters who were now grown up.

Amaya said she would give it some thought, and the queen threw her arms around the girl and kissed the shiny top of her hair.

"Do what's best for you," she repeated, but she hoped Amaya would stay.

That afternoon, Ehli-nikkalu, impatient, headed down to the chancery to see what Ili-milku might have found. She was in the corridor passing the royal apartments and, on the other side, those of Niqmaddu's concubine when a door opened and Pu-haddu stepped out, holding by the hand her six-year-old son, the crown prince. Ehli-nikkalu drew away from her in a way that made it clear she didn't fancy sharing the same air, and Pu-haddu smugly eyed her up and down.

"See, my son?" she said to her boy, but her eyes were on the queen. "There's your father's older wife."

She's as bad as Sharryelli, the little nothing. She never opens her mouth without saying "my son" or "my child." She knows that's the only thing she has over me.

But in fact, as far as beauty went, Pu-haddu had it over almost any woman. She was plump and full of curves, with a striking oval face, luscious lips, and seductive eyes. Ehli-nikkalu had to admit she could understand Niqmaddu's attraction. He certainly wasn't looking for an intellectual equal. The queen would have felt a certain hostility for a woman who used her beauty so shamelessly, in any case, but the concubine seemed particularly bent on flaunting herself in front of Ehli-nikkalu. *She's well aware she isn't worthy to tie my belt. Who even knows her family? Some nobodies.*

She was formulating a cutting reply when the little prince said in the innocent way of a child, "Hello, Queen." He looked up at her with such uncritical cheerfulness that she melted.

It was hard to keep her voice cold as she said, dropping into a slight bow, "Hello, my prince."

"Mama's going to have a baby! Isn't that wonderful? I'll have a baby brother to play with."

Ehli-nikkalu bit down a crude remark and said in a perfectly expressionless tone, "How wonderful." She shot a glare at Pu-haddu, who smirked. "If you'll excuse me, I have something important to do..." Without waiting for leave, the queen sailed past the pair and down the corridor, her steps clacking forcefully on the stone tiles. She heard Pu-haddu murmur something to the boy that ended in a laugh.

Still simmering, the queen entered the open door of the chancery writing room. A long table stretched down the middle, and twenty or so scribes sat hunched over it, writing on the damp clay tablets they had taken from a pile in the middle, kept moist under a damp cloth. The room was bright but not yet blistering with light from the west-facing windows. At the end of the table, Ili-milku looked up and, seeing the queen, rose. The others noticed and popped up one by one, sweeping into a collective bow like a field of wheat in a breeze.

"Ili-milku," said Ehli-nikkalu, "a word with you."

The tubby little chief scribe extracted himself from the bench and followed his queen to the doorway.

In the vestibule, she turned to him. "Did you find any properties in the north that belong to me?"

His brown eyes lit up. "Yes, my lady. You have vineyards and farmlands. There's a stud farm as well—it belongs to the crown, of course, but the profits are for your use. I'm sure there are houses attached to these properties. I was going to do a little more research before I reported back to you."

"Send word to whichever is nearest Apsuna—that's a fair-sized town, I believe—and tell them I'm coming for an indefinite time."

"Yes, my lady. Apsuna's in the mountains. It gets chilly at night, so I suppose you'll want to bring appropriate clothes."

She nodded, thinking eagerly, *How I miss the mountains!* Her homeland was mountainous—high and cold. It would be a delight to say goodbye to the oppressive humidity of the coast for a while. *It would be a delight to say goodbye to this place forever.*

"Now I have to ask permission of my august husband, I suppose. He'll be only too happy to grant it." With a caustic smile, she turned and made her way back down the corridor, grateful to see it empty of any trace of Pu-haddu.

However, when she entered her vestibule, she was surprised and displeased to find Sharryelli waiting for her, chatting with the handmaids, who giggled appreciatively at whatever she was saying.

"Don't let me interrupt anything," Ehli-nikkalu said frostily and made as if to pass her mother-in-law.

But the dowager queen turned her smiling rosy face to her daughter-in-law and said, as if the other woman's tone had been even half-welcoming, "Why, Ehli-nikkalu, my dear. Just the person I was looking for. Shall we go inside?"

Ehli-nikkalu led Sharryelli into the inner chamber and turned to face her, arms crossed. "Why did you lie to me about my father's emissary?"

"Lie to you?" Sharryelli looked sweetly confused. "What do you mean?"

Almost before the other woman had finished speaking, the younger queen snarled, "You told me he was coming in a matter of weeks, and only a few days later, he had come and gone. You knew what I wanted to say to him, and you didn't want him to hear it."

"I don't remember saying that, my dear. You must know, we're in a very stressful moment in this kingdom—well, perhaps you *don't* know, since you seem to take so little interest in our affairs—but the pretender who is threatening Niqmaddu's place on the throne has been active again. We need to be very vigilant. Then, Niqmaddu has to go on his annual vassal vigil to Our Sun right in the middle of this. That means I'll be in charge while he's away for weeks, and there's so much to be seen to." Sharryelli sighed, as if in resignation to her martyrdom.

Ehli-nikkalu bit her tongue. *I suppose it's too much of a burden to make an annual visit*, she thought sarcastically.

Sharryelli shook her head. "It's a very touchy situation that my son has to negotiate, you know. If I may say so, your father's exactions are getting rather heavy. We're facing enemies on all sides, and our ships are locked up with taking that grain from Mizri to Hatti Land. Meanwhile, the Assyrians are looking hungrily at our coast."

Of course, Ehli-nikkalu thought as the light dawned. *It's the Assyrians they're selling out to, not Mizri.* "Who is this pretender?"

"You may or may not remember, but Niqmaddu's grandfather had two queens. The first one was the grandmother of Niqmaddu, but the other one was a princess of Amurru, whom your father made the legitimate queen. Her mother was an aunt of yours."

"And?"

"Our Sun deposed and beheaded Queen Taduhepa for treason, and her son was exiled back to Amurru. He's claiming the throne now." The dowager queen shook her head. "What can he be thinking?"

"No doubt he's thinking, 'This is rightfully my kingdom,'" said Ehli-nikkalu dryly. The mistrust settled like frost between them. *I'll bet she holds me responsible for this nephew's—whom I've never even seen—ambitions.*

"So, what did you come to see me about, my mother?" Ehli-nikkalu finally asked with a burr of sarcasm.

"Oh, dear. I've quite forgotten. You see what the burdens of a kingdom do to one." She laughed briefly in self-deprecation.

The younger queen stepped in quickly. "Well, I have something to tell you." *I will not ask.* "I'm going to make a little visit to my properties in Geru province and spend some time there. It's much cooler than the city."

At first, Sharryelli looked at her blankly, then she put out a hand and touched her daughter-in-law's arm. "Oh, my dear, I wish you could put it off awhile—until Niqmaddu gets home from his visit. Your security is just one more thing to have to worry about at a bad moment. I'm sure you understand. I'll ask my son, but I feel sure he'd want you to postpone it for the good of the kingdom."

Ehli-nikkalu's face burned. *You can't miss a chance to disappoint and humiliate me, can you?* "Very well," she said in a clipped voice.

She turned away in dismissal, but Sharryelli cried, "Oh, *that's* what I had come about. Did you ever find a secretary?"

"Yes." Ehli-nikkalu turned her back once more.

"Who is it, my dear, if I may ask? We need to be sure he's recompensed for the extra work."

"A man named Teshamanu."

Sharryelli stared at the ceiling for a moment, as if trying to place the name. "Is that Rab-ilu's brother? There was some scandal about him a few years ago. Are you sure he's suitable?"

"Quite. I'm not sure losing his whole family at once amounts to a scandal."

"Before that, I mean. He was a gambler, as I recall, and always after the, er, women of ill repute. A frequenter of low places. He lost almost all his property in gambling debts—quite unbecoming for a maryannu." Sharryelli's face reddened—no doubt with embarrassment for speaking of such defects in a member of the ruling class.

"Sounds like an interesting man." *He can't be any worse than Hattatamu.*

That left Sharryelli without words. She shrugged and smiled amiably, as if to say, "All right. The consequences be upon you. But don't say I didn't warn you," and made her exit.

The next day, as soon as the girl had emerged from her little room and before the children were awake, Ehli-nikkalu broke to Amaya the news that their journey had been delayed.

Amaya concealed her disappointment and said breezily, "That's all right, my lady. The weather won't turn for a month yet."

But the queen seemed less inclined to dissemble her frustration. "Sharryelli's doing this just to trammel my independence. What difference does it make if Niqmaddu is in Hattusha or not?" She tore off a piece of bread with her teeth as if she wished it were her mother-in-law's head. "And why couldn't they send *me* with the delegation, by all that's holy? Didn't they think I might like to see my father and grandmother after all these years?"

Being unaware of the duties of the royal family, Amaya had no answer, but she gave the queen a rueful look of understanding.

They finished their breakfast together, then Amaya went off to waken and dress the twins. When she came back out, Uncle Teshamanu had taken his seat at the table and was readying his wax tablet to make notes. His face unsmiling and troubled, he looked up briefly at her entrance but didn't acknowledge her.

Lady Ehli-nikkalu began to dictate a letter, and Uncle bent his head over his work. There was something very twitchy about him. After a while, as the queen paused, he asked her under his breath, "Do you read, my lady?"

She looked surprised. "Yes. Why?"

He bent to the tablet once more and pecked out some words. The queen, leaning over his shoulder, took them in then straightened, a look of alarm on her long face. He wrote a few more words, and a grim expression settled on her mouth.

"So," she said at last in a quiet, contemptuous tone. "I shouldn't be surprised. Every woman in that antechamber is probably a spy—and my chamberlain too." She raised her voice. "And they're probably listening in right now."

Uncle lowered his eyes, looking gloomy. At last, he leaned over again and wrote a few more words, which Ehli-nikkalu read. Amaya saw compassion in the queen's face as she looked at the back of Uncle's bent head.

"Thank you for your honesty," the queen said softly.

He managed to meet her eye for a fleeting moment then said in his flat, rough voice, "Will there be anything else, my lady?"

"No, except to assure you that your job is secure." She gave a conspiratorial little smile. "We'll see to it you have something to report."

The secretary folded his tablet and made his way out the door with a bow. Ehli-nikkalu saw the curious faces of the handmaids turn toward him as he passed and thought bitterly, *Not one of you had such courage.*

A bitter and triumphant smile on her face, the queen turned to Amaya. The girl looked up expectantly, too well bred to ask what had just gone on.

"Thanks be to the gods your uncle is an honest man, Amaya, my dear. He just revealed to me"—she drew closer to the girl and lowered her voice to a near-whisper—"that Shipti-ba'al approached him yesterday evening to ask him to spy on me."

"Oh, my lady!" cried Amaya in horror.

"Teshamanu pretended to agree, but as you see, he told me about it. The queen's attack dog threatened to blackmail him, proposing on one hand to expose his debts and on the other to pay him off well if he cooperated. He was acting for *her*, clearly."

"And she was acting for the king, I suppose. Poor Uncle."

"But he proved himself an honorable man, and now I trust him." Ehli-nikkalu's gaze softened. "Your father would have been proud."

Author Note: The Umman-manda are a group of marginalized people—refugees and outlaws—who have banded together and live at the edges of society, sometimes robbing caravans, sometimes even attacking settlements.

Nobody asks women of the royal families of the Bronze Age who they want to marry—they're sent where a treaty is needed. They don't have to be happy to be useful.

Fortunately, despite his reputation as a wastrel, Teshamanu turns out to have something left of his maryannu honor.

Chapter 6

A few days later, Ili-milku visited the queen with the latest from the council meeting. The Great King wasn't happy with the loyalty of his vassal and was considering appointing a Hittite mayor for the kingdom.

"Replacing the king?" Ehli-nikkalu's heart leaped in malicious glee. It seemed almost too good to be true. *Maybe my letters have had some impact after all.*

"No, no. Just another layer of supervision. A delegate of the viceroy who would live on-site and supervise everything. He would have to second decisions and such. Needless to say, the council greeted it with extreme, well, hostility. Outrage, you might say." Ili-milku waggled his tufty eyebrows as if to suggest that "outrage" was an understatement. "The king was apparently livid. Let's just hope he doesn't show his anger too overtly while he's at court."

The queen gave a bark of caustic laughter. "I daresay he *was* livid. May the gods help anyone who he thinks isn't showing him sufficient respect. But what kind of respect does my father owe a paltry vassal like him?"

At last, he brought forth a letter addressed to the queen that the latest courier from the imperial capital had delivered. She seized it eagerly, her heart in her mouth, and cracked off the clay envelope with a tap of her spindle. It was written in Neshite, in Akkadian script. Alas, she could not decipher it, only recognize the phonetically spelled names.

She held it out to the chief scribe. "Do you mind reading this for me, Ili-milku? It's from my grandmother, and I don't want to wait until Teshamanu gets here."

"But of course, my lady. I, uh, I don't speak Neshite, but I can read it and translate it for you."

So long had passed since her last letter home that Ehli-nikkalu wasn't even sure what she had said. Certainly, the warning about Niqmaddu's disloyalty and the proof thereof had never made it to Hattusha, so this had to respond to some earlier attempt to put her father on his guard against the machinations of his vassal.

She seated herself on the spinning stool with her hands folded in her lap—as if, she realized with amusement, her grandmother were going to speak to her in person. The children had always listened to *Hannah*, Grandmother, with the most respectful attention. Except once, when one of her younger brothers had danced around, chanting, "Hannah, hannah, *tawananna*." It must have been Shuppiluliama, the baby. He was always a little troublemaker. She smothered a laugh. Such wonderful memories of childhood and home trailed along with the thought of her grandmother.

Ili-milku cleared his throat and glanced over the script then began to read haltingly as he translated into Ugaritic. "'From Puduhepa, the tawananna in Hattusha, to her granddaughter Ehli-nikkalu, queen in Ugarit. Peace to you. I am well, and your father and brothers are well. I hope you are well.'" He drew a deep breath, scanning ahead. "'I have received your latest letter, and I have to tell you how... how disappointed I am.'"

Ehli-nikkalu felt an icy frost creeping up from her feet toward her chest that she feared might stop her heart when it reached it. The scribe had fallen silent, looking up at her, unsure, and she urged him with a brush of her hand. "Go on."

He continued in a voice that grew quieter and quieter. "'To hear you complaining like a little girl about everything in your life, letter after letter, displeases me. Perhaps your mother didn't teach you well, but what did you learn at my knee? Must you divulge the most intimate details of your marriage to the whole world? Think, my dear: you are a princess of Hatti Land, a daughter of the Sun. Where is your dignity?'" He stopped again, his brow furrowed with distress. "My lady, do you want me to go on?"

Ehli-nikkalu controlled her burning face and said a little harshly, "Of course."

"'We have ambassadors who bring us news of the court and its political positions. Pray control this barrage of generic accusations. We know our vassals are self-interested, my granddaughter. How would they not be? You say you want to be admitted into the political life of your kingdom, yet you show yourself disloyal and unworthy to carry its secrets. What I would like to hear is that you have borne your husband a son. It's not too late—I was ten years older than you when I had my last child. But if you speak of him with such hostility, no wonder he finds no pleasure in your company.'" Ili-milku swallowed hard and licked his lips, as if deeply embarrassed by the words he was reading.

As well he might be, Ehli-nikkalu thought, steeped in shame and misery. She mastered her desire to weep and set her face stiffly. "Continue."

The scribe heaved a sigh. "'We have serious need of your kingdom in these times, and the cracks you are causing in our relationship are troubling to your father, who has difficulties enough without having to worry about you.'"

In spite of herself, Ehli-nikkalu sucked in a great, gasping sob. She bit her lip. After a moment, she was able to control her voice and instructed the scribe, "Go on."

"'I hope your next letter demonstrates that you have learned something, my dear granddaughter.'" Ili-milku looked up, his chubby face with his big brown eyes melting with pity. "That's all, my la-dy."

She sat as rigid as a statue on her stool, staring ahead of her. "Thank you, Ili-milku."

With a hopeful spread of his hands, the scribe murmured, "Perhaps it doesn't sound quite so harsh in Neshite, my lady. Perhaps my translation was..."

But Ehli-nikkalu gave a wry bark of laughter. "It would sound harsher in Neshite, believe me. My grandmother spares no one." She stood up, walked stiffly to the loggia window, and stared out into the garden, where autumn had begun to fade the leaves, although it was still hot. She wanted to say something offhand, to sound as if she were used to that sort of treatment from her family, as if it didn't mean so very much to her. But she felt as if her soul had leaked out through her shoes and that nothing was left of her but a shell without feeling. She was numb, as icy as a stone.

Do they hold me in contempt at home too? Am I a disappointment to them, too, because I have not borne a child? Don't they see how this has stunted me, twisted me, made me critical and bitter about every-thing? It wasn't the real Ehli-nikkalu in the words of that letter she had sent, of all those letters—it was the cold, soulless shell who had been such a disappointment to everyone, the one that had turned in-to a living complaint, a bottomless well of bile. She could feel it ris-ing up like a black tide through her middle, wanting to claim her and disfigure her, to make her its soot-black acid-pocked creature, brittle and disintegrating, to blacken her all.

"Is my lady unwell?" Ili-milku asked behind her, concern trem-bling in his voice.

She shook her head. She wanted to dismiss him, to say, "I'm fine, Ili-milku. Please don't speak of what you have heard here." But even more, she wanted him to tell her that her grandmother was wrong. That she was a good queen, a good daughter of Hatti, and that her subjects loved her. That her father still loved her. *Oh, Father. I wouldn't heap more trouble on you. I only want to help. I love you, my father.*

She could feel the burning tears brimming in her eyes and raised a wrist to brush them away, but it was like trying to hold back the River Marasshantiya with an apron. So she let them fall and run down her face and her chin and into the neck of her blouse. She didn't make a noise, but her shoulders jerked, and her mouth was stretched down into a sickle like the waning moon.

After what seemed like a long time, Ehli-nikkalu drew a breath again. She wiped her face with a corner of her veil and sniffed a few times. When she felt she could speak once more without embarrassing herself with a breakdown, she turned to Ili-milku, who still stood behind her, his face anxious, his tufted eyebrows rippled with compassion. "Thank you for translating that, my lord," she said, all propriety. "I believe that will be all for this morning."

"Of course, my lady." He bowed and started to leave, then he added quietly, "If my lady has need of anything, I am here to serve."

She nodded stiffly, and he was gone. She stood in her bedchamber alone, her eyes gritty and tear-boiled, her nose stopped up. *Don't act like such a child,* she told herself. *You know how Hannah can be when her temper is up. After she's savaged you, she'll kiss you and say she didn't mean it.* But usually, she *did* mean it. "It" was simply one of those painful truths one shrank from hurling at a beloved child until one was angry enough.

So Ehli-nikkalu was at fault for many of her miseries. It was her fault that the king kept as far away from her as possible. She forced herself to accept that—painfully, as it stuck a dagger in her pride. *But does that give him the right to treat me with disrespect? To jerk me around like a slave? Was I wrong to offer my father whatever I knew about the intentions of his vassal? How could I—or Hannah—know what the Great King's ambassadors or spies or the viceroy and his men knew?*

Yet Ehli-nikkalu had to admit that she was probably the least well-informed person in the kingdom, certainly until Ili-milku had decided to help her. Maybe she was nothing but officious to think that she alone could pass along any profound insights. *Generic accusations.* For these had Rab'ilu died, she realized with shame. And she had thought she was so helpful, that her father would be grateful and say, "No one could have done a better job, my daughter." What naiveté. The fact was, she hardly knew her father. He was a remote, almost divine figure who looked at her with a kind of aching, awkward affection once in a while but rarely even said hello. A jet of self-pity squirted up through her control, and she pushed it back down with a stern hand. *Very well. I can at least take criticism like a Great Lady of Hatti Land.*

But her self-esteem smarted the most beneath one thought—that no doubt Sharryelli and her henchmen had read the letter before it was delivered. She could picture her mother-in-law's smug pink smile, her scarcely concealed enjoyment of Ehli-nikkalu's humiliation. And the dowager would turn it against her: "See, dear? Even your own family thinks you're disloyal and obsessive."

Could they have altered my letters? Did they make me look even more immature and whining? Ehli-nikkalu couldn't endure it. She had some self-respect, after all. Anger began to smolder under her breastbone, staining her soul with its bitter black soot.

She had planned to dictate to Teshamanu the juiciest court gossip she could find—or manufacture. But now she was afraid of what would happen if they were, in fact, delivered. Her own dear Hannah had joined the circle of enemies that had closed in on her. The queen told herself sternly that she would write no more letters home, except to describe breezily anything of interest that had happened—whatever that might conceivably be in her joyless life.

It seemed like very little time had passed before King Niqmaddu returned from his vassal visit to their overlord in Hattusha. So much so that Ili-milku wondered if it hadn't been cut short. But instead of presiding over the council meeting in person, the king had pleaded weariness from his travels, and it was Lady Sharryelli who stood before the men who collaborated in the rule of Ugarit, ready to brief them.

Ili-milku cast a surreptitious look about the council room, with its red-painted dado and high windows. Except for him, present by virtue of his office, those present were all *maryannuma* of the highest birth—and the most impressive wealth. Merchants, shipbuilders, owners of vast agricultural holdings or of dye works that produced the priceless purple dye for which the city was renowned, men who had value apart from the favor of the king. The late Rab-ilu had sat on the council, but his presence had become as welcome as a vulture at a wedding, always reminding the men, just by being who he was, of their dead honor. That memento mori had disappeared now, and venality woke from its hibernation.

"My lords, my lords!" cried Sharryelli in her high-pitched voice. She carried a tablet in either hand. "Let me report for our king on his visit to Hattusha." The buzz of voices didn't subside, and she turned to her son-in-law at her side. "Make them be quiet, Shipti-ba'al."

Shipti-ba'al let out a piercing whistle, and the chatter died immediately. All eyes focused on the small, pretty, pink-cheeked woman who stood before them, tablets pressed to her bosom.

"Well, gentlemen," Sharryelli said with a thin smile, "you will remember that we received two messages from our king in his absence. This one"—she held up one hand—"signed by Niqmaddu with his birth name, says everything is going well, and that the face of Our Sun shone upon him. Isn't that wonderful?"

The men nodded, curious and a little suspicious. Such was the message they had expected.

"But this one"—she held out the other hand and brandished the tablet at her interlocutors—"which is dated a mere day later, says something very different. It comes from Queen Puduhepa, the tawananna, the Hittites' dowager. It appears that our dear king's reception was far from warm. He completely omitted the visit to the tawananna, and his presents for the vizier were—and I quote—'insultingly insufficient despite clear instructions from the Foreign Office.' Niqmaddu's two ambassadors, our own dear Tuna and Dagan-ba'al, were arrested! Maryannuma lords, prominent sons of Ugarit, locked up overnight!"

Something has gone wrong, thought Ili-milku uneasily. *What in the world could have happened?*

"Now that our king has returned home, we have at last the explanation of this strange discrepancy. My lords, our kingdom has been dealt a grave insult. You all know about the mayor to be imposed upon us, in addition to the viceroy."

A rumble of displeasure arose.

"Another layer of burdensome servitude, even while our overlords are draining us dry—siphoning more and more of our grain, commandeering our fleet to the point we can scarcely carry on commerce."

Predictably, that reminder awoke in these seafaring merchants a hot reaction. Someone cried out, "Is there no limit? What are the Hittites doing for us?"

"Niqmaddu, as the brave and loyal man he is, expressed his displeasure to the court at Hattusha—forcefully, my lords. He was speaking for all of us. And what did they do to him? They humiliated him in public. Their tawananna savaged him—*in public.* Imagine the shame to our kingdom, our king dressed down by a woman." Sharryelli stared around at her countrymen, eyes blazing.

It was quite a remarkable performance, Ili-milku thought. The queen wasn't a figure on whom righteous indignation sat comfortably, but she was doing a passable job at implicating them all emotionally in the king's humiliation.

"And so, to make it clear that we were not anybody's footstool, Niqmaddu refused to turn over the gifts he had carried for the tawananna. He brought them right back to us. And those for the vizier too."

The men erupted into a loud babble of bellicose approval, but a shiver ran up Ili-milku's spine.

Those diplomatic gifts were set by protocol; to leave off a part of them like that would be interpreted as a calculated—and unpardonable—affront. *Dear gods of our city, help us now.* He noticed from the corner of his eye that Shipti-ba'al was unusually quiet.

"I say let us offer our good king a token of our approval and loyalty," drawled a gray-bearded merchant. "Show we're ready to stand by him if there are reprisals. How would those bastards like it if we stopped shipping their grain?"

After permitting the hubbub to mount excitedly, Sharryelli finally patted the air for quiet. "We will meet again when Niqmaddu has had time to recover from his exhaustion. He can tell you personally how he was treated, and you can judge for yourselves whether he did right." She stared around the room, looking each man in turn in the eye. "Consider how we can make our grievances heard."

"We must stand up to the northerners," Lord Yabni-shapshu cried in his nasal, drawling voice. He was not a man Ili-milku liked or respected—a sycophant of the worst sort. "Our Sun has had his chance. Let's change our vassalage to Mizri. They would never treat us this way." The maryannu turned to his colleagues, especially the junior ones, to see how they received his words.

"Ah," Shipti-ba'al said at last, "but my lord Yabni-shapshu seems to have forgotten the visit of the Egyptian minister last week. Mizri doesn't seem to want us as a vassal." He recrossed his legs and leaned back in his chair.

"No," Sharryelli confirmed sadly. "They gave us nice gifts, but it was all a polite way of saying, 'No thank you.'" She laid the tablets on the table and dusted her hands. "It's been a hard week for the prestige of our dear kingdom, my lords."

"Go over to Assyria!" shouted another of the maryannuma. "They want a coast—there's nothing they won't pay us for access to the sea."

"We'll discuss this when the king is among us." Her face aflame with fervor, Sharryelli favored them with a look of brave resolution, and the council members filed out, still grumbling and expostulating among themselves. The dowager queen and Shipti-ba'al brought up the rear except for Ili-milku, who, with a sick sinking in his middle, mulled over the gross imprudence of their king's action and what it was likely to mean. In his distraction, he dropped his stylus and tablet. With an oath, the chief scribe got down laboriously on his hands and knees and crawled under the table to retrieve it.

As soon as he dodged out of sight, he heard the door close quietly, and Sharryelli said, "Let's step back in here for a moment."

Ili-milku froze.

Shipti-ba'al hissed in an intense undertone, "Is he crazy? Does he realize what terrible repercussions his childish fit of pique is likely to bring down on us?"

"Now, now, my dear. Don't be so negative. There are other suzerains out there. You heard what Yabninu just said. Assyria would do anything to use our coast."

Lord Ba'al Haddu, protector of our city, help us! Ili-milku could feel the cold sweat spring out on his temples. Lady Ehli-nikkalu was right. Treason had reared its ugly head at the very top of the kingdom, an asp whose bite might well kill itself rather than its intended victim. He licked his lips and looked around for a way to escape. He had a feeling things wouldn't go well for him if the queen found out he was witness to her seditious conversation. But there was no place he could crawl that he wouldn't be seen—assuming his middle-aged knees could endure such a trajectory across the stone paving. Scarcely daring to breathe, he tried to settle himself less uncomfortably.

"I think that's a very naïve evaluation of Assyria's real intentions, my mother. Our Sun is in the middle of a war against Alashiya. A landlocked nation is attacking an island. *Who* would you say is really willing to pay 'anything' for the use of our ships?" Shipti-ba'al's tone was distinctly sarcastic. "If you want my advice, we should do everything we can to make up to Our Sun and convince the king not to repeat that terrible gaffe in diplomacy."

"Shipti-ba'al," Sharryelli said icily, "when I married you to my daughter, I assumed you would put your talents to the service of the crown. You yourself have told me how much goodwill with Alashiya this war will cost us. When ships show up on their shores filled with Hittite soldiers, the Alashiyites will know where they came from. Then what happens to our oldest trading alliance?"

"I'm a lot less afraid of Alashiya than I am of Hatti, my lady. If they decide to destroy our ships in harbor, where is our livelihood? We have to stay on their good side," Shipti-ba'al growled.

After a moment of silence, Sharryelli said sweetly, "I'm surprised you're such a supporter of the Great King. You know how many constraints they have put on trade with Mizri—and you of all people have an interest in that not happening. They don't call you 'the Egyptian' for nothing, my dear."

Ili-milku, huddled painfully under the table, let out a cautious breath. He wanted desperately to be somewhere else. Then, to his horror, he heard footsteps approaching, and someone drew a stool out from the table not a cubit away from him. A second stool slid out with a screech, and the feet of the dowager and her son-in-law were thrust under his nose.

His heart was caught in his throat. *If they find me here...*

Another long silence. Sharryelli said as cheerfully as if she hadn't been arguing against it, "Well, we need to find some method to win our way back into Our Sun's graces. You must think of something, Shipti-ba'al. For sure, nobody else will be devoting any energy to it."

He gave a snort of disgust. "You'd think it would be Niqmaddu doing that, wouldn't you?"

"Well, he won't. After making his stand, my son isn't likely to back down and grovel." She made as if to stand up but stopped. "Maybe I have an idea myself. We'll talk again. I'll need your help. I'm not sure anyone else would go along with it."

"Are you so sure *I'll* go along with it, my dear queen?" There was a curious snide note in his voice, as if there were a whole unspoken meaning beneath his words.

And the queen's reply was laden with the same weight of significance. "Now, Shipti-ba'al, dear. You know you'd do anything to please me. My daughter is pregnant, and pregnant women are often touchy and suspicious. Would this be the best time to let drop that her husband had his way—with her own mother?"

A stunned silence fell. Ili-milku suppressed a yelp of shock and suddenly found it hard to breathe. *What is this?* He had heard remote rumors—more snickering wagers than serious reports—that there was more than a filial relationship. *That certainly explains his loyalty to the queen mother.*

Shipti-ba'al snarled, "You would do that? To your own daughter? You are an evil vixen, aren't you?"

"I have a duty to this kingdom as its queen. And I, a princess of a country that no longer exists, am attempting to carry it out without any of the native advantages of you maryannuma," Sharryelli said with pious self-righteousness. "I'm a little woman in a big man's world, and I must use whatever tools I have at hand. If you were digging a hole, you wouldn't refuse to use a shovel, would you? I make sacrifices for Ugarit myself, and I expect others to as well. Is that so evil?"

"So that's what I mean to you? A useful tool? Someone you'd willingly ruin, along with breaking your daughter's heart?" Shipti-ba'al made a noise of disgust.

Sharryelli didn't reply, but Ili-milku thought he heard a little laugh. *Oh, dear gods, let them leave. Let me get out of here. My life isn't worth a donkey turd if they find out I'm listening.* His knees screamed. His back clenched up. He couldn't hold this crouch forever. *Let them leave.*

At last, the two stools scraped back, and Sharryelli and her son-in-law rose. Without a sound—but with a chilliness that was almost physical—the two left the council room and shut the door forcefully behind them.

Author Note: We know historically that Niqmaddu muffs his interview in Hattusha by not delivering all the gifts and almost provokes reprisals from Hatti. Alashiya is the island kingdom of Cyprus.

Chapter 7

Ili-milku was eagerly on his way home for lunch, crossing through the empty ceremonial dining rooms to the main entrance of the palace, when he heard someone calling his name. On edge from his narrow escape, he jumped and gave a little cry. But it was only the queen. On her long legs, she came toward him out of the darkness at a quick pace like a colt galloping for the barn.

"Ili-milku, what happened at the meeting?"

He shushed her urgently, staring around him in terror, and she cocked her head in surprise at his seeming disrespect.

Her voice dropped. "What is it?"

"Not here, my lady. Can we go somewhere private?"

"Meet me in my apartments in a few minutes."

Oh no, oh no, he thought. *I want out of this bargain.* But he liked her, and he felt she was mistreated by being kept in ignorance of the affairs of the city. *And what harm could it do just to tell her what everybody else in the royal household knows?* So he gave Ehli-nikkalu a few minutes to reach her rooms, then he proceeded up the scribe's staircase and headed toward the royal residences from the other direction.

In the upstairs corridor, he passed the king's chief concubine, the Lady—loosely speaking—Pu-haddu, with her eldest son, the crown prince, a robust little lad of six. Ili-milku bowed respectfully at the waist and heard the prince say as he went past, "Look, his head is shiny."

He stared after the departing pair, fascinated despite himself by the undulating derriere of the royal mate. He thought of poor Ehli-nikkalu, doing battle against such competition for the king's favor, and decided she deserved at least a bit of information. After all, if Sharryelli's suspicions were correct, the queen might be up against more than a little feminine rivalry. If she really was, well, tattling on her husband's government, there was no telling what they might do to her.

Ili-milku was in an anxious state again by the time he knocked on the queen's door, and the eunuch chamberlain admitted him.

Ehli-nikkalu looked both eager and worried, red spots alight on her pale cheeks. "Is something wrong, Ili-milku? Is anybody following you?"

"I doubt it, my lady, but there was talk today of someone having undermined the king's mission to Hatti, and everyone seemed to look at me."

"Did it go badly, then, the mission?" A hopeful smile played across her face.

"Apparently." He recounted in brief the dowager's report.

"But it sounds like the gifts were wrong. That's not anyone's undermining. Niqmaddu just didn't do it right. He didn't even visit my grandmother."

"I hope you're correct, my lady. Please be careful. The council may start to suspect you. If they decide your priorities are stacked against Ugarit, they won't spare you."

She drew herself up, mantled in her full dignity. "They wouldn't dare attack the Great Lady of Hatti Land officially."

But Ili-milku shook his head. "Oh, my lady, don't rely on that to save you. Why, only seventeen years ago, another queen—and she was a princess of Hatti, too, through her mother—was put to death for conspiring against the king."

"I remember that," Ehli-nikkalu said, suddenly uneasy. "She was my cousin, only two years older than I was. Aunt Gasshulawiya's youngest." She fell silent, her brow troubled. Then she looked up and, partly defiant, partly pleading for affirmation, said, "But she was working against my father and the treaty, not for it. She shamed us."

Ili-milku sighed yet again. He felt he couldn't draw a breath with all the weight that lay upon him. *Us. Those are the people we call* them. "Just be careful, I beg you."

He listened to his stomach growl as a thud, a scream, and a scuffle came from outside the door to the loggia, and two flapping, fluttering missiles seemed to drop from the sky and crash to the floor in the doorway. The queen cried out in horror and ran toward the scene. Already, half the wild pair had taken to its wings and rowed strongly back up into the air with a shriek of triumph—a hawk. Left in its wake was a dove, struck down in flight by the larger, swifter bird. It lay dead, its gray plumage strewn all over the floor near the door, its poor little feet curled helplessly, pointing upward. Its obsidian eyes were veiled with transparent lids. Blood spattered its breast.

Ehli-nikkalu gave a sob and knelt to cradle the bird in her hands. Ili-milku was overcome with gut-sinking sorrow. It seemed like a terrible omen of some sort. He had never seen the queen weep. She was always cool and self-contained, even haughty, in public. But she was crying like a child, shaking her head and stroking the dead bird's plumage with her long fingers.

Finally, she laid it gently down and covered it with a shawl. "I can't bear to look at it," she said in a trembling voice and turned away.

They stood silent for a long time, during which he tried to think of something consoling to say, but he was frankly overcome by the fear of what an augur would read into this.

At last, sniffing and tight-voiced, Ehli-nikkalu said, "This may interest you, Ili-milku, as a poet. We have a song at home called 'The Moon That Fell from Heaven.' Once upon a time, the Lord Arma—you call him Yarikh—fell out of the sky, where it was bright and beautiful, and he reigned as king of the night. He fell all the way to earth, and he landed in the mountains." Her voice cracked, but she continued. "He... he lay broken on the rocks, flailing around in pain, and bits of himself, like... like silver feathers, were thrown all around and stuck to the rocks." She began weeping again, mucus running down her lip, her shoulders shaking. "The other gods sprayed him with water and shot lightning at him, but nothing could pry him loose or make him whole again. Until his beloved wife, Nikkal, called him, and he rose back up to the sky. But ever after, bits of his silver have been found in the rocks of the mountains, and you can see how parts of his shining silver face have been peeled away." She covered her face with her hands, bent over, and wept as if her heart would break.

Ili-milku felt as if bits of him were stuck all over the rocks too. If she had been anyone other than his queen, he would have taken her in his arms and comforted her, but nothing like that could possibly happen. He stood, wilted with compassion, wondering what awful sorrow gnawed at her that the sight of a dead bird could awaken such a reaction. Gods help him, but he wondered if he could use any of it in a poem.

The more she ruminated over that encounter with Ili-milku in the days that followed, the more Ehli-nikkalu was deeply embarrassed by her tears. *What came over me?* All at once the tragedy of her own situation had struck her like that hawk dropping from the sky. She, who had always been so strong and cheerful, had fallen from her happy life at home into this underworld of miserable exile, where the gods had thrown at her all the sorrows in their arsenal. She had spent so much energy flailing around in outrage that whole bits of her nature had peeled off. *Does contempt and isolation do this to every-*

one, or has some secret flaw in my person cracked open under the stress? She felt she must get away—from her unkind husband, from her oleaginous mother-in-law, from the resentful looks and bland contempt their childless queen read in the eyes of the maryannuma. The time had surely come for her and Rab-ilu's children to go to Apsuna. She would be free in the country—could almost tell herself that all that heartache in the city no longer existed. Amaya would love her, even if no one else did.

However, Ehli-nikkalu dreaded asking Niqmaddu's permission. He had returned from Hattusha in a black mood, lightened only by his satisfaction with himself at having played the noble patriot—a satisfaction stoked by the queen mother and the councilors. He might be glad to see her go, or he might refuse just to thwart and hurt her.

She had to make an appointment to speak to him just like any subordinate. When the queen was finally admitted to the royal apartments, she saw, to her annoyance, that Pu-haddu was there. The concubine lounged at Niqmaddu's feet, a slight smile on her lips, her sultry eyes half closed. She made a point of drawing an arm around the king's legs, just in case the queen had missed the intimacy she enjoyed.

"I want to speak to you alone," said Ehli-nikkalu to her husband in an icy voice, refusing to look at Pu-haddu.

Niqmaddu hesitated then pushed the younger woman a bit, gently, and she rose and sashayed away, hips swinging.

His eyes followed her for a moment until he drew them back to his wife. They were as cold as chips of obsidian. "What?"

"I want to visit my properties in the north. You'll no doubt be glad to be rid of me for a few months."

He stared at her for a moment, a strange smile starting across his face that left uneasy prickles up the queen's arms. "My mother had mentioned that. Go, then."

Caught off guard by this easy victory, Ehli-nikkalu returned his gaze suspiciously then bowed.

"Who are those children who follow you around?"

Ehli-nikkalu's heart nearly stumbled. *So people have noticed them. We're barely getting away in time.* "Just some maryannu children. I'm training them as pages."

Niqmaddu nodded, but his eyes narrowed, and that mysterious smile continued to curl his lip.

The queen had turned in silence to make her way out, but the king said to her back, "I'll see to it you have a guard." She nodded without looking at him, not wanting to witness again that sly—dare she say—gloating expression. He clearly intended to enjoy her absence.

But just as the heavy doors closed behind Ehli-nikkalu, she heard Niqmaddu's voice raised in anger. "I told you to leave. You were listening to the whole thing?"

Pu-haddu said in a small voice, "I... I..."

Then, the sound of a slap and muttered curses. Ehli-nikkalu felt a little thrill of satisfaction at the humbling of her rival.

The morning of Ehli-nikkalu's journey to Apsuna arrived. In the royal plaza, wagons lined up alongside her private carriage as grooms backed mules and donkeys into the shafts, and royal equerries hitched them tight with leather lines. A continuous hubbub of preparation arose: the rattling of harnesses, the rumble of wheels on the paving stones, and an occasional bray of protest from one of the pack animals. Now and then, a groom would shout out an order, or a frantic clacking of hooves would resound as a mule was pushed into its hitch.

She watched from the parapet over the royal gate, too nervous and excited to stay in her room, yet not wanting to get underfoot.

From her vantage point, the boiling brew of men and animals looked like an army preparing to march. She wondered if the king had over-done the security demands. *Look at them all, in their crimson tunics, stowing spears and quivers full of arrows as if they were arming for war.* They were the special mercenaries Niqmaddu employed as his body-guard. She supposed there could never be too many soldiers as they entered into the territory harassed by the Umman-manda. The main purpose of the journey, after all, was to protect the children, to get them to safety with their grandmother, even if it had turned into a pleasure trip somehow in her mind.

And what fun it's going to be! Amaya would learn how to be a lady-in-waiting, and it would make her a more attractive bride for some maryannu looking to improve his credentials.

The weather was changing. The autumn morning was crisp, the stickiness of late summer suddenly a thing of the past. Ehli-nikkalu drew in a deep breath, filling her lungs with the smell of leather and animals and the damp clay of water jars that sat ready to pack in straw on one of the supply wagons. She could hardly believe her escape was really going to happen. Something about Niqmaddu's expression as he'd granted her permission had made her suspicious of a trap—she had fully expected him to rescind the go-ahead just to crush her with disappointment. But here she was. The mountains already called to her, offering healing from the wound her grandmother's letter had left in her soul. Perhaps the king was just glad to be rid of her for a while.

She looked up and saw a block of scribes crossing the bridge from the palace to the city ramparts, no doubt wanting, like her, to watch the preparations. Three reedy young ones and two older men, includ-ing Ili-milku, walked together. She smiled at his round, trundling fig-ure, although he didn't see her yet.

Chattering, the men approached the parapet where Ehli-nikkalu stood. Suddenly, one of them noticed her, and they all dropped into an obeisance.

She drew herself up and nodded a gracious greeting. "You've come to watch the caravan get ready, I see."

"Yes, my lady," Ili-milku spoke for them. He beamed happily. "We wish you a safe trip and a pleasant sojourn."

"Thank you for permitting Teshamanu to accompany us," she said.

"Your needs are paramount, my lady. He's there for your service. We'll manage without him."

Whether she needed him was a debatable question. Ehli-nikkalu hadn't written her family since the infamous letter. She might send them a happy, news-filled bulletin from Geru, might thus intimate to Puduhepa that she accepted her rebuke and would mend her ways. But in general, the scribe's presence at her side was a luxury she could best justify as a responsible party for his nieces and nephew.

She looked down again at the plaza and saw the king standing on the porch, his hands on his hips. He was accompanied by some of his young maryannuma friends and by Pu-haddu, who had Ammurapi, the six-year-old crown prince, in tow. They were talking and gesturing in turn, pointing to one thing or another. Ehli-nikkalu saw the little boy jump up and down with excitement and Niqmaddu open his mouth in laughter, although she couldn't be sure whether she heard him or only fancied it. He put his arm around the concubine. The sight filled her with sudden poignant jealousy. That scene of family happiness should belong to her. *But no.*

She wondered if Niqmaddu was as disagreeable around the mother of his son as he always was in her presence, or if Ehli-nikkalu had something in her, as her grandmother had suggested, that brought out the worst in him. Or if Pu-haddu, with her earthy beauty and fawning, unintellectual ways, simply offered him what he wanted in a manner that Ehli-nikkalu could not, not with all the good will upon the black earth. She was almost ready to believe that perhaps the young king wasn't such a bad sort, that maybe she was part of the fraught relationship between them—but then she remembered how he had cruelly twisted her arm, and her heart grew hard again. *Don't forget, you Zawalli gods: I want my vengeance.*

The sun was completely up, and Ehli-nikkalu made her way across the bridge to the palace, leaving the five scribes leaning on the parapet, observing. She descended the stairs, her shoes thumping on the wooden treads, her heart beginning to beat fast to the cadence of adventure. Her handmaids and chamberlain were gathered on the porch, while the king had disappeared. An officer of the guards called out orders, and his men formed up, stamping their boots and shouldering their spears.

Amaya, with the children in tow—Ba'aluya clutching her doll—came up the steps at a brisk pace. Their faces were as bright as the autumn-morning sun starting to creep across the walls of the palace and touch the shadowed plaza, their big, dark eyes as round as plates. Amaya threw herself at Ehli-nikkalu and hugged her in excitement. Ba'aluya snuggled her more quietly, shyly wrapping an arm around her hips.

Yanakh whacked around himself with an imaginary sword, crying, "Die, enemies of the queen!"

Teshamanu watched, his scowling face anxious.

"My lady and her party can mount now," the officer called in an accented voice. The man was tall—he must be one of the mercenaries.

Ehli-nikkalu took little Ba'aluya into her arms. Amaya and Yanakh joined hands, and they all made their way to the mule-drawn carriages prepared for them. The secretary followed them, where he hoisted the girls expressionlessly over the driver's seat. The guards would walk alongside.

Then they were squeezed tight on the seat of the carriage, the children's warm bodies next to hers, Ba'aluya's sharp elbow in Ehli-nikkalu's ribs. Teshamanu rode in another vehicle behind them with the servants. The mules began to move, their bells jingling, their steady hooves clopping on the paving stones. Ehli-nikkalu pushed back the linen curtains that hung on either side of the tentlike shelter of the carriage and watched the royal porch pass from view as the gate from the palace precinct into the city swallowed them up. In a moment, they were swaying and bumping down the street past the north wall of the king's house, leaving it behind. Her journey had begun.

Author Note: The Hittite poem, The Moon That Fell from Heaven, *is known today only in an incomplete version. It may be intended to explain the presence of silver on earth.*

Traveling is slow and dangerous in antiquity, especially at this period when so many dissatisfied people are roaming the wilderness. A short trip from the city of Ugarit to Apsuna in the north of the small country can take days.

Chapter 8

By the time the caravan had passed over the bridge across the drainage ravine and the city walls had receded behind them, Amaya had already traveled farther than she ever had in her life. Her eyes were almost frozen open, she had widened them so, not wanting to miss a single new sight. Ba'aluya drank in the sights just as eagerly, her doll forgotten in her lap, while Yanakh argued out loud with himself in some kind of imaginary play.

For the first few hours, the queen led the younger children in games, like seeing pictures in the clouds or being the first to spot a certain bird. But then Ehli-nikkalu became as silent and observant as Amaya, swaying drowsily to the movement of the animals and the rhythmic tinkle of bells as they crossed through olive orchards and pastures and fields of stubble. Everything was golden somehow, even the dusty air, and a wonderful, sweet smell followed them through the fields—not flowers but more like honey, only not so sharp. It was the smell of grassland in autumn, Amaya supposed—or the little gray-leaved, stickery bushes along the road—with something of hot mule skin in it. How she wished her mother could be there to see it all. No doubt Father had passed down that road many times. How she missed him. How she missed her mother.

Amaya glanced at the queen out of the corner of her eye and saw that Ehli-nikkalu was almost asleep, her heavy-lidded eyes drooping, her slim neck bent under the weight of her head. They had let the curtains fall back, and she had taken off her veil and cap. Her long hair fell over her shoulders like the fleece of a brown sheep. *She has such pale skin.* Uncle said that was because she was from the north. Amaya could see blue veins under the surface of her temples and under her eyes. She thought the queen was very beautiful, despite what other people might say. She loved the queen's long face and long, thin nose with a knob on the bridge. Everything about her was long and stretched out—her hands, her feet, and her back.

A greenish eye opened, and Ehli-nikkalu smiled. "Was I asleep?"

Amaya smiled. "I think so. It's nearly midday. We're getting into the hills."

At her side, Ba'aluya rubbed her eyes and slid up to a sitting position. "I'm thirsty," she murmured, still half drowsing.

"I'd like to have some water too. Wouldn't you others?" The queen caressed the girl's sleepy face.

"Shall I go tell the chamberlain?" Amaya offered. "There's water in the wagon with Uncle and the servants."

But the queen said, "No, it's too hard to get out while we're moving." She leaned out through the curtained opening of the carriage and called to one of the soldiers walking alongside.

He turned and stretched his neck a bit to see her.

She said loudly, "Tell my chamberlain in the wagon we want some water."

The soldier gave her a grin that was not altogether pleasant and wasn't very respectful, for sure. Amaya could feel the queen tense beside her.

Her long face grew severe. "Do you understand me, man?"

But the soldier replied something in a foreign language with a kind of nasty laugh. Amaya guessed he *didn't* understand. She began to feel uneasy. Something wasn't quite right. But then, what did she know about the etiquette of traveling?

The queen fell silent, her face stiff and thoughtful. When she turned again to look out at the passing fields, her expression was still uneasy, her eyebrows pleated. She kept looking at the soldier as long as he was in view.

Finally, Amaya asked, "Can't he speak Ugaritic?"

"I don't know, my dear. He must be one of the mercenaries the king hired. I'm not sure what language that was."

The queen had told Amaya that the bodyguards were mercenaries—men of all nationalities and of none—who hired themselves out to fight for anyone who paid them. They must speak many languages.

She forgot all about the strange soldier as the day wore on. They stopped for lunch by the side of the road, under some old olive trees, huge and wrinkly like ancient grandfathers, with a canopy of fine silver leaves overhead. The cicadas were so loud one could hardly talk, but everybody was tired and hot, anyway, and didn't have much to say. The cool morning had given up early, and it felt like summer again. Amaya was glad her hair was braided. *The poor queen, with her long mane.*

Uncle Teshamanu joined them for lunch, and they all sat on a blanket on the ground while the slaves unpacked their picnic of olives and chickpea spread and flatbread with pickled turnip slices. Although he was fat and old and probably felt the day's journey more than anyone, the chamberlain, Shamumanu, had to keep working. He served clusters of grapes after lunch, and Amaya and her brother and sister ate them to the very last. The queen seemed to have a wonderful time throwing them into Yanakh's mouth. To the delight of the others, he could catch them from the air like a dog and was extremely proud of himself. Uncle looked tired and introspective, a pleat between his eyebrows revealing some inner anxiety. He said little, speaking only when the queen addressed him.

They didn't even stay for a siesta but piled back into the litter after they had eaten and relieved themselves under the trees with the servants standing guard. The mules had to be yelled at and whipped a bit because they didn't want to start up again. Still, before long, the party had taken up the swaying, rocking pace of the journey once more. The mountains were closer, near enough to see the darkness of the forests on their flanks. She could hear the queen fighting back a yawn. Amaya yawned, too, and despite her intentions not to miss a thing, her eyes sagged shut, and she drifted off to sleep.

When Ehli-nikkalu awoke, they had entered the forest. It must have been the middle of the afternoon—long shafts of mote-shimmering light sifted through the leaves of oak and plane and chestnut already going a little golden with the end of summer. The two girls slumbered at her side in the heat of the tented carriage, their mouths open. The pace of the mules had grown labored as the road, which had become not much more than a trail, unspooled perpendicular to the slope but pushing steadily upward. She could hear the creak of wheels behind her, the jangle of harnesses, the dull, patient clopping of hooves, and the shuffle of booted feet in the dry leaves.

She closed her eyes and opened her nostrils to the perfume of the woods—the elusive sweetness of bracken and the pungent hint of fir now and again as the hardwoods began to give way to the darker conifers. *So rich in memories.* Cicadas droned. An occasional animal crashed through the underbrush, but no human voices could be heard. Ehli-nikkalu thought of the black forests that surrounded the city, perched between the high plateau and the higher hills, where she had been born. In her homeland, the mountains themselves were divine. Her father was named for the god of a mountain. Surely anyone could sense the sacredness of the place through which they sailed in their lumbering, rocking bark of a carriage.

She opened her eyes once more and, in a state of tender nostalgia, watched the passage of age-old trunks, of dense shadow and brilliant clearings, and of the brief flash of wings as a jay or pigeon fluttered from branch to branch. The swaying of the carriage almost lulled her into a state of wakeful dreaming.

Thus, at first, she wasn't sure how to react when, much later in the afternoon, Teshamanu appeared at the side of her wheel. He was a bit winded from having bypassed the intervening mules at an uphill trot. To stay abreast of her vehicle, he had to walk carefully sideways to avoid being scraped off the road by the trees, which enclosed them more and more tightly.

"My lady," he said with ill-concealed alarm, "I think we've taken a wrong turn."

"What? What makes you think so?" She became wide-awake.

"I've been to Apsuna many times, my lady. This is certainly not the road. We're heading east, up the mountainside." His dark eyes were wide with concern.

Ehli-nikkalu's first instinct was to tell him that was non-sense—the soldiers had to know the way. And indeed, there seemed to be no contradicting such an obvious fact; the king would never have confided them to guards who didn't even know the way to their destination. *Or at least, the animal drivers must know...* Less sure of herself, she asked, "What do the muleteers say?"

"I asked one fellow, and he said it looked to him as if we were off the route, but he wasn't that clear on where we were heading."

She fell silent, a niggling tendril of doubt working its way up her gullet. After a moment, hoping he had an answer, she asked, "How could that be? Perhaps there's a detour."

He shrugged and said nothing, but his eyes pierced hers and infected her with his doubts.

She whispered, "What's going on, then?"

The secretary looked around him and said uneasily, "Perhaps nothing, but—" He was cut off suddenly when he had to step back into the woods to avoid striking a tree that crowded the passage of the carriage.

A moment later, a high-pitched scrape sounded as a wagon bare-ly passed through the narrowing road, and a muleteer let out an out-raged cry. "What in the name of all that's holy! This can't be the right way!"

She stuck her head out the window of the litter and called out, "Officer, come here a moment."

Beside her, Ba'aluya sat up and rubbed her eyes. "Are we there yet?"

Ehli-nikkalu waited a decent space of time, measured by the thudding of the mules' steps, but no one responded. She saw Teshamanu had fallen back to the wagon where the servants rode, and he walked alongside its driver. Shamumanu stuck his head out the front of the wagon. The three of them were talking.

She called again loudly, "Soldier! You there! Tell your officer to come back here. I want to speak to him."

The man was only a few paces in front of her, at the side of the righthand mule. He turned his head, grinned at her, and turned back, never breaking stride.

Fear fluttered its wings in her heart, a gray dove that saw the shadow of more powerful wings overhead.

"What's wrong, my lady?" Amaya asked.

But Ehli-nikkalu had no answer. She knew only that something was gravely amiss.

Ahead of the carriage, the mule's driver plodded at its side, flick-ing it absently with his folded whip. Ehli-nikkalu watched the man's sweaty back flex with each climbing step and the appearance and reappearance of his heels in their dirty boots.

She cried out imperiously, "Muleteer! Stop this vehicle. I want to get out."

But he seemed to be deaf. His steps continued at the same trudg-ing pace.

"Do you hear me, man? It's the queen who commands. Stop the mules."

But nothing.

This is unnatural—like a nightmare where you want to scream for help but can't make a noise. She called out and called out, and no one seemed to hear. *Have I died? Am I nothing more substantial than a ghost lamenting in a voice no living being can hear? Or is something more physical—and more sinister—taking place?*

Amaya, at her side, asked, "What's going on?" The girl's voice seemed to echo, as if she said it again and again.

Those words hammered in Ehli-nikkalu's head like a pulse. She calculated her chances of climbing out of the litter as it moved, but the trees, which were little more than saplings, were closely serried, crowding in around the vehicle. The scrapes and curses behind her grew more frequent, but the path had become so steep that she suspected the carters feared to stop their wagons lest they roll backward.

She looked back at the wagon that followed, where Teshamanu and the muleteer and the chamberlain still appeared to converse heatedly, waving their hands and pointing. She could hear only "wrong road!" and "going on?" and "tell the king."

"What's happening?" she shouted to them.

Teshamanu slipped into the trees and began to squeeze his way through their slim trunks toward her.

In an anxious, high-pitched voice, the chamberlain called, "No one is sure, my lady."

Her secretary drew level with the carriage and hoisted himself awkwardly into it with his one hand. She drew the girls to the side to make room before he fell over her legs.

Amaya caught at him, crying, "Uncle, what's happening?"

That seemed to be the only thing anyone could say, the thing that consumed all their thoughts. The younger children awoke and stared openmouthed, infected by the adults' fear.

"What's wrong with the soldiers? Why don't they respond to me?" Ehli-nikkalu demanded.

The carriage had barely enough room for four people on the bench, even if two of them were small. Teshamanu struggled to the bed behind them and knelt there, holding on to the back of their seat. He said under his breath, "My lady, it seems to me that our guards have turned against us and are taking us over. The muleteers have no weapons and dare not stop the convoy on this slope. You may have noticed that the soldiers are all foreign mercenaries. I think they've rebelled. Perhaps they plan to hold us for ransom."

The blood drained from Ehli-nikkalu's face, and she put her arms defensively around little Ba'aluya's shoulders. "Oh no!" The children were under her protection. She couldn't let those barbarians harm them. "What can we do?"

"Try to survive. Promise them whatever they want." He drew his little penknife from his belt and hefted it. "Sell our lives dearly, if it comes to that."

Ehli-nikkalu fell silent, a knot of freezing fear inside her. If they wanted a ransom, it was she they would hold. *What will happen to the children and Teshamanu? To my innocent servants? To the grooms and mule drivers?* She was responsible for their welfare. They never would have found themselves in danger if not for her.

Then a more chilling thought assailed her. *Who will even care what happens to me? Will Niqmaddu or his mother? They would be only too glad to see an end to me. Will my own father, the Great King? Will my grandmother, the tawananna?*

She could imagine Puduhepa saying tartly, "Well, she *had* to go to Apsuna, didn't she, knowing it was dangerous up there? Let her figure out by herself how to get out of it. We're not paying the ransom. What good is she to us, anyway?"

She collapsed against the back of her seat, drained, her heart beating so heavily that she could feel it thumping against the leather cushion.

The trees grew sparser and thinner until, little by little, they gave way to a kind of clearing. It had long ago been cut over, but the forest was closing in fast once more. Bushes and bracken had reclaimed much of what was not bare rock, and whippy little saplings bent before the passage of the animals. The road, such as it had become, seemed to trickle to an end there. At the far end of the clearing stood the ruins of an old building, mostly its socle of stone, the mud bricks above them long melted out, the wooden beams fallen and rotted.

Tents had been erected within the ruins, the linen ghostly white in the fading twilight, while others stretched around them. Donkeys and even horses, raising their ears curiously at the arrival of the caravan, were picketed in the clearing. Four men stood up from a campfire they had been stirring. Others drew near from around the tents. They were all armed. Ehli-nikkalu saw upon one of the tumbledown walls of the old house a man with a bow drawn, its arrow nocked and aimed at the approaching party.

Teshamanu stared out through the curtains of the carriage, squinting into the fading light.

"Who are these people?" Ehli-nikkalu whispered.

When he answered, she was surprised she had spoken aloud.

"Brigands of some sort, I suppose. Maybe Umman-manda."

"But what does that mean? Who are the Umman-manda, exactly?"

He turned to her. "No one's quite sure. Refugees. Renegades. Deserters. Perhaps we're about to find out."

"Are they as bad as everyone says?" Amaya asked, a tremor in her voice. She turned a pale face to the queen.

"We'll see," her uncle said, and his voice sounded less sure than it had a moment before.

"I'll fight them off," promised Yanakh, brandishing his wooden sword.

But Ba'aluya snapped at her twin, "No you won't, silly. This isn't a game."

The officer of the king's guard walked calmly to meet the men at the campfire, and they exchanged words Ehli-nikkalu couldn't hear. Someone shouted orders, and the soldiers began to round up the grooms and carters, who were too stunned to resist. They dragged Shamumanu and the two terrified handmaids out of the wagon to a salvo of gross laughter and what were clearly obscene suggestions.

Ehli-nikkalu cried out in indignation, "Don't you dare hurt them. Those people are under my protection." But her words only seemed to provoke more laughter, and the men stared at her. They had mockery in their eyes; they didn't care that she was the daughter of the Sun. To them, she was just a helpless woman. She shrank back, her heart clenching with fear.

Teshamanu slid to the ground and drew his penknife. Confronting the ogling men, he cried, "Anyone who would touch the queen of Ugarit must deal with me first."

"No," she begged him in a low voice. "Don't try to be brave. You said give them what they ask for." *Dear gods, he may have been a soldier, but he only has one arm. I can't have his blood on my hands.*

Her grip tightened around Amaya's and Ba'aluya's shoulders. Ehli-nikkalu heard Amaya gulp, although she was clearly trying to behave calmly.

The tall officer swaggered up to the carriage on the other side from where Teshamanu stood menacingly. "My lady," the soldier said with a brief salute and a dry smile. "Welcome to our palace. You and yer people will be our guests for a while. If everythin' goes as planned, no one'll be hurt." He looked around and called out an order in another language.

To Ehli-nikkalu's amazement, she understood his words.

She was so stunned she hardly reacted when he turned back to her and said, again in Ugaritic, "Call off your guard dog."

Overcoming her shock, she begged her secretary to relinquish his knife, and he dropped it on the ground, his face growing thunderous.

To the officer, she murmured in disbelief, "You're Luwian? What are you doing here?"

"Aye, from Taruisha. Servin' the king of Ugarit seemed better than starvin' at home, my lady."

The Luwians were vassals of Hatti Land—the men of the West, whose populations had been scattered all over the empire through deportation. They were never content under the yoke of Hatti, but their western kingdoms were in a constant state of revolt.

Are all these people Luwians, then? But she had heard other languages she hadn't understood...

The officer said in a loud voice, "You're our guests, not our prisoners. Long as you don' try anything, you'll be left more or less free. But know that we're watchin' you. You're worth more to us unharmed, but don' trade on our goodwill, eh? Eh, little scribe? Because an arrow shoots a lot farther than you can stick with your little knifey."

He laughed, and the men around him picked up the sound, crude and uproarious.

Ehli-nikkalu's hair rose on her neck. *Luwians. No friends of the Hittite royal family.* She straightened and tried to look dignified despite the pounding of her heart. *It could hardly be worse.*

Someone pulled Amaya out of the carriage and set her on her feet. Ehli-nikkalu quickly swung her own feet out and slid to the ground before anyone could touch her, then helped the younger children out. She and the girls drew together, and Teshamanu edged toward them as if to stand between them and their captors.

Yanakh ran toward him. "Uncle! Are these bad people?" he cried, sounding partly excited and partly frightened.

"I'm sure they're not, my dear," Ehli-nikkalu murmured reassuringly. But she wasn't sure at all.

The soldiers hustled the two adults and the children toward the tents, and the servants shuffled behind them, one of the girls whimpering and praying aloud.

Don't give them that gift, Ehli-nikkalu thought. *Don't let them see you're afraid.* She said it to herself because she was desperately afraid, her innards clenched so tight she worried she would soil herself.

They made their way through the gathering darkness, their skirts catching in the brush, their feet slipping on rocks. Amaya held onto her siblings' arms. As the captives drew into the circle of the fire, the rest of the clearing sank into the night behind them. The crickets pulsed in the invisible trees, and it began almost immediately to grow cooler. Ehli-nikkalu looked up and saw a full moon rising just above the deeper darkness that marked the mountaintops. Its silvery light filled the eastern sky like milk, like foam, and began to cast shadows stronger than those of the fire across the clearing. *Lord Arma, Lady Nikkal, rescue us. I'm under your special protection, my lady. Don't let us die here,* she prayed.

A woman handed the new arrivals clay bowls of thin soup, and behind her, a boy passed out flat pieces of bread. Ehli-nikkalu took hers without demur. Despite everything, she was hungry. *Surely they wouldn't feed us if they intended to kill us.*

Ehli-nikkalu helped the younger children seat themselves on the ground with their bowls, and she ate standing up, but eventually, she sought a place to sit and found a pile of crumbling masonry that was close enough to the fire not to provoke the suspicion of her captors yet far enough away to feel herself bathed in the moonlight. She looked up at the face of Arma, his brilliant silver tarnished and peeled in places. *Poor thing,* she thought, her throat closing danger-ously. *Exiled from your beautiful heaven, broken and suffering.*

She thought of her homeland, shimmering under the same moon somewhere to the northwest; of the limpid moonlight on the walls of the capital, the gauzy mists rising from the spring that ran at its roots, like a divine city that had descended from heaven upon the foothills, still trailing clouds; of her brothers and sisters, wherever they might find themselves that night; of her grandmother; and of her father. *Is he on the battlefield somewhere? Does he ever think of me?* She pictured him as she had last seen him—when the delegation from Ugarit had come to Hakpish to take her away with them—so much taller than the Ugarites, a tall man even among a tall race, with his long face and quiet, hooded eyes. She remembered the love she'd seen in those eyes, pained with the inability to express it, because her father was not a man who could easily show his emotions. She felt her heart would burst with sorrow and longing. At last, with the silver moonlight stroking her back, the queen put her face in her hands and wept quietly.

*A*uthor Note: *Mercenaries are often former soldiers who hire them-selves out as fighters or guards. They have loyalty only to whoever pays them.*

Almost all of Ugarit (modern Latakia, Syria) is hilly, but some really serious forested mountains cut off the coastal plains just behind the city. Taruisha is the city known to us as Troy.

Chapter 9

In the camp of the Umman-manda, the days passed in a strangely quiet rhythm of domesticity. It was not the brigands' main settlement, whose location they were at pains to conceal. The men in the uniforms of the king's guard were rarely around, but one evening, when their officer was present, he seated himself beside Ehli-nikkalu at supper. She stiffened at his pungently unwashed body's proximity, at his muscular bulk, and at the ostentatious clank of his sword at his waist when he sat, not convinced he meant her no harm. But the man seemed friendly enough. He seemed, in fact, to want to talk.

"So here y'are, Our Sun's daughter. Is our hospitality to your taste?" He spoke in Luwian, a language she had spoken from childhood, like everyone else in Hatti Land.

"Why are you doing this?" she asked him frankly. "You have to know what will happen to you when the king comes after you."

The man grinned. "Only if he catches us. And though you've probably never known hunger, I c'n tell you, it's a powerful motivation, my lady. We're doin' it for food."

"Food? You mean you're asking a ransom in food?"

He nodded, a grin on his face that seemed to defy her disbelief. But his smile was replaced by a grimmer expression. "Two years ago, there was an earthquake in Taruisha. Lot o' people died. Property was ruined. People lost their livelihoods. Plenty o' misery. Along with the drought, you c'n imagine how it made the famine worse. People my age hardly remember a time without famine." His jaw clenched, the muscles in his bearded cheek taut. After a moment, he continued, "And d'you know what yer daddy did for us?"

She shook her head, afraid to hear the answer.

"Nothing. Big fat nothing. Except to take what little grain we had and ship it inland so's his horses could eat."

The man gave a cough of rancorous black humor, and Ehli-nikkalu felt a wave of pity for his bitterness and pain. Of course, her father had no idea what things were like in the far corners of his empire. He had to feed the chariot horses if they went to war, and the Lukka—to mention only one enemy—were constantly on the attack. The situation seemed so cruel, so complex, so insoluble.

She wished she couldn't understand it from the Taruishan's side. "But if you work for the king of Ugarit, doesn't he feed you?"

"Oh, aye. He feeds *me*. But not my cousins. Not my neighbors. We're thousands, my lady. We're tens o' thousands."

"All of you here are Taruishans?" Her eyes widened with incredulity. She had thought that Taruisha was loyal.

The officer laughed. "Not hardly. Same thing's going on all over the black earth. Him?" He pointed at a man stirring the fire. "He's a nomad from the east. Hungry, him and his tribe. That woman? She's Teukrian. Pair of them brothers is from Karkisha. All hungry. All tired of being squeezed so somebody else can eat. Runaway deportees, outlaws, deserters. There's actually some real Umman here and there. They're hungry too."

He subsided into dull anger, staring into the fire. Ehli-nikkalu's eyes were riveted to the man's rugged, sunburned face. *He was probably a farmer facing crop failure year after year.* He had seen his world sliding into the abyss. And no one could help him because they were struggling to stay alive too. Even the Great King. *Dear gods, is this the end of the world?*

After a moment, the officer heaved a sigh and pulled himself heavily to his feet.

Wanting to see him as a person and not just the villain who had kidnapped her, Ehli-nikkalu called after him gently, "What's your name?"

But he looked at her with an accusing grin, as if he thought she was trying to trick him, and answered, "It's Ba'alanu for now, my lady. What's yours?" He strolled away into the darkness.

Ehli-nikkalu was profoundly disturbed by the officer's tale. Lots of misery, indeed. Her small troubles grew suddenly insignificant. Yet instead of feeling lightened, she felt so heavy that it seemed the black earth must yield under her feet and swallow her. She rose, dusted her skirts, and drifted away from the fire. Women carried stacks of empty soup bowls off toward the tents, which glowed with the faint orange luminosity of lighted lamps through the linen. Around the fire, men whittled or fletched arrows or did the myriad tasks that an army encampment must do. Yet they were not just an army. They were a people, a vast, starving, embittered people.

Is anyone in charge of them? Have they a king?

Outside the pale light of the fire, the clearing darkened rapidly. She drew her shawl about her shoulders, chilled. The moon had just begun to rise over the mountains, swallowing up the stars in its cold, milky light. Ehli-nikkalu stumbled over the rough ground toward an outcropping of rocks, where she had grown accustomed to seeking solitude in the evening after the children had gone to bed. She had just groped her way to the rock, which retained some warmth from the afternoon, and settled herself upon it, tucking her heavy skirts around her ankles, when she saw a shadow approaching. It was a man's outline but in a long tunic, thus not one of the soldiers or muleteers. Certainly, Shamumanu would have been broader, so she guessed that it might be Teshamanu and called his name.

"My lady?" His voice was flat. He drew closer and stopped, still distant and silhouetted, then stammered, "I can go somewhere else. I didn't mean to disturb you."

"No, don't go away on my account. There's plenty of room for you here too. I won't talk." She smiled. "I like to come here and think in the evenings."

He murmured thanks and took up a perch on the other side of the rock, his back to the moon. They sat thus for a long time, back-to-back. The crickets chirruped in the forest, and somewhere, an owl hooted its desolate call. Quiet sounds of life drifted from the camp. Near the fire, someone took up a harp and began to sing. It had to be one of the Luwians. He was singing—in Neshite—"The Moon That Fell from Heaven."

Ehli-nikkalu dropped her head and clutched her shawl close about her, filled with sweet, aching melancholy that was both pain and consolation. Her chest was so tight she could hardly breathe. Thinking of the dead dove, of the Lord Arma, and of herself, fallen from her dear homeland and the love of her family, she heaved a sigh that seemed to empty her soul. She stared up at the tarnished silver face of the moon and saw that its perfect disk had worn away in only a few nights. Nothing endured. No good thing lasted, while pain seemed to go on and on.

"My lady?" Teshamanu asked with concern.

Ehli-nikkalu took hold of herself. "I'm all right. It's that song. It's from my homeland." She took a deep breath and added unsteadily, "It's... it's about loss. And love."

After a moment, he said, "Oh," and she remembered his loss and feared that she must have said something terribly hurtful without intending to.

"Forgive me. I didn't mean to..." She turned to face him, but he was all but invisible in her shadow.

"It's..." He had lowered his face in the darkness, and he sat that way, unmoving, for so long that she wondered if he had fallen asleep. But finally, he looked up at her, the moonlight glittering in his eyes, and said, scarcely above a whisper, "How much do you know about my past, my lady?"

"Only that you... lost your family all at once. And your hand, in trying to save them."

He swallowed hard and murmured, "I'm not a very good man. I don't know why—our family was fine, supportive. No one was ever unkind to me. But I disappointed them. How could I compete with Rab-ilu? He was so solid, so upright, always working, devoted to his family. I refused to do any of the things he did so well. It would only mean failure. So I did what he did not and joined the chariotry. That was honorable. And I became a good soldier. I fought with the bravery of one who had nothing to lose. I thought my family would be proud of me. But I started gambling, leading a dissolute life." His voice shuddered, and his face was strained and white with shame in the harsh light of the moon. "You deserve someone better as your secretary."

Ehli-nikkalu, thinking of Hattatamu, said kindly, "There's no moral standard for royal secretaries, Teshamanu. You're a good scribe and loyal—that's all that matters."

"I shouldn't be telling you this. I guess I suspect we may not get out of here alive, and I want someone to know the truth about me."

But thinking of Sharryelli, the queen thought that more people probably knew the sketchy past of Teshamanu than he realized. "Of course. Say whatever you want to say. I promise I'll never hold it over you."

The secretary took a deep breath. "My wife began to complain about how frequently I would leave the house at night. Once, she followed me and showed up on the doorstep of... of where I had gone. I was furious. You can imagine how guilty I felt, but I took it out on her. The next night, I—had the steward set a bar on the outside of the door to stop her from going out after me when I left."

"You locked her in?" Ehli-nikkalu gasped, knowing where that had to lead.

Teshamanu nodded. His dark hair, silver in the moonlight, dropped across his face, but she could still see the strong arch of his nose, the thin, downturned line of his mouth. His heavy breathing punctuated the stillness of the night, mingled with the sad, distant chords of the harp.

"There was a fire. The slaves got out, but my wife tried to save the children. By that time, the door into the courtyard was blocked with flames, and the front door... the door was... I had barred it..." He bit his lip with bared teeth and seemed to have been turned to stone.

Ehli-nikkalu reached out and took his arm in silent pity.

"I can't forgive myself," he whispered. "I didn't know how much I loved her until she was gone. I wasn't worthy of her love. I was unworthy... unworthy..."

A terrible compassion seized Ehli-nikkalu's heart and crushed it in a torturing grip. "That's not true. You must forgive yourself, Teshamanu. You've paid, after all—with your hand, with your career."

"If there were any justice, I would have died, not them."

"Your wife wouldn't want that, would she? Forgive yourself. You can be happy again. You'll see. You can remarry, fall in love again, redeem yourself. Don't let this ruin the rest of your life." Her eyes were wet with tears.

But he shook his head, disjointed, like a man who was too exhausted to hold himself upright. "I made a vow to the gods, my lady. I swore I would never again look at a woman if they would forgive me. I've kept that vow, to my misery. But lately... I've started to wonder. How do I know if they've accepted my offering? If I feel attracted to a woman... does that mean the vow has been rejected? If they can't forgive me, how can I forgive myself? How? How, dear gods?"

A vow? She felt a chill of disappointment run down her spine that she scarcely dared acknowledge. Her voice, when she could speak, was tense with something close to fear. "But, Teshamanu, is that a vow that pleases the gods? Do they ask that of anyone? They... they want us to be fruitful. Perhaps you're trying to force your own will on them." *He feels attracted? Could he mean to me?* The thought confused her, but she was not displeased. *Don't be ridiculous. He's just your employee, your subject.*

Teshamanu hung his head, facing into the darkness once more. The strains of the distant song seemed to grow louder. The singer had reached the verse in which the loving call of Nikkal reached out to her husband, awakened his last breath of strength, lifted him from the rocks of the earthly mountains, and drew him upward through the liquid night. *Such a night as this...*

Oh, Nikkal, rescue me too. Rescue Teshamanu. Rescue all these angry, starving people who don't know where to go or what to do. But love is the rescue, isn't it? And no one loved her, not there on the silver-strewn mountains of earth. She had a husband who mocked her and held her in contempt. A mother-in-law who lied to her and tricked her. No daughter to say she was beautiful. No son to defend her...

And Teshamanu—his case was even worse. He'd had love and lost it, destroyed it with his selfishness. It was hard to imagine—he who was so efficient, had so honorably reported to her the commission to spy on her. And he had sworn never to love again. *Whoever heard of such a thing?* Perhaps it was cowardice. Her heart went out to him in pity. *Someone needs to love him. That would be his rescue.* She tried to imagine herself being in love with Teshamanu, but she realized, disappointed, that in fact, she just felt pity for him. *Is pity the same as love?* It seemed they were confused in her mind. Yet she loved the children without pity. But that aching desire to protect them, that fear that they would be hurt by life, that they would grow old and die—*isn't that a kind of pity for their poor, limited mortality?*

Ehli-nikkalu heaved a sigh that seemed to loose her very soul into the night air. The song at the campfire was finishing, and she couldn't remember how the last verse went.

The next morning, Ehli-nikkalu and Amaya sat on the rocks, trying to make themselves useful to their captors, while the younger children played below. One of the Umman-manda women had given them spindles and distaffs and, without intelligible words, made it known to the captives that they should produce some thread for the cause. For the first time in her life, Ehli-nikkalu was grateful to have spinning to occupy her. She bent close to Amaya and demonstrated, as best she could, the kind of controlled grip on the unspooling wool that kept it in a tight feed. It occurred to her how dirty they were all getting. The girls' hands were taking on an overall dinginess from the sweat and the smoke and the dust and from eating with their fingers with no water to clean them afterward. Hers were no better, crescents of grime marking the quicks of her short, blunt nails. Yanakh had willingly descended into grubbiness, his knees black, his neck creased with dirt.

From somewhere on the other side of the tents came a racket of hooves and rattling wheels. Voices were raised in greeting, laughter, and excited conversation. She wondered what was happening. It sounded far too jolly to signal the arrival of rescuers.

A brief while later, an adolescent-sounding voice called out, "Where's the queen?" and a small, slim, good-looking youth with wildly disheveled hair strode toward her from around the rock. He was dressed in what had once been fine clothes of rich, expensive colors but which now showed severe signs of wear, and their last trip into the river to be beaten clean had clearly been some time in the past. "Are you the queen?" he asked cheerfully.

She drew herself up and nodded with dignity. "Who inquires?"

The young man made a flourishing bow. "Utri-sharrumma son of Ammishtamru."

Then, when Ehli-nikkalu remained sitting, he prodded, "Aren't you going to bow to me now?"

The queen stared at him in confusion. "Who are you?"

He spread his hands as if to present himself for her inspection. "I am the king of Ugarit."

Ehli-nikkalu froze. *The little man must be moonstruck.* She said carefully, "Excuse me, but the king of Ugarit is Niqmaddu son of Ibi-ranu. My husband."

"Wrong, my dear lady and cousin. Niqmaddu is the *false* king of Ugarit. I am the *real* king." He climbed up on the rock beside Ehli-nikkalu and, taking in her look of astonishment, threw back his head and laughed. "I'm the son of Taduhepa of Amurru, the wife of Ammishtamru, whom he had cruelly put to death. My grandmother is your aunt Gasshulawiya."

She wasn't sure what to make of her eccentric young relative. She smiled hesitantly. "Hello, my cousin. I don't think I quite understand..."

"No, because it's unjust and incomprehensible. Let me summarize by saying that despite having been my father's heir, I was demoted with my mother, and Ibi-ranu took my place in the succession. Of course, it was all very open-minded. I was four years old. They gave me the choice: either I could remain in Ugarit with my father—my big, scary, bearded father, his face bursting with anger—and rule or I could crawl away with my dear, comforting little mama and give up my chance to be king. Guess which choice I made. But, well, they did ask me." Despite his over-bright smile, he was clearly deeply angry, rotten with anger.

"What are you doing here, with the Umman-manda?"

"Planning my revolution." He grinned. "I can say this to you because you have no idea where we are and can't send anybody back here to kill me." Utri-sharrumma scratched his head at length and with a ferocity that indicated he had lice.

She drew away a little.

"You can tell my nephew, the false king, that I'll be seeing him—with an army at my back."

Ehli-nikkalu sat silent, not sure what to think. Internecine struggles were familiar to her dynasty, the gods knew. Her grandfather had taken the throne from his nephew, too, unleashing a generation of civil war that still dogged her father. She wondered if the strange, dirty youth would make a better king than Niqmaddu. Ehli-nikkalu had to admit, she didn't even know what kind of king Niqmaddu made. She could testify that he was a dreadful husband and not much of a human being, but perhaps his governance was effective.

"So you're using the Umman-manda as your army?"

"That's the plan. They need a leader, someone to legitimize them. I need swords. So far, most of our supporters have been in the north. But that's not to say that I have none in the city. There are more people than you might think who found the persecution of my mother to be highly distasteful."

She had heard about uprisings in the area around Apsuna, mysterious sabotage of dams and bridges, people killed or seized on the roads. "Was it you who ordered my kidnapping?" she asked.

"Ordered? Hmmm, too strong a word. Let's say *recognized the value of*. It takes a lot to feed a revolution. You're worth a great deal of food, cousin." He gave her a horse trader's look that was somehow too evaluating and too intimate to be courteous, then he laughed uproariously, a shrill, cawing laugh.

Ehli-nikkalu found Utri-sharrumma disturbing. She eyed him surreptitiously. He was a small, wiry man scarcely out of boyhood, with glittering gold-brown eyes and a reddish beard. His fine features were almost femininely perfect.

She wanted him to go away, but she said blandly, "How is my aunt?"

"Not happy with me, of course. Somewhat brokenhearted. She gave me the best upbringing she could, and I love her for it. But she does believe in law and order. Curious, for a woman whose father stole a kingdom, isn't it?"

"It was the Lady Shaushga who wanted my grandfather to become king of Hatti Land," Ehli-nikkalu said, feeling obliged to defend him.

"And no doubt she wants me to be king of Ugarit," he concluded cheerfully. Utri-sharrumma slid off the rock and bounced to his feet. He seemed to see Amaya for the first time. "Who's this?"

"My lady-in-waiting," the queen said uneasily. She didn't like the way the boy stared into a woman's face.

"How would you like to be a queen, little beauty?" He pinched the girl's cheek between his grubby fingers.

Amaya shrank back against the queen, her eyes flashing with anger and alarm, and Ehli-nikkalu felt protective fury rise within her.

She said in a voice scarcely polite, "Don't touch her. She's under my protection."

Her cousin's face grew sharp, like a fox in ambush, and his grin was dangerous. "I wouldn't antagonize me if I were you."

Author Note: Readers of The Sun at Twilight *will remember Ehli-nikkalu's father, Tudhaliya IV, and his love for her. And also the troublesome Luwians, grudging vassals of the Hittites.*

Later, the pressures of starving groups like the Umman-manda will destabilize Hatti, bringing it down, along with Ugarit and many other kingdoms. This will be the end of the Bronze Age.

Utri-Sharrumma, the pretender to the throne of Ugarit, will be familiar to readers of The Queen's Dog, *where he is banished from the kingdom with his mother as a toddler.*

Chapter 10

Amaya had trouble falling asleep that night. The odd, dirty young man had looked at her in a frightening way, and his pinch had left a white mark on her cheek. She was glad the queen had been with her, although there was little either of them could do if Utri-sharrumma decided he wanted Amaya for his own. She prayed that their rescue would come soon, before she had to defend herself against him and risk whatever reprisals such a madman might concoct.

She lay on the blanket that served as her bed, between the queen and the twins. Old Shamumanu snored on the far side, his belly a quivery mountain that rose and fell in the darkness. They barely had room to roll over, and if anyone had to relieve herself, she had to step over the others to get out. Amaya didn't know what it was usually like to be kidnapped, but their experience hadn't been too terrible. People were nice enough to them. They were fed at least something—the same thin soup over and over—and if they had a chance at a bath, it would be endurable. Except fear always hung over her head—things could get worse. She thought again of the foxy little man and shivered, a chill that didn't want to let go of her. If only her father were there to protect her.

At the memory of her parents, a deep, hollow pain throbbed inside her. *Wherever you are,* she reached out to them silently, *watch over us, please. Watch over the little ones. Watch over the queen. Get us out of here safely. I love you, Mother and Father.*

When morning finally came, Amaya didn't feel very refreshed. The west side of the mountain stayed in shadow until nearly midday, so it was still quite dark when the Umman-manda rousted them all out of bed. Amaya and the queen jumped up and put on their shoes while the two maids pulled Shamumanu to his feet and the little ones rubbed sleep out of their eyes. The eunuch wasn't as fat as he had been when they'd arrived only a few days or maybe a week ago. Amaya figured none of them were—her belt hung loose on her. She sometimes shared her food with the little ones so they wouldn't cry.

Ehli-nikkalu pinned her cap and veil on top of her long hair, which she had started braiding because it was so hot. Together, the four of them made their way to the perpetual campfire, where women handed out the same old bowls of soup. No bread that morning—her heart sank into the emptiness of her stomach. But the Umman-manda didn't have any more to eat than the prisoners did, which somehow made it seem more bearable.

Amaya saw her uncle crawling out of one of the tents on the far side of the ruined houses, and she called to him. Uncle Teshamanu barely caught her eye, but he made his way toward them, his face gloomy.

"My lady," he mumbled, making a small bow to the queen. He kept his focus somewhere near her feet. Amaya would almost have said he was embarrassed.

Ehli-nikkalu seemed equally reluctant to look Uncle in the face, so it made an odd dance, with the two of them nodding politely and avoiding one another's eyes. Amaya wondered what was going on. The queen had crept into the tent late the night before, snuffling. It was hardly imaginable that they had been up to something together—the queen was too proper, and Teshamanu was too surly. He was good-looking enough, but she couldn't imagine anyone being attracted by his glum, silent manner.

Every day, the weather became a little less summer and a little more autumn. It was still dry, but the mornings were cool, the afternoons pleasant if she wasn't exercising. Uncle went to gather wood with the men, off in the forest someplace, and at the queen's orders, took the children with him, although it seemed distasteful to him. But they needed to get out and run.

Amaya and the queen brought their spindles and distaffs to the big rock where they liked to work, far enough away from the fire that nobody bothered them. Amaya found that if she stood upon the rock, above its sharper face, her whorl could drop a very long way before she had to rewind, so the spinning went faster. She was doing pretty well with the fine thread, but sometimes it went thick on her unexpectedly. She cried out in dismay as a puffy spot slipped past her fingers and made its way down the lengthening string.

The queen looked up and smiled. "What happened?"

"I let it get thick on me. Should I rewind and do that part again?"

Ehli-nikkalu seemed distracted, her eyes a little vacant even while her skillful hands continued to manipulate the wool. "Well, you should, but I think it will be fine. I can't imagine these poor people are very particular."

"Are they 'poor people'?" Amaya asked pensively. "I thought they were bandits. Why don't they just steal more if they're hungry?"

"It's more complicated than that, dear girl." The queen was silent for a long time, then she murmured, as if to herself, "So much suffering. Can't we save anyone?"

Amaya darted a glance at Ehli-nikkalu's face and saw that it was stretched down into a troubled mask, her hooded eyes shadowed.

"Who needs saving, my lady?" she asked quietly because the queen looked far away with her thoughts.

"Everyone, I think. Your uncle certainly does. The Umman-manda do. You and the twins do. I do, too, I'm afraid." She looked up and smiled, a deeper smile that stretched her mouth wide and erased all the little lines around her lips. "How can we help them all, Amaya?"

But Amaya had no answers either. It worried her to think that everyone in the world seemed to need saving. *Where could I turn for help?*

It must have been midday—because the sun had begun to shine in their eyes—when raised voices and the clashing of metal came from the woods, followed by an ear-splitting whistle. Amaya stopped her thread and stared downhill, where a flash of something bright caught her eye. She and the queen gaped at one another. Around the tents, the Umman-manda had begun to boil like ants when someone stepped on their hill. The other women ran toward the ruined house, but when the queen slid off the rock and started after them, they gestured at her and yelled things in some language Amaya couldn't understand.

Finally, one of them cried in Ugaritic, "Stay! Stay!"

But they were laughing and talking breathlessly as they ran away. They didn't seem frightened at all.

"What's happening?" Amaya asked the queen in a whisper. Her heart sat uneasily in her throat.

Ehli-nikkalu cried, "I think it's the king's men!"

Sure enough, out of the woods burst the royal guards in their crimson uniforms, shouting and beating on their shields, shaking their spears and making piercing whistles. The bandit men waved their arms and ran away, bellowing, into the forest. A few of the guards went after them, but mostly, they stayed and rounded up the horses and mules, knocked down the white tents, and kicked dirt over the campfire. They seemed strangely without rancor.

Someone roared, "Where's the queen?"

Ehli-nikkalu waved her arm, and the person who'd yelled waded toward them through the chaos.

Amaya saw that it was the big officer who had conducted them up the mountain. She shot a confused look at the queen.

But Ehli-nikkalu managed to conceal whatever surprise she felt and said calmly and majestically, "Is this our rescue? They've given you the food?"

The officer nodded and grinned. "We're here to take your party back to the city, my lady. Hope it wasn't too rough."

"No," she said dryly. "If anyone I know ever wants to be kidnapped, I'll recommend you."

He roared with laughter. "Better you don't say nothing, actually." Then he raised his voice so everyone around could hear and added, "All right, ladies. Let's go. In the king's name. Double-quick, all you ugly bastards over there."

No one wasted any time. The soldiers and muleteers harnessed up the wagons and carriage and put the packsaddles on the donkeys, but Amaya saw that everything was empty. The Umman-manda had stolen their supplies, including all their beautiful new dresses. Uncle Teshamanu was shoved forward, and he suppressed an offended snarl as he shook a soldier's hand off his good arm, then he and Shamu-manu climbed into their wagon and helped up the handmaids. Finally, Amaya and Ehli-nikkalu crawled into their wagon with the little ones. It was hot and cramped inside after the pleasant days of liberty in the encampment. The mules took a few lazy steps forward, and the soldiers guided them toward the downward path.

From the edge of the clearing, the foxy little man watched, his hands on his hips. He blew a kiss in the direction of the carriage.

Amaya shuddered, but then something else caught her attention. "Look, my lady," she murmured, pointing to their muleteer. "The soldiers are driving some of the wagons. What happened to the rest of our men? Did the bandits kill them, do you think?"

"No," the queen said just as softly. "I think the men joined the bandits."

"I don't understand. Something strange is going on. They didn't even fight when the guards came to rescue us—they just ran away. And some of the guards are the same men who kidnapped us."

Ehli-nikkalu smiled approvingly and patted her on the arm. "You're very observant, my friend. These soldiers are all foreign mercenaries hired by the king. Don't say this to anyone, but I think they turned on Niqmaddu and kidnapped us on their own. They're desperate for food. That's all they asked for ransom."

Amaya wondered if they needed food so badly as to risk kidnapping the Great King's daughter, but she thought of the watery soup and how the bread had run out, and she saw that things were probably sufficiently desperate. At home, she had heard the slaves talking about famine in the empire all the time. Still, one thing puzzled her. "What's that little man who says he's the real king got to do with them?"

The queen sighed, and her eyes strayed out the opening of the curtain. "I'm sure I don't fully know, either, Amaya."

Ili-milku shaded his eyes and stared around the square as the west gates clanged open to admit the carriage and wagons of the returning captives. Sharryelli had arranged a welcome ceremony to advertise the successful rescue of the queen and her party. As the king's guards entered the Royal Gate with Ehli-nikkalu's carriage in the lead, the palace musicians broke into a dramatic fanfare. The slaves and scribes and functionaries, ranged around the ramparts and hanging from the upstairs windows, cheered and whistled and banged on the windowsills with patriotic pride, according to instructions. On the banner-draped porch, between the *karubuma* columns, the king waited at his mother's side, arms crossed, tapping his fingers on his sash as if he would rather be anywhere else. Sharryelli had apparently convinced Niqmaddu to leave Pu-haddu and their son out of the official welcome party, but Prince Zuzuli was present, representing the viceroy, and the entire council, including Ili-milku, stood by in appropriately admiring postures.

The chief scribe watched Zuzuli uneasily out of the corner of his eye. The Hittite's mien was stiff and carefully inexpressive, a bad sign in a diplomat. Ili-milku shot a quick, curious glance at Shipti-ba'al, but the merchant stared around at the crowds, eyes narrowed against the sun. No doubt calculating what he could sell them.

"Give your speech now, dear," the dowager prodded her son.

Niqmaddu looked around with an appearance of utter boredom that didn't match his nervous fingers. "I thank all you brave soldiers for delivering our beloved queen from the hands of the Ummanmanda." Then he turned his back and went inside, leaving the others to welcome his wife in person. He hadn't left much doubt as to how little he cared about the return of Ehli-nikkalu. No wonder she hated him. Ili-milku sneaked a glance at Zuzuli, who maintained his bland expression but was taking everything in.

The plaza had become extremely crowded with wagons and mules and pack animals and soldiers and carters and grooms. People from the royal stables had come to lead away the mules, but it was too chockablock to get them unhitched and pass them through the press of humans, so they just stood around, adding to the congestion. The minutes stretched on. Looking straight at the dignitaries on the porch, one of the pack asses indulged an indignant bray, causing some murmurs of amusement from the ramparts. At length, the curtains of the carriage drew back, and the queen unfolded her long frame and stepped out.

A wrinkle of distaste at the filthy condition of her daughter-in-law twitched Sharryelli's nose. Still, she let loose the full flower of her beaming maternal smile and rushed to embrace her. "Ehli-nikkalu, dear. Thanks be to all the gods that you're back safe and sound! We were so worried. Was it terrible?" She clasped her arms around the woman.

"No." The younger queen, who was a great deal taller than Sharryelli, looked down at her with a rigid smile that suggested she was only just tolerating such a gesture of affection.

Ili-milku, watching the dowager with more interest than the returning party, saw a little shiver of ice pass across her face. But outwardly, she beamed and dabbed at tears and hung onto Ehli-nikkalu's arm. Her eyes flicked toward Amaya and the children, but she quickly returned her attention to her daughter-in-law. "I know you want to bathe and rest. I'm sure it was traumatic, my dear. Make way, everyone, for our dear queen to come home."

The councilors parted, smiling and calling out their encouragement—"Well done, my lady!" "Welcome back!" "Long live the king!"—and Sharryelli hustled Ehli-nikkalu inside the vestibule. The viceroy's man stepped aside into the shadows to let the women pass. He loomed over everyone else, a tall, grim gray figure like a messenger of death, and Ili-milku feared the worst. *Why is he really here?*

The assembled council sat uneasily in the small throne room, waiting for Prince Zuzuli to join them. Niqmaddu crossed his legs and swung the upper one in a nervous rhythm. He was installed in a fine chair on the dais, but it was the viceroy's representative who would occupy the throne in the middle. Ili-milku uneasily patted the tips of his fingers together and rested his chin upon them. Neither he nor anyone else had failed to observe the coolness of the viceroy's ambassador, and he wasn't sure why that should be, except for the obvious fact that the queen of Ugarit had just been carried off by brigands. He felt rather as he had as a student scribe years ago, waiting for the master's report on his first dictation. He watched the queen mother, who sat peaceably, smiling as usual. She leaned in to say something to her son-in-law, who suddenly shot from his chair. Ili-milku looked around and saw that Prince Zuzuli had entered.

Everyone surged to their feet with a scrape of chairs and a rustle of skirts, Niqmaddu included. At least he had that much sense. Once, a mere ambassador would have risen for him, but the power of the viceroy leaned more and more heavily upon their kingdom, and his man was the equivalent of his own presence. The viceroy, Talmi-tesshub, was in their midst, even in absentia.

Ili-milku found the prince to be impressive in his own right. He was experienced and articulate, a holdover of his late brother-in-law's distinguished reign. Tall, clean-shaven, with long gray hair and shrewd, heavy-lidded eyes, he cast an appraising glance around the room then took his seat on the throne with perfect dignity. The others sank into their chairs. Sharryelli's smile grew frayed.

"My lord king, my lady, lords of Ugarit," the ambassador began in his deep, measured voice. "The viceroy has directed me to convey to you his felicitations on the safe return of your queen, his cousin."

He allowed a moment of silent digestion. Ili-milku suspected that citation of the queen's kinship with the viceroy, a prince of Hatti, had some purpose: a reminder of her dignity, of the esteem in which the viceroy—and his overlord, the Great King—held her, of the jewel that her possession entrusted into the hands of a mere vassal. King Niqmaddu's handsome face was frozen in a studied look of indifference, but he shifted imperceptibly in his chair.

"Certainly, the rescue of this great lady of Hatti Land does credit to your kingdom. The viceroy is not unmindful of the gratitude that he and all those who profess allegiance to the royal family of Hatti must feel on this occasion. However..."

Oh dear, Ili-milku thought. *Here it comes.* He shot a glance at the king, whose chest inflated with a deep breath as if he were bracing for a blow.

"One must ask oneself how it happened that this great lady—this estimable daughter of our suzerain, need I remind you, gentlemen—came to be kidnapped in the first place.

"The viceroy has many times warned his children in Ugarit that the safety of roads is a primary duty of a vassal. The unity of the empire demands the possibility of safe and timely passage from one end of it to the other." The ambassador tilted his head and looked from person to person, the picture of reason. "Is it not so?"

The councilors vied with one another in nodding vigorously.

"This issue of safety in your kingdom has been a repeated source of anxiety on the part of the viceroy. How often have merchants reported being attacked by brigands in the mountains or lonely stretches of the eastern desert? How many fines and reimbursements have you paid to those whose property or persons have been damaged by predators because you have not kept your roads safe?"

Ili-milku watched his colleagues squirm. They were all merchants and had had convoys attacked, caravans disappear into the desert sand, cargoes lost, indemnities paid by the crown. Sharryelli wiggled a little, and Ili-milku thought she was getting ready to say something, but Shipti-ba'al elbowed her. Niqmaddu stared into his lap, his face dark.

The ambassador's voice rose, not angry but exceedingly firm. "It must stop, gentlemen. It must stop now. Whatever resources you need to devote to this endeavor, apply them. There must be no more of this lawlessness within your borders. The viceroy is already unhappy with you because of the embarrassing incident in Hattusha—"

Ai! Ili-milku flinched. *That kicked a few people in the balls.*

"—and his patience is growing thin. He knows you are not happy about the impending addition of a regional governor or a local mayor. Is this the way to assure him that such steps are not needed?"

Zuzuli looked around him gravely, seeming to see into the soul of every person present. Then a smile twitched at the corner of his thin mouth. "We have a parable in Hatti Land: the jailer said to the prisoner, 'Tomorrow you will be released,' and that night, the prisoner hanged himself." He stood up, a tall adult towering over the huddled children at his feet. The others in turn got to their feet, red-faced, and bowed as Prince Zuzuli descended from the dais and left the room.

When Ili-milku rose from his bow, the others had begun to stare at one another, suspicious and confused, and to murmur.

Niqmaddu said in loud disgust, "What, by all that's holy, does *that* mean?"

Sharryelli cast an anguished look at her son-in-law but recovered quickly and said with sweet good cheer, "Isn't he a lovely man?"

Urtenu the Younger, one of the councilors, shook his head. "Half my holdings to anybody who can figure out what he means by that parable."

"Why didn't one of us ask him?" Dagan-ba'al cried, his gaunt face bleak. "You don't want to get these people on the wrong side of you, believe me. I still have nightmares about that stay in Hattusha."

Tuna lowered his many chins and looked grim.

Ili-milku had a feeling he knew what the parable meant. They had just inflicted upon themselves incalculable harm. They had been on the edge of an exception, perhaps—but it was done for. They would have their mayor.

After the meeting, Ili-milku headed for the queen's apartment as usual. His delight at her return had certainly been squashed by the viceroy's rebuke, but the man had a point. *What kind of world is it when a queen, by all the gods, can be carried away right in her own country? What kind of safety can anyone count on?* The more he thought about it, the more lightly he realized they had gotten off. Something like that could have precipitated a war.

The grubby and travel-weary woman of the previous day's ceremony was clean and refreshed. She welcomed him into her chamber and closed the door carefully behind him, peering around it to be sure they were alone.

"Welcome back, my lady," he said with sincere pleasure. "How was your experience of captivity?"

She smiled, but her eyes were sad. "I learned a lot, Ili-milku. Tell me about the council meeting, and I'll tell you about my captivity."

Author Note: There really is some documentary evidence that suggests Ehli-nikkalu was kidnapped, although scholars debate the translation.

Karubuma are mythological winged lions (Biblical cherubim). Zuzuli's cryptic parable is historically documented.

Chapter 11

He described the meeting with the viceroy's ambassador and how, so far from praising the king for his wife's rescue, the prince had peeled off Niqmaddu's skin for letting her be captured in the first place.

She couldn't repress a grim little smile. "It's actually worse than the viceroy thinks. Let me tell you my theory about what happened."

And Ili-milku listened, his jaw dropping, to her story of renegade mercenaries and hordes of starving deportees and refugees roaming the mountains.

"You mean to tell me the king's soldiers were part of the Umman-manda?" he cried, his heart leaping into his throat. "We must tell him!"

"To do what? Dismiss them? So they'll be unemployed and hungrier than ever? Ili-milku, all they wanted was food. *Food.* They're starving, trying to feed their families. Are we going to punish them for that?" She faced him, her nostrils white and her mouth taut with passion.

"But, my lady, I... I..." His protests subsided helplessly. He murmured almost to himself, "From Taruisha, all the way down here? This is an unbelievably enormous problem. Whatever can resolve it?"

Ili-milku's heart sat like a ball of lead in his stomach. He thought of the worsening famine. At first, it had been Hatti's problem, up on their high, cold plateau. But their vassals, like the Luwians—and like Ugarit—had kept them supplied. Then they had had to ship grain all the way from Mizri. Then the drought had begun to spread, and dearth came to the semi-desert interior of Ugarit itself. The crops were shrinking even along the rich coastal plains. It wasn't only the lack of rain. Terrifying rumors of locusts to the south were spreading like, well, locusts. It was as if the jaws of some ravenous monster were closing in on them. Perhaps the whole world was going to starve.

He thought of his children and their little children, who would have to face such a terrible future existence, who might tumble down the dark maw of that monster to their deaths, and he almost whimpered. He stood, head bowed, his lip in his teeth, for a long time.

At last, the queen said, "Ili-milku, what do you know about a Prince Utri-sharrumma?"

He looked up quickly, welcoming the distraction of another train of thought. "He was the much younger half brother of King Niqmaddu's father, my lady. The son of that queen I've mentioned who was put to death."

Ehli-nikkalu nodded, seeming to remember the story.

Ili-milku continued, "He was sent off to Amurru with his mother when she was exiled, but after her husband decided to execute her, well, I don't know what happened to the child. I suppose he stayed in Amurru. Why do you ask, my lady?"

"Is he the rightful king?" she asked.

He blew out a troubled breath. "That depends. He wasn't the eldest son by a good twenty years. However, when your father married Ammishtamru to the Amurrite princess, it was under the condition that her children inherit the throne. I guess that's always the way these treaties go, isn't it? But it gets still more complicated. At the time of the queen's exile, her son was given a choice of staying with his father and remaining the crown prince or going with his mother and losing his chance at the throne. He chose to go." Ili-milku's face crumpled in a dubious frown. "Although I don't know that that would hold up in a law court. The prince was only a small child..."

"So, is he the rightful king?" Ehli-nikkalu asked again, her face expressionless.

But Ili-milku put up a protesting hand and cried in horror, "Oh, my lady, don't ask me that, I beg you. How can you ask me such a question?"

"I was just curious, Ili-milku. I didn't mean to put you in a corner."

He mopped his temple with the towel that hung at his waist to wipe the clay from his hands. Icy perspiration had broken out all over. "Will that be all, my lady?"

"Thank you, my friend, yes."

Ili-milku scuttled from her apartment, a sense of relief washing over him like the sweat that trickled down his sides. *Whatever possessed the queen to pose such questions?* Of course, if there were any justice in the world, Utri-sharrumma *would* be the real king. The child had been tricked, and Ili-milku knew it well because he had stood right there in the throne room and seen it happen seventeen years ago. He had a terrible, sick feeling that the sins of his rulers were about to fall on their heads. Ili-milku remembered the omen of the dove struck down in the queen's very chamber. It promised nothing good.

He set off at last for home and a hot meal, glad to be on his feet and moving because remaining inside the palace had become an ominous and oppressive ordeal. He couldn't help but think, with a frisson of dread, about all the weights hanging over the head of his country, civil war and famine not the least. *Ba'al, help us. Will we ever again have a normal rainfall, a normal harvest? How long has it been?* All the rumors of dearth from other parts of the empire had started to close in even around their fertile little corner of the earth. As he walked, his footsteps took on a kind of rhythm, and before long, he thought, growing gradually excited, *This would make a great dramatic episode in the poem! Somebody lays a curse, and Ba'al withholds rain.*

No one was around him on the street. Ili-milku stretched out a hand and began to declaim in an orotund voice, "'Seven years Ba'al is absent; eight, the Rider of the Clouds.' I like that!" He repeated it silently a few times, trying to feel where it was taking him, then he improvised in a deeper and more tragic baritone, "'No dew, no downpour. No swirling of the deeps. No... no welcome voice of Ba'al!' Yes, I like that."

Amaya and the twins sat in the garden kiosk with the sheer linen curtains drawn against the sun. She and Ba'aluya played with the beautiful jointed doll the queen had given to the child while Yanakh built a castle out of pebbles retrieved from the garden path. Amaya had done her best to provide silent activities for the twins. It was risky to bring them to the garden to play, but the confinement of the queen's apartment after those ironic days of freedom in captivity was weighing heavily on all three of them. *To have come so close to safety with Anani-nikkalu in Geru...* Somehow, that check had brought home to her the burden of their condition—not just orphans but hunted, in danger. Even though she had seen no faces, her father's murderers couldn't know that.

Lady Ehli-nikkalu has been so generous to us, she marveled. Not just anyone would have inconvenienced themselves for strangers, as she had done. *And look at the way she stood up for Hattatamu and welcomed Uncle, despite his unsavory past. She's a good woman.* Amaya begged her parents to look down with protection on the queen as well as on their children—because, despite her prestige, Ehli-nikkalu seemed to need protection desperately.

A sudden crunch of footsteps on the gravel outside made Amaya look up, her heart pounding. She hastily started to gather the children for a flight indoors, but before she could open her lips, the curtains flicked back, and the dowager queen stood in the aperture, her mouth open in surprise.

Little by little, a smile spread across her pretty face. Lady Sharryelli said pleasantly, "Why, hello there. Who are you, my dears?" Her eyes shifted especially to Amaya, who was frozen like a rabbit hoping to avoid discovery if only he could stand still enough.

"I... I... Amaya, my lady. I'm the queen's new lady-in-waiting." She forced herself to bow.

The two children gaped curiously at the dowager.

Yanakh blurted, "Who are you?"

Sharryelli laughed in delight. "I'm the king's mama. Who are you, you adorable thing?"

"Yanakh son of Rab—"

But Amaya poked him, horrified. *Dear gods, he still doesn't understand that we're in hiding.* Ba'aluya rolled her eyes furiously at her twin.

Sharryelli's own eyes widened in recognition. "Oh, you're Rabilu's children. You just lost both your parents, didn't you, my dears? I'm so sorry," she said in a voice melting with compassion. She reached out and squeezed Amaya's hand. "It was such a shame the way your father died in the mountains. It must have been scary being a prisoner in the mountains after that, never knowing." She sat on the stone bench and patted the seat beside her.

Amaya gave her siblings a push, and they exchanged a glance then took to their heels.

Unable to disobey the king's mother, Amaya sat, her back stiff and upright with discomfort.

The girl stared across the garden, hoping desperately that something would interrupt and free her from this uneasy proximity to Ehli-nikkalu's enemy. "Yes," she said, and her mouth pressed firmly shut. "That's what they say." *Died in the mountains? Is that what people think? Who's spreading such a lie?*

"They?" Sharryelli asked. "I thought that was what happened. How did he really die, my dear?"

"I don't know." The girl felt flushed with desperation. *Does the dowager really not know how Rab-ilu died?* This whole conversation struck her as strange in the extreme. Looking everywhere but at Sharryelli, she said, "It may have been in the city. His death was reported almost immediately."

"Did you really see it happen, as they say? It must have been dreadful for you. And you have no mother to talk to about it." Sharryelli stroked her hand. "Don't hold it in, or it will fester, my dear. You need to confide in someone."

Amaya was growing more and more nervous. *What should I say?* She had no experience of the careful phrasing of diplomacy. The queen was after information, and Amaya was inclined to suspect her intentions because Ehli-nikkalu disliked her so. *Anyway, how does Sharryelli know I witnessed the murder unless she spoke to the killer?* But in fact, Sharryelli was the mother of the king; the girl felt she couldn't simply refuse to answer her questions. *Mother, what would you do?* "I don't know, my lady."

Sharryelli gave a regretful smile. "My daughter-in-law has told you to avoid me, hasn't she? I'm afraid she's a very unhappy person and suspects all of us of intending her harm. After seven years, I don't think she can believe that I really just want to be friendly. Your father was very dear to us all, and we want to help his family. It's that simple."

Amaya lowered her head and said faintly, "That's very kind of you, my lady." *She seems nice, but the young queen says she's a liar. I don't know what to think.* She wanted to excuse herself and run off, but etiquette demanded that the dowager rise first.

And at last, Sharryelli did. "I do hope to see you again, my dear. You're a lovely young woman. I could be helpful in finding you a husband."

Now that I've inherited so richly from Father—I'm sure you could.
"My lady is too kind." Amaya bobbed a stiff bow.

The dowager queen departed through the filmy curtains, and Amaya heard her footsteps crunching off down the path. Little by little, the girl's frantic heart stopped pounding. "I must tell Lady Ehli-nikkalu we've been discovered," she told herself. "If one person knows who I am, everybody will soon."

She gathered the children's abandoned toys and edged out of the kiosk to see if the twins were somewhere in the garden. She saw no sign of them, but she did hear voices talking beyond the shrubbery—a man's and a woman's. It was the dowager queen speaking in an undertone. Amaya couldn't make out the words. Then the man responded and laughed sarcastically. And all at once, Amaya recognized that deep, cultured voice. She had last heard it in the moon-washed street near the city gate on that terrible night last summer. It belonged to one of her father's murderers. Lord Shipti-ba'al.

Her heart in her throat, the girl backed up into the kiosk once more and desperately pushed open the interior door. Into the dark palace she ran as if the demons of the underworld were at her heels.

Ili-milku was trundling through the empty throne room toward the bright opening of the smaller court when he saw ahead in silhouette the figure of the dowager queen.

"Ili-milku? Is that you?" she called, shading her eyes.

"It is, my lady. Can I help you?" The chief scribe scurried up and bowed. The mental image of that dead dove struck from the air wouldn't leave him alone, even after all these days, and had begun to swell in proportion after the visit of the viceroy's emissary. Nothing was going well. He hoped these reverses weren't like the minor shaking that heralded some huge earthquake.

"We were just talking about you, my dear," Sharryelli said with her cheery smile.

"Nothing bad, I hope." He chuckled uneasily. "Actually, you might be the person I need to see, my lady. I was heading to find the high priest of Ba'al, but you might be... that is..."

"What's the problem? Apart from the problems we all share these days." She arched her eyebrows as if to let him know that she referred to the dressing-down they had been collectively delivered—and that she took it lightly.

"It may be related, and I just regret that with everything that's happened, I haven't reported it to anyone sooner. I was in the queen's apartment just before her unfortunate kidnapping—"

"I didn't know you were close to the queen."

"Er, a letter was delivered to the chancery for her, so I just took it up. You know..." He could feel the sweat dampening his armpits. The younger queen was political poison, and he certainly didn't want to get a reputation for being her man. It still rankled that everyone had looked at him so suspiciously in the council meeting. *Do they think I sabotaged the king's vassal visit on Ehli-nikkalu's behalf?*

She nodded in understanding, and he continued. "And while I was there, a hawk attacked a dove and left it dead, right on the floor at her loggia door."

"Oh dear."

"I didn't think about it at the time, but after she was kidnapped, it occurred to me that that was probably a sign, something significant."

"I should think so." Sharryelli looked unnerved. "I hope it was just a warning about her kidnapping."

Ili-milku took a deep breath. "I just returned from the augur priest. He couldn't be specific, but he felt it was a dangerous omen still to be fulfilled."

"You should have let me know sooner."

"I should have, my lady. Forgive me."

"But you did well to tell me, Ili-milku," she assured him, sobered. "These are dark days. We need to arm ourselves with foreknowledge, don't we? Thank you. I'll convey this to the king."

"Thank *you*, my lady." He thought he could remember those words about arming oneself with foreknowledge from a priestly harangue not long ago. No one could accuse Sharryelli of being original.

The chief scribe toddled off into the interior of the palace. He had a feeling he should warn the young queen, too, about the reading of the omen, since it had taken place in her apartment. Hopefully, its effects were already discharged and his imagination was just preying on him.

When he was admitted to her chamber, he saw the girl Amaya and the queen seated together in conversation, spindles in hand.

The face Lady Ehli-nikkalu turned to him was blanched. She sprang to her feet and wrung her hands. "Ili-milku, something dreadful has happened. Amaya's identity has been exposed, and she recognized the voice of the murderer as Shipti-ba'al. That means Sharryelli and the king are involved. What can we do to hide Rab-ilu's children now? That vixen is trying to pump Amaya for information. She wants the girl to confide in her."

Ili-milku's stomach dropped within. *Now I'm caught in warfare between the two royal women. Ba'al protect me.* He wanted to back out the door and pretend he had never entered. "What can I do, my lady?"

"We must think of someplace else to hide Amaya and the children. I'm afraid to try to get them to Geru province again. The roads are clearly not safe."

"Perhaps you should turn them over to their uncle to hide. It's his duty to protect them."

A strange, pained expression overtook the queen's face. "I'm not sure he'll take them, Ili-milku."

"Whether he wants to or not, it's his duty before the gods to raise them. He can remarry and give them a normal family life."

Ehli-nikkalu turned sadly and drifted toward the loggia door. "He probably won't get married again. For one thing, he said he was in terrible debt. He may not feel he can give them a good home."

Ili-milku remembered saying that himself some time ago. But now duty—and danger—seemed to outweigh convenience. He said forcefully, "The children share a substantial inheritance. Surely they can afford to retire to some country property of their father's. We should talk to Teshamanu. I believe he's the administrator of his brother's estate. It would be in the children's interest to do this for them."

But Amaya sprang to her feet, her big eyes flashing. "I don't want to go with Uncle, and I don't want him to be the administrator. He hasn't shown us any family support. Let someone take us to our sister, whatever the danger. She, at least, loves us." She turned to the queen, adamant. "I don't want Uncle touching our gold. I don't want to marry him, and I don't trust him not to take some of our inheritance to pay his debts."

She was both furious and pleading, Ili-milku saw in pity. He and the queen exchanged anxious looks.

"We have to get her out of the palace, Ili-milku," the queen said wildly. "I'll tell Teshamanu myself—I'll command him. He has to take them."

"If you feel we can trust him enough not to tell Sharryelli..." Ili-milku wished his fear had not intruded itself into his head. But the secretary was desperate for gold. His honor might or might not survive another temptation.

Amaya stared triumphantly at the queen, but Ehli-nikkalu said in a firm voice, "He can be trusted."

Amaya turned away angrily, her lip in her teeth and a mist of tears dampening her eyes.

Why am I involved in this, dear gods? thought Ili-milku with a sigh. "We can bind him to a strict written accounting of where every shekel is spent. I can oversee it, just to be sure. Amaya, my dear, we must do something to protect you. And *they* could use the children against you somehow—make them betray your whereabouts or hold them for ransom."

"Please don't send us away," Amaya begged in a tight voice.

Ehli-nikkalu looked anguished. "Why do you dislike your uncle so, Amaya? Has he... has he ever done anything to you?"

"No," the girl said, turning back to face them. "But he isn't our father. He cares nothing about us. He doesn't want us—you know that. And we've—I've been so happy here." She hung her head, clutching her hands together.

Chapter 12

Ehli-nikkalu, her mouth trembling, threw her arms tenderly around the girl. They stood there, clasped tight, for the space of a heartbeat, then the queen said in a pleading voice against Amaya's capped head, "Try to find a little pity in your heart for Teshamanu, Amaya. He's had some terrible experiences, and I suppose he's not altogether himself."

Amaya said nothing, but Ehli-nikkalu could feel her body jerk with suppressed sobs of misery. *Perhaps I'm asking too much of a young person. Finding pity sometimes takes a lifetime.* "Ili-milku, you can go now. Oh—what did you come to see me about?"

The chief scribe looked nervous. "I wanted to tell you I had an omen taken from that dove struck down a week or so ago. The priest didn't find it very encouraging..."

That was no surprise, but it plunged a dagger of fear into the queen's heart nonetheless. She had been brought up to take omens very seriously, and yet she had completely ignored the meaning of that event, seeing in it only the image of her banishment from home. *You selfish creature,* she told herself sternly. *The whole kingdom may be in danger, and you're feeling sorry for yourself.*

"Perhaps it was just our kidnapping. Yes, that was probably it." She didn't want to frighten Amaya—the gods of heaven knew she didn't need any more fear than being hunted down by the dowager and her henchmen.

When Teshamanu appeared the next morning, ready to work, Ehli-nikkalu sat him down and posted herself before him with a grim air. "Look here, you must take in your nieces and nephew, Teshamanu. It's a scandal that you haven't. You're their only male relative."

His face grew red—with shame, perhaps—and his eyes sought to avoid hers. "I cannot. I mustn't, my lady. Forgive me, I want to obey you, but—"

"Then obey me. I'm giving you an order," she cried in exasperation. "They're in danger here at the palace. Sharryelli knows who they are and that Amaya witnessed your brother's murder. Do you care nothing about them, man?"

"I do. I do, and that's why I can't—"

She shot back angrily, "You coward. Are you afraid to be responsible for them because of what happened to your own children? You're likely leaving them to death if you make me keep them here under the king's roof. Send them to some country property. I don't care where, but do it. They think their own uncle doesn't love them, the poor children."

He sprang to his feet, his eyes flashing, his fist clenched. "I *do* love them. They're all I have of my brother. And that's why I can't take them." The secretary reined in his anger and said in a more restrained voice, "I told you I was in debt. The man I owe is not gentle. He might well harm the children to pressure me. I can't let that happen, don't you see?"

Ehli-nikkalu turned away, her thoughts churning. *Can it be there's no safety anywhere for those poor young ones?* Perhaps they needed to marry Amaya off so she could take care of the little ones herself. The queen faced Teshamanu once more. "How much do you owe? Perhaps I can help you."

He snorted. "You don't want to know how much I owe. It seems to grow with every breath I draw. Perhaps I could pay it back from Rab-ilu's legacy, but I'm not sure. Anyway, that belongs to his children."

"Well, at least *that*'s spoken like a man," Ehli-nikkalu said caustically.

Teshamanu's head jerked up as if she had slapped him, but it was fury—and perhaps desperation—in his eyes, not pain. "I told you what kind of person I was, my lady. You said you wouldn't turn it against me. I can't make the past not exist. I've done what I've done, and very unpleasant consequences haunt me still. I cannot take the children." He gave a sarcastic bow. "If you'd rather not have such a wicked man in your employ any longer, I understand."

But her face aflame, Ehli-nikkalu caught him hastily by the empty sleeve. "No. I'm sorry. I... I spoke in anger, Teshamanu. I'm desperate. I can't think of any place your nieces and nephew will be safe. Believe me, no one will be sorrier to see them leave the palace than I. But we must think of them. We can't be so selfish about their fate."

"Send them to their sister. If the governor of Geru province can't protect them, who can?"

The queen remembered her own kidnapping, how the guards had been complicit, how she could trust no one. And she thought of the three innocent orphans in the clutches of the Umman-manda. In the clutches of Utri-sharrumma, that madman. Each solution was worse than the last.

Ehli-nikkalu turned and walked to the loggia door, where she stood breathing heavily, staring out into the garden. There was a fresh touch of autumn in the air, a gauzy veil of high clouds that spoke of changing weather. Another reason why taking Rab-ilu's children to Geru wouldn't be practical. *Am I just being selfish after all? Do I just want them to remain in the city so I can see Amaya? Dear Lady of the Night, show me the way...*

Behind her, Teshamanu still stood poised to leave, his jaw tight. She stared at him, at his arched nose, at the obsidian-dark eyes and high cheekbones that reminded her of Rab-ilu.

He's a handsome man, she thought irrelevantly. *But he has more than his share of problems. No one could ever live with him. Perhaps he's right—the children cannot go to their uncle.* "But then what?" she asked herself. And more loudly, "All right, they'll have to stay here for a while. However, I want you, as her legal guardian, to find a husband for Amaya, someone who will see to it she's protected and will take in the twins as well."

"Yes, my lady." He nodded, a stiff, expressionless gesture.

"But she must have a say in it. I won't have her married to someone she doesn't care for."

"Yes, my lady." He shot the queen an unreadable look.

Perhaps he's being sarcastic. She wondered. "Now, if you're ready to take dictation..."

Ehli-nikkalu opened her outer door to let Teshamanu out at the end of the morning—only for him to almost walk straight into her husband, who was passing with a coterie of his young friends, all dressed for the hunt. Niqmaddu eyed the scribe up and down, a thin smile compressing his lips as Teshamanu made a low court bow and continued on his way.

The king turned his hard gaze to his wife. Gesturing to his companions to stay put, he hustled Ehli-nikkalu back into the vestibule, shutting the outer door behind him. He eyed the empty room. "Where are your handmaids, my dear? Do we closet ourselves with men these days with no chaperons?"

"They're not my chaperons. They're my servants. I didn't need their services. They're in the garden."

Niqmaddu eyed her narrowly, and her flesh crept under the calculated hostility of his expression.

"You've certainly become a problem to me," he said as reasonably as if discussing the cut of his clothing. "Stirring up trouble with your family, colluding with the viceroy—"

"Colluding? Stirring up trouble? Stop blaming me for your own stupidity. That's what's brought the viceroy's wrath down on you. I had nothing to do with any of those things." She started to turn away.

Suddenly, he grabbed her arm and jerked her toward him with a snarl. "Must you contradict everything anyone says? I've read a good many of your letters home, my dear. You're not free of guilt. I suppose nothing would please you more than to see my kingdom humbled under your father's boot heel, eh?" He gave her a shake and slung her away from him.

Ehli-nikkalu felt rage mounting in her like a corrosive tide. She brushed off her sleeve contemptuously and drew herself up to her full height. "How dare you manhandle me, you pitiful little kinglet. My family ruled the world when your ancestors were hauling in fishing nets."

With a roar of frustrated fury, Niqmaddu lunged upon her and, to her horror, sent her reeling against the wall. He slapped her first with an open palm then with the heavily ringed back of his hand. A cry of pain and surprise escaped her as she tried to protect her face.

"I've had enough of your mealy-mouthed criticisms, your hypocrisy, your disloyalty," Niqmaddu snarled, breathing heavily. "As the gods are my witnesses, I've endured it as long as I can. Go back to your family—you certainly feel more loyalty to them than to us. Get out. I divorce you."

Crumpling with fear and pain as she was, Ehli-nikkalu still felt a surge of relief, of delight almost. *Divorce? I'll be free of him. Of this place, with its hostility and disrespect. Home again!*

She wiped her burning cheek with the back of her hand, and it came away bloody. "I knew you'd show your colors one day," she gloated, wiping it on his chest. "Pretending to be such a reasonable gentleman while I'm the screaming shrew. Now we see what you are!"

Niqmaddu yelled in her face so loudly his voice broke, "I've had enough, do you hear? You've brought everything down on our heads with your spying and prying. Enough!"

He clutched at her shoulders and, teeth clenched, shook her violently with a kind of manic savagery until her head knocked against the wall, mercifully cushioned by her thick hair and veil. At last, he gave her a final shove and strode away toward the outer door, heaving as if he'd run across the mountains on foot. He slammed the door after him so hard that the frame shook.

"I curse you!" she howled, fists raised to the air he had occupied a moment before. "May the Zuwalli gods hound you and bring your sins down upon your head. May the Inarawantesh, the Violent Ones, destroy you. I want my vengeance!" She stared after him, her heart pounding.

Something had broken loose in him; that facade of amused uncaring had evaporated, baring his impotent anger. She had goaded him to a real fury, and it gave her a perverse sense of satisfaction. Although her face was throbbing and blood dribbled down her chin, she could rejoice—she had heard the words she had longed to hear for seven years: "Get out."

I'll sail home before the winter storms. And Amaya and the children can come with me! The idea came to her as a gift from the gods.

Ili-milku exited his office in the chancery and stood for a moment in the writing room. A few scribes were seated, heads bent, at the big table, pecking away at tablets of clay or wax on wood. *Oh, to be one of them again,* the chief scribe said to himself with a sigh. *With no more responsibilities than the document you're writing.*

He wanted badly to get back to his poem, which he'd been working on for years—every time he was ready to let go of it, some new idea popped into his head. And now he had so many administrative tasks that it seemed he would never be able to sit down with a stylus and get them on clay. He sighed again.

As he drew out into the corridor, Lady Sharryelli hustled toward him, her face anxious. "Ili-milku, come with me, please." She latched onto his arm and steered him down the hall toward the royal apartments, her little steps pattering along beside his own.

"The council meeting hasn't started yet, has it, my lady?"

"No, and we have just the time to do what we need to. We must stop the king from going hunting." She cast a nervous look around.

Ili-milku said in confusion, "He's going hunting this afternoon? But we have a meeting…"

"He insists he doesn't have to be present. But *hunting*, Ili-milku! Remember the omen? What is he thinking? We must stop him. I'd take Shipti-ba'al, but Niqmaddu doesn't like him much. I'm afraid he'd do just the opposite of whatever his brother-in-law said."

"I'm not at all sure he'll listen to me." Ili-milku's neck prickled. The king didn't like to be thwarted—*what young man does?*—and his displeasure tended to take the form of a long, cold vengeance.

Sharryelli and the chief scribe strode purposefully down the corridor, sunlight casting its rhythmic bars of brightness across them from the clerestory windows overhead.

They were admitted to the king's apartment to find him arming for his hunt. He was dressed in boots and a short patterned kilt with silver acorns weighting down the closure. Niqmaddu's face was thunderous and as red as a pomegranate. He shot them a glare of aggravation. "What now?" he asked ungraciously.

Sharryelli motioned the king's valet to withdraw.

While Ili-milku stood behind her, his cheeks on fire, the dowager said with remarkable calm, "Niqmaddu, my dear, this really isn't a good time to go hunting. There's so much business to attend to..."

"No reason it can't wait a few hours, is there?"

"Er, actually," Ili-milku said hesitantly, "there is a bit of urgency, my lord. Your uncle, the pretender, has been seen in the vicinity. It seems he may be preparing some sort of attack on the capital."

"Well, he won't be taking over this afternoon, will he? I'll deal with him after I get back. Over a good roast boar dinner."

Oh dear gods, no—boar?

"But that will take until sundown, my dear. You can't take a whole afternoon off to play right now." Sharryelli forced a lighthearted smile to her lips, but it wobbled a little.

"I'm the king, Mother. Kings hunt," he said irritably, then he smirked. "I am the king, am I not? And I can do whatever I like. Here, man, will you put that thing on me so I can get out of here?"

The valet scuttled up and hastened to strap the bandoleer over Niqmaddu's shoulders and tied it at his waist. The king pushed past his mother and headed for the door, his acorns jingling. She caught at his arm, and he jerked himself out of her grasp. Ili-milku watched helplessly. The king was already in a bad mood; the scribe felt he dared not intervene further.

But Sharryelli cried after him in a tone of anguish, "Don't go, son. Please. There's been a bad omen, and I'm afraid for you."

Niqmaddu froze in the doorway for a moment. He turned and gaped at her, a whole squadron of emotions chasing one another clearly across his face: superstitious fear, annoyance at a killjoy mother, the desire to look brave, longing to indulge himself. At last, he said with his icy smile, "But I want to kill something, Mother." He turned away and walked out with a jaunty step.

Ili-milku's stomach lurched. If the dowager followed him and pleaded, the cause would be lost. *Lord Ba'al, protector of kings, take care of him. That's all we can do.*

They should have published the omen reading and made it a major public event so no one would collude with Niqmaddu to do something dangerous—they should have set up a slave as a false king, to draw the gods' wrath away from the real one. They should have consulted the oracles immediately to find out the cause of the hovering evil and take it away.

At the bottom of it all, Ili-milku should have told someone much sooner. *Dear me, before the queen's kidnapping? Why did I wait so long? I haven't handled this at all well.* At his side, Sharryelli made an anxious little noise and set off down the corridor toward the stairs, Ili-milku at her heels. Time for the council meeting.

A*uthor Note: The historical Ili-milku, chief scribe (or vizier), is author of a series of poems called the Ba'al Cycle, found in Ugarit. The words quoted here are from it* (Ugaritic Narrative Poetry, *ed. Simon Parker, SBL, 1997).*

The people of antiquity believe strongly that the gods warn them of their displeasure through signs or omens. Augurs, specially trained priests, deal with omens revealed by birds.

It is taken for granted that a man will support his late brother's family. If Rab-ilu's wife were living, Teshamanu would be expected to marry her as well. No one would think it odd if he married Amaya.

Chapter 13

The more she thought about the confrontation with Teshamanu that morning, the guiltier Ehli-nikkalu felt. It preoccupied her all through lunch, although she didn't feel she should trouble Amaya with it. After all, the row had centered on the fact that Amaya's and the children's presence was undesirable to their uncle, and the girl seemed bitter enough already on that score. But in her mind, the queen told herself, *You abused his confidences—that was so unworthy. And the poor man has suffered so much.*

At last, she sent the chamberlain to find her secretary and bring him back, to tell him that she had a project she wanted to discuss with him. She would act as if nothing was the matter, as if her flash of temper had been a passing thing of no substance.

In the first stroke of good fortune for quite a while, Teshamanu happened to be in the writing room of the chancery, and so scarcely any time elapsed before he was bowing at her door once more. She had sent the handmaids out into the vestibule to spin, and Amaya and the children were playing with the crown prince's cat in the garden.

"I want to apologize," she greeted him before he could say so much as "my lady." "I was offensive and intrusive this morning—you have all the freedom in the world whether to take the children or not and no need to tell me the reasons. It was unfair of me to command you."

Teshamanu looked serious but not angry. In fact, Ehli-nikkalu thought she detected a whiff of weariness, as if he'd fought this battle for a long time. "Nor do you owe me any apologies, my queen," he said. "I am your servant."

Ehli-nikkalu felt her shame lighten and fly away. He had accepted her apology with the magnanimous spirit of a true *maryannu*. "I have a project I would like you to help me with, Teshamanu. I want to learn to read and write Neshite."

He nodded expressionlessly. "I can teach you that. It's difficult, though. It will take years to become proficient."

"It won't discourage me—I'm stubborn. But then"—she couldn't repress a rueful smile—"you know that."

They sat side by side at the table, each with a wax tablet.

"Here's how the system works—it's different from Ugaritic, even though the symbols are the same. There are many more of them, and they stand for ideas or words rather than sounds. Usually. Lots of exceptions." Teshamanu pressed a few signs into the wax.

The queen laughed. "It already sounds difficult!" *Why didn't I think of this years ago?* she wondered. *It's so much better to fix my attention on something positive like this than on all the things I'm prevented from doing. Father will be proud of me.* She took up her stylus and tried to imitate the marks her secretary had made.

The room was getting dark. The long rays of the late-afternoon sun were blocked by the west wing of the palace, so the garden was already in shade. She called to Shamumanu, who waited in the vestibule, to bring her a lamp. The chamberlain set it on the table between the two and a little ahead so they wouldn't knock it over with a careless hand. It occurred to Ehli-nikkalu that fire might be an unsettling element for Teshamanu, but he seemed to pay the lamp no mind. They set back to work, she imitating each mark he impressed upon the wax. It gave her pleasure—and it gave her pleasure to sit beside Teshamanu, his dark head bowed seriously over the table, his stump bracing the wooden tablet frame with some effort.

Then, from far away or close upon them or deep below, a thundering noise began. It sounded like chariot troops approaching.

Ehli-nikkalu looked up, half-alarmed and half-amused. "Are you kicking the table?"

"No, my lady." Teshamanu held his feet up off the floor to show they were innocent.

Then the lamp started to rattle on the table until the oil splashed out. The tablets chattered, and one fell off the edge of the table with a crash. The ewer on the queen's clothes press danced crazily in place. The tiles seemed to liquefy, undulating under their feet. Nothing was solid. Everything was in flux. The most substantial stool vibrated, rattling louder and louder. Boxes and vessels fell from the shelves. Ehli-nikkalu heard a cry from the vestibule and felt one rising in her throat.

"E-Earthquake! Tarhunta spare us!" she stammered. *Should we flee? But where does one go when the earth itself heaves?* She tried to stand, but it was like being on the deck of a ship. Her heart bobbled in her mouth.

Then it was over. She and Teshamanu confronted one another, white-faced, clinging to the table as if to hold it down.

"Dear gods!" she said with a half laugh of relief and embarrassment.

The secretary blew out the lamp for safety's sake.

A frightened cry came from outside the door. "My lady? Shouldn't we go outside?"

"Yes. Outside, everyone!" she called. Earthquakes were frequent in her homeland too. She knew the ritual.

They rushed for the door, ready to follow the handmaids, when Ehli-nikkalu remembered Amaya and the children in the garden.

"Oh, they'll be frightened."

She turned to the room again to call from the loggia, but Teshamanu held her back. "I wouldn't walk out on it if I were you."

He kept hold of her hand, and she followed him once more toward the antechamber to flee.

Then the infernal rumbling began again, as if the very lords of the world were shifting their vast weight, stretching in their blind sleep. From the foundations of the netherworld right up through her feet came the immense roar of some cosmic beast arising that turned her very flesh to liquid. The floor swayed and buckled in a wave. The bed slid into the wall, and the table rose and fell as if it wanted to take flight. She felt the tiles roll beneath her feet, toppling her to her knees, her stomach lurching with seasickness.

The noise grew, a great shearing sound, as of cliffs caving into the ocean that surrounded the black earth. A line of daylight opened between the wall and ceiling. The brick and rubble wall on the garden side of the chamber leaned outward—slowly, slowly, curtains fluttering, lintels melting—and plunged with majestic deliberation into the garden, and a vast detonation of sound swallowed her, obliterating all her senses. She was no longer upright but sliding down, her hand loosed from the secretary's, spread full-length on the floor, which was horizontal no longer.

"Teshamanu!" she screamed.

Then the world sped up, and everything fell in on top of her.

Ehli-nikkalu must have lost consciousness for a time because she only gradually became aware of herself again. The twilight sky stretched serene and violet through a gauze of white dust. She was lying on her back on some hard and uncomfortable surface, her skirts up over her waist, her bare legs exposed, white with dust, bruised and bleeding. It took her several tries to sit up. The garden and its low wall were gone, filled with a flattened mountain of mud brick and splintered beams, upon which she had been deposited, with a scattering of stones, tablets, furniture, and pottery all around. Straw and chunks of plaster, caught in her hair and on her shoulders, fell away in a small avalanche as she rose awkwardly to her feet. Her cap and veil had scraped off somewhere in the course of her slide.

The other wing of the palace seemed to be standing, despite the fissures in the wall. Smoke billowed from what must have been the kitchens, and a few alarmed voices and the sounds of beating came from what seemed impossibly far away. Perhaps someone was trying to extinguish a fire. She felt she had been deafened—it seemed too silent.

Ehli-nikkalu shook her head and wiped dust from her eyes, and her hand came away sticky with blood. Little by little, what had happened came back to her—an earthquake, and all in the space of a few minutes, everything had fallen apart. She had been with Teshamanu. Her heart constricted, and she tried to cry out his name in fear, but her voice didn't seem to work, and she ended up coughing until she gagged. She staggered a few steps, dizzy and sliding on the rubble. Finally, she dropped to all fours and crawled down the debris, away from the destruction behind her. *Amaya and the children! They were in the garden! Oh, surely they aren't beneath all this...*

Somewhere to her left, a part of the outside wall of the garden court stood, the wooden gate still intact. Staggering and crawling, she made her way toward it, hoping to get out of the palace before aftershocks came.

She heard pounding and banging, and the gate fell sideways in its frame with a crack. Soldiers and servants hovered in the opening.

"Help!" she cried, but her voice sounded like a whispering breeze. She tried to wave her arms, but it occurred to her vaguely that perhaps she was injured. She didn't seem to be able to lift her hands very high. The soldiers ran toward her and began to wade over the debris at what seemed like a comically slow pace.

"Teshamanu? Amaya?" she tried to call again, but suddenly, the ground began to hum, and all the debris beneath her feet started trembling and rattling. She gave a hoarse cry of bone-deep fear and fell on her face painfully. After a space of several heartbeats, the earth was still once more, but she could hear behind her driblets of clay as they dropped from the dangling ceiling and pebbles flowing down the hill of rubble. Her heart hammered.

At last, the men reached her and pulled her up by her arms, making comforting noises that her mind couldn't interpret as words. One of them threw her over his shoulder, and they made their way unsteadily out the gate and into the street. They set her down on the paving stones and started into the garden again.

"Teshamanu?" she cried weakly.

Through the veil of dust, she stared back at the wing of the palace that had foundered. The outer wall was gone, and she could see into the room above, the floors canted at a steep diagonal. She saw her bedchamber, the concubines' rooms, and some offices emptied out as if the contents had washed down a drain. *Where are the people who were in there? Were they able to flee down the staircases?* Tears of hopelessness and fear began to gather along her eyelids, and they rolled down her cheeks through the coating of dust.

A hoarse voice behind her cried, "My lady? Oh, you're safe! Thanks be to all the gods!"

Ehli-nikkalu turned, and her heart leaped up to impossible heights of joy as she saw Amaya running toward her, her arms outstretched, the twins at her heels.

The girl threw herself upon Ehli-nikkalu, who sat dazed in the street, and hugged her so tightly it seemed she wanted to climb into the queen's clothes with her. "I was so scared!" Amaya sobbed against her neck. "I was afraid you and Uncle had been killed, but I didn't know what to do."

"We were almost squashed!" Yanakh cried in a shout of nervous excitement.

Ba'aluya sobbed with a wide-open mouth, as if the horror of the situation had just penetrated her.

Ehli-nikkalu laughed in a shaking voice, tears in her eyes. She felt numb and stupid still, unable to think clearly or find her words. Her Ugaritic seemed to have left her. "W-Where were you?" she stammered. "I saw the garden gone and feared..."

"We were playing with the crown prince's cat, and all of a sudden, she jumped up and climbed over the wall. I was afraid we'd get in trouble if she ran away and was lost, so we followed her out. But then the ground started to shake, and we couldn't get back in, and I saw the palace fall apart and... and... oh, my lady!" She buried her face in her hands. "Is the Lord Ba'al angry with us?" She drew away a cubit's distance and asked, her face twisted with concern, "Is Uncle all right?"

"I... I don't know," Ehli-nikkalu murmured dully. "I don't know."

From time to time, the rescuers brought forth more people, limping or borne brokenly in the soldiers' arms, weeping with shock. Sometimes it was a dust-whitened body they carried out and laid on the pavement. But Teshamanu was not among them.

As her wits returned little by little, Ehli-nikkalu could see that the massive ashlar stones of the palace's outside walls had held, despite some fissures. Only one interior wall had fallen—only that one wing. Elsewhere in the city, who knew what damage the quake had wrought. Plumes of smoke rose here and there from fires that had started as ovens ruptured, lamps spilled, and beams fell into forges. She heard the men speaking of parts of the city's defensive walls that had collapsed and whole blocks of houses that had gone down right next to others that were untouched. The tower of the temple of Ba'al had toppled, but no one had been inside. The granaries had fallen, the grain all buried in dust and straw and stones.

Not long after Amaya had found the queen, another wave of tremors came, and they clung to each other with shuddering fear, the children pressed between them, their very bodies remembering the horror of the great upheaval.

Evening was coming on, and one of the slaves called out to Ehli-nikkalu as they left, "That's all we can do now, my lady. It's getting too dark to see." But she didn't know what to do or where to go.

At last, Ili-milku came trotting down the street with an entourage of maids and helped her to her feet. "My lady," he said in a kindly, distracted voice, "Lord Yabni-shapshu's house just behind you has been vacated for the use of the royal family tonight. These women will help you change clothes and settle in."

"What about my staff? Have they been found?"

"I don't know, my lady. We can't search anymore until daylight."

He was in a hurry to be off, so Ehli-nikkalu bit back her questions and docilely let the women lead her and Rab-ilu's children down the broken street to the house assigned to them. Her heart seemed to be underwater, numb to the dread that haunted her. *Where is Teshamanu?* She got Amaya and the twins settled in the care of the handmaids and turned back to the street. Staggering, she headed for the palace.

Ili-milku had just gotten home when the earthquake struck, and his first terrified thought was *Here is the disaster!* His second thought was *Thank the gods Niqmaddu was stubborn enough to go hunting.* Ugarit was no stranger to quakes, but this one was bad, he could tell. *Please, let the crown prince be safe.*

As he staggered out his door, surrounded by his wife and younger children and a coughing, weeping crowd of servants, he could see that buildings here and there had suffered varying degrees of damage. His house seemed more or less intact, but the tower of the temple of Ba'al on the hill opposite was no longer visible, replaced by a tower of smoke. The air was opaque with dust, like a thick fog, with a wisp of indigo sky drifting above it and the first stars of the evening. He hugged his family and started for the palace, where duty called—but almost toppled when another surge of tremors struck, rolling the pavement under his feet like a wave.

He collected himself, heart pounding. "Dear gods, help us," he murmured, feeling his way forward, fearing the earth might buckle beneath him again. *Oh, let my married children be all right.*

The royal plaza was a seething beehive. People who had been caught inside when the quake had struck were being evacuated into the open, where they sat or lay weeping, white with dust, many blood smeared. Slaves and functionaries rushed to and fro. As if they had rained from the sky, stones were strewn about. The Royal Gate still stood, but its massive lintel sagged—they would have no way to close the city at night. Great rifts fissured the wall of the palace, and one of the *karubuma* columns on the ceremonial porch was cracked.

Dear me, all this will need to be rebuilt as soon as possible. We won't be able to pay the Great King to get out of our army levy this year. And little Ammurapi, the king's heir—was he able to get out? Then he thought in irritation, *Wouldn't you know, the king is out enjoying himself while his capital falls in ruin. It would certainly be nice if he were here to show himself compassionately in charge of things.* He wanted with all his heart not to be responsible for supervising the rebuilding of this himself.

"Can I go inside? I want to see the damage," Ili-milku called to a group of chancery officials who had gathered in front of the main entrance.

They were talking and waving their arms and directing slaves, who staggered out of the palace with victims over their shoulders or pieces of furniture in their arms. Someone thrust a torch into his hand.

Ahead of him, a short, plump figure and a tall, thin one turned. It was the two queens, standing side by side, a sight he had rarely seen. "Be careful, Ili-milku," Sharryelli called. "There could be aftershocks. But I think everything but the residential wing is safe, if you don't stay long. We may have lost the archives—all the tablets slid off the shelves."

"Oh dear. Any of the scribes injured?" asked Ili-milku.

"We haven't found Teshamanu," Ehli-nikkalu said in a numb voice. "He was in the room with me when the wall fell. We were sitting at the same table."

Sharryelli ignored her and replied to Ili-milku, "So far, not seriously. But a number of them are unaccounted for. We can only hope. All the banquet halls and storerooms on the ground floor of that wing are gone, of course. If anyone was inside, I don't give them much chance."

A twinge of anxiety rippled through Ili-milku as he mounted the steps and entered the dark maw of the main door. At any minute, another shock could roll underfoot, bringing the weight of all that stone and wood down on his head. But a ruler had to inspect the damage, and since the king was away, disporting himself in the mountains, that meant the dowager and the young queen—and the chief scribe. Ili-milku trailed behind the women with his torch.

"Here, my ladies, let me accompany you," he called, his words ending in a choking cough.

He drew abreast, torch held high, and they proceeded cautiously through the throne room. The private staircase behind it had loosened from the upper floor and hung skewed in its well.

"Nobody got down that way," Sharryelli murmured uneasily.

They passed into the largest ceremonial banquet hall, dark and cavernous, the stacked tables and couches toppled in streams, as if they had been shoved. The atmosphere was suffocating, claustrophobic. Ehli-nikkalu held a hand over her mouth and nose and tried to control the shiver that seemed to paralyze her body. It was eerily silent except for the distant sounds of shifting rubble as rescuers dug in the garden. A faint light of torches filtered in from the open door. They stood for a moment in the porch of the smaller banquet hall, and Ili-milku could see beyond it the mountain of crushed brick and stones that filled the garden. His breath caught in his throat. *Dear gods!*

Sharryelli put out a hand to steady herself against the wall as if faintness had overcome her.

"It's bad, my lady," Ili-milku agreed in a subdued voice.

They headed toward the larger staircase in the direction of the Court of the Royal Dead, but from a corridor ahead, the sounds of panting and grunting and rocks crashing as someone evidently dug through the rubble came to them. That was where the fall of the upper story had ended. The ceiling sagged on splintered beams. Big ashlar stones had dropped, and smaller rocks from the interior wall packing had torn away with the loosening of the floor above. The hall was scarcely passable.

"Help!" a man cried out breathlessly in the darkness ahead. "Anyone! Help! The king! To me! The king!"

Sharryelli froze. Ili-milku's heart stopped in his mouth. But that wasn't Niqmaddu's voice—he was hunting in the woods someplace. *Has someone found little Ammurapi?*

Ili-milku and the two queens clambered with haste over the rocks, their torch guttering as if the dust were so concrete it could bend flame. Sharryelli's foot slipped, and a cataract of plaster and pebbles threatened to take her feet out from under her. She gave a cry of alarm.

"Careful, my lady." More loudly, Ili-milku cried, "We're coming! Hold on!"

They stumbled and crawled forward in the fluttering darkness until they saw a man crouched over the debris, his dust-masked face wild. It was Teshamanu.

"The king," he repeated, his voice failing as exhaustion overtook him. He fell panting to his hand and knees. A person in a short kilt was stretched out face down in front of him, partially covered with rubble.

A horrible presentiment raised the hair on Ili-milku's arms. Sharryelli threw herself forward with a cry and began to dig into the plaster and stones wildly with her hands until she could see the fallen man's battered profile. It was Niqmaddu.

A great primal howl of horror poured out of her mouth, and she dug faster, in a frenzy. Ili-milku and the other scribe threw aside the rocks, panting and gasping with exertion, oblivious to their bleeding hands. At last, they uncovered the king, still and limp, bloodied from the hail of stones that had poured down on top of him.

"Niqmaddu!" Sharryelli wailed, throwing herself upon him. "Oh, my son, my son! What happened? You weren't supposed to be here!" She collapsed, sobbing, upon his lifeless back. "Why did you listen to me? Why didn't you go?"

Ili-milku felt a shiver of holy fear run up his back. Here was the ineluctable hand of the gods at work. No one could escape his fate. Sharryelli had thought to spare her child danger by keeping him home, and after all, home was where the danger lay.

Off to the side, in the darkness, Lady Ehli-nikkalu stood staring, first at Teshamanu then at her late husband. No one could have interpreted her stunned expression.

The two scribes let the dowager weep until yet another tremor shook them, then taking her arm gently, his voice uneasy, Ili-milku said, "My ladies, you need to get out. Teshamanu and I will bring the king." He thrust the torch into a crevice in the rubble, and he and the secretary began to drag the king's body into the clear. He shot a worried glance at Teshamanu with his one arm. "Can we do this?"

"Help me get him over my shoulder. I can carry him alone if we get him positioned right."

The men struggled to fold the king's dead weight into Teshamanu's embrace then up over his shoulder. He rose to his feet with a grunt. Ili-milku snatched up the torch, and together they picked their way through the rubble toward the main doors of the palace.

Like figures in a nightmare, the women stumbled ahead of them over the debris. It was clearer by way of the Court of the Dead, and somehow, as if hardly conscious of her surroundings, the dowager found her way to the throne room and out the porch door. Ehli-nikkalu dragged after her with exhausted footsteps. In the light of rescuers' torches, Sharryelli stopped, drained and frozen, upon the top step. Someone called up to her, but she didn't seem to know what they said. People turned to her with concern, but still, she stood there, swaying.

"The king," she whispered then tried again, louder. "The king..."

Ili-milku and the secretary came shuffling and panting in her wake. Teshamanu managed to unload his burden and laid Niqmaddu's body out on the porch.

"The king!" Sharryelli wailed, and she sank to the pavement.

*A*uthor Note: Divorce in the ancient world is a simple matter of saying "Leave, I divorce you." This divorce possibly really happens, according to historical sources, despite Ehli-nikkalu's status.

Earthquakes are very common in the eastern Mediterranean, and archaeological evidence shows Ugarit suffers a big one in the late 13th century.

Chapter 14

No catastrophe is comparable, Ili-milku thought grimly, *to the death of a king.* It was upheaval on a cosmic scale. When it was a young king, whose heir was only six years old, how much more of a disaster his death guaranteed. And if that were not enough of a curse, the city lay half destroyed by an earthquake, its grain stores compromised. *What have we done to deserve this?* he thought in helpless misery, then a chill crept up his neck because he remembered thinking not so long ago that their rulers' sins were going to be brought down upon their heads. *Oh, please, you Great Ones, I'm only a poet,* he reminded the gods. *I don't mean things literally.*

He was seated at a makeshift table in Yabni-shapshu's house, where the chancery was carrying out its duties in the interim. That worthy councilor had happily withdrawn to his country estate and turned his vast mansion over to the royal family to serve as a residence and workspace until the palace could be rebuilt. *Hmmm,* Ili-milku thought suddenly. *The building of a palace. That has dramatic possibilities for a poem.*

At Ili-milku's side, head bent over the table, sat Teshamanu. The other scribes had already left for lunch. Presumably, they had intact homes somewhere.

Once he had determined that his family was safe, Ili-milku and his staff had set to work trying to reestablish the king's chancery. Foreign affairs wouldn't stop just because the world was in ruins. Lots of archived texts had fallen and broken. They would need to recopy what could be read and clear out the hopeless remains. Everything could be stored in the north annex with the older cases until the palace was once more safe to inhabit. They could move the writing room there as well.

Ili-milku and the other palace bureaucrats had been busy without stopping all night long. Rescuers had pulled out as many victims as could be safely removed for the time being. *Kalliu* messengers had been sent out at breakneck speed to the viceroy, notifying him of the calamity and begging for aid. Priests and musicians and mourning women had been rounded up for the late king's obsequies in the morning and the coronation of his little successor. The dowager, too, was managing to function, keeping things moving forward. It was she who would rule the kingdom under its six-year-old king. Ili-milku wished he felt more optimistic about that. She had certainly proved her strength, but he had doubts about her honesty. However, in that regard, nothing much had changed—Niqmaddu had permitted his mother a dangerous degree of liberty; she was almost a ruler of a parallel kingdom. Ili-milku regretted the absence of kinder thoughts about the dead, but there it was.

"What do you say we stop for a bite to eat?" he suggested to Teshamanu, who was bent diligently over a tablet as he recopied its text. "My family has probably already eaten, so we may just have to grab a bite in the kitchen here."

"With pleasure, my lord." The queen's secretary laid down his stylus and straightened the tablets before him. He did his best to wash the clay from his hand in the bucket that sat beside them and dry it on his hip. There was no concealing the clay stains on the elbow of his empty sleeve, where he had steadied the tablet.

Ili-milku couldn't help but notice that even water was in short supply. The earthquake had disturbed a lot of people's wells and ruptured the cisterns.

As he scooted out his stool and got to his feet, he eyed his colleague surreptitiously. Both the men were shaven, in a gesture of mourning, which seemed to make wholly unfamiliar people of them. Teshamanu's face was bruised and scraped, one eye half swollen shut, but he seemed to be holding his own after the trauma of the quake and of finding the king. Nonetheless, a grim pleat sat between his eyes.

The two scribes made their way down to the kitchen, and Ili-milku said, "How is it you happened to find Niqmaddu, anyway, my friend? He wasn't even supposed to be at the palace yesterday morning."

"After the queen's floor collapsed, I took off through the door, intending to head down the stairs to get her from below, but the nearest staircase had fallen," Teshamanu explained. "So I went all the way down to the main one by the Court of the Dead Kings. I saw someone below me running for the exit, then another tremor hit, and parts of the ceiling that had been holding fell, all in a rush, and I fell too. I could see the man had been covered by rubble and rocks, so I started digging, hoping he was still alive." He dropped his eyes. "But he wasn't. As soon as I got the face uncovered, I realized it was the king. I dug and dug, then finally, I heard footsteps, and I called out."

Ili-milku clapped a hand compassionately on his shoulder. "That was quite a day, wasn't it? Did you find the queen?"

The scribe smiled slightly, as if he were embarrassed, his cheeks coloring. "Yes. When I found out she'd been taken to Yabni-shapshu's, I came back—so she'd know I was alive. Amaya was with her and told me the children were well and their house and servants had been spared."

"How's the queen doing?"

"Unhurt, except for some minor injuries. Some cuts and bruises on her face."

Ili-milku said, "We owe a grateful offering to the gods, despite everything. I've heard the casualties weren't as high as one might have thought from the amount of damage. But then, surprises are probably still waiting for us under the rubble."

They approached the doorway, where the appetizing smell of lentils welcomed them. Almost none of the staff was still eating, and the kitchen slaves had begun cleaning up, but one waved at them and yelled that he would bring them a bowl. They found a place on the floor in the corridor and sat against the wall.

"Amaya said they even found the crown prince's cat." Teshamanu grinned, an expression Ili-milku thought he'd never seen on his colleague's face. But the habitual look of fixed gravity returned immediately.

"Now, there's a lad whose life has changed suddenly. Where do we all go from here, I wonder?" Ili-milku couldn't help wondering if the viceroy might find this interregnum an appropriate moment for a change of dynasty, and he wasn't sure he objected.

Then the kitchen slave pressed a bowl of lentils into his hands, and the chief scribe fell to, eating gratefully.

Engineers determined that the vaulted tombs of the royal dynasty, built against the north wall of the palace, with its five- or six-cubits-deep courses of ashlar stone, had not been compromised by the earthquake. Thus, the funeral of King Niqmaddu took place in the Court of the Dead, as the exequies of Ugarit's monarchs had done time out of mind. It was a somber crowd of the royal family, palace functionaries, priests, and nobles who gathered nervously in the enclosed space. Ili-milku looked like a dead man himself—his beard nothing but a dark memory, his protruding eyes black-ringed—and Ehli-nikkalu suspected he had not slept much since the finding of the king. She took her place on the dais beside her late husband's mother, concubines, and children, a grim coterie in black. Little Ammurapi, who was the new king, sat stiff and scared looking, but he made a praiseworthy effort at dignity. Ehli-nikkalu had good hopes for the lad, who had always seemed a cheerful and intelligent young fellow. But he wasn't *her* child. She was not the queen mother, and even if Sharryelli joined her ancestors that very day, Ehli-nikkalu would not be the queen mother. Her role was supremely unclear—more unclear than it had ever been.

Can I even call myself a queen any longer? She was no longer the wife of a king, and Sharryelli was officially the dowager of the kingdom. Ehli-nikkalu watched her mother-in-law from the corner of her eye. As little as she liked the woman, she couldn't help but feel sneaking compassion for her. None of the usual studied effects were at play upon her duplicitous little face. It was blanched and empty with undramatic grief. She had wailed and torn her hair and made all the customary responses to the outrage of death, but now she sat drained and bereft. Her eldest son had died, after all. And he had been very young.

Ehli-nikkalu looked at Niqmaddu's body stretched out upon its bier in the center of the court. She had to admit, he was like a statue of a mythological king, dressed in rich violet, with an embroidered diadem around his head, a bow lying in the crook of his arm, and a sword on his hip. She couldn't help but notice the terrible bruises and purple-mouthed gashes on his face from where he had been hurled to the floor by falling debris. They reminded her too poignantly of the bruises he had left on *her* face.

Everyone spoke of Niqmaddu as if he were handsome, and Ehli-nikkalu supposed he was, in an unexceptional way. As for her, she had never been able to see anything beautiful in him. *Yet who am I to hold in disdain the imperfect bodies of others?* No, it was more than pickiness. She had not been able to separate his body from the mean-spirited, sneering soul that had inhabited it, oozed out through that body's pores, and glazed it with malice, like the thin, shiny-blue crust of Egyptian faience. She had no good memories of her late husband's body. She hadn't even liked his smell.

As for Niqmaddu's soul, they said it had become one of the Rapi'uma, the divine royal ancestors. They would pray to him henceforth, and he would guide his little son in his duties. *I hope he's wiser in death than in life,* Ehli-nikkalu thought caustically.

She would not miss him at all and had no real grief for his death. *Yet the death of any mortal is a sorrow. We're so transient, so contingent. We're born. We barely taste life's joys, then we're gone.* Niqmaddu was just a youth—who would never see old age, never know his grandchildren. And he was a king. Mourning lay upon the whole city, upon the whole kingdom. The death of its divinely chosen ruler had rent the very earth of Ugarit, toppled its buildings, and crevassed its fields. *Who could not read some mighty sign from the heavens here? But what? And what of me?*

The funeral rites were beginning. The choir sang. The priests prayed. Sacrifices were offered. Voices invoked the ancestors of Niqmaddu, who would admit him to their deified number. Ehli-nikkalu's thoughts wandered. If it had been the death of a Great King, the rites would have gone on for fourteen days while the whole world stopped. She remembered clearly her grandfather's funeral—she had only been thirteen or even less—and could still see Hattushili's long, thin body stretched out in splendor, garmented like the sun god himself, in the scarlet-and-gold skullcap of kingship, with the royal bow in the crook of his arm and bands of thin, beaten gold laid over his eyes and mouth. When her turn had come to kiss his icy face, she had meant it. She had loved him, and his loss had been real to her.

Her father had wept—he the calm, the impassive—tears running down his face despite his efforts to conceal them. It had shocked her and torn her heart. He had loved his father so much that his mask had fallen off in spite of himself. Oh, her poor father, so full of love and so unable to show it. He had something broken inside him, she felt, and perhaps that was what made her love him so.

Do I love Teshamanu? That seemed like an odd, almost impertinent question. Despite her gratitude to him for trying to save her and the pleasure her writing lessons gave her, she decided she did not—she just felt sorry for his tragic past. That she even asked herself such a thing was a mark of the new freedom she felt with the death of her husband. No one knew Niqmaddu had divorced her, but it no longer mattered. She was a married woman no more.

She gazed up into the filmy blue sky and watched the curling smoke of incense drifting toward the heavenly palace of the gods. Niqmaddu's soul must be rising too. The marshals led her to sprinkle the body, and with the rest of the late king's family, she followed it on its richly draped stretcher to the vault where the royal dead were laid. Seven times, the celebrants lowered the late king's body toward the earth. Seven times, they raised it high again, until finally, he was set inside the open sepulcher, and the tomb was resealed. She heard Ammurapi's treble voice crying aloud, "Papa!" and the suppressed weeping of others, no doubt Sharryelli and Pu-haddu. Tears came to her own eyes but not for Niqmaddu.

At last, Ehli-nikkalu drifted from the Court of the Dead, pensive. She spotted Sharryelli's back, drooping beneath its mourning veil, and heard the sounds of sniffing.

Suddenly, the dowager whipped around. Her face was momentarily twisted with the need for comfort, but then she realized who stood behind her, and she stiffened. "Oh. It's you," she said, not with hostility but with resignation. Her small eyes, naked of kohl, were red, her mouth tremulous.

Ehli-nikkalu felt a tide of something akin to pity tug at her. She nodded. "I... I'm sorry for your loss."

The two women stood facing one another, making no effort to touch.

"It's no loss to you at all, is it?" Sharryelli asked after a moment.

Ehli-nikkalu shook her head. They continued to face one another, not looking directly into each other's faces out of a kind of modesty.

Sharryelli said in a weary voice, "We should have been friends, shouldn't we? But frankly, I couldn't abide the way you always treated Niqmaddu with contempt. You could never unbend, just be one of us."

"He belittled me, struck me, and never had a kind word for me. How *should* I have treated him?"

"Did you ever consider that he had feelings too?" Sharryelli asked. "How do you think it felt to have his wife constantly reminding him that he was only her father's vassal? He had his pride." The dowager's lip trembled, and she lowered her head.

Why should I feel sorry for him? Ehli-nikkalu thought rebelliously. *What did I ever do to him?* But then, she recalled how she had cursed him when he had struck her—and not just mildly but with furor, begging the gods of vengeance to take him, calling upon the Violent Ones to wreak their worst upon him. To bring their vengeance down upon his head—she could hear her very words suddenly and shivered with the fearful power her curse had given her. She remembered how the face of the king upon his bier was purpled and split with bruises, as hers had been. She couldn't make herself feel contrition, exactly, but a certain sense of futility descended upon her. It was no victory she could enjoy. Death alone was the winner.

She said in dull wonder, "You're really sorry he's gone, aren't you?"

Sharryelli's eyes flashed with a spark of something. "Yes, my dear. He was my son, my firstborn. Mothers do, in fact, love their children. If you had ever borne one, you'd realize that."

"Worthy or not?" Ehli-nikkalu could recognize the rise of bitterness up her throat. "Even if they are unkind and violent? Dishonest and selfish?"

"Children don't have to earn their mother's love."

Another silence overtook the women. In the distance, people were calling in the courtyard, and boards crashed where workmen were already dismantling the ceremonial platform.

"And do you love only your son? Does *his* death alone give you sorrow? What about men like Rab-ilu and Hattatamu? Do their deaths mean nothing?"

Sharryelli looked at her, almost pitying. "People die every day, my dear. One cannot sorrow for everyone." She shook her head slowly. "You're still as naïve as ever."

But Ehli-nikkalu persisted. "Why did Rab-ilu die? Wouldn't he play your game?"

"His chariot went off the mountainside, didn't it?"

Ehli-nikkalu made a rude noise of disbelief. Anger was mounting within her, heating her cheeks, and she turned away. *I'll return by another route. This can only end in an argument.* She could feel Sharryelli's eyes on her back, and she walked away with the dignity of her simmering fury.

On the stairs, she overtook Pu-haddu, recognizable immediately by the sway of her well-rounded buttocks. Ehli-nikkalu drew away as she passed, as if the woman's commonness might be contagious. Pu-haddu glared out the corners of her eyes at Ehli-nikkalu. She didn't look so very bereaved, despite the mourning clothes.

"My condolences," Ehli-nikkalu said dryly as she drew ahead.

"You're the one who'd better be sorry, my lady," the concubine said in her uneducated voice. "I'm still the king's mother. What are you now?"

Ehli-nikkalu turned and glared at the woman. She could feel all the resentment of their seven-year rivalry, all the flaunting of the woman's beautiful, fertile body, creeping up her throat. She said acidly, "I'm the daughter of the Sun. Being married to a paltry vassal kinglet didn't take that away from me."

The days that followed the earthquake were strangely free after the cloistered routine at the palace. Yabni-shapshu's house, while luxurious, certainly didn't provide the same kind of privacy for the royal family as had their real residence, where substantial rebuilding was underway, a constant source of dust and noise that didn't spare the residents of the mansion across the street. After the coronation of little Ammurapi, the queen and her charges took refuge more and more frequently at the summer palace at Appu, on the coast, which they had to themselves except for the slaves. She had managed to shake off the ministrations of her handmaids, which in itself gave her a sense of freedom—at least they wouldn't be reporting her every action to Sharryelli. And Rab-ilu's twins could play outside along the shore and climb the rocks and, for once in a long time, be children, not hunted prey.

She and Amaya spent long hours together, spinning and talking, sometimes on the sea's edge and sometimes in the queen's quarters. But now, fall was upon them, with its storms, and the indoor days were growing more frequent. The two women were seated on stools, spinning and listening to the rain lash the shutters and the more distant slamming of the surf.

"How is it you're not married yet, Amaya? At eighteen, I might have expected you to have found a husband. Especially since you're such a beautiful girl, and from a respected family." The queen wound her latest length of yarn around the spindle. It was getting hard to see by the little lamp on the table beside them.

Amaya looked down, her eyes veiled with sorrow. "I stayed home to take care of my mother, my lady. She was sick for several years, and Father was gone all the time. Anani-nikkalu is married and lives in Apsuna, so I was the only one. Somebody had to mind the children too." Then she raised a defiant face. "But I don't regret it. My mother's courage is a lesson that will stay with me all my life."

"You don't lack courage, my dear," Ehli-nikkalu said, her voice rich with affection. "You've had some terrible experiences these last years, and they haven't broken you."

"You, too, my lady."

Ehli-nikkalu said nothing. She was still in mourning clothes, but that was the extent of her grief.

The hammering rain had ceased, and the queen rose to her feet and unlatched the shutters, pushing them back. She drew a deep, liberating breath of the scoured air. Outside, indigo clouds were boiling away to the east, and a brave ray of late-afternoon sun gilded the buildings below them, transfiguring the royal compound into something glorious.

"I want to get married now so I can take care of the twins and not have to depend on Uncle, who is clearly never going to do the right thing by us."

"He has his reasons, I'm sure."

Amaya looked dismissive. Her soft mouth hardened in resolve. "Maybe it's just as well. I don't want him telling me who I have to marry, my lady. I want to have a say in the choice. I don't want someone who is just after my land and ships."

"I'm sure Teshamanu will respect your wishes. He seems like a well-intentioned man."

"I don't know what kind of man he is." Amaya was silent for a long beat, then she said with less rancor, "I want to feel sorry for him, but I think that makes him angry."

Ehli-nikkalu thought that was a rather perceptive observation—one she needed to internalize herself. She said airily, "I rather miss my writing lessons. But I guess it will be a while before the chancery has all the archives recopied. And anyway, I won't be here much longer." That thought made her less happy than she expected, and that astounded her.

"Will they send you away now, my lady?"

"Probably. My father will no doubt marry me out to someone else—unless he thinks I'm too old."

She turned away from the window and smiled at Amaya to hide her bitterness. "You'll make a wonderful wife and mother. You've had ever so much more experience caring for people than most young women your age. I just hope marriage will be kinder to you than it was to me." She cast her gaze out the window once more and leaned against the casing. "Oh, I shouldn't say that to you. I should give you something to look forward to. All men aren't like Niqmaddu, I know."

Amaya went to her side and put her arm around the queen's waist. They watched the pigeons on the flat roof below, drinking from the rain that stood in puddles here and there.

Suddenly, Amaya gave a startled cry. "Oh, look! There are seven of them! They're the Katharat!"

"Where? Those birds?"

"Yes, my lady, see?" Amaya pointed. "They're the seven daughters of the new moon, the Katharat. They're the goddesses of marriage and childbearing, and they appear as birds. I wonder if this is an omen."

"I don't know, but I hope so. We call them the Hutellura. They never listened to my prayers, but I hope they'll hear yours." After a moment, she said, "The daughters of the moon?"

"The new moon, yes: Hilalu, Lord of the Sickle."

"May the Lady Nikkal make them responsive to your prayers, my dear girl."

They continued looking at the pigeons strutting and pecking and scrapping with one another until, one by one, the birds flew away, and what was left was only a pair of iridescent gray-violet pigeons with pink feet, who didn't look like goddesses at all. Ehli-nikkalu wondered if they had brought a message for Amaya or if the Katharat were somehow speaking to her.

*A*uthor Note: It does seem the real house of Yabni-shapshu is used as the chancery at one point. Many of the preserved tablets that tell us about the history of Ugarit are found there.

Earthquakes are so traumatic that their victims often suffer from PTSD. It must be all the worse for societies where they're viewed as evidence of the anger of the gods.

Chapter 15

Ili-milku was in the new chancery writing room, squeezed into the north palace annex. Conditions were cramped, but at least they had a roof over their heads, a place where the newly written-out archives could be kept away from the autumn weather. The room was filled with scribes at the moment, all bent over the table, concentrated on sufficiently piecing together the documents that had been smashed in the earthquake to recopy them.

I should stay and help, Ili-milku thought a bit guiltily. Everyone was worn to a frazzle by the extra work in the last week or so, but he had asked the dowager queen for a moment of her time; he had something to tell her.

Lady Sharryelli had set up an office on the second floor of the same building, so, in next to no time, Ili-milku was knocking on the door. Shipti-ba'al opened it. He gave Ili-milku a friendly smile, his dimples bared by the absence of his beard.

"Here's the chief scribe, my lady," he called back into the room.

"Show him in, my dear."

Ili-milku entered and made an obeisance. Sharryelli was seated at a large table, which looked as though it might have been commandeered from the kitchen. She greeted him brightly. "Ili-milku, my friend. What's on your mind? Your note sounded urgent."

"Perhaps not urgent, my lady, but something that must be dealt with." He hoped this wouldn't rake open the queen's sorrow, but she would understand its importance. "Were you aware that Lord Niqmaddu was in debt to somebody named Iwiri-muza? The man's just brought a claim against the late king's estate for seven hundred silver shekels. And when I went back through the books, I found Niqmad-du had been dishing him big sums for nearly six years."

The queen looked nonplussed, her mouth hanging open. "Seven hundred shekels? That's an enormous amount. Whatever can that be about? Was he gambling?" She looked at Shipti-ba'al. "I didn't think he had the patience for *senet*. Dogfighting, perhaps?"

"It's a lot of silver." Lord Shipti-ba'al, who had been listening closely, pursed his lips. He seated himself on a stool, leaving Ili-milku standing alone, like a schoolboy before his masters.

"We can't afford things like that right now," said Sharryelli. "Anything. The Great King is not going to help us at all with rebuilding. The viceroy says Hatti is in no position to help anyone else—they're in desperate straits themselves at the moment. Then there's this ridiculous pretender making trouble—we'll have to campaign against him. We can't let private creditors peck apart the treasury." She knit her brows and stared hard at the tabletop for a moment.

Ili-milku could almost see the thoughts churning within her.

"Tell me, Ili-milku," she said at last. "Can you have some research done into that business with the queen of Ammishtamru seventeen years ago? I need to know how the banishment of Utri-sharrumma was carried out. And also how they went about offering indemnity for the queen's life. It was paid to her brother, right? Does that all go to the individual, or does the crown get some? Oh, and who is the chief judge while the king's a minor?"

Ili-milku shrugged modestly. "Well, I can probably answer personally any of my lady's questions about the trial. I was working in the legal archives at the time and was actually involved, in a strange way. At least, with the assassination of the king that followed. I don't mean *involved*, you understand..." He laughed and gave an apologetic grimace.

"Oh, tell me everything, Ili-milku," Sharryelli said avidly. She shot a sideways glance at Shipti-ba'al.

"Well, Queen Puduhepa was accused of treason by virtue of being involved in Ammishtamru's brothers' uprising. And she also, er... adultered with one of the king's brothers. There was no trial, really; it was a matter of state, and she was caught red-handed. It was Ini-tesshub, the viceroy, who sentenced her. But it didn't all happen at once."

"Oh?"

"No. At first, the viceroy ordered her to be expelled and sent back to her brother's court in Amurru. But then Ammishtamru decided he wanted her executed—as was his right, even though Ini-tesshub had hoped to avoid such a divisive event between vassals. Ammishtamru went over the viceroy's head to the Great King himself, and of course, because Tudhaliya needed Ugarit's friendship, he agreed. So she was extradited and put to death, and Ammishtamru did the right thing by offering her brother an indemnity of fourteen hundred gold shekels."

Shipti-ba'al whistled and raised his eyebrows.

"Goodness, that's a lot of gold."

"Well, she was a princess of Hatti through her mother."

Sharryelli sucked her teeth for a moment. "How complicated. Do I need to go to the Great King with this? But he hardly speaks to his vassals anymore. The viceroy rules us almost independently. What we *can't* do is wait until we have yet another layer of governance—that awful mayor right in our city, checking our books. What would he think of Niqmaddu?"

"What have you in mind, my lady?" Ili-milku asked.

Shipti-ba'al was silent, watching the dowager with a sharp, probing stare.

After a moment of gnawing her lip thoughtfully, Sharryelli said, "What would the indemnity have been if the queen had been simply a local aristocrat? Some *maryannu*..."

"Oh, I couldn't say, my lady." Ili-milku scratched his scalp. "It depends in part on what their family demanded. An ordinary ransom for a hostage, a commoner, is something like fifty silver shekels. But I feel sure that in any case, it would be much less than the queen's indemnity."

"Do men cost more than women?"

"Well, perhaps, if it means the supporter of a family, yes, I would think they might ask more."

"As much as seven hundred silver shekels?"

Shipti-ba'al's eyes narrowed, and a thin smile twitched at the corner of his lips.

Ili-milku twisted his mouth in thought. "Don't quote me, my lady. It's been years since I worked with law cases. But I would say easily a thousand silver shekels, depending on the number of children left orphaned and such factors."

She smiled cheerfully to show she was satisfied with his information. "Thank you, Ili-milku. That helps me. And what about the court? How do we carry out trials until the king comes of age and can sit in his own name?"

"Well, presidency on the court rotates, my lady. At the moment, it happens to be mine." He laughed and rolled his eyes. "If anyone wants to claim it, I'd be happy to turn it over to him! Of course, the king always has the last word, no matter his age. One assumes that some adult would help him understand his duty."

Sharryelli made a reflective nod, her eyes lowered. Then she looked up. "And that brings me to something I wanted to talk to you about—Utri-sharrumma has apparently gone to the viceroy to make an appeal for the throne."

Ili-milku's eyes popped in astonishment.

She replied with a grim smile. "Yes. Can you imagine? Do you think he has any legitimate claim, dear? Is Ini-tesshub conceivably going to listen to him?"

The chief scribe gnawed his lip, troubled. "He could certainly make a good case, my lady. He was tricked out of the succession, I'm afraid. It will be a matter of the viceroy's judgment."

Shipti-ba'al snorted darkly. "That doesn't sound good. If Ini-tesshub is sufficiently peeved with the current dynasty, he might well rule in favor of Utri-sharrumma, who has the double advantage of being a prince of Hittite blood."

"A pox on that Ehli-nikkalu—if only she had given us an heir. Dear little Ammurapi can claim nothing more than a working-class concubine for a mother. It isn't a fair fight." Sharryelli's eyes shriveled in distress, as if she were on the edge of tears.

Ili-milku sank into thoughtful silence, debating with himself, then he said in a low voice, "My lady, were you aware that Utri-sharrumma is associated with the Umman-manda?"

Sharryelli cried out in horror, "Oh, no! What makes you think so?"

"The queen spoke to him during her kidnapping."

Sharryelli grew suddenly pale but managed a smile as she said, "Really? I'll bet the viceroy doesn't know that."

"The queen has a theory about the affair. She thinks the Umman mercenaries who accompanied her party went rogue and kidnapped her for food. They're apparently refugees from far and wide who have fled the famine."

Sharryelli said more calmly, "And Utri-sharrumma is involved how?"

"He's leading them, my lady. He finds them food, and they offer him their swords to help him regain the throne."

Sharryelli goggled at him, an angry pink flushing her cheeks. "Were you ever going to tell me this, Ili-milku? This is serious."

Ili-milku squirmed. He could feel the sweat breaking out on his face. "It seemed to be hearsay, my lady. Purely interpretation on the young queen's part." *Forgive me, Lady Ehli-nikkalu, but she already hates you.*

"She's not a queen anymore," Shipti-ba'al reminded him pointedly. "Your loyalty is to the regent, Lady Sharryelli."

"Yes, my lord," the chief scribe said, chastened.

Sharryelli turned to her son-in-law. "This is worse than we thought. We need to deal with the Umman-manda immediately." To Ili-milku, she said, "And does Niqmaddu's widow know anything else that might be useful to the kingdom? Since *she* seems uninterested in sharing that with us..."

"Not that I'm aware, my queen."

At last, the dowager dismissed the chief scribe, and he tottered in relief from her presence, wiping his forehead. *I think it must be lunchtime,* he thought, not caring if it were true or not. *I'm going home.*

When Ili-milku returned to the makeshift chancery that afternoon, he realized he needed to look into something else. *What had those six years of debts to the fellow Iwiri-muza been about?* If it was something frivolous, the government might perhaps brush aside the present demand for seven hundred shekels in the interests of the national well-being. Perhaps the creditor could be convinced to forego them if sufficient persuasion were applied—verbally, of course. Some appeal to his patriotism. If not, they would simply have to find the silver. *With all this rebuilding to do? May the gods help us.*

Amaya had made one of her periodic visits to the city to check on the house and the servants. To her relief, everyone seemed to be managing. They assured her that Teshamanu was regularly disbursing funds for the running of the household. It disgruntled

Amaya seriously that her wishes had not prevailed over those of Ili-milku and the queen—no one ever listened to a woman or took her desires seriously—and that her uncle had been appointed adminis-trator of the estate after all. How she wanted to come back to her own house, restore the twins to the familiar scene of their happy life before. She was just leaving by way of the front door, remembering that headlong flight after her father so many months ago and the nightmare it had loosed upon them, when she almost collided with a man raising his hand to knock at the door—Teshamanu.

Her face chilled. "Uncle," she said curtly, still simmering with thoughts of annoyance toward him.

He looked at her with an unreadable expression, nervously push-ing back his drizzle-dampened hair. "Amaya."

"I was just leaving. If you'll excuse me." She started to shove past him, but he extended his hand and caught at her sleeve.

"Wait, don't go. I want to talk to you."

Well, I don't want to talk to you. "About what?" She folded her arms.

He dropped his eyes for a moment in a way that looked suspi-ciously like shame. "I know you don't like me, but I'm not sure why. I certainly haven't been a good uncle, but I've never done you harm."

Amaya had to admit that was true. When she was a child, he and his wife and children had been much more involved in the family. He had been a pleasanter man altogether. Then they had died, and Teshamanu had recovered from his burns at Rab-ilu's house. He had grown embittered and nervous, had argued with his brother again and again, then he had moved out as soon as he was able to care for himself. Where exactly he had gone, she didn't know—some room somewhere. He hadn't shown up at their house again. Her father had taken to shaking his head hopelessly at the mention of his twin.

"I know. I just feel you could have—should have—done more for us after Father's death. I had to arrange the funeral. I had to try to find a safe place for the twins. You should have taken them in, Uncle. It was your duty. Do you think for a moment that Father wouldn't have done right by your family if it had been you who had died and not them?" *Where is this cruelty coming from? Am I that angry at him?* But she stared at him defiantly.

He looked so haggard and downcast that Amaya almost relented. His beard was just growing in, and he had the air of a scruffy street dog, despite his well-shaped features.

"You're fully justified," he agreed dully. "I wish I could make it up to you. I've failed everyone who has trusted me, including you and the children."

Amaya found herself disarmed by this humble acknowledgment. She bit her lip, unable to think of a comeback. "Well, I know you've had a hard time of it."

"Stop making that an excuse for my irresponsibility. You and everyone. I've made bad choices from the beginning, and I've brought hard times down on myself."

Amaya was herself an adult, but somehow, this breast-beating in a relative of her parents' generation embarrassed her as it might have a child. Perhaps that was why she didn't like him—his shipwreck of a life made her uneasy. Everything in her own young life had crashed down around her in the last year, and the one last person who should have been a source of support was a broken spar. Now, they would all be swept away like a trading vessel in a storm. She could feel helpless tears prickling in her nose.

"Don't cry," Teshamanu said in a gentler voice. "I don't want to make all this harder for you. Do you need silver? I can have it sent to you."

She bit her lip to control its tremor and shook her head. "Silver won't replace my loss, Uncle. Silver won't make me happy again." She turned away as if to go.

"Amaya, I *can't* take in the children. I want you to know that. I can't. It might endanger them. And at the very least, my present quarters are not suitable for them." He stared at her with pleading eyes.

"We're already in danger." She strode away, her steps quick and brittle, leaving her uncle standing in the street before the door. She didn't know what to feel.

She was still staying with Lady Ehli-nikkalu in Lord Yabni-shapshu's house when she had need to come to town, and the queen would be waiting for her in their temporary apartment. Across the street, most of the clearing out of the palace garden had been accomplished, she saw. The courtyard looked clean, despite the gaping unwalled chambers that hung dizzily above. Of the beauty of the garden, though, nothing was left—of the trees and kiosk, of the flowers, of the neat gravel paths. It had become a desolation of mud and rubble, tramped over continuously by an army of workmen, the blows of whose tools clanged without cease, even in the drizzle. Wrapping her shawl about her, Amaya drifted toward the site curiously. *Dear Lady Nikkal, what were you trying to tell us?*

There was no longer any gate in the cracked wall of the service court, and Amaya passed in. She and the children had been sitting right about there, playing with the crown prince's cat, when the animal had bolted fearfully over the wall. And then...

"Amaya, my dear? Is that you?"

The girl turned, expecting Lady Ehli-nikkalu, but instead, it was the queen regent holding the little king by the hand.

The child beamed at Amaya. "Hello, pretty lady."

Despite her pounding heart, Amaya was touched by the little king's gallantry. She dropped into an obeisance. "My lord king. My lady."

"You're getting all wet. Come inside with us." Sharryelli smiled, to all appearances full of uncalculating goodwill.

But Amaya's back was icy, prickling with warning. "I was just leaving, my lady. I need to get back."

"Back to where? Surely in this weather, nothing too urgent is happening. Your king commands you, don't you, my sweet?" She ruffled her grandson's hair.

He was a charming boy, with a handsome, round face and an innocent air, an adorable dimple in his chin. He said with a big grin that bared an absent front tooth, "Yes!"

Amaya felt downright conflicted. She didn't trust Sharryelli at all after the way the regent had treated Ehli-nikkalu, and there was a good chance that the woman had been involved with Rab-ilu's murder. But she could hardly disobey the king, even if he was six years old. She trailed them into the kitchen corridor, where the overhanging second story of the intact wing protected them from the rain. There, she stood uncomfortably while Sharryelli reached out and straightened the girl's cap in a motherly gesture.

I never should have come over here, Amaya thought ruefully. *She could have me killed right here, and who would be aware of what happened?*

"You know, my dear, I've been thinking about what I told you all those weeks ago. About helping you find a suitable husband. I have a son, Talmiyannu, who is sixteen—that's about your age, isn't it? He's a very handsome boy. Perhaps we could introduce you to him and see what happens."

A wave of panic started to rise in Amaya's throat. "Oh, my lady," she stammered. "It's... it's too much honor for a commoner."

Sharryelli laughed. "That's the first time I've ever heard a *maryannu* claim they weren't equal to the ruling dynasty! No, my dear. You're from one of the best lineages of Ugarit. You'd make him a splendid match. And wouldn't it be nice to become a princess? We'd so love to have you as part of the family." She all but winked at the girl, her face wreathed with conspiratorial good humor.

Within, Amaya shrieked, *But I don't* want *to marry a prince I've never met and probably won't even like. I want to be happy, like my parents, and not be looked down on if I have daughters and not sons. And what's Lady Sharryelli up to, anyway? Is she trying to buy my silence about Father's murder?* She struggled to keep a pleasant expression on her face, but her heart was thundering. *Mother, what should I say?*

The regent must have seen her turmoil because Sharryelli said in understanding, "I know this is sudden. You don't have to make up your mind right now. And there will be negotiations to make with your uncle—dowry and things like that."

"My uncle?" Amaya cried in surprise.

"Well, he is technically your guardian, dear, even though my son's widow seems to think you've become her property."

The king tugged impatiently at Sharryelli's hand. "Come on, Grandmother."

Sharryelli turned to him. "How would you like Lady Amaya to be part of our family, Ammurapi? Wouldn't she and Uncle Talmiyannu look sweet together?"

"Or I could marry her," he suggested innocently.

Sharryelli smiled with grandmotherly tenderness, but Amaya could hardly force herself not to draw away in horror. *I don't want anything to do with these dreadful people. They killed my father.* She bobbed a quick bow and fled across the street.

*A*uthor Note: *We have historical evidence of the royal funerals of Ugarit. Shaving the beard (or letting it grow, in the case of clean-shaven societies) is a typical gesture of mourning.*

The dead kings of Ugarit, like those of Hatti, are considered to become divine upon their death. While alive, they are chosen by the gods but are not themselves gods.

Since the Ugarites have no real money, standard weights of silver and gold form the basis of value. The shekel is about 7-17g (it varies over time). An unskilled laborer might earn 10 silver shekels a year. Niqmaddu's debt is historical.

Readers of The Queen's Dog *will remember the punishment of the queen and Ili-milku's small part in the episode.*

Chapter 16

When Amaya regained the queen's apartments, her flesh still creeping with fear, she found Ili-milku there, too, a tablet in his hand.

"My lady, I just ran into the regent and the little king," the girl cried breathlessly.

Ili-milku looked uneasy. "I'll be going, my lady, unless there's anything else you need me for."

But Ehli-nikkalu held him back. "I want your advice, Ili-milku. Don't go." To Amaya, she said, "What did she want?"

"She's talking about betrothing me to her younger son. I think she's trying to buy my silence."

The queen and the chief scribe exchanged a concerned look. Then Ehli-nikkalu's anxiety gave way to a pensive expression. "You know, that might be your best hope of safety."

Amaya gaped at her. "Can you mean that, my lady? She's the very one who wants to kill me."

But Ili-milku, who was clearly following the queen's thinking, said, "Maybe not, my girl. In the first place, we don't know that she's involved at all—"

"But I recognized Lord Shipti-ba'al's—"

"Shipti-ba'al, yes. But do we have any proof of the regent's collaboration?" The queen snorted. "Little as I like Sharryelli, she may, in fact, have had nothing to do with Rab-ilu's death. The fact that she knows where you are and has tried nothing against you makes me wonder."

Amaya stared from one face to the other in distress. "Why would Shipti-ba'al have killed my father? It had to have something to do with those messages, and it was the late king and his mother who had the motive to stop him from delivering them. You told me as much."

Ili-milku looked conflicted as he listened to her speak. "Our queen is right, my dear. We don't really know that Shipti-ba'al wasn't acting alone. Perhaps he thought he could render his... er... brother-in-law a favor by taking things into his own hands."

"I can't believe this!" All the fear Amaya had felt in the regent's presence met her sense of betrayal by those she trusted and melded into anger. The heat went roaring up her cheeks, and she stamped her foot in frustration.

Lady Ehli-nikkalu put a kindly hand on the girl's shoulder, her face crumpled with sorrow. "Even if she is guilty, Amaya, she may honestly think that once you're part of the royal family, you wouldn't dare betray her. Surely she wouldn't do anything to such a visible member of society as her daughter-in-law. It may honestly be your best chance for safety—you and the children."

"I'm expected to sell my honor for safety?" Amaya wanted to cry, "I thought better of you!" but she could never have said that to the woman she loved and admired so.

Ehli-nikkalu and Ili-milku looked shamefaced, but the chief scribe said earnestly, "You must think of the children, my girl."

I must sell my hope of happiness for the children. I must marry a man I don't love for the children. I must walk into the lion's den for the children. She thought her heart would incinerate—after all the years of sacrificing herself to care for her mother, just when the freedom to be happy and have a normal life opened up.

But she knew what her mother would have done. Amaya drew a deep breath and said in resignation, "All right."

Only the next day, something happened that seemed to redress the gloom of Amaya's forced betrothal.

She was alone with Yanakh and Ba'aluya while Lady Ehli-nikkalu saw to some business she had been called to deal with. As the girl was playing cat's cradle with the twins, Lady Sharryelli appeared in the door of Ehli-nikkalu's apartment, all intimate smiles. His hand in Sharryelli's, the little king stood beside her, dancing on his toes at the sight of other children.

"I believe my daughter-in-law is occupied with some of her properties this morning. Is that not so? I actually had her called away because you're the one I want to talk to, Amaya dear." The regent made her way into the room while Amaya sat frozen in suspicion, her siblings staring up by her side.

At last, Amaya jumped to her feet and dropped in a bow.

"It's the king," Yanakh blurted.

His twin sister gave him a dig with her elbow. "We should bow," she hissed, and the two youngsters scrambled to their feet and folded over.

Ammurapi laughed happily. "Hello, little boy. Hello, little girl. Can they play with me, Grandmother?"

"Indeed, they can, my love. Maybe the three of you could run down to the courtyard and play tag while there isn't any rain for once." She beamed at the king and shot a conspiratorial wink at the twins, who, after staring questioningly at their elder sister, followed the younger boy out with a thunder of footsteps. Amaya could hear their voices raised in dares and challenges as they clattered down the stairs.

Trying to maintain an appearance of adult calm despite her hammering heart, Amaya said neutrally, "What can I do for my lady?"

"My daughter—may I call you that? It won't be long before it's true. Your uncle and I are talking already about the betrothal. We need to bring you and Talmiyannu together to meet one another.

Isn't it exciting? A girl's wedding day is the happiest day of her life." She stretched out a hand and stroked Amaya's arm fondly. "I've thought and thought about what to give you as a wedding gift, and it seems to me that revenge for your father's death would be the thing that made you happiest. Am I right?"

Amaya's jaw dropped. She didn't know what to say. *Can this be sincere? Lady Ehli-nikkalu seems to have backed away from the idea of Sharryelli's complicity, but I still don't trust the regent.* She finally managed to stammer, "That would... yes, it would be wonderful. I... I would be most grateful." In spite of herself, she dropped to her knees and reached to kiss Sharryelli's plump pink hand.

Sharryelli patted the girl's cheek and said with great earnestness, "Tell me who it is, and I promise you he'll be brought to law."

Amaya stiffened. As she got to her feet, she kept her face downward, hoping the regent couldn't see the play of hope and suspicion that chased one another within her. *Is this a trap to make me reveal I do, in fact, know who the murderer is? Can she honestly not know?*

"Perhaps Lady Ehli-nikkalu should be present," Amaya murmured uncertainly.

"But you were the witness, my dear. And you're an adult—you don't need her to tell you what to think. I can assure you, your uncle is eager to see justice done. It's on his head to see his brother avenged, after all. But he's not the witness." Sharryelli smiled, looking so sweet and caring that Amaya felt shame for her suspicions.

I don't know what to think. At last, she drew a deep breath and said hesitantly, "It was... it was Lord Shipti-ba'al, my lady."

Lady Sharryelli shook her head, looking troubled. "What a scandal—my daughter's husband. But justice must be served, or the gods will continue to be angry with our kingdom." She sighed in resignation. "Would you be willing to testify in court, my daughter? He'll be tried by the council with Lord Ili-milku presiding."

Somehow, the idea that the kindly Ili-milku was involved reassured the girl. "I will, my lady." And now that she had committed to it, the thought of punishing her father's killer sounded better and better. She said resolutely, "I will."

When Lady Ehli-nikkalu returned from the chancery later that morning, she had the chief scribe in tow. Amaya ran to her, excited but full of trepidation, to tell her the shocking developments. The others looked stunned.

"Ili-milku, can we trust Sharryelli to go through with a trial?" the queen asked. "Is this somehow a trick?"

"Maybe not, my lady. If she wants our Amaya to become part of the royal family, she may actually think this is a minimal gesture of goodwill. Or the price of Amaya's loyalty." Cautious hope lit Ili-milku's big eyes. "With a firsthand witness, I don't see how he can be acquitted. I think this may be our best chance of obtaining justice for Rab-ilu."

May the gods grant us this, thought Amaya. *Oh, Father, no matter what I have to do to get it—even marry that awful prince.*

After so many days of rain, a morning finally dawned as bright and crisp as a day in the land of the blessed *Rapi'uma*. It seemed criminal to spend it indoors, and they had walked along the sea so frequently that the shore was almost tiresome. Ehli-nikkalu's eye craved green. She craved trees and mountains, and the smell of pine.

"Amaya," she said, as the girl pinned the queen's cap and veil on her hair. "I know the children are playing with the king today, but what if you and I have a picnic in the country? I have a lot of property in the neighborhood of the capital, so we wouldn't have to travel any distance. There's no danger this far south." Eyes sparkling with excitement, she looked up at her lady-in-waiting standing behind her. "It's such a beautiful day. There may not be many more of them this season."

"Oh, my lady," the girl cried in delight. "That would be wonderful! Will the regent let you do it?"

Ehli-nikkalu said in a hard voice, "I don't have to ask permission of anyone just to visit my orchards for a few hours."

Besides, she felt guilty about Amaya. It had clearly been a terrible blow to the poor girl to believe her protector was throwing her to the wolves, but in fact, Ehli-nikkalu had thought—and still thought—that the bosom of the royal family might ironically be the safest place for Rab-ilu's children. Her real fear was that the prince would be like his older brother. She wasn't sure she could endure the guilt of having forked Amaya over to such a life.

Ehli-nikkalu needed something soul restoring to take her mind off such thoughts, and so did Amaya. The queen threw herself into her preparations. They rounded up shawls and dragged blankets out of the bedding chest. A file of slaves came to carry everything to the courtyard and pack it on a donkey. The mules had been hitched to her litter. Under a sparkling sky as blue as Egyptian glass, a soldier unbarred the wicket. And off they set through the city, past the deafening worksite of the palace, along market streets lying half in ruins, and out the south gate.

Over the rattling wooden bridge across the Rahbanu they passed and down the road, clopping along, bells jingling to the rhythm of the mules' hooves. She wasn't even sure where they were going, just "to the orchards." *To the orchards!* Olive trees closed in around the road on both sides, filled with workers, men and women, busy with the harvest of the ripe fruit for oil. Somewhere, her own trees grew, the precious olive trees that paid for her life of comfort.

They swayed and rocked at the animals' gentle pace until the sun had reached halfway up the eastern sky. The city was far out of sight. Trees stretched endlessly, climbing up the foothills on narrow terraces, billowing over the level fields like a frothy silver sea. Then the drivers took them diagonally into the stony white orchards, between the trees with their spume of silvery leaves.

The normally peaceful groves seethed with activity during that season. Men with long poles beat the trunks and branches in a loud storm of clacking. Others climbed into the crown of the trees to shake the boughs with hands and feet. And all around beneath them, a rain of black fruits pattered to the ground, where women and children scrabbled about, gathering them into big baskets. Some of the men sang to pace their work. Ehli-nikkalu felt a fierce thrill of energy, a peace born of fresh air and the smell of the cold earth and the subtle fragrance of ripe olives. She resolved not to let her failures overcome her. The world was alive, divine. Richness, benevolence, and plenty were all around her. She filled her lungs with the clean perfume of winter and swung her feet to the ground. Amaya slid out of the litter behind her.

The foreman of the harvest made his way toward her, bowing even before he had reached her. "My lady," he called. "How can we serve you?"

"We're just here to watch and spend the day," she said. "We don't want to get in your way. Is there a place we can spread our lunch?"

He led them toward the little stone building that stood at the edge of a block of groves. A line of women carrying baskets full of fruit on their heads made their way toward the edifice, and at the door, men received them, hoicking the baskets up and passing them within. Everyone worked rhythmically and efficiently. The olives would be crushed by hand in a deep mortar to form the very best oil, the foreman explained, and the bruised flesh of the fruit would then be dumped into the openwork fiber baskets of a press. Two other men readied the heavy bar that would be lowered over the baskets and hung with stone weights until yet more oil ran from the press. Already, golden-green liquid stained its edges and dripped into the stone basin beside it. Another man ladled oil from the basin into a tall jar to add to the army of sealed jars that stood at attention. A growing pile of pits and crushed olive flesh mounted to one side as the press was emptied again and again while boys with yokes over their shoulders shoveled the pits up and took them away.

"They burn that dross in the pottery kilns. Really hot flame. Be careful you don't dirty your clothes, my lady," the foreman cautioned, leading them past the door. "Now, over there, on the other side of the press house, we've cleared those trees, so you can sit wherever you like and bother nobody. Of course, they're *your* trees, so you're no bother." He grinned and bobbed his head to defuse his seeming disrespect.

She smiled back. It would take more than that to curdle her good mood. The sweet, appetizing smell of olive oil filled the air. The little party spread its blankets under the stripped trees, at a remove from the percussion and singing of the harvesters. Some little bird twittered in the branches overhead, and a crow flew squawking across the orchard.

Ehli-nikkalu drew a deep, contented breath. "Shall we walk a little first, Amaya? Warm ourselves up a bit?"

The two of them drifted off through the trees, hugging their shawls about themselves, while the handmaids and other slaves prepared the meal. Behind them, their pack donkey began the laborious inhalation before a mournful bray, and Ehli-nikkalu laughed. She was unaccountably reminded of Teshamanu with his moody silence. She saw him too rarely those days and admitted it had depressed her a bit not to have those writing lessons to look forward to. Going out into the countryside had been a good idea—to remind herself that the world went on despite earthquakes, loneliness, and the deaths of kings.

She shielded her eyes with a hand against the bright winter sun. The hillside was all white caliche and silver leaves fluttering delicately in the air. If she squinted, she could imagine it was snow.

Below them, toward the road, she saw other colors, dull but variegated. "What's that?" she asked almost to herself. "Why, it's people." Indeed, a whole crowd of people in a straggling mass trudged at a determined pace toward the orchards, into the orchards. Bronze gleamed among them now and again. *Are they the next shift of workers with their tools, come to relieve the others?*

"Who are they, my lady?" Amaya asked, anxiety catching at her voice. "There are certainly a lot of them."

"I don't know..."

The people filtered among the trees, and the harvesters began to notice them. People from both sides shouted out, but Ehli-nikkalu could make nothing of the words. The singing ceased. The line of women heading for the press house slowed and broke. The women dropped their baskets and started to run away into the orchards. A tentacle of fear crept up Ehli-nikkalu's spine. She'd had that feeling before. Something was wrong. She clutched Amaya's elbow.

The newcomers had weapons as well as tools, while the harvesters were armed only with their long poles, which were too unwieldy to be of much use in a showdown. Her men faced off with the crowd, tossing their heads and yelling brave words, but suddenly, one of them flew into the air and dropped to his back on the ground. Red blossomed where his face had been. People cried out in dismay. One of the newcomers hefted a rock in his hand as he prepared to drop it into the deadly leather pocket of a sling. *Slingers!*

The other workmen drew back. They had women and children to protect, and no one wanted to grapple with a slinger who could kill from *ikus* away. Ehli-nikkalu's heart rose in her throat. *Who are these people?* Clearly no army—they were in civilian clothes, worn and ragged at that. Some looked as if they might be Ugarites, but others were dressed differently. She saw women among them too—women with slings, clubs, scythes, and shepherd's crooks. They yelled, making warlike, warbling noises, and their men closed in on the harvesters, who held their ground for a moment then turned tail and fled.

The newcomers cheered and whistled victoriously but didn't pursue the fleeing workmen. Instead, they fell upon the baskets of olives, dropped to their knees, and began gathering fallen fruit. Others mounted the trees, resuming the beating of the branches. Some of them took off toward the press house.

"They want the olives," Amaya cried with amazement. "They're hungry!"

"They're Umman-manda," Ehli-nikkalu murmured. She wanted to yell, "Run!" yet they had nowhere to go. They could never outdistance an angry mob at the genteel pace of a mule-drawn litter.

Nonetheless, the two took off toward their picnic site. At the very least, they could warn the slaves. But the slaves had already seen—and gone. The animals stood aimlessly cropping weeds. The picnic lay spread upon a rug on the ground, but not one of the seven men and women who had accompanied Ehli-nikkalu was anywhere to be seen. A wave of mingled fury and terror broke over her.

Umman-manda here, only a few leagues from the walls of the city itself? And that wall down in places, the gates wedged open until repairs can be made. There must be hundreds, perhaps thousands, of the ragtag dispossessed swarming the orchards, breaking into the press house, carrying off the jars of fresh gold-green oil. *My oil.*

Amaya and Ehli-nikkalu were alone, undefended. Perhaps no one would know who they were, but if anyone recognized her, she would be taken for ransom again. The prospects might be even direr for a pretty young girl like Amaya.

Ehli-nikkalu swallowed with difficulty, not knowing what to do but deeply grateful that the twins hadn't accompanied them. "Let's go up the terraces and try to hide. Those trees have been stripped. The Umman may not be interested."

They ran in their heavy skirts and soft-soled slippers, stumbling over the rocks and hard clots of soil, their shawls slipping from their shoulders and snagging in the dry weeds. Growing wearier and more breathless by the step, they zigzagged from tree to tree until the air tore in Ehli-nikkalu's throat. They hauled themselves up the low stone walls that formed terraces, bruising themselves on the stone, falling, faces flat in the dirt, sobbing and exhausted. Ehli-nikkalu felt as if her heart would explode. It roared in her chest until her eardrums echoed with its beat. Finally, she could run no more.

"Keep going if you can," she gasped. "But I'm done for."

She lay on her back, panting, and Amaya fell beside her.

"I'm not leaving you alone, my lady. Let them get us both."

They dragged themselves behind the broad gray bole of a tree and tried to flatten into the ground. The thunder of Ehli-nikkalu's pulse seemed to fill the air. She wondered if she could pretend to be dead, but surely, the heaving of her back would give her away.

After what seemed like an excruciatingly long time, she raised her face and peered downhill. Below them, the orchard to the other side of the press house still echoed with the shouts and clatter of the Umman-manda harvesting with enthusiasm. Around her, everything was silent. A chilly breeze ruffled the leaves about her with a faintly metallic sound.

Amaya still lay with her face to the ground, her eyes squeezed shut. "How long should we lie here, my lady?" the girl whispered into her forearm.

"We may have escaped without being seen. Let's try to find our way back to the road by the long route and walk back to the city." Ehli-nikkalu pushed up to her knees and began to climb to her feet.

Author Note: In this patriarchal culture, Teshamanu would certainly be the one to negotiate a marriage for his niece. Prince Talmiyannu is a real person (although some believe that is Niqmaddu's birth name).

Avenging a family death is very important to the Ugarites, but because they are such good businessmen, this sometimes takes the form of a fine rather than execution.

Chapter 17

"On the other hand," a youthful male said behind her, "you may *not* have escaped without being seen."

Ehli-nikkalu spun, fear leaping into her throat. She knew that voice. And there he stood: Utri-sharrumma, still dressed in the same filthy tunic of their previous encounter months before. An apple—one of their picnic apples—was in his hand. He threw back his matted head and cawed with laughter. Desperation overwhelmed her. If there was one man upon the black earth she didn't trust, it was that one, with his mad eyes and sudden malevolent laugh.

She drew herself up to her full height, trying not to show how deeply he unsettled her. "Ah, cousin. Are these your people, then?"

"They are, cousin." He took a bite of the apple and began to chew with gusto.

"Then I welcome them to my olive groves. I freely give them the harvest." She hoped her show of control wouldn't rub him against the grain, but she suspected that to cringe would be to provoke his cruelty.

"How gracious of you, cousin." He made a little bow and, crossing his legs, seated himself on the ground, motioning for her to do likewise.

Her eyes on his neat, bony ankles, she sank uneasily and drew her skirts around her feet.

"I daresay there's more food in the city, am I right?"

"Of... of course. But the granaries were destroyed by an earthquake. There isn't as much as you'd think."

Utri-sharrumma nodded, considering. "Yes, we'd heard. Yet you still ship it to Hatti Land. Must not be too scarce. And they still pay you, right? So there must be other commodities in the city. Gold, perhaps. Purple textiles. Things of great price. Perfumes." He laughed raucously. "I'm sure you'd agree that my need for perfume is acute." He reached out a small, delicate hand and flicked a thistle off the front of Ehli-nikkalu's blouse.

She drew back, unable to conceal her fear.

Utri-sharrumma gave her a piercing and malicious grin. "Don't worry, cousin. You're a little long in the tooth for me." He tossed aside his apple core. "But," he continued, facing Amaya as she tried to look inconspicuous behind Ehli-nikkalu, "this one is just right." He sank into a long, reflective silence, his amber eyes fixed with unsettling intensity upon her.

A chill ran up Ehli-nikkalu's spine, and suddenly, she wanted with painful urgency to get the girl out of his sight. She and the pretender sat silently side by side. Ehli-nikkalu saw the dirt ingrained above Utri-sharrumma's collarbone. A louse bounded into view on his knotted hair.

"Don't you ever take a bath?" she murmured, grimacing with disgust.

"It isn't easy, living rough in the mountains, cousin." Utri-sharrumma's pretty face was as sharp as a knife, and anger flickered under the surface like the fire inside a coal. "There is rather a dearth of slaves to heat the water for you and pour it over your head and towel you off afterward. But I'm sure you remember that." He brightened and turned out his hands in a dancer's theatrical gesture. "So I wear my dirt as a sash of honor."

"Forgive me. I was rude," Ehli-nikkalu said, more fearful of his reaction than ashamed. "I spoke like that because... because I'm afraid."

"Good. I like my cousins to be afraid." He watched her reaction through glittering eyes, then he spread his lips with the dangerous good humor of a fox. "Fear is what keeps people alive."

"Not Niqmaddu," she said. "He died because he was afraid."

"Ah, the false king. The divine, late, false king. What was he like in bed?"

She jerked away from him, staring at him in alarm.

He explained, grinning, "I feel compelled to excel. That's what happens when you grow up as an afterthought."

Ehli-nikkalu groped for an answer but could think of nothing and smiled weakly. Amaya shrank away and managed to get to her feet unaided, without taking her wary eyes off his face. Ehli-nikkalu swallowed with effort and rose hurriedly, thrusting herself in front of her lady-in-waiting.

"Leave her alone, Utri-sharrumma. She's promised to the king's uncle," she lied. "The royal family will impale you if you touch her."

"Ooh, that just makes it so much more of a challenge."

The wild glitter was back in his eyes. She never knew what to say to him or what would set him off.

"If she has a penchant for false royalty, then the real king will be that much more to her taste." He drew close to Amaya and bent down—but not by much—to address her.

Amaya recoiled subtly, and Ehli-nikkalu hoped Utri-sharrumma did not notice.

"It will be hard for the first few years, my beauty, but once I'm back on the throne, things will look up." He rose and turned back to Ehli-nikkalu. "What's her name?"

For some reason, the queen felt that was too intimate a request. Amaya's name was something she could not share with that moon-struck man. "Ask her, my cousin."

He fixed Amaya with his mad golden eyes.

"It's... it's Pu-haddu, my lord," she said defiantly.

"And you may call me Utrishu. Or Utrishushu. That's what my mother used to say." He cackled like a jaybird then distracted himself from his laughter by catching a louse, which he cracked between his dirty fingernails with great concentration. "Now, what do I do with you ladies?"

Ehli-nikkalu interposed hastily, "Let me... let me serve you from within the city. Let both of us. We have influence with the royal family. We can support you. I'll speak to the viceroy on your behalf. I can—"

"Don't expect miracles from him, cousin. He is the master of airy promises." Utri-sharrumma drew something airy with his hands.

"The king is just a child. I can influence him. We won't do you any good outside the city. I'm not worth anything now that Niqmaddu is dead. It won't be like before. They won't pay you ransom this time."

He drew back, eyeing her with a dry, foxy smile. "I didn't get any ransom for you last time. I didn't kidnap you at all."

She froze, nonplussed. "The Umman-manda weren't under your command?"

"Oh, yes. But we were just the hands, so to speak. The head was someone else altogether. You didn't know that? Oh, I thought you were more perspicacious! Let's play a guessing game, then. Who kidnapped the queen? Was it Utri-sharrumma? No-o-o. Was it...?" He urged her on, waving his fingers. "Go ahead. Guess."

She wanted to cry out in anger, *You madman! Who wants to play guessing games?* But she dared not. She said faintly, "Mizri? Assyria?"

"No, no, no!" Utri-sharrumma beamed with delight. "Closer to home."

Ehli-nikkalu was so distraught and furious with him she could scarcely contain the resentment in her voice. "The king?"

"Getting warm!"

"The queen mother?"

"Yes, yes, yes! Well guessed!" He clapped his little hands with glee, yet his eyes were sharp as he caught her expression of shock.

"B-But..." she stammered. "Why? She had to pay ransom..."

"No. She paid, but it wasn't ransom. Let's call it a business deal—you know these Ugarites. Business, business, business. And winning your father's favor would have made it all up to her."

"My father's favor?" Ehli-nikkalu felt she was hearing words in a foreign language. They seemed to make no sense.

"You know, the man on the throne in Hattusha. If he thought the Ugarites had rescued his kidnapped daughter, he would favor them—or so she thought."

It occurred to Ehli-nikkalu that Sharryelli must be crazier than Utri-sharrumma. She repeated incredulously, "She paid you to kidnap me?"

"Food, mostly. I refer you to our conversation in the mountains of Geru, where I explained how much food it takes to feed an army—especially during a time of universal crop failure."

Suddenly, with the vigilance of a deer at a water hole, Utri-sharrumma's head jerked up, and he stared toward the road. Almost before Ehli-nikkalu knew what had happened, the pretender had disappeared—volatilized into the sunny orchards like a drop of water on a hot rock. She never heard a retreating footstep, but he was gone. Ehli-nikkalu looked around and saw pouring through the silver of the trees the bloodred tide of the king's men and a chariot bouncing over the uneven ground toward her.

Ili-milku was returning from lunch to the newly arranged archive room in the north annex of the palace. They had finally set up a dedicated space for the chancery and were no longer in the overcrowded confines of Yabni-shapshu's house along with the royal household. The king himself was established with his grandmother and mother in Lady Sharryelli's residence just beyond the royal plaza, to the north.

It was chilly, despite the welcome sun—especially in the shadow of the buildings—and he had wound his shawl around himself, although without much effect. It didn't seem to go around as many times as it used to.

As he approached the doorway, Teshamanu and a few of the other scribes came up, ready to set back to work. Teshamanu, he saw, walked alone, his mouth grim, his eyes fixed on the ground, his hand clenched on the hilt of his penknife.

"Is everything all right, my friend?" the chief scribe called with a smile that attempted to dissemble his concern, while the others passed him by and disappeared into the building. "Can I help in any way?"

"No, I'm fine," Teshamanu said curtly.

Ili-milku had a sudden recollection of a moment seventeen years ago when he'd had the same exchange with another friend. That friend had ended up dead. He eyed the secretary. *You're about to get involved in someone else's life again*, he warned himself. That was, he supposed, the price of caring about his subordinates.

"You look... preoccupied. I think we have the archives under control now if you want to return to the queen's service." He clapped his colleague on the shoulder.

Teshamanu shook his head. His lips were compressed, as if in anger, but his black eyes looked hopeless. "My life is in such a stew that no one can help, Ili-milku. Can I turn around in a month a problem that's been brewing for years? The less I have to do with the queen, the better for her. I should probably resign anyway." He stared at the street as if reluctant to meet Ili-milku's gaze.

Ili-milku cast a quick look around then drew Teshamanu toward the wall, where they would be less in the way. "What is it?" he asked under his breath.

With a huge sigh that trembled a little at the end, the secretary said, "I'm in debt, Ili-milku. Enormously, unimaginably in debt. I've somehow managed to get myself entangled with the most pitiless element of the underworld. I keep paying and paying, but the amount I owe seems to rise rather than be reduced. The gods know what interest he's charging. I'll never be able to clear this." He pushed back his hair in a nervous gesture.

Ili-milku pursed his lips reflectively. "That's bad, all right."

"And now I'm administrator of the children's inheritance. Do you know how much temptation there is to deturn some of that to get this creditor off my neck? It's tearing me apart. I've tried to resist, but..."

"I'm so sorry. I wish there were something I could do."

"There's nothing anyone can do—including me. I'm not sure even selling myself into slavery to this man would satisfy him." Teshamanu's anguished expression softened momentarily. "Lady Ehli-nikkalu offered to help me pay it off. Can you imagine? She's a good woman. But I can't drag her into this, let her be splashed with the muck of my dishonor."

Ili-milku nodded, dispirited. He thought of the late king and his monthly payments, which threatened to continue even after his death. *Why do these young noblemen let themselves get into such a trap? I could understand fast horses or even women, but to throw away good silver on gaming and have nothing to show for it?*

Teshamanu gave a bitter snort. "There's no depth to which I wouldn't sink at this point. I've even agreed to marry one of the king's aunts—for her dowry."

"Lady Sharryelli's daughter?" Ili-milku was taken by surprise. "Were you aware that she wants to marry Amaya to her son?"

"Of course. We've already agreed to discuss dowries. I'm hoping the princess's dowry to me will pay back my little loan from Amaya's estate so I can turn over her dowry in full. Sharryelli won't sell cheap."

Ili-milku fanned his face, which had suddenly grown inexplicably hot, despite the weather. He said kindly, "Don't be too hard on yourself, Teshamanu. Any *maryannu* would give his right... er, leg to marry into the royal family. It will mean concessions and tax advantages and all sorts of perquisites for the rest of your life."

"The only hitch is that... that I've sworn never to touch another woman, Ili-milku. What kind of marriage will that be for the poor girl?"

"You've what? Is this because of your wife?" The chief scribe stared round-eyed in disbelief at his colleague. "I've never heard of such a thing. Get a priest to lift the vow from you, man. Make an offering instead. This is unnatural."

Teshamanu shook his head slowly. "Further evidence of my terrible judgment. You can't know how I regret it—although not because of this marriage."

"Get the vow lifted—I'll pay for it. This must offend the gods. Shaushga, the Lady of Love, must be furious. Perhaps that's why your debts keep mounting."

Teshamanu had opened his mouth to say something when Ili-milku heard footsteps pounding at a run toward him.

"My lords! My lords!" a young man cried out, breathless and wild.

The two scribes looked up to see a slave half stumbling to their feet.

"The queen! The bandits! She's in... the olive groves and..."

"Where?" Teshamanu cried, suddenly erect, grabbing the man by the tunic and holding him up. "Where is she?"

"The orchards just east of the city. Her property. Near the press. About three leagues away. The Umman-manda overwhelmed the harvesters, and we don't know what happened to the queen. She and that girl wandered off, and we had to run or be captured." The slave panted so hard he was scarcely comprehensible.

"Amaya too?" Teshamanu's face drained of color. "Tell the captain of the king's guard." He turned to Ili-milku, suddenly crackling with purposeful energy. "Let's go."

"Go?" Ili-milku stammered, but he was already running after the slimmer man as best he could, not being much of an athlete.

They hammered down the block, pen cases banging at their waists, and across the square at the head of Market Street then on to Rab-ilu's house, which wasn't far away. Ili-milku had begun to flag by the time they careened through the wicket gate, his breath raking in his throat.

Teshamanu yelled for his brother's slaves at the top of his voice. "Hitch up a chariot! Now! Now! And bring an ax."

"You can drive?" Ili-milku panted, bug-eyed. He stared uneasily at Teshamanu's empty sleeve. *How can you drive without two hands?*

But it was clear that the *maryannu* could. As soon as a pair of horses had been wrestled into the harness and he had thrust the battle-ax into his sash, Teshamanu sprang upon the flimsy bentwood-and-leather box and grabbed the lines in one hand. "Help me," he ordered curtly.

Ili-milku breathlessly hauled himself up beside Teshamanu and assisted the former soldier to tie the reins around his waist, scarcely daring to think about the foolhardiness of their actions.

The horses wheeled under Teshamanu's lash and, guided by the shifting of his whole body, sprang out of the gate with a clatter of hooves. Down Market Street they galloped, scattering shoppers in terror. Foam sprayed from the animals' mouths, and they tossed their heads as if they relished nothing better than a pell-mell career through a crowded city. Ili-milku hung onto the rail for his life, nearly toppling with every turn, his bones jolting, his midriff bouncing, his heart stuck in his throat.

At the city gate, Teshamanu shouted, "The queen is in need! To her orchards! Assemble the guard!"

He whipped up the horses again, and out they flew, then across the rumbling bridge and down the road, a trail of dust rising after them like the wake of a ship. But at the first crossroads, Teshamanu leaned back to rein in the horses.

The men stood for a moment, gasping, while the animals switched their tails and blew, then the secretary said uncertainly, "Do you know where the queen's olive groves are, Ili-milku?"

Ili-milku was drenched in sweat and rattled half to jelly by their wild ride. He gasped, "I have no idea." He mopped his head.

"Maybe we'd better wait for the guards..."

"I think that would be a good idea." Ili-milku had a vision of the two scribes careening up to a battle, minimally armed. *What would we be able to do against a whole gang of bandits, anyway, even if Teshamanu is a former soldier?*

They waited at the intersection for some minutes before they saw a body of crimson-clad guardsmen coming toward them at a jog, then they peeled off after them. As soon as the groves came into view, Teshamanu whipped up his horses again, and they charged into the orchard.

Things looked peaceful enough. Men and women harvested, beating the trees to dislodge the ripe olives and carrying baskets of fruit to the press house. But as soon as the Umman-manda saw the soldiers approach, they scattered, many of them dodging off into the silvery distance, others drawing weapons and attacking the king's men, while the women made away with the olives. Teshamanu drove past them like a madman over the clods and rocks, branches whipping in his face, and Ili-milku hung on, his heart in his mouth, as they rocked and wove and tipped between the gray boles.

"Where are we going?" Ili-milku yelled breathlessly.

Teshamanu pointed with his whip. On a terrace above them, some distance away, stood two women, a tall one and a small one, frantically waving their arms.

*A*uthor Note: *Olives and olive oil are very important products in the ancient Near East, just as they are today in that region. Olives are harvested in the winter, when they're ripe.*

The name has great power in antiquity. To know the name of someone gives a person power over him (cf. the biblical gift of the right to name the animals given to Adam).

Marrying into the royal family is a coveted honor. But Teshamanu's vow is in the way. Procreation is so important in those days that such a vow must have looked downright impious.

Unlike the toy slingshot of today, the ancient one is swung around and around before releasing until it has deadly centrifugal force. It is even used as a weapon of war.

Chapter 18

Ehli-nikkalu had rarely in her life experienced the rush of knee-weakening relief that flooded through her at the sight of the royal guards. Some of the Umman-manda made off into the surrounding trees without a fight. Others mounted a stiff resistance, desperate, perhaps, not to lose their recently won food supply. She watched, holding her breath, as slingers and wielders of various farm tools held the armed soldiers at bay, but at last, the crimson-clad guardsmen seemed to overwhelm the marauders.

At that moment, a chariot broke out of the melee and thundered toward them, the horses stumbling and scrabbling uphill but still relentlessly bent upon the two women. Ehli-nikkalu yelled and waved her arms with Amaya chiming in. As the vehicle drew near, the queen saw two improbable figures in the box. Teshamanu drove the horses, his hair flying like their manes, and beside him, frozen to the rail, bounced the rotund shape of Ili-milku.

She laughed for sheer joy and relief and the wonderful absurdity of it all. "Look! It's the chancery come to rescue us!"

Amaya stared in disbelief. "Uncle! He's got Father's courier chariot!"

Teshamanu leaned back to rein in the team as they approached the terraces, and he and Ili-milku spilled out and started up the hill, even as Ehli-nikkalu and Amaya ran downward, sliding among the rocks. Amaya was less fearful of falling and reached the men sooner. She threw herself around her uncle's neck, and he embraced her, his face buckled with emotion, and swayed her back and forth. But his eyes were on Ehli-nikkalu, who hesitated behind the girl.

Ili-milku, as red as a pomegranate yet grinning, cried out, his arms extended, "My lady! Your slave told us what happened, so we called out the guard. It's like an epic, isn't it?"

Ehli-nikkalu threw back her head and laughed. "Now I know—if I want a dramatic rescue, find a poet!" But her attention was on her secretary.

As soon as Teshamanu could detach his niece, he dropped to his knee before Ehli-nikkalu and said in a voice gruff with what might have been embarrassment, "My lady. I'm glad you're safe."

Her face burning with relief and excitement, the queen cried, "Thank you, Teshamanu. That was quite an entrance! It's a good thing you have a military background. Those were the Umman-manda, you know. Utri-sharrumma was with them."

The two men exchanged an uneasy look. "The wall is still breached, and the west gate hasn't been rehung yet," the chief scribe murmured. "Teshamanu, better tell the regent that the usurper is at her door."

Teshamanu took off in his brother's chariot back to the city ahead of the returning soldiers, while Ehli-nikkalu, Amaya, and the chief scribe awaited a carriage sent out from the palace. It was late as they rolled back in through the ruined gate, heavily guarded by the king's men. Now that the soldiers knew the Umman-manda were in the area, they would be doubly watchful.

Amaya recounted to Ili-milku the adventure of their surprise encounter with Utri-sharrumma and his frightening attentions, but Ehli-nikkalu sank into pensive silence. She had a lot to occupy her thoughts—brigands who stole olives, not gold, pretenders who had been cheated of their destiny, and women who felt disproportionately happy that their secretary had bothered to come personally to their rescue.

Ili-milku both dreaded and was eager to see how this convocation of the governing council would go. Today was the day Lady Sharryelli had told Amaya she planned to call out her son-in-law for the murder of Rab-ilu. Shipti-ba'al was smart and well-liked, and his partisans might well rise up in his defense—chaos, even armed violence, could break out if he resisted the indictment, and his wrath might turn upon the presiding magistrate. The chief scribe wondered if the merchant had gotten wind of what was coming.

Lady Sharryelli sat primly beside her grandson, the king, whose legs dangled off the edge of the throne. He swung them back and forth in rhythm. The lad was attending his first full council meeting. Ili-milku thought that if Ammurapi understood how serious the matters they were preparing to discuss were, he might not have looked so eager and cheerful.

It was Lord Uzzinu's turn to preside over the meeting, which he called to order in the name of the king. Ili-milku looked around surreptitiously at the faces of the men he had worked with for more than twenty years. Tuna and Dagan-ba'al were problematic—they were business partners of Shipti-ba'al and might rally around him. Urtenu was a partner, too, but he had been a friend of Rab-ilu's. He might nonetheless turn on Ili-milku because Urtenu was among the *maryannuma* who mildly resented the ascension of a commoner into their midst, talented though he might be. Yabni-shapshu, on the other hand, was Shipti-ba'al's chief trade rival, and the latter's downfall would profit him enormously.

Amidst the elderly faces sitting around the table, so familiar to Ili-milku, he spotted the fresh, youthful visage of Sharryelli's younger son, Talmiyannu. The prince was still an adolescent, although he had a decent beard, and he stared around him in frank interest with much the same innocence as his little nephew. Ili-milku wondered if

Sharryelli hadn't arranged this as a subtle way of introducing him to Amaya.

Teshamanu, too, sat on the council for the first time, elevated by his impending marriage into the royal family. *Not*, Ili-milku thought sourly, *that he doesn't have good enough birth to be a councilor on his own account.* But his reputation had been frayed by his ill-spent youth. He sat, seemingly at ease, with his erect military posture, but Ili-milku saw him brush at his hair from time to time in an uneasy gesture.

Ili-milku himself was so nervous about the coming confrontation that he barely heard the discussion of harbor taxes and indemnities for damaged goods. He perked up when someone referred to the growing problem of the Umman-manda.

Sharryelli called, "Ili-milku, dear, tell the council what you told me the other day about their connection to Utri-sharrumma."

The chief scribe rose and, clasping his hands, said, "It seems he's at their head."

A cry broke out among the councilors.

"That's terrible!" Urtenu the Younger stated the obvious.

The others murmured and railed. The little king watched with round eyes, taking in everything. They discussed the dangers. Someone wondered if an effort couldn't be made to pay the Umman-manda to leave the kingdom alone, but others countered that that was exactly what Utri-sharrumma would never let happen. He would take the bribe and still attack.

"And pay them with what? Our Sun is draining us with all these new levels of governance."

Ili-milku's neck prickled. Surely they weren't going to get into this uncomfortable discussion again.

Then Yabni-shapshu got importantly to his feet, a jug-shaped figure with a plump little mouth and a cloud of fluffy gray hair. "I see Teshamanu, son of Mut-ba'al, sits among us today. Welcome,

Teshamanu. We compassionate the recent loss of your brother. But where did he go? I want to ask these reverend councilors assembled here what has happened to our colleague Rab'ilu. Does anybody really know?" he demanded in a suggestive drawl.

The change of subject is strangely abrupt. It occurred to Ili-milku that Sharryelli had put the merchant up to this opening. Yabni-shapshu wasn't very bright, and he was loyally in the regent's camp. Still, he was doing well as a royal stalking horse. Yabni-shapshu looked around, playing it up nicely. The chief scribe was aware of Shipti-ba'al tensing, but the regent's son-in-law continued to lean casually upon his elbow, his face expressionless.

"Do you know, Yabni-shapshu?" someone asked.

"We've been told he died in the mountains in an accident on an official trip to Hattusha, but there are witnesses who tell a different story, gentlemen. His daughter saw the whole thing."

Shipti-ba'al froze, and color suddenly leached from his bearded cheeks. Teshamanu's gaze flew to Shipti-ba'al, and his eyes narrowed, his jaw tightening.

Yabni-shapshu is doing splendidly. His natural pomposity lent the whole revelation the weight of something momentous. Ili-milku saw Sharryelli smile surreptitiously to herself.

Yabni-shapshu continued in his nasal voice, a sententious finger in the air, "And he was murdered, gentlemen, in cold blood!"

A gratifying roar of outrage and shock arose from his colleagues.

"Murdered... by one of our number. Right here in the city."

The outcry grew. The men stared at one another, sudden suspicion in their eyes.

Uzzinu cried, "Who, Yabni-shapshu? Don't keep us in suspense!"

Sharryelli laid a hand to her mouth, as if she, too, were on tenterhooks. The king gaped, owl eyed, at the speakers in turn.

"We all know Rab'ilu was of the party that wanted to strengthen the Hittite alliance. Who among us stood to lose the most from that policy, my brothers?" Yabni-shapshu glared around from face to face with a ferocity that would have been comical on his fat, chinless features were it not so effective. "Who but the man we call 'the Egyptian'? Shipti-ba'al, son of Tsidqi-ba'al!"

"Now just a minute, Yabni-shapshu." Shipti-ba'al shot to his feet, his face as white as curds, his voice trembling with suppressed rage. "You'd better have some damned good proof for an accusation like that!" He shot a furious glance at Sharryelli, but Ili-milku wasn't sure if the anger was aimed at her or if it was a plea for rescue.

The regent gasped aloud with horror and clapped her hands to her face, as if such an idea were too scandalous to be borne. Teshamanu sprang up from his chair, quivering, his face taut and grim.

Yabni-shapshu demanded smugly, "Is the word of a *maryannu* girl who saw the whole thing with her own eyes sufficient, gentlemen?"

They cried out for the witness to be brought forth. People stared at Shipti-ba'al as if he had shown symptoms of leprosy, only Tuna and Dagan-ba'al gesticulating to him to say something. Ili-milku thanked the gods for the rivalry that always simmered below the fraternal surface of those merchant nobles. They were happy enough to turn on one of their own when they faced no external threat.

All thoughts ceased when the doorkeeper admitted Amaya, who had been kept in readiness in an antechamber. Amaya made the perfect witness, the embodiment of all that those men valued in their daughters and wives. Beautiful, demurely dressed, just frightened enough—her eyes flew to her uncle—but brave and wanting to see her blood vindicated. She wore the cap of a virginal adult woman, legally capable of testifying. Everything was calculated to make her credible, an honorable victim.

Young Talmiyannu's eyes fastened upon her in awe.

Teshamanu murmured to his niece, taking her by the shoulders. "Are you sure you want to do this?"

She nodded resolutely. It all added so much to the impact of her testimony. Sharryelli couldn't have planned it better herself. Ili-milku thanked all the gods that the child was willing to go through with it; Rab-ilu's family deserved some closure.

For his part, Shipti-ba'al turned a look of furious disbelief upon the regent, his lips drawn back from his teeth. It occurred to Ili-milku all at once that the queen *had* been in league with him and had turned on him—to his manifest astonishment.

The regent laid her palms to her face, as if in disappointment, and seemed to whisper to her son-in-law imperceptibly behind her hand.

She must be unsure of what he may say if he thinks she's double-crossed him.

"Ili-milku," Sharryelli called over the hubbub, "you're the president of the court. Do you need to summon the witness officially?"

"In the king's presence and under the eyes of Shapshu, who sees all, I do convene this court of the council," the chief scribe said hastily, rising and coming forward. His heart hammered in his chest. "Let the witness come forward, and under oath before Shapshu and all the gods of Ugarit, let her make her statement."

He held out his hand to Amaya, and the girl went and stood beside him, her face set resolutely. The king watched, spellbound, his feet no longer swinging. They swore Amaya in, and she began to tell her tale, omitting nothing, even how she had reported her suspicions to the young queen and to Ili-milku as soon as she had identified the murderer. When she had finished, no one even needed to ask how she had recognized the killer. Everything was perfectly clear.

Ili-milku thought he had never in his life been part of such a strange drama. Sharryelli had clearly decided to abandon her henchman, but Ili-milku couldn't quite figure out why—or what came next. He felt that one false move on his part could have terrible consequences for someone... and he didn't know for whom.

He was glad enough to bring Shipti-ba'al's criminal guilt into the open, but he didn't want to see the man executed for what he now believed was the dowager's crime. And she would never be prosecuted, not in ten thousand years. Nor was he sure she should be, whatever her guilt. She was the regent for a six-year-old monarch. *Who knows what would happen to the kingdom if she fell under suspicion of a crime?* Perhaps the viceroy would put Utri-sharrumma on the throne.

The councilors yelled and waved their arms at one another all around Ili-milku. Tuna and Dagan-ba'al seemed to try to make excuses for their partner, but he declined to explain himself, sitting steaming with rage, occasionally roaring, "This is a travesty!" and turning wrathful eyes on the regent.

Finally, Ili-milku realized he needed to draw the hearing to a conclusion. "Is there anyone who isn't satisfied that the accused is guilty as charged?"

No one raised a hand, including Shipti-ba'al's supporters. Amaya's testimony had been devastatingly clear.

The chief scribe said to the accused man more gently, "Lord Shipti-ba'al, have you anything to say?"

"The gods see the truth of this matter, even if you can't," the queen's son-in-law spat. "May their curse be upon all of you who have widowed my wife and orphaned my children."

Ili-milku had to admire Shipti-ba'al's loyalty. Even staring death in the face, he didn't implicate the regent, although his flaming eyes sought her out for his curse.

Then Sharryelli herself stood up, tearful and magnanimous, to say, "My lords, don't put this good man to death for a personal rivalry that turned fatal. He has served our dear kingdom well for so many years, and... and... he's the father of my grandchildren." She buried her face in her little hands, and the men could hear her suppressed sobs.

Yabni-shapshu's nasal drawl cut through the chaos. "If the family of the deceased is agreeable, we can accept indemnity for Rab'ilu's life instead. No need to deprive the kingdom of yet another of its sons."

It seemed to be a popular compromise. Everyone turned to Teshamanu, upon whom the final decision rested. He looked uneasy, flushed in the face, his eyes glittering.

He needs that silver, Ili-milku thought.

The secretary consulted with his niece quietly then raised his head. "We accept."

Ili-milku felt a flood of relief wash through him. No blood on his hands, at least. "What seems to the gentlemen of the court to be an appropriate indemnity for the life of a *maryannu*?" he asked, looking around at his colleagues.

Someone said, "Teshamanu? It's your family asking reparations."

They turned again to Teshamanu, who looked undecided. He had had no idea this was coming. "I don't know. My brother's life was beyond price."

Sharryelli said feelingly, "That's right. Rab'ilu was the father of a large family, who are now orphaned. We would dishonor him to ask any less than a thousand silver shekels, wouldn't we? Then there were the two slaves who were killed, the courier chariot damaged, and government documents destroyed. Is fourteen hundred in silver fair? Or say, four hundred gold?"

"We"? Amaya's dowry is in play, Ili-milku thought dryly. Shipti-ba'al stared at the dowager with a hate-filled hook between his eyebrows. Then Ili-milku remembered his own conversation with Sharryelli not so many days earlier. *Hmm. This unexpected turn of events was not so unexpected to her. She had no intention of letting her fellow conspirator—and lover—be put to death. He's one of the richest men in Ugarit.*

The assembled councilors nodded, evaluated, and weighed. He could imagine them biting the gold if it had been present. Then they all agreed, thinking, perhaps, that if Rab'ilu were worth such a sum, they would be too. The little king was made to say in his boyish voice that he willed it to be so. Teshamanu and his niece burst into smiles and hugged one another deliriously, then Sharryelli called Amaya to her side, and she hugged the girl as well and kissed her forehead. Ili-milku, despite a nagging sense of something out of balance, felt a great weight lifted from his shoulders as he prepared to sit back in his place.

But then Shipti-ba'al, who had been sitting hunched over in fuming silence, raised his voice rancorously. "I have a question. If this was such a heinous deed and my guilt was so manifest, why did Lord Ili-milku tell no one when he found out about it? It's been months. Maybe he wasn't so sure about it, eh? After all, there's no evidence, just the girl's recollection from a traumatic night."

Ili-milku's stomach fell. He tried to think of a way to explain without compromising the regent—a dangerous act. "As a commoner, I, er... I felt that a falling out between two *maryannuma* was not my business to report," he said lamely. He realized almost immediately that he should not have made a point of being lower class than his colleagues—that would unite them against him.

Sure enough, Urtenu the Younger said, "How did you know about the connection between Utri-sharrumma and the Umman, Ili-milku?"

He had ceased to be *Lord* Ili-milku. "The queen told me, my lord," he said. "But she didn't talk to me immediately. Some time had passed. You'd have to ask the queen why."

"I think that's pretty clear." Yabni-shapshu sniffed. "Utri-sharrumma's the queen's cousin. She's probably hoping he'll take over the throne."

A babble of outrage and suspicion arose. Ili-milku let out a heavy breath. *Please let Our Sun get her out of here quickly.* Perspiration trickled down his temples.

"Weren't you involved somehow with the Amurrite queen?" It was Urtenu again, looking belligerent, as if all his grievances had finally found a crack to spew out of. "My father used to say you had something to do with her and with the assassination of King Ammishtamru."

Ili-milku's eyes flew open in fear. "I had *nothing* to do with the queen or the assassination. I knew the assassin, that's all. He worked in the chancery." *Dear gods! Sharryelli must have told him that. Why?* He saw suddenly that she had set him up for something. She must know he suspected her involvement in Rab'ilu's murder.

But the queen mother stared at him in innocent horror, as if she had had no idea he knew the assassin up to that moment. He signaled her, *Why?* with a gesture of his hands. But she turned aside, fingertips over her mouth, her eyes mournful with confidence betrayed. Ili-milku, who was a mild fellow, felt a flicker of rage at her duplicity. "Should we remind ourselves of Lord Yabni-shapshu's involvement with the coup against King Ammishtamru too? These things are all in the past," Ili-milku cried hotly.

"Are you trying to sow dissension among us in these dangerous times, Ili-milku?" Tuna asked, swelling with outrage.

"Wait, I didn't start this…" Now they held it against him that he had sat in judgment against one of their own. His heart pounded like an animal's at bay.

"Gentlemen, please," Sharryelli interrupted with a sad, forgiving smile. "We all know Ili-milku has the welfare of the kingdom at heart. None of this brings back our dear dead. If he's had lapses in the past, surely he'll walk more carefully in the future."

And that's her message, Ili-milku thought. *"Be careful, Ili-milku. You're under observation."*

"Won't you, my dear?"

"Yes, my lady," he said docilely. *The vixen. She's been tricking us all along.*

Shipti-ba'al leered at him with a malevolent grin, happy to have dragged someone through the mud with him.

Teshamanu looked dumbfounded and outraged. "See here, what's that got—"

Only Amaya, with her innocent sense of honor, got to the heart of things. Her light voice cut through the rumble of masculine hostility. "Ili-milku's a good man."

Author Note: Women have many rights in Ugarit, including that of bearing witness (just not that of picking their own husband! But that's mainly for the aristocrats, for whom marriage means family alliances).

Ugaritic kings were not autocrats—their power was tempered by that of a council of bureaucrats and aristocratic merchants. Ili-milku was historically chief scribe, but possibly earlier than the time of this story.

Chapter 19

Ehli-nikkalu welcomed Ili-milku to her temporary apartment with a smile that faded as she saw how drained and wild-eyed he appeared. Sweat poured copiously from his scarlet face.

"What's wrong, Ili-milku?" she cried with concern. "You look like a lion chased you here."

"No, I left the lions in the council room, my lady." He blew out a breath and, patting his temples with his towel, sank to the stool she offered him.

She took her chair at his side and hung forward, her hands twisted together. "What happened? How did the trial go?"

He explained about how persuasive Amaya's testimony had been and how the penalty had been assessed at a walloping fine—more than enough to give Amaya a fat dowry that would pay off Niqmaddu's debts. Ehli-nikkalu's expressions swung from shock to an outrage that left her gaping with disbelief. Then Ili-milku told her how Sharryelli had primed Yabni-shapshu to bring up the affair while she pretended to know nothing about the crime, which she had characterized as a personal grievance. How furious Shipti-ba'al had been, and how he, Ili-milku, was sure that Sharryelli knew something about the murder after all.

The queen began to smolder with a bitter fire and let a dragon-like noise escape from her throat.

"That hypocrite! This confirms everything I've always known about her. She's let him pay the penalty for her misdeeds, just like she used to blame me for everything. Of course he's angry."

"Alas, there's more, my lady." Ili-milku took a deep breath and recounted how the councilors, like magpies with slit tongues, trained to talk, had turned on him, repeating everything he had told the queen mother in confidence. "Then she swooped in and rescued me, thus leaving me warned and in her power." He hung his head. "Amaya was the only one with the courage to defend me."

"Not Teshamanu?" she murmured, her heart sinking.

"Well, I think he was starting to. Undoubtedly so. But you, my lady—be careful. Don't attract anyone's attention as long as you're still here. Better stay away from me. They're looking for a scapegoat for their problems, I think."

Ili-milku stared up at her with his kind brown eyes, as honest as the full moon on a cloudless night, and she thought, *What sort of place is this? They don't deserve this man.* "Thank you, dear friend," she said. "I suppose that was the end of the meeting?"

"No, if you can imagine. We actually settled back down to discuss a few things. Shipti-ba'al has been missioned to Mizri to head the trade delegation there. It's exile, of course, but honorable exile. He'll grow even richer, we may be sure. Teshamanu has taken his brother's place on the council and been assigned to administer some of the queen's properties—in Shipti-ba'al's place."

Ehli-nikkalu snorted. "Not that he needs the gold anymore, with such an indemnity."

"Hmm, perhaps. But I suspect a large part of that will go with Amaya. I just have a suspicion, from the way Sharryelli kept upping the amount every time she took a breath." He chuckled, seeming to become more himself as the painful meeting receded into the past.

"I just hope we haven't endangered Amaya after all if Sharryelli was really involved in the murder." *Oh, make her happy, you Hutellura. Let her betrothed not be like his brother.*

"My lady, please don't take this amiss, but I think it might be more politic if I don't see you so frequently. Everyone's watching me

now. It might be misunderstood." He looked up at her apologetically, softening the words with a smile.

"Of course, Ili-milku. If they think I'm a partisan of Utri-sharrumma!" Ehli-nikkalu laughed at the very idea. She could think of
no candidate for the throne she felt less likely to support. Cousin or
not, the man was frightening and unpredictable. It was risible. "Stay
away, and don't taint yourself with me."

But she thought once more of what the pretender had said about
Sharryelli masterminding the kidnapping. She had laughed it off as
the meanderings of a madman, but now, she wondered.

Ili-milku started to say something mollifying, but she smiled to
show she had no hard feelings toward him. "You've been the only
person here who has shown me the least kindness, and I won't forget
you to my father the Sun. I wish you peace and health... and safety,
Ili-milku."

He bowed deeply then took her hand and kissed it. Tears shone
in his eyes. It felt like a real goodbye—she feared she might never see
him again. Her eyes were misty, too, as she watched him back from
the room, his shiny bald head down in full ceremonial departure.

Ili-milku thought he should probably continue his investigation
of the late king's creditor—it couldn't hurt to stay on the regent's
good side. He summoned the chief bookkeeper to Lady Sharryelli's
house and waited there with her until the man appeared.

The little old scribe who supervised the accounts of the royal
household doddered in, slowly making his way up the long room. He
toppled forward into something resembling a bow, and the regent
kindly bade him take a seat. In fact, she bade him twice before the
old man worked out what she had said. The fellow had been at la-
bor in the chancery since the reign of King Niqmepa, longer than
Ili-milku had even been in Ugarit. With his pale, glabrous head and
white-tufted ears, he had rather the air of something embalmed in

the Egyptian manner, but in his defense, the chief scribe could imagine the effect of long years spent desiccating among the accounts.

"Tell me, Shabilim, my dear, is there any way to know what these payments by the late king were made for?" Sharryelli shouted. She shot a helpless look at Ili-milku.

"No, my lady. Not unless an entry to that effect was made at the time. These were just entered as 'personal expense.'"

Ili-milku restrained a noise of chagrin. "And the claim of this Iwiri-muza upon the late king's estate? Can we investigate the man?"

Shabilim's face never changed expression, but a puffing noise seemed to emanate from deep within him: hnf-hnf-hnf-hnf. It was only after a moment that Ili-milku realized he was chuckling. "If this is the Iwiri-muza one supposes, my lord, we can guess what it's about."

"What do you mean, my friend?"

"He's an infamous pimp in the port, my lord, well known to the young billy goats of the bookkeeping staff. They think I can't hear them discussing their exploits, but I can."

Incredulous, Sharryelli cried, "Seven hundred silver shekels? What could it possibly be for?"

"Hnf-hnf-hnf-hnf!"

"And these other charges, the ones over the six previous years. How much were they for?"

"The same, my lady. Seven hundred a month for six years."

Starting well before Niqmaddu became king. *Dear gods! No visit to a brothel could have cost so much.* "So there's nothing else we can tell about these charges?" Ili-milku pressed him.

"Nothing, my lord. 'Personal expenses.' Hnf-hnf-hnf."

Sharryelli spoke up, looking unsettled. "How are the debts paid? Do we deliver the silver to some particular place?"

"No, my lady. A servant comes every month and collects the shekels in person."

That's odd, thought Ili-milku. *Surely this Iwiri-muza's place of, er, business must be easy enough to find.*

"Then that will be all, Shabilim. Thank you for your time." Sharryelli forced a smile.

After the bookkeeper's endlessly slow procession out the door, the regent heaved a sigh and sat back in her chair. Ili-milku, who was exhausted from the shouted conversation, watched her. Her face was puckered with distaste and anxiety.

"Someone needs to pay Iwiri-muza a visit. We need to see how reasonable he's willing to be."

The regent turned to Ili-milku. "But now that Shipti-ba'al has disgraced himself, I don't know whom to trust." Her melting eyes seemed to invite him to volunteer. "Can you see what we need to do, Ili-milku? This can't go on."

"No, it's clearly no longer a case of 'services rendered.' The late king is, after all—well, late."

The next morning, when the chief scribe went to the chancery to look again at Iwiri-muza's claim, he was astonished to find it had been paid.

Teshamanu betrothed to Sharryelli's daughter, Amaya to her son, and Ili-milku in self-imposed exile from the young queen's presence—suddenly, from the heights of happiness, Ehli-nikkalu's life had pitched back into the depths. Alone again. Thus, she was in a dispirited frame of mind when Shamumanu announced the next morning that Lady Pu-haddu was at the door.

The queen stared at him disbelievingly. "Pu-haddu? What does she want to see me for?" *Come to gloat, has she?* she thought, prepared to show her contempt.

"I don't know, my lady." His high-pitched voice dropped to nearly a whisper. "She seems very upset."

Curious in spite of herself, Ehli-nikkalu told him to send the king's mother in.

Pu-haddu appeared a moment later, imminently pregnant but not the gloating, flashily dressed tart the queen had expected to see. The king's mother was wrapped in a dark cloak and covered with a respectable cap and veil so that only her glossy bangs showed. She hung in the doorway, as if unsure of her welcome, until Ehli-nikkalu said dryly, "Come in."

Pu-haddu's striking face was tense, her kohl-expanded eyes round, like an animal that mistrusted every shadow. She advanced a few steps then murmured in an uncertain voice, "My lady." She sank in a deep reverence.

Drawn up to her full, formidable height, Ehli-nikkalu eyed her coldly. "How can I help you?"

"You must be wondering why I'm here." Pu-haddu laughed a little, nervously. "I'm not too sure myself. It's not like we've ever been friends."

She fell silent, hoping, perhaps, that Ehli-nikkalu would rescue her with a kind word. But Ehli-nikkalu said nothing.

"I have something to tell you and something to ask you. I can't tell Niqmaddu's mother because... because I don't know what she'd do."

Ehli-nikkalu was suspicious of the woman's sincerity, but because she had been brought up to be courteous to those lesser than she, she motioned Pu-haddu to a stool. "Please, sit." She held up her heavy skirts and seated herself majestically on her chair. "Say what you're here to say, please. I haven't got all day."

"There's... there's a man named Iwiri-muza. He's mixed up in all kinds of shady business. He owned me."

Ehli-nikkalu jerked upright in her chair and cried, "Owned you? You were a slave? By all that's holy!"

Pu-haddu swallowed uncomfortably. "He was my owner when the king met me, seven years ago. I mean, Niqmaddu wasn't the king then. He was the crown prince. He was only sixteen." Pu-haddu laughed with a weary air. "He fell in love with me. Believe it or not, that sometimes happens."

"Believe it or not, I'm aware of that," Ehli-nikkalu retorted. "Go on."

"What I mean is, men sometimes fall in love with a girl they hire. I was a prostitute. Iwiri-muza was my pimp."

Ehli-nikkalu felt heat flush up her cheeks. Those weren't words she had to listen to every day. Well-bred women, princesses, weren't even supposed to know about such things. But she wasn't as shocked as she might have been. Her instincts about Niqmaddu's tastes made the revelation seem obvious. Still, it was repugnant. He had shared the girl with the gods knew how many soldiers, travelers—slaves, even—and then he had entered *her*... Sickened, that was what she was. Her stomach heaved.

Ehli-nikkalu knew her downturned mouth and flared nostrils had betrayed her revulsion because Pu-haddu said in a tired voice, "I know, I know. You hold me in contempt. And so would all the rest of the royal family if they knew."

"They *don't* know?" Ehli-nikkalu was incredulous. "No one investigated you before they let the crown prince take you as an official concubine? They didn't know you were a prostitute? Did they even know you were a slave?"

"Was? I still am, my lady. Nobody ever freed me. They didn't know because we lied. Iwiri-muza told them I was his wife—an orphan he had taken in then married. That Niqmaddu paid him to divorce me. But then, the dog shit made the king pay him again, over and over, not to tell anybody the truth. And now that the king's dead, Iwiri-muza still wants silver every month—seven hundred shekel-weight of it—or he'll tell everyone that the new king is the son of a whore and a slave. That my Ammurapi is... a slave too."

Ehli-nikkalu reeled inwardly, as if she had been struck a blow. *That smart, charming little boy?* He was the only good thing Niqmaddu had ever done. *What will happen if Sharryelli or the council or the viceroy—or my father—demand that he be removed from the succession? Who will replace him? Utri-sharrumma? And if they don't replace him, and the secret of his birth becomes public... how many usurpers will appear, ready to wipe away the shame of the kingdom?* She felt faint with the enormity of the repercussions. *What sort of idiot was Niqmaddu?*

"And..." Pu-haddu hung her head. Her voice became almost inaudible. "Ammurapi isn't really Niqmaddu's anyway."

"Dear gods!" Ehli-nikkalu exploded. "What are you saying? Whose, then?"

"Some... someone else's. A *maryannu*'s. Oh, I'm not even that sure, really. Iwiri-muza said to pass him off as the prince's. Otherwise, I'd lose Niqmaddu. Iwiri-muza would lose him. But now—" Her voice broke and grew tiny with her tears. "Iwiri-muza's gotten greedy, and if the regent finds out..." She trailed off, too frightened, no doubt, to contemplate what might happen. As long as Ammurapi was on the throne, Pu-haddu would be honored as the king's mother, even if she never became the official dowager. If he should be booted out in disgrace, she would find herself servicing soldiers again. Her full red lips quivered.

Ehli-nikkalu covered her face with her hands. She didn't know what to think, let alone what to do about it. Her heart was like lead in her belly, her cheeks clammy. *Oh, would that I had not heard these words.* "Does the real father know...?" she asked faintly. *That would be a dangerous situation, for sure—blackmail to rival Iwiri-muza's. Or designs on the throne—controlling the king.* Each possibility was worse than the last.

"No, I'm sure he doesn't. I never saw him again after a few weeks or so had passed. He was an odd one, him. A cavalryman—but he knew how to read and write lots of languages. A really sweet, respectful fellow but troubled, you know? Always silent and distracted. He said his life was a mess. He had a bad conscience about us, on account of his being newly married. I guess I felt sorry for him. Like I could save him if I showed him I really loved him. Maybe I did. I don't know. You're not supposed to. But we saw each other for a few years. We were getting pretty fond of each other. Then he disappeared."

The queen thought she had already fallen to the bottom of the well of horror, but Pu-haddu's words kicked the ground from beneath her feet, and she dropped again—down, down, down, dizzily. *Lady Nikkal, my dear protector on high, say this man isn't who I think he is...* But she thought of the king's little dimpled chin... and of someone else who, she had recently discovered, shared that trait. Ehli-nikkalu couldn't manage to say a word. She just tried to breathe deeply so she wouldn't faint right out of her chair. The room seemed to spin.

After a moment, Pu-haddu said dully, "I guess you're wondering why I'm telling *you* all this, my lady." She looked up, and her painted eyes were drained with desperation. "I don't know where else to go. For silver, I mean. If somebody doesn't pay Iwiri-muza, he'll say something. And then..."

Ehli-nikkalu forced herself back to the conversation, but her pulse hammered in her temples. *Can I even be sure Pu-haddu isn't lying?* Part of her wanted to cry out that it was all lies, that there had never been a gruff *maryannu* who left a whore pregnant with a king. "How do I know you're not just trying to get gold out of me?"

"Why would I do that if all this wasn't true? I'd have all the gold in the world. But I understand why you might not believe me." Pu-haddu sighed heavily. "It sounds too awful to be true. I can try to sell my jewels, I guess. Niqmaddu gave me a lot of them. He liked to see me all hung with gold. I used to flaunt that at you, didn't I?" The concubine stood up and turned, shoulders drooping, and extended her hand toward the door.

"Wait," Ehli-nikkalu said. She found she could hardly say what she meant to, nor could she tell why it should make any difference to what came next. "Did Niqmaddu ever... ever hit you?"

Pu-haddu laughed bitterly. "Do you want to see the scars?"

Author Note: We have no reason to think the real Ammurapi wasn't legitimately the son of Niqmaddu... but who knows? Certainly Utri-sharrumma is legitimate, so this would make him even more dangerous.

Not only are Ehli-nikkalu and Pu-haddu rivals for the king's affection, but they are from the opposite extremes of the social scale. Slaves are considered chattel, property, with few rights. But they're both women.

The children of slaves are slaves themselves unless they are formally freed. Otherwise, slaves tend to be prisoners of war; no one group is associated with the stigma.

Chapter 20

The next day, the queen summoned her husband's concubine to her apartment once more.

"I paid the silver Iwiri-muza was demanding," Ehli-nikkalu said to Pu-haddu, "but he's just going to ask for more in a month. We need to think of a way to silence him for good."

The two women sat knee to knee before the crack in the shutter that let a minimum of chilly daylight into the temporary royal apartment. If anyone had suggested even two days earlier that the queen and her hated rival would be coconspirators in an effort to save the throne, she would have laughed them scornfully to shame. Yet there they were, united by the violence of their late husband.

Ehli-nikkalu looked at Pu-haddu and saw, for the first time, not the smug, painted common woman who flaunted her youth and beauty but an uneducated girl socially in over her head who walked on the edge of a precipice, who loved her children, and who had suffered at the hands of a man who loved her yet abused her. Why, it was almost exclusively envy that had made Ehli-nikkalu hate the concubine, she realized. She felt her expression go soft as she gazed, the cold, corrosive pain growing dull as the envy trickled out, and Pu-haddu, watching, tilted her head as if in response to a question.

"Nothing," Ehli-nikkalu said with a smile. "I was just thinking that we should have been friends a long time ago. Now it's almost too late. I'll probably be called back to Hatti. So we have to take care of Iwiri-muza soon."

"Kill him, you mean?" Pu-haddu seemed to take savage satisfaction in the idea. Bloodthirst sat incongruously upon her pretty face.

Ehli-nikkalu hung her head. "I'd rather not unless there's no other way." *But what other way could there be? Dear Nikkal, inspire me with something so I don't have to descend to Sharryelli's level and kill my enemy.* "Are you sure no one else in court has recognized you? What about... the father of your son?"

Pu-haddu smiled crookedly. "I've seen a few of my former 'clients' over the years, my lady, and believe it or not, they didn't recognize me. I mean, it was generally dark when they saw me before, but even more, they just don't expect it to be me here. Maybe they say to themselves, 'The king's concubine is almost as pretty as that girl in Mahadu,' but they wouldn't believe it was me if you told them. And it's been more than six years, after all. I've grown up since then. My son's father? I've hardly seen him except off in the distance. He hasn't had much to do with the court."

"You must have lived in fear, though, always wondering if somebody would make the connection."

Pu-haddu sniffed. "It's not the first time I've lived in fear. Iwirimuza is the one who really scares me, though. He's into all sorts of serious bad business: gambling, smuggling, extortion—I don't know what. He stops at nothing to get what he wants."

A knock at the door made Ehli-nikkalu stiffen in a flash of panic, but it was only Shamumanu.

"My lady, the lady Amaya is here with the children. May she come in?"

"Of course," the queen said, relaxing.

Amaya and the twins entered, laughing and full of energy from being out of doors, but then Amaya saw the visitor and drew back. "I'm sorry. I didn't know you were occupied. We can see you later. The children just wanted to show you some pretty leaves."

"That's all right, my dear. This is Lady Pu-haddu, the king's mother."

Amaya bowed, but her eye caught Ehli-nikkalu's. No doubt she wondered why the two rivals were sitting companionably face-to-face.

Yanakh cried enthusiastically, "The king is lots of fun, my lady. We've been having a good time together, even though he's a little child."

Pu-haddu smiled. The twins, clearly, weren't that much older than Ammurapi. "I'm so glad. He's rather grown-up for his age."

Amaya said to the queen in a more subdued voice, "My lady, we just ran into the regent. She wants me to meet her son tomorrow."

"Niqmaddu's brother," Ehli-nikkalu explained to Pu-haddu, who looked at her in confusion. "Tesh—the girl's uncle has betrothed her to Prince Talmiyannu."

"He's a nice boy, nothing like... you know. I hope you'll be happy together," Pu-haddu said sincerely.

"I'll go now, my lady. I don't want to keep you. I just wanted to see you and tell you how things were progressing." Amaya lowered her eyes, and her cheerful expression slipped; Ehli-nikkalu could see the toll this sacrifice was taking on the girl's dreams, and it ripped a piece out of her own heart.

Have I given her the wrong advice?

Ehli-nikkalu sat there pondering. A funny thing about youthful dreams. *Do they ever come true?* she wondered. *Why are there always such high hopes and an eventuality so much less glorious?* All she had ever wanted was to love and be loved. One moment of her father's shy affection had been enough to make her willing to die for him. That was the way she was. She would so gladly have given her whole body and soul to a husband who loved her. But the Gulshesh had not apportioned such a lot to her.

"What is it, my lady?" asked Pu-haddu quietly.

"Oh, just remembering what it's like to be young. But you're still young, Pu-haddu. I guess there aren't so many memories."

"Too many, if you ask me," the king's mother said sadly. There was a wistfulness about her that hinted at how little comfort her memories offered.

"Was your life so unhappy?"

"I was a slave, a whore, my lady. I grew up in a brothel. I guess you can't even imagine."

And Ehli-nikkalu recognized that she could not. For all the basic qualities of womanhood the two of them shared, an enormous gulf of experience stretched between them. She asked herself why that should be. She didn't want it to be so. She wanted, when someone said, "You can't imagine," to be *able* to imagine. She wanted to feel everything Pu-haddu felt, to suffer with her, to inhabit her in some way. Just as she had wanted to do with Teshamanu and with her father. As if, somehow, by sharing their pain, she could alleviate it. It was like an excruciating itch inside her that could only be relieved by shouldering the other person's burden. Perhaps that was naïve—everyone was always telling her she was naïve. Perhaps she wasn't strong enough. Perhaps such a thing wasn't even possible. *Is that love, or is it pity?*

"Surely, between the two of us, we can think of a solution to the Iwiri-muza problem, Pu-haddu. You know him. How can we make him stay silent?"

The younger woman rose, her mouth downturned with discouragement. "I'll try to think of something, my lady. But I'm afraid the only silent Iwiri-muza is a dead one. I'd better go look in on the little ones now." She arched her back and stretched, her belly projecting heavily ahead of her. Pu-haddu was halfway to the door before she turned. "I was wrong about you, you know," she said shyly. "You're kind. Thank you for helping me." She opened the door and disappeared into the vestibule.

Ili-milku read the queen's summons with a prickle of fear up his spine and wondered if she had not quite understood how danger-ous it was for him to be seen with her. He glanced surreptitiously around the chancery to see if anyone was watching him in a suspi-cious way. No. All the scribes were going about their own business. No one was hanging over his shoulder to read the message written in the queen's earnest, childlike hand. He turned the wooden tablet over on its face as a precaution and sat for a moment, trying to decide what to do. He seemed incapable of saying no. She was his queen, af-ter all. But even more, she was a fellow human being with a problem of some sort. So he wrote in the wax on the back, *Yes, but meet me on the parapet of the south gate at noon. The streets will be empty.*

"Here, my boy," he said to the pageboy who had brought the mis-sive. "Take this reply back to the sender."

Then he tried to settle to his work again, but he was completely distracted. He read the line *Parched are the furrows of the field, O Shapshu*, four or five times, but he still couldn't think of where to go from there. It was as if he had no connection to those words, al-though they had come forth from him. *What did I even mean?* He rested his chin on his hand and sighed.

At last, the page returned, panting, and handed Ili-milku the same letter with an additional word scratched in the margin: *Yes.* The scribe promptly rubbed out the entire content of both sides with his erasing stone.

Ili-milku waited until he heard the meal clapper sound down-stairs in the kitchen, then he shot out of the interim chancery ahead of everyone else and sped off down the street. He passed the worksite of the palace, emptied of workmen, who were all eating their lunch somewhere at that hour. He flagged as he walked through the empty Market Street, with its shuttered shops and dismantled stalls. The smell of food from someone's cooking lunch wafted out, and his stomach growled. *Dear gods, whatever made me suggest a meeting at noon?* His wife would wonder where he was. He should have told the pageboy to take her a message.

By the time Ili-milku reached the wall at the southern end of the city, he was weak with hunger and panting for breath. The great gate stood open, its plaza vacant. A soldier passed from time to time across the parapet. *Why did I think of this as an appropriate meeting place?* It was a spot no civilian had clearance to go except someone like the queen, so he had figured they would be unseen and undisturbed.

He knocked on the door of the little staircase that led up to the walkway over the gate, and a soldier appeared. "Excuse me, my good man, but is the queen up there yet, by any chance?"

"She is," the soldier said. "What's your name?"

"Ili-milku of Shubanu, chief scribe. Here is my seal."

He held the roller out to the man, who probably couldn't read anyway, and the fellow bade him follow up the stairs. Their footsteps resounded on the planks. Ili-milku was hauling himself up using the banister by the time they reached the door at the top. He stopped to mop his face, sheeted in sweat despite the chilly temperature, and stepped out onto the windswept parapet as the soldier left, closing the door behind him.

The queen stood looking out over the bridge and the groves beyond the crenellations, her back to him, dark against the sunless gray sky. Her long veil and skirts whipped in the cold air. At the sound of his heavy expulsion of breath, she turned and caught his eye anxiously. "Oh, my dear friend, thank you for coming. I so didn't want to get you involved with this, but I didn't know whom else to talk to."

She was wrapped in a heavy cloak of the Hittite fashion, and Ili-milku realized he had on nothing but his tunic and a shawl over one shoulder. His perspiration was starting to chill.

"My lady, how can I serve you?"

"You're always so willing, dear man. Here's what has happened. And it's worth all our lives if this gets out." She gestured to him to sit beside her, and the two of them slid to a seat on the packed-clay floor, their backs against the outer crenellations so they could see if anyone came up the stairs from below.

Leaning close to his ear and speaking in a voice scarcely above a whisper, Ehli-nikkalu began to recount how Pu-haddu had come to her, the story she had told about her past, and the trick she and Iwiri-muza had played on the late king about her status. Ili-milku felt his blood rushing away from his face and was glad he was seated. *What ungodly history is this? The danger! The scandal!* He felt quite faint at the thought of what it might open up, with Utri-sharrumma on the prowl.

The queen must have seen his aghast expression, and she paused to let him exclaim, but he was speechless. At last, he sputtered, "I can hardly believe my ears!"

"I haven't told you the worst yet, Ili-milku. But you see why I'm so at a loss."

"You must tell the regent, my lady."

"Do you really think so?" She smiled dryly. "Let me finish the story."

Then she told him how Ammurapi wasn't really Niqmaddu's son, how Iwiri-muza had been blackmailing the late king, and how, since Niqmaddu was dead, the pimp was extorting even more from the king's mother to keep his story quiet.

"But who's paying him these days? Sharryelli must know."

Ehli-nikkalu shook her head. "I've been paying him."

"Oh dear," Ili-milku groaned. "Oh dear, oh dear." *This is truly terrible. Yielding to his demands will only embolden such a man. And Ehli-nikkalu has let herself get involved, no doubt thinking she can save Pu-haddu.* "Perhaps you should just tell the queen mother and let some soldiers go arrest the fellow—lock him up or exile him somewhere. Better still, let Pu-haddu tell her so you can stay out of it."

"I don't know if he's working alone, Ili-milku. According to Pu-haddu, he's not just some little brothel owner in the port. He's a powerful figure in his way, an organizer of black-market transactions on a large scale, an importer who scorns the customs taxes. He's got a hand in all sorts of nefarious schemes. Besides, what would Sharryelli do if she found out little Ammurapi wasn't really her grandson—and was legally a slave at that? Would she pass the throne down to his younger brother? Put another of her own sons on the throne? It scares me to think about the chaos."

"Sharryelli would do whatever benefited her most," Ili-milku agreed.

He realized that he had turned some kind of corner. Once—even very recently—he would never have breathed such cynical words aloud. But the dowager's attack in the council meeting had alienated him to the core. *Yet why? That's what rulers do: play their adversaries off against one another.* He just wasn't accustomed to thinking of himself as anyone's adversary. His days of comfortable neutrality seemed to have ended.

"But why should we assume it wouldn't be what benefited the kingdom as well? She's pretty able, as much as I hate to admit it." Ili-milku heaved a deep sigh and shivered. The drying of his sweat had chilled him. Or perhaps it was fear. "So how do I come into this, my lady? Is there something you want me to do?"

"Could you go to Iwiri-muza and negotiate with him? Threaten him—I don't know. But we have to stop him. At some point, I'll be called away, then Pu-haddu won't be able to pay any longer."

"Perhaps some *maryannu* would make a more persuasive negotiator, my lady. Teshamanu has become a powerful man all of a sudden."

"No!" she cried sharply. "Anybody but him."

Ili-milku stared at her, surprised by her vehemence.

"He's... he's not eloquent enough," the queen added hastily. "He's too much the blunt soldier."

An uncomfortable silence fell between them. Ili-milku felt a little hurt on behalf of his fellow scribe, that the queen should dismiss him so readily for what hardly seemed to be a fault.

But finally, shame and dread at war on her face, the queen approached Ili-milku's ear and explained, almost pleading, "He's the father, Ili-milku."

Ili-milku's jaw dropped, and he gaped at the queen with round eyes. But she just stared back at him in grim confirmation, her lips compressed.

"Ba'al's beard," he murmured, feeling suddenly flushed with a wave of burning heat. For a long while, he could say nothing, only stare into space, imagining all sorts of horrible consequences.

At last, he rallied himself. It was him or no one, then, for the mission. "All right. I'll do it. What am I supposed to tell this ruffian? 'Stop asking for silver because you could cause the kingdom to fall apart'? He knows that only too well. That's his handle on us all."

Ehli-nikkalu shrugged helplessly. "I'd hoped you could come up with a plan, Ili-milku."

They sat silently, each revolving their own despairing thoughts. Ili-milku pondered lunch waiting for him at home and the easy companionship of his family. He imagined himself bearding that Iwirimuza. One version made Ili-milku the successful hero, reducing the criminal to blubbering jelly with his eloquence. The other version depicted Ili-milku retreating in disgrace, just ahead of a rain of sling stones. He felt he couldn't get a satisfying breath of air.

After a long space of pondering, he said, "What if I tell him everybody already knows his secret and nobody cares?"

The queen's heavy-lidded eyes brightened. "That might work."

He crawled to his feet, and the queen followed. The wind hit him like the lash of a chariot whip. "Gods help me for a fool, but I'll do it tomorrow. If I'm not back by sundown, better send someone to look for me."

Ehli-nikkalu looked so grateful his heart melted. She was like a tall, thin, long-legged crane with a pointed beak—no one's idea of womanly beauty—but not altogether unattractive when her mouth wasn't pursed into a haughty crescent. At that moment, she had a girlish air of vulnerability about her. The wind lifted her veil and the light-brown mass of her hair floating behind her hips. He realized that he had never before seen her hair in all its length.

"Oh, thank you, Ili-milku," she cried. "You're a high functionary at the palace. If you say nobody cares, he'll believe you." She reached out her hands and took hold of his, gave them a conspiratorial squeeze, and whispered, "The gods go with you, my friend."

The next day, Ili-milku bade his wife goodbye as if he might never see her again. He took one of his slaves and set out for the port in the foggy chill of early morning, departing by the Royal Gate. None of the scribes was around at that hour, so he wouldn't have to answer any questions regarding his destination. The two men trudged along side by side, silent except for the crunching of their feet on the gravelly road and the *huff-huff* of their unsynchronized breaths. The whiteness wrapped them softly like a fleece, erasing the world around them. Only a blurry aura surrounded the pair—the dark fuzzy shadow of a tree, the dimly perceived guardhouse at the end of the curtain wall. From time to time, a pack animal would emerge from the fog and clop past them then sink back into the featureless nothingness of white.

After a while, the slave said, his voice ringing in the fog, "Master, have you any idea what we're gonna run into down there?"

"None, Anani," Ili-milku admitted. He had thought to seem less threatening without arms of any kind, but he regretted that decision. Not that he was sure what weapon he could have employed—he didn't know the first thing about physical mayhem. He had only brought his slave because Anani made a kind of guard of honor that seemed to lend an official air to the mission.

Ili-milku had to chuckle. Anani was undoubtedly the most disreputable-looking guard of honor ever, with his bowed legs and toothless grin. But he was faithful to the bone. "You know, this man has been blackmailing the king's mother. Our lady the queen made the mistake of paying him off, and now we have to convince him that his secret is out and nobody will pay him anymore."

"Blackmailer, eh?" grunted Anani knowingly. "Them's a bad lot."

"Apparently, that's the least of his crimes. He may be quite dangerous. I think it's only fair you be aware of that, Anani. If he tries to take me prisoner or something, run for it."

"I couldn't leave you, master," the man objected, his eyes round.

"No, you must, if it comes to that. Somebody has to report back to the queen."

Anani looked unconvinced, but he said, "Yes, master."

They trudged on.

At last, the ghostly cubes of buildings began to hover closer in the mist. A clang of hammers echoed from somewhere. People started to emerge more frequently out of the whiteness, and the heavy smell of fish and other more acrid industrial odors floated in the opaque air. From a distance sounded the clapping of water against the docks and the irregular knocking of vessels, one against the other, as they bobbed at anchor.

The day before, Ili-milku had sounded out his scribes about the location of the infamous house of Iwiri-muza. He had not lacked for volunteers to accompany him, and he wondered how it was that no one had informed Sharryelli about the man's sinister identity before the old bookkeeper.

Ili-milku and Anani marched down the main street toward the docks, and when nothing remained before them but the stone quays and the ghosts of masts and furled sails hanging cloudily in the mist, they turned right. The second house from the end of the block was large and featureless. It might have been a chandler's as easily as a house of ill repute. A big stone anchor sat tipped against the wall, as if it were one of those regular stones set there to protect against collisions by vehicles. Resigned, Ili-milku drew a deep breath and knocked on the hobnailed door. Behind them, an oxcart passed with the slow rumble of wheels.

A portly, balding man opened the door, scratching his belly and yawning. "Whaddya want at this hour? Ya think people never sleep?"

"I'm looking for Iwiri-muza." *He has a nice, fashionable Hurrian name that sounds more like some young scribe of good birth than a depraved criminal,* Ili-milku thought.

"He's busy. Unless y'owe him money."

"Well, he may *think* I owe him money," Ili-milku said dryly.

The man appeared to reflect, then he opened the door. Anani passed through in Ili-milku's wake, shooting the doorkeeper a look of disdain.

The small vestibule was dark except for the pale light of a foggy morning filtering in through the half-closed shutters. A steep staircase rose into the shadows of a corner, and the floor, wet from their steps, was of smoothed plaster, painted to look like precious stone. A closed door on the inner side of the room let a white line of daylight penetrate at its threshold. A stale, heavy fug of perfume and sweat and something that might have been vomit hung in the air.

"What's yer name?" growled the burly man.

"Ili-milku of Shubanu, chief scribe of King Ammurapi, son of Niqmaddu," Ili-milku said, dangling his big sealstone.

The doorkeeper opened the panel in the rear wall, and the vestibule suddenly flooded with dull light. He disappeared into what was clearly a room on an interior court. Voices murmured within. Ili-milku and Anani exchanged triumphant looks tinged with nervousness. The pimp was there, and in a moment, Ili-milku realized, he would have to confront him.

In fact, an instant later, someone called from inside, "Come in."

*A*uthor Note: *The sealstone, pressed into clay or wax, serves as a signature and badge of identification. Readers of* The Queen's Dog *will remember Ili-milku's slave Anani.*

The Hurrians are inhabitants of Mitanni, a land in inland Syria. Lots of people in Ugarit and throughout the Hittite Empire have Hurrian names (for example, Ehli-nikkalu), but real Hurrians are also found, many as refugees (cf. The Singer and Her Song*).*

Chapter 21

Ili-milku entered, his guard of honor at his heels. Two men sat at a table within the room, silhouetted against the fleecy white light from the window. Nothing was visible in the courtyard. Three other fellows stood against the walls, raggedly dressed but focused and formidable. *A different kind of guard,* he thought uneasily. An aura of violence hung in the room, a sense of power that filled the atmosphere and made it hard to breathe.

He bowed with as much pomp and as little subservience as possible. "Which of you is Iwiri-muza?" he asked.

One of the seated men dipped his head. "Have a seat," he offered.

Ili-milku lowered himself to a stool. He could see his interlocutor at last, but he would scarcely have been able to describe him a day later. Iwiri-muza was of middle age, middle height, and middle build, with a bland, undistinguished face of slightly pale complexion. His hair and beard were graying brown. He could have been a merchant, an aristocrat, or a slave with equal probability. His smallish eyes were neither vicious nor intense. In short, he radiated no clue that he was a powerful and crooked personage who exploited the vices of others. The look he turned upon Ili-milku was cool and intelligent, curious rather than intimidating.

"What brings you here, my lord?" he asked in an ordinary voice of medium pitch. "Are you seeking a girl?" The pimp had a slight accent—he probably really was Hurrian.

"I come to you to discuss your business affair with the royal family," Ili-milku said. He glanced at the other man. "Perhaps you'd rather carry out this conversation alone."

"Ooh, the royal family. I'm so interested," the other man said in an adolescent-sounding voice.

Ili-milku eyed him uneasily. That person was by far the more distinctive—and disturbing—of the two, a small, thin, birdlike fellow with a russet beard and a mop of impossibly matted hair. He had about him a striking feminine beauty. Were it not for the beard, Ili-milku would have suspected he was a woman in poorly executed disguise. The youth's eyes were an intense amber shade of brown Ili-milku had seen before, although not for years. Suddenly, he realized who this was.

"I knew your mother, my lord," he said to the young man. "She was a beautiful woman."

"Oh, look, he knows who I am," the youth cried delightedly. "Who am I, scribe? Tell him."

Ili-milku was thrown off balance by the fellow's strange manners, but he said, "You're Prince Utri-sharrumma, are you not? The son of our late Queen Taduhepa?"

"He gets the prize, doesn't he, Iwiri-muza? Except it's King Utri-sharrumma now."

The pimp nodded thoughtfully without registering any particular emotion.

Ili-milku could feel the sweat running down his sides despite the cool day. He could remember Ehli-nikkalu's description of the man's crazy unpredictability. But more heartrending, he could remember him as a curly-haired toddler, frightened and confused, torn between his parents, tricked into giving up the throne. Enough to curdle a person's sanity, surely. Ili-milku's mission had just become doubly delicate.

And Utri-sharrumma is here with Iwiri-muza? They're in league? Dear gods, give me eloquence... "Do you... do you want me to speak freely, Iwiri-muza?" he murmured, catching the saner man's eye.

Iwiri-muza tipped his head in a silent nod, calmly lacing his fingers around his crossed knees.

Ili-milku began, "The payments that you have been exacting from the crown are no longer worth anything. Your secret is now known to all, and it has caused no particular scandal. The queen instructs me to cease all transactions." He fell silent, confused by the pimp's complete lack of response.

After an uncomfortable moment, Iwiri-muza said, "Is that all?"

"Yes, if you accept. If you persist in making demands, the king's men will be paying you a visit. No doubt if there's an investigation, all sorts of irregularities can be found in your business ventures." *And this,* he thought, his heart hammering, *is the moment when they slit my throat.*

But Utri-sharrumma cried, his golden eyes glittering with curiosity, "What's the secret, Iwiri-muza?"

"Consider whether it serves your best interests to tell him, Iwiri-muza," Ili-milku cautioned the Hurrian desperately. *Dear gods, all we need is for this wild-eyed pretender to get wind of the king's irregular status.*

"Oh, the late king took one of my girls as a concubine," Iwiri-muza said off-handedly.

"Do you have a reply for the royal family?" Ili-milku pressed, hoping it would be a promise to back off.

"Tell them... tell them the Umman-manda raided my establishment and took you hostage." The pimp raised a hand, and the three men against the wall threw themselves at Ili-milku.

"Oh no, ya don't!" Anani cried, thrusting himself between the ruffians and his master.

But they pushed him aside and grabbed Ili-milku by the arms. Ili-milku could scarcely repress a squeak of fear. He pulled back, but they outnumbered him and outmuscled him, twisting his elbows behind his back so that he couldn't struggle. One of them knocked the slave's feet out from under him and pinned him on the ground with an "oof!" Ili-milku and his honor guard were left helpless, panting, the scribe's heart hammering more from terror than exertion. Everything had gone wrong so quickly.

"So, slave," Iwiri-muza said calmly to Anani as the latter lay on the ground with one of the pimp's henchmen kneeling on his kidneys. "I want you to go back to the city and tell the royal family that their official is held hostage by the Umman-manda. If they want to see him alive, they need to reconsider their plan to renege. And if they do renege, I can always tell the real king here the full truth about Pu-haddu."

"Pu-haddu!" Utri-sharrumma cried, his eyes lighting up. "Oh, I like that girl. Send her along for me, will you, slave, since I'm holding the scribe hostage? I want to talk to her again."

They picked Anani up and manhandled him to the door. He cast an anguished look back at his master.

Ili-milku shouted, "Do what they tell you, man!"

The door slammed behind the slave, and Ili-milku was alone with his captors.

The worst had happened. There he was, held by a cold-blooded professional extortioner and a madman. His heart thundered in his ears and filled his throat. Perhaps he would never see his wife and children again. If only he had refused the queen's mission. He should have seen how doomed to failure it had been, how poorly they had thought things out.

"We won't be here when he comes back, of course," the Hurrian said matter-of-factly. "You'll be in the real king's custody. I'll be out of sight. Too bad someone upset the cart like this—it was all very businesslike, no one endangered. Now"—he gave a thin smile of regret—"someone *is* in danger. The real king is rather unpredictable."

Utri-sharrumma threw back his head and cawed like a lunatic jaybird. "I am that. Why, even I don't know what I'll do next."

One of the henchmen threw a sack or cloak or something opaque and smelly over Ili-milku's head, wrapping it around his throat so he couldn't shake it off. They bound his wrists before him and hustled him outside. The mist closed in around his body, cold and clammy on his hands and ankles. He stumbled blindly across the paving stones, held up by his captors' grip.

"Are you the Ili-milku who wrote those songs about Ba'al?" Utri-sharrumma asked cheerfully as they staggered along. "I'm a bit of a poet myself. I want to see how you go about putting together the lines. You'll have to write a poem for me."

Half-suffocated and wholly terrified, Ili-milku could only grunt. He bumped into something hard, and they pitched him up over the top and into it like baggage, bruising his shoulders—he assumed it was a cart of some sort. It creaked and lurched as others got in with him, then came the clopping of hooves. The cart began to move. He tried to right himself, and someone patted him companionably on the bottom. *Oh dear gods, where are they taking me? Will Anani ever find me? Will I die here, blindfolded, without ever seeing the beautiful light of Shapshu again?* He had so many regrets. He could feel a tear leaking from his eye.

Ehli-nikkalu resented the necessity of having to speak with her mother-in-law even occasionally, but like it or not, she had to discuss the disposition of her properties when she was recalled to Hatti Land. Thus, in a rare moment, Ehli-nikkalu happened to be talking with Sharryelli when the chief scribe's slave burst into the regent's presence. The two women gaped at the bow-legged little man who stood before them, wringing his hands. He was almost in tears, to the point that Ehli-nikkalu could scarcely understand what he was saying, but what he seemed to tell them was horrifying. The younger queen's heart seemed to choke her speechless with dread. *Dear lady Nikkal, what have I gotten Ili-milku into?*

"Could you please repeat that, my dear?" Sharryelli asked, looking stunned. "I must say, it's almost unbelievable."

"My master's Lord Ili-milku. Him and me, we went to talk to that ass turd, Iwiri-muza, an' while we was there, the Umman-manda come in and captured him. I'm afraid they'll do 'im in if nobody ransoms 'im, my lady. They was serious, and that king of theirs is a loony bird if ever there was."

"The Umman-manda in Mahadu?" Ehli-nikkalu echoed, her heart sinking.

Sharryelli gasped. "So close to the city? Dear me. What if they damage the ships? Burn the port?" She glanced at her daughter-in-law—*was there suspicion in that look?*—but addressed the slave. "My dear, what was your master doing at Iwiri-muza's? Do you know?"

The slave explained, "He was tryin' to talk that son of a jackal outta blackmailin' Lady Pu-haddu. Then the other little one, the one they calls the real king, he says, 'Ooh, send 'er along. I like 'er.'" He spoke the last words in a high-pitched voice.

Sharryelli's eyebrows rose in a look of total confusion. "Blackmailing Pu-haddu? Was that what those payments were about? But why? And why is Ili-milku involved? And Utri-sharrumma likes Pu-haddu? How does he know her?"

Ehli-nikkalu's throat closed up so she could hardly swallow. She knew only too well how all this had happened and could just hope the regent wouldn't ask her any questions. She felt suddenly deep in over her head, swept out to sea on a current too strong for her. *How could I have been so foolish, so arrogant, as to think I could control these desperados?*

Oh, how I wish Ili-milku were at my side—someone knowledgeable to discuss things with. But of course, there would be nothing to discuss if he were free and present. The whole situation was so bizarre—and it had come up so suddenly—that she felt she was caught flat-footed. *Teshamanu is a soldier. Perhaps he would know what to do about this. I have to get Ili-milku back before that madman does something to him, or I'll have his blood on my conscience for the rest of my days.* She wanted to flee Sharryelli's presence and send out a rescue party before the regent figured out what was going on.

Sharryelli wrung her hands. "We need desperately to get him back unharmed. This is a disgrace to the kingdom. Whatever possessed him to go alone into the lair of that blackmailer?"

Ehli-nikkalu stiffened and said nothing.

"He's a valuable man to the conduct of the government. If only they could have captured Yabni-shapshu instead." The regent looked wild-eyed with distress. "Send out the army!"

"If we send troops, won't they kill your master?" Ehli-nikkalu asked the slave, thinking aloud.

"They's gone, my lady. They took off even b'fore I left. Shapshu knows where they got him now." The slave's face crumpled with extravagant distress, and tears began to trickle from his eyes. "I shoulda stayed and fought..." He began to weep miserably.

"No, no, my dear. What could one man have done?" Sharryelli called out for her chamberlain, who appeared at the door. "Gather a unit of the guards. Tell them to go to the house of Iwiri-muza in Mahadu, and double-quick. I suspect at least some of them will know where that is." She turned to the slave. "And you—go with them. Show them the way, in case they're a bunch of virtuous young fellows." She called after her own servant, "Tell them to arrest Iwiri-muza and the leader of the Umman. And bring Ili-milku home safely."

But Ehli-nikkalu thought about Utri-sharrumma's demand. With a sinking in her middle, she remembered Amaya identifying herself to the pretender as "Pu-haddu" and knew who he really wanted. There was no way she would send that young girl to Utri-sharrumma. She wondered instead how much it would endanger the real Pu-haddu to let her go along as bait—under heavy guard, of course. She was carrying the king's brother, after all.

Sharryelli stood for a moment in the doorway as the others scattered to their tasks. Ehli-nikkalu, behind her, stayed silent, hoping to attract no questions. She was damp with cold sweat.

The regent passed a hand across her brow. "Dear me, I feel quite faint. I've never heard a more incredible scenario. What upon the earth is happening? Clearly, whatever it is, nobody thought to inform me." She shot Ehli-nikkalu a look that might have been challenging or simply a plea to the universe to answer her questions. "What has Ili-milku to do with the payment of those debts to Iwiri-muza, which apparently involve blackmailing Niqmaddu's concubine? What has she done? Oh, I knew from the first that she was unsuitable, that common girl."

Ehli-nikkalu shrugged, feigning ignorance, but her heart was pounding against her breastbone. It would not go well for her if the regent found out this whole imbroglio was due to her. *Oh, Ili-milku, what have I done to you?*

Sharryelli, still fluttering, called her litter bearers, and they took off with her across the royal plaza. Limp with relief, Ehli-nikkalu watched her go. *I must think of some way to get Ili-milku out of this without jeopardizing Pu-haddu.*

As the younger queen entered the corridor, death in her heart, she saw a sturdy one-armed figure passing at the end of the hall, on his way to the staircase. She felt an inexplicable need to see her secretary again. "Teshamanu," she called in an unsteady voice. "Something dreadful has happened. I need to talk this over with someone who understands campaigns and strategy. Please follow me to my apartment."

With quick steps, she led the way, and the old eunuch let them in, eyebrows raised in curiosity. But she shooed him out and barred the door. Ehli-nikkalu and the scribe were left standing face-to-face. A look of alarm passed over him at the sight of her expression, which she knew must be distressed in the extreme.

"Teshamanu, something dreadful has happened, and it's my fault. We have to undo it, preferably before the regent calls out the army. There's been another hostage-taking."

Teshamanu's eyes flew open, and his jaw dropped. "Not you, at least, my lady. Who, then? Not... not Amaya?"

"It's Ili-milku." The queen was so overcome with guilty misery that she could feel tears burning in her eyes. She wrung her hands, which were none too steady.

"Ba'al's beard! Who? The Umman-manda again?"

"So it seems. And that Iwiri-muza. This happened right in Mahadu, in broad daylight."

Teshamanu's face grew sharp, almost wild, suddenly. "Him? What's he got to do with the Umman?"

"We don't know." But she had caught his change of expression. "Are you afraid to confront him? I know you owe him gold..."

"No. I'd like nothing better than a chance to put an end to him," he growled, dropping his eyes. "He's a piece of scum, with a finger in every dirty business in the kingdom. It doesn't surprise me he's in league with the Umman-manda. If Iwiri-muza can make any kind of profit off these people..." His face had grown dark with contempt, and a peculiar grimness settled upon his mouth.

Ehli-nikkalu clutched at his arm. "I need some advice, Teshamanu. Sharryelli has sent soldiers to the port, but the slave who told us about this says the kidnappers were already vacating the premises when they sent him off. So her men probably won't find anyone there. I don't know how the kidnappers plan to collect their ransom for Ili-milku. I have to find him. We can't let them kill him."

Teshamanu murmured something that sounded like a curse. His hand clenched on the hilt of his penknife.

"But then he said that Utri-sharrumma—"

"That mad dog is there?" the *maryannu* interrupted.

"Apparently. He said Utri-sharrumma wanted to talk to Pu-had-du—"

Teshamanu looked up in confusion. "Pu-haddu? Which Pu-had-du?"

"Well, the king's mother—who else? Not some washerwoman, surely." Ehli-nikkalu didn't know how to avoid telling him she knew his history, and this stress just added to her abruptness.

"Oh. Of course. Iwiri-muza wouldn't have to go looking for the other one..." He stared about, nonplussed. "But why? What does he want with her?"

The queen fixed him with anxious eyes. "He thinks that's Amaya's name."

Teshamanu jerked back in horror.

"Utri-sharrumma took a fancy to your niece, and I guess he thinks we'd do anything to get the chief scribe back. But I won't send him a young girl like that, Teshamanu, even just to talk to him. He's a strange and dangerous man. Do I explain the mix-up or tell Sharryel-li to let the king's mother go to him? Under guard, of course. I don't want to jeopardize the real Pu-haddu either. She's carrying a child, af-ter all." Her mouth trembled. "But what if he won't release Ili-milku unless we show her to him?"

Teshamanu looked worried, his brow corrugated with indeci-sion. "I... I... don't know what to say, my lady. I wouldn't trust Utri-sharrumma, that's for sure. And Iwiri-muza is even worse, although he's not mad."

Ehli-nikkalu turned away from him and heaved a deep, agonized breath. *What to do?* "Think, Teshamanu. I'm afraid of how Sharryelli may carry this out. She doesn't know how volatile the pretender is. If she refuses to let him talk to Pu-haddu at least, he may take it out on Ili-milku. And I'm the one who got him into this danger. Oh, why do I have to fix everything, save everybody?"

"We must act, my lady. As soon as you know when and where Iwiri-muza plans to collect his ransom, we must forestall him. Set a trap. Offer him bait. Then close the trap."

Chapter 22

By evening, Ili-milku was more than ready for release.

They had imprisoned him in a hovel someplace, a one-room cabin with only a single shuttered window. It held furniture of a rough sort—a table and a pair of stools—and a clay brazier filled with small logs burned down to charcoals that radiated enough heat to make the air wiggly immediately above them but not to take much chill off the room. The reed-and-clay ceiling leaked in several places, and he could imagine how miserable it would be to spend the night there. Other than a few cooking vessels and wooden utensils, it held nothing else, no sign of bedding.

Certainly nothing that could serve as a convincing weapon. His captors had unhooded him and untied his hands, so they clearly considered him no danger. But just in case, one of Iwiri-muza's henchmen sat in front of the door, cleaning his nails with the point of his dagger, and Utri-sharrumma, who had a long, gold-sheathed knife at his hip, never left Ili-milku. If any of them had to relieve himself, he did it into a basin in the corner.

Ili-milku's torture consisted not of any physical brutality but of the endless recitation of amateur poetry by Utri-sharrumma, who wanted the scribe's commentary on everything he had ever composed. Which—for a man with only twenty-one years behind him—was a lot. Every word was committed to his exceptional memory. They sat at the table, upon the hard stools, side by side. The stench of the unwashed pretender at such proximity was overwhelming.

"What's wrong with this line, Ili-milku? I've never been satisfied with it," the prince said, tapping his fingers aggrievedly upon his knee. "Why do yours sound so much stronger?"

"If I may suggest, my lord—while this is an excellent line—it would profit from simplification. Especially when you consider it with the next line, which parallels it. So: 'In his face, he became hot'—that's enough, you see? Because then—'In the strength of his loins, he became warm.'" Ili-milku watched Utri-sharrumma's face closely. He had already learned to gauge the young man's reactions and try to head off the eruptions of anger—an exhausting exercise. "It parallels."

The pretender seemed to consider his words seriously and said, "Yes, you're right. It's better. Could I do the same thing with this one: 'Is my appetite like unto the lion's appetite in the wilderness?' Should that become, 'Is my appetite the lion's appetite in the wild?' Because then it goes, 'The appetite of the dolphin in the sea.' Or maybe, 'the appetite of the lion'?"

"Much better, my lord. You catch on very quickly."

Utri-sharrumma shrugged, as if the praise didn't matter much to him, but his expression brightened. "I suppose I have some natural ability. But what about this one:

> They hitched their chariots,
> They yoked their horses,
> They raised the standards.
> They mount their chariots,
> They come on their stallions...

I'm not sure where I want to go after that, but how does it sound so far?"

Ili-milku could barely suppress a groan of exhaustion. *For how many hours have I been rewriting the man's poetry?* His eyes were falling shut, and his buttocks were growing numb on the hard saddle of his stool. Perhaps it was exasperation that made him risk saying, "Very good, my lord. But it sounds rather like something someone else has already written. Perhaps with your formidable intellect, you could find an alternative for some of these images—"

"Alternate image?" Utri-sharrumma cried, his voice shooting up, his face growing red. "What alternative is there to a horse? What alternative image is there to a chariot? The gods are going to war here, Ili-milku. I can't say 'hitched up their donkey to a cart,' can I? Are you making fun of me?" He stared into Ili-milku's face with his too-bright eyes ablaze, and Ili-milku realized he had miscalculated badly. An explosion was on its way. His heart began to pound. Utri-sharrumma's fingers were twitching on the hilt of his dagger.

"N-No, my lord is quite right," he stammered, drawing back uneasily. "'Horse' is the only possible choice. Or 'mare' perhaps, since you've used 'stallion.'"

"No, Ili-milku. You're betraying your low birth. No one hitches mares to a war chariot. Only stallions. And I've already used that word, as you so astutely point out."

"Forgive my ignorance, my lord. You're absolutely right. Perhaps 'sons of mares'... but what you have is perfect." *It was perfect when Yabni-ilu wrote it fifty years ago, and it's still perfect,* he thought wearily, but he would never have expressed such an honest thought out loud. He found he slid into subservience easily.

Utri-sharrumma bolted to his feet, his face flushed, and turned away from the table, as taut as a wire. Ili-milku drew a difficult breath and struggled to keep his face set in a meek, admiring smile. He was very conscious of the pulse beating in his temple, the sound of life in his veins. Which might come to an end any minute if Utri-sharrumma decided to plunge that pretty dagger into his heart. The ruffian at the door sat, impassive, seemingly unaware of the other two men and the tension that twanged between them.

The moment stretched out while the pretender struggled with his demons and Ili-milku tried not to whimper.

All at once, a hammering at the door broke their tension. The guard sprang to his feet, and Utri-sharrumma drew his knife and whipped around. But it was Iwiri-muza and a pair of his men.

"You can put that blade away, my lord," the Hurrian said dryly, closing the door behind him. "Everything is going as planned. The royal troops have stormed my house in Mahadu, finding only the girls. One of them presented the officer with the tablet we left for the dowager queen, giving her the location of the field where we will return the king's chief scribe—"

"The *false* king's chief scribe," Utri-sharrumma interrupted, but his anger had evaporated. He slid his dagger back into its gaudy sheath.

"The false king's chief scribe. In return for another seven hundred in silver and the girl, Pu-haddu."

"What fun!" The pretender turned to Ili-milku, cheerful once again. "Won't that be fun, Ili-milku? Although I may grow attached to your company. Perhaps I won't let you go..."

Anguish seized Ili-milku's heart, sending tears to his eyes. "But, my lord. I have a family..."

"And so will I, once I marry the lovely Pu-haddu." Utri-sharrumma spread his hands in a happy gesture.

Iwiri-muza shrugged and said blandly, "The fewer hostages we have to keep track of, the better, it seems to me. They slow us down."

"I'll think about that. Let's get out of here, though. It's such a trap. I think we should take our positions in the hills well before nightfall."

The pimp agreed. His men grabbed Ili-milku's arms and pulled him to his feet, and someone slid the hood roughly over his head again, its coarse textile rasping against his nose and beard. Hands seized him by the elbows and hustled him to the door, then they were out into the biting cold of a winter night. Their footsteps crunched over the dead leaves and gravel. Breath wheezed in the men's noses, but no one spoke. He could see nothing, could hardly inhale. Somewhere, an owl hooted a dismal commentary on life.

Dear gods, get me out of this alive, Ili-milku prayed.

It was late in the evening when a knock came at the door of Rab-ilu's house. Uncle Teshamanu had brought some silver for the household expenses and seemed strangely reluctant to leave. He sat on the stairs, staring at the wall with a fierce and troubled expression on his face. When Amaya asked him why he was so nervous, he said merely that he was awaiting word from the queen. Amaya herself had just helped the nursemaid prepare the twins' bed for the night and was directing the clearing of the kitchen after supper. A strange tension reigned over the household—a sense, almost, of foreboding. When the knock sounded, Ba'aluya, in her night tunic, rushed to answer before the servants could get there, and Amaya, following her, was amazed to see the regent in the doorway.

"The king's grandmother!" cried the little girl. "Is he here to play?"

Amaya pushed aside her sister, the hair suddenly rising on her neck. "How can we serve you?" she said tensely, forcing a bow. *What can this mean at such an hour?*

"Hello, my dear." Sharryelli enfolded the girl in her arms, but her hug was distracted. "Your uncle wasn't at home. Is he by any chance here?"

"Yes, my lady. Just a moment."

Even as the young woman turned to call him, Teshamanu appeared at the foot of the staircase. He looked up, surprised at the appearance of the regent. "My lady."

Sharryelli rushed across the vestibule and seized his hand urgently. "Oh, Teshamanu, dear, I need your advice. Where can we go to talk?"

Uncle ushered her into the salon, his twitchiness mirroring the anxious expression upon the queen mother's face. Amaya hustled into the kitchen to prepare a tray of refreshments and, a moment later, followed the other two into the salon, bearing the cups and pitcher, which clinked softly as she walked. She set them down, silently and without fuss, upon the table, positioned a second oil lamp, and retreated to the door.

"You know I told you about the business with poor Ili-milku taken hostage by the Umman," Sharryelli said in a low voice.

Amaya's heart stopped, and she froze in place at the door. *Oh no! Lord Ili-milku has been captured by that awful Utri-sharrumma.* Out of the corner of her eye, she saw Uncle nod, his shoulders tense with concern.

"My soldiers just overran Iwiri-muza's place of business, but of course, all the men had fled. Only the girls were left, and they knew nothing. However, one of them had been directed to give the officer this tablet." Sharryelli drew the patty of clay from her shawl and handed it to Uncle. She was breathless with anxiety as she said, "Can you read this for me, my dear?"

He turned it right side up, tilted it toward the lamps, and read in a strangled voice, "Tonight at midnight, bring the seven hundred silver shekels and the girl Pu-haddu to the queen's olive orchard, one hundred cubits uphill from the press house. Send her out alone with the silver, and Ili-milku will be sent out from our side. Any tricks and your chief scribe dies." In the lamplight, Amaya saw Uncle's profile with its crescent nose and thick lashes tipped up toward the queen mother. He had gone white.

Amaya was swallowed by a wave of confusion. *Utri-sharrumma wants Pu-haddu? The king's mother?* But then with a sinking of her stomach, she remembered: that was the name she herself had given him when he had asked her. She couldn't have said why she had misled him, except that at the time, she'd been thinking what a mistake she had made identifying herself to the queen mother in the garden. *And now, what will happen to the real Pu-haddu?* Sweat beginning to trickle down beneath her bangs, she stayed very silent and listened to the older pair, hoping they had forgotten she was there.

The queen mother said in a frightened voice, "Do we dare send Pu-haddu, dear? I just don't know what to do." Her voice broke, her head lowered, and her hands plucked helplessly at her shawl. "We need Ili-milku, and it would be a terrible dishonor to the kingdom to lose a high official like that. The viceroy would never trust us again after all the grief he gave us before, when the queen was kidnapped."

"You'll never get him back unless the woman at least appears," Uncle said, biting his lip. "But there has to be some way not to turn her over to Utri-sharrumma. They say he's a dangerous character."

Amaya thought with anguish of the beautiful Lady Pu-haddu sitting with the queen the other day. She was ready to give birth. They couldn't make a pregnant woman go to Utri-sharrumma—he would be furious. Because the person he really wanted was Amaya, and in his disappointed rage, he might hurt the king's mother. Tears of panic sprang to her eyes. *Oh, what have I done? And how can I undo it?*

Uncle said, rising, "I'll go with you, my lady. Tell your soldiers to get into place early and have their arrows aimed at the other side, so if anyone moves to take Lady Pu-haddu, you can hold them off. Let her throw the silver out to them. But not until Ili-milku is far enough away from them that he can run."

Amaya thought of the bouncing little Ili-milku and wondered how far or fast he could run—certainly not faster than an arrow. And he might be tied up. But Uncle must know more about such things than she did. She knew what *she* had to do.

"I'm going, Teshamanu. Join the troops when you can. You know the site of the exchange." The dowager rushed out the door of the salon so hastily she seemed not even to notice Amaya's presence.

Uncle swept out behind her with a grim smile at his niece, scarcely seeing her. "I'm going to tell the queen," he murmured. In the vestibule—a man with a task to perform—he called for Rab-ilu's sword.

As soon as her uncle had left the house, Amaya, too, slipped out the door, not even telling the slaves where to look for her. She had her own task to perform—to offer herself in Lady Pu-haddu's place. Then Utri-sharrumma would let Ili-milku go.

It was late when a hammering at her apartment door made Ehli-nikkalu start up from her spinning. She hustled Pu-haddu into the bedchamber, not knowing who had come. The chamberlain announced that Teshamanu wanted to see her. She sprang to her feet as the secretary, his face wild and a sword at his hip, rushed into the room.

"My lady," he cried with no preamble, "we have the meeting place for the exchange of Ili-milku against his ransom. Iwiri-muza and Utri-sharrumma have repeated their demand for Lady Pu-haddu as well."

The queen gave a moan of horror. Her heart sank to her feet. "Oh no—what have I done to them both?" She buried her face in her hands. "Oh no. Oh no…"

"We have to act immediately. The queen mother is sending soldiers right now, and they're looking for Lady Pu-haddu to take her along, under heavy guard. Apparently, no one can find her. I have to go, but I thought you'd want to know."

"Where are they?"

"The exchange is to take place at midnight in your olive groves, above the press house. If you see Lady Pu-haddu, let someone know. Forgive me, my lady, but I need to be off..." He edged toward the door, his hand on his sword hilt. Teshamanu was blazing with grim energy. He seemed quite a different man from the gruff, silent scribe who came every day armed with nothing more ferocious than his stylus and penknife. It crossed Ehli-nikkalu's mind, even in her present state of distraction, that this was really the person he was.

"Fly, Teshamanu." It hardly mattered to her at that moment that he had become the dowager's man. "Fly. And save Ili-milku."

The door slammed behind him, and she sank into her chair, suddenly too wobbly to stand. In her innocence, she had sent her friend into deadly danger. *Even if the queen mother pays the ransom Iwiri-muza and the "real king" are demanding, will they let Ili-milku go?* Her nose began to burn.

From the inner chamber, Lady Pu-haddu peeked out. "He's gone?"

"Yes, my dear. It seems my attempt to hide you didn't work. And I didn't tell you everything about their demands."

"I heard him," the king's mother said, her face white. "I didn't want to come out till he'd gone." She emerged with dragging steps and sank onto a stool, face-to-face with the queen. "I... I heard him." She rubbed her big belly. "It's not Lady Amaya they want at all. They want *me* to go to them. To Iwiri-muza."

"Oh, my dear!" Ehli-nikkalu clapped her hands over her mouth. "That's right. This is even worse for you than it would be for anyone else. It's your former owner... Oh, what have I done to everyone?"

The two women sat silent and fearful. Finally, Pu-haddu said unsteadily, "I guess I should go."

"No, no, you're carrying a child! Let me go."

But the former whore gave a puff of lugubrious laughter. "You're worth more than a chief scribe and all the chancery together, my lady. I'll go. At least it will end the blackmail he's been demanding."

Ehli-nikkalu clutched at her hair in misery. "When I told you Utri-sharrumma had demanded Amaya, I... I didn't tell you that she had said her name was Pu-haddu.'"

The king's mother looked quizzical. "Why did she say that?"

"I have no idea, my dear. I guess it was the first name that sprang into her mind. I think she was afraid to give my cousin her real name. He's quite strange, and he showed a disturbing interest in her. She was scared of him."

"So now it's me who gets thrown to the wolves," the real Pu-haddu said, trying to laugh, but she looked desperate.

"No, no. I'll go. I'm the one who made this whole mess. And we can't very well hand a virginal young girl over to him."

"No, my lady. It wouldn't be proper. You're the Great Lady of Hatti. Don't worry. I'll do it. Teshamanu said under heavy guard. I'll be all right." She smiled wistfully. "Amaya's a sweet thing. I wouldn't wish Iwiri-muza on any good girl." Pu-haddu looked sadly at her belly. "Well, I'm off." She stood up and gave a bitter laugh. "I've always had rotten luck. Of all the names on the black earth, she thinks of mine."

"I'm coming too. I'm responsible for this horrible situation."

Ehli-nikkalu ordered Shamumanu to call up a unit of guards and a carriage for the two women—a litter wouldn't be fast enough—and they grabbed up cloaks and precipitated themselves down the stairs.

Author Note: Mahadu, "port", is the port of Ugarit. It's only about an hour's walk from the city (nothing in ancient times) and its ships are the source of Ugarit's wealth and power.

The poems given here as Utri-sharrumma's are real, written by a Yabni-ilu, found in Ugaritic Narrative Poetry, *ed. Simon Parker, SBL, 1997.*

Chapter 23

The evening passed like a nightmare for Ili-milku. They took him in the bumping cart somewhere into the countryside. The wheels rattled on the paved city streets then gave way to the dull crunch and thud of rural roads. Once they were outside the half-walled city, his captors took off his hood, but he was almost as blind without it in the pitch-black of a winter night before the moon rose. Only the group's few torches flickered and smoked, casting wavering shadows of one man against another. They seemed to number about twenty—rough, piratical fellows with grim faces. Nobody spoke.

The silence grew awful, menacing, freighted with fatal possibility. Ili-milku's imagination populated the darkness with leering demons and slavering beasts. His skin crawled with imaginary fleas that he couldn't scratch. Because his hands were behind him, he toppled this way and that with the movement of the cart, unable to balance himself. He could smell Utri-sharrumma's unwashed body and see him slipping his dagger in and out of its sheath. The prince's eyes glittered like a wild animal's in the torchlight. Iwiri-muza stifled a yawn.

At some point, they pulled off the road, and the wagon lurched violently this way and that over uneven ground. Iwiri-muza had said the place of rendezvous was the queen's orchards. Ili-milku imagined their vehicle bobbling over the rocks and clods, moving uphill toward the press house. He was overcome with the urgent desire to urinate, to yield to all the instincts of vacating his body before the worst happened to it and he was sent down below the earth, a hollow shell.

Thoughts of his wife and children and grandchildren, their faces deformed with grief, haunted him. *Dear Lady Shapshu, who sees all, don't let me die here in the darkness, far from your light. Not without my loved ones around me.*

He was not altogether surprised to discover how unheroic his last thoughts were, how lacking he was in any ambition to go down with defiance or sell his life dearly. He was trained as a scribe, a scholar. He was the son of a scholar and of a scholar's daughter. No one had ever inculcated in him those pretty ideals of the warrior class he'd seen even in a scribal *maryannu* like Teshamanu. No. Ili-milku wanted unashamedly to live. He wanted it so badly he figured there wasn't much he wouldn't do to make that happen. He would have begged. He would have shoved a woman in front of him. But even such a sordid commerce seemed to be denied him. He was as helpless as an egg.

After what seemed to be endless ages of movement, the cart stopped, and two of the ruffians pushed and rolled Ili-milku painfully over the edge to the ground, where rude hands just prevented him, his stomach in his mouth, from crashing with all his weight upon the stones. The others climbed out. Utri-sharrumma and Iwiri-muza exchanged words, but he couldn't distinguish what they were saying. The men hustled him over the uneven ground uphill, branches whipping him in the face, unavoidable in the flickering darkness. Their breath steamed from their noses in the cold air.

"Are the men in place?" the pretender said in a loud whisper to one of the others.

Someone mumbled a reply. Then everything grew still again—absolute, waiting stillness. At that time of year, no crickets were to be heard. All the animals were safe in their lairs. The torches sputtered, but the shadows that appeared came from the other direction, and Ili-milku realized the moon had begun to rise over the eastern mountains.

From off in the olive groves came a faint thumping and shuffling, as of numerous feet. Torches approached, flashing through the trees. Then a voice called out from a distance, "Are you there? We are the king's men. We have the silver and the Lady Pu-haddu. Show us the scribe."

Someone pushed him forward. Another bravo grabbed him by the upper arm and forced him to walk, stumbling, out in front of the group.

"Here he is," Iwiri-muza called from behind him somewhere. "We meet in the middle."

I'll be free in a minute. I'll be free in a minute, hope whispered wildly in Ili-milku's ear, but his reason warned him how many things could go wrong even at the last instant. His heart was in his throat in a choking, throbbing lump. Ahead of him, shadowy in the torchlight and the growing brightness of the moon, were a cluster of soldiers and, before them, figures he recognized: Teshamanu, the queen, and a shorter woman who must be the king's mother, wearing an enveloping cloak.

Iwiri-muza called out in his dry voice, "Why, is that Teshamanu I see? We meet again."

"Ooh, do you know him?" Utri-sharrumma asked, irresistibly curious.

"Turn Ili-milku loose," the *maryannu* cried grimly. "He's done nothing to you."

Ili-milku swiveled his head, staring at one side then the other. *What's going on? Can't they set me free* then *have a conversation?*

"Mighty brave tone of voice, my friend. Don't forget you still owe me silver," the Hurrian said. His flat voice was tinged with mild humor, as if he enjoyed the situation.

Oh no, Ili-milku thought. *That's who his debts are to.*

"You know I'm serious about collecting it. If you should forget, I'll keep sending you reminders." He paused then added, "Remember the fire, Teshamanu? Where are your wife and children?"

The silent night grew all at once immensely more silent. Inside the heart of every one of them who knew Teshamanu's tragedy echoed a huge unspoken gasp. Ili-milku stared with horror at the *maryannu*. Even in the pale moonlight, he could see the man's mouth fall open.

The queen murmured, "Oh no!"

Utri-sharrumma cried in admiration, "You set it? Nice touch, Iwiri-muza!"

The sheer lunacy of his comment against the horrible somberness of the moment chilled Ili-milku's blood. He was still the prisoner of a madman and a man with no conscience. He might yet die.

Teshamanu had grabbed for his sword and lunged forward with a snarl, but the queen and soldiers held him back.

Someone murmured, "Let the exchange go through, my lord."

"Just a reminder, friend," Iwiri-muza called out in his disturbing monotone. "Send out your people with the silver and the girl. They'll meet in the middle."

Two soldiers took the king's mother by either arm and began to walk her forward. She clutched a heavy-looking bag in her hands.

"Is that her? She's all wrapped up," Utri-sharrumma murmured suspiciously.

The pretender's voice was receding—only Ili-milku was being pushed forward to the place of exchange. He tripped in his nervousness and nearly fell but was sustained by the rough hands of the men at either side of him.

"Wait, that's not her. She's too tall. Look, Iwiri-muza—she's pregnant. It's not her! Stop!" The pretender's voice had grown loud and agitated.

"Of course it's her," Iwiri-muza said. "You just can't see by the moonlight. Of course it's her, my lord. I know her well. Don't stop the exchange now."

But Utri-sharrumma cried shrilly, his voice cracking, "Stop! Bring back the scribe. It's not her. I've been tricked!"

The men guiding Ili-milku jerked him to a halt, and one yelled, "Do we stop? What do we do?"

Ili-milku cast an anguished glance back at the Hurrian and his men.

Utri-sharrumma's voice rose in a breaking howl, "You've double-crossed me, damn you, Iwiri-muza!" He slid his dagger from its gaudy sheath and raised it in a mounting frenzy.

"What? I've done no—"

The Hurrian broke off with a strangled grunt as the pretender thrust his blade into the other man's belly, just under the breastbone. He pulled it out savagely, and Iwiri-muza buckled and slid wordlessly to the ground. Two of his men bent over him, but others closed in on Utri-sharrumma with menacing cries. Some of the Umman thrust their way forward. It looked as if a brawl were going to erupt.

"What about me?" wailed Ili-milku, who was still held between the two parties.

"Kill him!" the pretender screeched.

Then suddenly, a small brave cry cut through the deep roar of men's excited voices. "Here I am, my lord. I'm the one you wanted."

Ili-milku's head jerked up, and everyone in the queen's party turned as well, taken completely by surprise. From the darkness of the trees walked a small, slim figure in a cloak, her braids capped but unveiled. It was Amaya. She glanced at her uncle and the queen but marched courageously out between the two parties. Pu-haddu stopped and looked around at Ehli-nikkalu, clearly not knowing what to do.

"No!" Teshamanu yelled wildly.

"No, Amaya!" the queen cried out simultaneously, clapping her hands to her mouth.

"Go back, my child!" Ili-milku moaned. What a nightmare. He would be killed, and that young girl too.

But she called out in a voice of unwavering assurance, "Let her go. I'm the Pu-haddu you want."

In the torch-flickering darkness, with the moon barely risen, the whole scene was as unreal as a nightmare. Amaya seemed, to herself, to be moving in a dream, where her actions had no real-life consequences—indeed, were carried out by someone other than herself. That was the only way she was able to stay calm, to tell herself that none of this was really happening. She had asked her mother and father what they would have done, knowing that someone else was innocently going to pay the price of her actions, and she knew what she was doing was right. And so, her parents had protected her from fear by this sense of dreamlike trance.

She walked serenely toward the little clot of men with torches. Ili-milku, between two ruffians, was gaping at her, his eyes like plates. Behind him, in the shadows, Utri-sharrumma grinned in foxy delight. Everyone seemed to be frozen in place, and only the crunching of her own footsteps through the dry grass and gravel broke the stillness of a winter night. On she walked.

Behind her came a cry, a snarl, and a chorus of "No!"

With maniacal ferocity, Teshamanu pulled loose from those who restrained him and rushed forward, sword raised. That was like a signal. The king's men broke ranks and poured up the slope, brandishing their weapons. So fast that Amaya hardly knew what was happening, Utri-sharrumma darted forward and grabbed her roughly by the arm.

As if she had just awakened to find her nightmare real, fear flooded through the girl. The little man was surprisingly strong, his thin fingers like a vise of bronze, dragging her uphill. She smelled his pungent odor, heard his breath heaving in and out through his teeth in fury. She cried aloud, terror sizzling through her, but she had enough presence of mind to strike at Utri-sharrumma with her fist, kick wildly at his legs. Still, rage had given him more-than-human strength. He hauled her away stumbling, like a hawk fallen upon its helpless prey, then dragged her when she fell.

Amaya screamed in pain and terror as she raked along the rocky ground and bumped over the terraces. But she never stopped fighting, grabbing at her captor's ankles, eventually managing to pull off his shoe. At that, he threw her down roughly and shrieked in a high-pitched animal voice, "Ungrateful little vixen!" He kicked at her and hobbled away into the body of his men, screaming orders. Amaya lay for a moment, stunned and exhausted, her body throbbing. Then, she scrambled to her feet and ran back toward the king's men for all she was worth, the shoe still in her fist.

Ili-milku, too, began to run, fearing at every moment to feel an Umman spear in his back. Freedom was so close. He was so vulnerable, so unbalanced with his hands bound at his back, feet stumbling in the near darkness on the rolling rocks of a terrace. He thought he might have whimpered aloud in fear as he ran, the king's soldiers pouring past in the other direction.

Arms reached out to grab him. Ehli-nikkalu hugged him, sobbing. Lady Pu-haddu was hustled back by her guards, and all of them huddled together, weeping and praying, finally safe. In the chaos of the moment, nobody realized that Amaya was not among them.

The night air struck Ili-milku's burning cheeks, cold and sweet, freezing the sweat and tears and mucus on his face. From the hillside came the sounds of fighting but only briefly. The light of the moon showed that Iwiri-muza's men had no stomach for a battle once their master was dead, and Utri-sharrumma seemed to have scarpered off at the first attack. Ili-milku thought he saw Teshamanu wading out of the fray with his sword in his hand and something round beneath his arm.

A soldier cut the rope that bound Ili-milku's hands, and he pressed them to his face, tears finally flowing. "It was horrible, my lady. That Utri-sharrumma is a monster. He read poetry to me all day long!" Suddenly, the scribe began to laugh, wild with relief. "I swear I'll never make my wife listen to lines again, poor woman!"

They walked toward the press house, where the king's mother had already withdrawn.

Ehli-nikkalu laughed, too, but then she grew contrite. "I'm so glad everything turned out all right, Ili-milku. I exposed you to such terrible danger."

He couldn't stop laughing, weak and shaken though he was. "It's nothing, my lady. Just something to write about, since it turned out well." It all seemed so ridiculous now—now that the danger was past.

A big fire was blazing in a brazier in a corner of the press house, well away from the oily press. The lady Pu-haddu was there already, warming her hands.

At her side was Anani. He ran to his master, threw himself on him joyously, and wrestled him back and forth. "Master! You're safe!"

Ili-milku clapped the tearful Anani on the back and said, "But you ladies. You must have been terrified. Why are you both here?"

Ehli-nikkalu explained, "Pu-haddu was bait, of a sort. Utri-sharrumma asked for her as part of the exchange." Ili-milku nodded. He was aware of that part.

"But I understood he really meant Amaya. She had identified herself as Pu-haddu once when he asked her name."

Suddenly, everyone seemed to realize the girl wasn't among them.

Ili-milku's heart leaped into his mouth. He saw the two royal wives exchange a look of wide-eyed horror.

"Sweet Lady Shaushga! They have her!" Ehli-nikkalu turned toward the door and began to run.

At that moment, Teshamanu entered the press house, his arm around his niece, supporting her. He was splattered with blood, the hem of his tunic soaked. He looked like a butcher at the end of the workday. And Amaya—she was alive! Filthy, bedraggled, her dress torn... but alive and smiling. In her hand was a worn shoe.

"Thank the gods you're safe!" the queen cried, throwing herself on the girl. Amaya clung to her, half weeping, half laughing with relief.

Everyone crowded around.

"And you, too, Teshamanu," Ehli-nikkalu added in a quieter voice. "Thank the gods *you're* safe." It seemed to her for an instant that no one else was in the room. Everything else had grown soft in focus, and only Teshamanu was etched in clarity against the ruddy light of the brazier, his dark eyes glittering beneath their strong brows, his nose casting a shadow across one cheek. From around Amaya, who was clinging to her, she reached out and took the *maryannu*'s bloody hand. She locked eyes with him, and a flash of something passed between them. Understanding? Gratitude? *Something deeper?*

Amaya said breathlessly, "Utri-sharrumma grabbed me, but I fought him. Eventually, it was too much for him to drag me up the terraces, and he ran away."

The queen and the king's mother guided her gently to the fire and made her a place to sit down. Amaya limped over and settled herself gingerly. With a gesture of disgust, she flung the shoe into the flames.

"Oh, you poor thing. Are you hurt? You must have been terrified," Ehli-nikkalu squatted at her side and brushed the girl's disheveled hair back with a tender gesture. "You were so brave—I've never seen anything so brave."

"I knew what Mother and Father would have done. Oh, Lady Pu-haddu, I'm so sorry I used your name to that awful man. I don't know why—it was just the first thing to come out."

The others took their place once more within the warmth of the brazier.

Beaming, Ili-milku said, "You're our own little Anat, the virgin warrior!"

The queen added with a smile, "And you were brave, too, Ili-milku. It was like a story about the heroes of old!"

The poet laughed as giddily as Ehli-nikkalu herself felt with the relief of everyone's safety.

"What happened finally?" she asked. "Did the king's men catch Utri-sharrumma and the others? Is Iwiri-muza dead?"

Teshamanu stood and said with grim satisfaction, "He's dead. And his wicked head has been separated from his body."

Aha, Ili-milku thought. *That's what he was carrying. I can't say that I blame him.*

Teshamanu continued, "Iwiri-muza's thugs and the Umman had a falling out, as you saw. Utri-sharrumma escaped, and I'm sure we haven't seen the last of him. But he knows the king's men are ready for him now. He may leave the capital alone for a while."

"Teshamanu," the queen said in a hesitant voice, "did I understand Iwiri-muza to say he started the fire that...?"

"Yes, my lady." Teshamanu looked down for a moment then raised his head and began to speak in a low, intense voice. "I know I've told you this in part, but it may make sense of everything. I owed the bastard silver, lots of it, for a long time. I'm ashamed to say I gambled and let myself be drawn into all sorts of schemes to make the silver back that just ended up impoverishing me more. I was a wreck of anxiety. Where could I get such a sum? I had small children to support, and I had spent all my family wealth. I was just earning a cavalryman's salary. He played me for the young fool I was. Iwiri-muza was... he was the one who suggested I lock her in to keep my wife from following me again to his establishment."

For an instant, Teshamanu hung his head and seemed overwhelmed. But then he set his jaw and continued. "The moment came five years ago when I was against a wall. The dowry my wife had brought me was exhausted. My brother had finally refused to bail me out of my folly yet again. I went to Iwiri-muza to beg for more time, and he said what he just said tonight: 'I'm serious.' And when I got home, my house was in flames. I had my suspicions, but it was hard to believe that even he could do something as gratuitously cruel as that."

The women gasped with horror. Ili-milku felt a wrenching stab of pity for his colleague, so desperate and harried for so long. No wonder the sense of culpability had struck him so hard.

"In my guilt, I forgot all about my suspicions of Iwiri-muza. I just felt the gods had turned their backs on me, wretch that I was, and every bad thing was going to happen to me from then on. I felt I couldn't continue to live. Rab-ilu and his family nursed me back from complete despair, but I haven't been the same since. Because the debts have still been there. Iwiri-muza was still on my heels. 'Serious.'"

"Only now, he's dead," the queen murmured. "You're free."

"I'm finally free." He smiled. His shoulders were back, his head high. The *maryannu* squeezed Amaya to him again. "I'm free."

"I hope," Ehli-nikkalu said softly, "that you haven't lost your freedom yet again to the dowager, Teshamanu. She'll try to use you, you know, once you're her son-in-law."

But, his smile deepening, Teshamanu said, "I don't need the gold anymore, my lady, thanks to that settlement for Rab-ilu's murder. She has nothing over me any longer. The twins can live with their married sister in Geru province, and Sharryelli won't be able to touch them. Once they're safe"—he stared the queen fearlessly in the eye—"I'm breaking off the betrothal."

"Oh, good for you, my friend," Ili-milku cried, his heart swelling with happiness for his colleague. He saw a tearful smile break out on the queen's face.

"I can't let an eighteen-year-old girl show more courage than a grown man, a *maryannu*," Teshamanu said with a fond caress of Amaya's hair.

But Amaya looked up, her face troubled. "What about me, Uncle? If you move away with the little ones, do I go too? Or must I go through with the betrothal to that prince?"

Everyone stared at Teshamanu, whose decision would determine the girl's fate. He dropped his eyes, uncertain. "I won't make you do anything, but I think you should at least meet the lad, see if you like him at all. It would be a prestigious match for our family."

Ili-milku saw the stubborn anger reddening the girl's cheeks. "So would your marriage, Uncle. But you seem to be free to break it off. Why not me?"

Ili-milku had to admit she had a point. But that was the way the world worked. And then he remembered Teshamanu's vow. *We must get that lifted. Surely he can't consider himself guilty of the death of his family any longer.*

A uthor Note: *A cubit is the length from a man's elbow to the tips of his fingers, thus, about two feet.*

The historical Ili-milku is from the neighboring kingdom of Shubanu, which no longer exists as an independent state. In the story (cf. The Queen's Dog*), he is a non-aristocrat who has worked his way up to high office by his skill.*

Anat is the sister of the god Ba'al, a rather bloodthirsty war-goddess in Ugaritic mythology, who is virginal, like Athena.

Chapter 24

The king's mother had stood quietly through all that, a little distance from the fire, her face shadowed by her veil. She pushed it back to wipe her eyes, and Teshamanu stared at her with a quizzical expression. Ili-milku realized that the man didn't quite place his former girl. Or didn't dare assume that a royal wife was also a common whore.

Ehli-nikkalu, too, had seen the secretary's curious glance. "Yes, you know her," she said. "Or you knew her in her former life."

Teshamanu murmured in astonishment, "So it *was* you. When they spoke of 'Pu-haddu,' I wondered..." He faced her with a frank smile of happiness. "I'm glad you got away from that life. You were too good for it."

Lady Pu-haddu returned the smile reluctantly. "Things have looked up for me in the last six years. And a lot more in the last few hours. Now that Iwiri-muza's dead, I'm free too."

Ili-milku noticed for the first time how the dark-lashed eyes of the *maryannu*, no longer averted and grim, resembled the eyes of the little king. If only that sordid story could be kept secret. But then, none of them there were likely to reveal it, and Iwiri-muza, who—unknown to almost everyone—had held the entire kingdom hostage for years, was dead.

Eventually, the captain of the guard came to the door of the press house and reported to the queen, "We've chased them all out, my lady. Unfortunately, the pretender escaped, but that pimp from the harbor was found decapitated. Looks like they turned on each other. Can my men escort you back now?"

"Yes. Thank you. It's been a long night." The queen turned to Ili-milku. "I think we can fit into the carriage together. Tomorrow, we'll hear all about your adventure, Ili-milku, but I imagine Sharryelli will want a report first."

"I'll walk with the soldiers, my lady. I'm too filthy to ride in a carriage," Teshamanu offered.

Ili-milku thought that the man might welcome a chance to stretch his muscles in the open air, like a butterfly bursting from its chrysalis. He noticed Teshamanu touch his hand to the sword at his hip.

"Thank you, my lady." Ili-milku's frenetic excitement was wearing off, and exhaustion had overcome him all at once. "I need to get home. My wife must be frantic."

"Oh, I had her notified that you were on a diplomatic mission and might be late, but she'll certainly be worried by this hour. Go straight home to her, my friend." The queen smiled wearily, and he wondered if Sharryelli would have been so thoughtful.

The four of them climbed aboard the carriage, willingly suffering the crowded bench, and the mules set off, accompanied by Teshamanu and the king's troops. The full moon reigned, serene in a cold, cloudless sky, and the olive trees took on a silver shimmer in its pale light against the dark puddles of their shadows. *How beautiful is the land of the living.* Ili-milku drank up the majesty of his surroundings, grateful to still be able to take in the sights of the world. *How good it is to be alive.*

The next morning, Ili-milku appeared in the chancery once more, all in one piece and rather effervescent after his ordeal. Lady Sharryelli looked quite delighted at seeing him, although the best of all must have been the news her men had brought her the previous night—that Iwiri-muza had been killed. The blackmail was over.

It had been nearly dawn by the time the soldiers and the hostages had returned to Ugarit, and the regent assured the chief scribe that she had not slept at all until she had seen them back safely. "Ili-milku, dear! It's so good to have you back," she cried. "Perhaps we've finally driven those Umman away this time."

Other scribes looked up with curiosity and excitement as the story of their chief's nocturnal adventure spread.

He chuckled modestly, letting her draw him by the arm to the doorway.

"Let's step out here, where we can talk." But the corridor of the temporary chancery was filled with coming and going as well.

"Better in my office," she murmured. "I want to talk to you about the situation… you know." She smiled significantly and led him across the plaza and around the palace wall to the mansion of Yabni-shap-shu, where they mounted the stairs. The writing room saw less activity since the damaged files had been carted away for recopying. The corridor was all but deserted. She led him to her office and pushed open the door. "Now, my dear. Do tell me in more detail what went on. How was it Iwiri-muza died?"

"Utri-sharrumma killed him in a fit of pique. He was unhappy that the wrong girl had been brought to him. He had requested 'Pu-haddu,' as you know. But while we all thought that meant the late king's concubine, Lady Pu-haddu, he really meant the Lady Amaya, who had told him her name was Pu-haddu when she encountered him in the orchard some weeks ago."

Sharryelli stared at him, confusion rendering her speechless for a moment. "I-I'm not sure I understand," she stammered finally.

"And when Amaya heard you and her uncle discussing the demand for Pu-haddu last night, she realized what had happened and set out on her own to give herself up in Pu-haddu's place."

"She did?"

"She did indeed, which was a very brave thing for a young girl to take upon herself, it seems to me." Ili-milku beamed with pride for the girl and her exploit.

"Well, I certainly must congratulate her," Sharryelli said, her face proclaiming that she understood many aspects of the ordeal not at all. "Now if you could just enlighten me about how the queen got involved in this affair, Ili-milku..."

He nodded, looking a little guilty. "I believe the queen became part of it through her desire to help Lady Pu-haddu."

"Since when have they been friends?" Sharryelli demanded crossly. No doubt, the only relationship she was aware of was the concubine flaunting her pregnancies in front of the queen, who had looked down her nose in disgust at the younger woman. "And why did Pu-haddu need help?"

A flush of red rose in Ili-milku's chubby cheeks. "Er, it seems that Iwiri-muza knew something about her past that she preferred not to be noised about. He was blackmailing her."

"All these years?" Sharryelli's nose wrinkled. "She was hardly a suitable person, even for a commoner."

"I don't know how long, but certainly during your son's reign," Ili-milku said. "He paid the man's blackmail until his death. Then I think the Hurrian addressed his demands to the late king's estate. I suppose that's how they came to your attention."

"And my son's widow?"

"She paid the first posthumous exaction herself."

"Ohhh." Sharryelli must have seen now why the debt was marked *paid* in the books. She looked as if she found it annoying.

"Ehli-nikkalu is such a busybody, always saving people, whether they want it or not."

"But Ehli-nikkalu realized that couldn't go on forever because she's likely to be recalled any day by her father. So she sent me to negotiate with Iwiri-muza. Unfortunately, when I presented myself to him, he was in conference with Utri-sharrumma." Ili-milku made a grimace that said *What luck*.

"Oh, that awful young man. He seems to be everywhere at once lately. I'm so afraid the viceroy will make him king, Ili-milku." Aggrieved, Sharryelli heaved a breath and sat back in her chair.

Ili-milku looked skeptical. "Even if Talmi-tesshub thinks he's associated with the Umman-manda? I thought the viceroy rather disliked them, since he suffers from them as much as we do."

"He may see that as a way of solving two problems at once. Perhaps putting Utri-sharrumma on the throne would make him call off his brigands. Don't you see?"

But Ili-milku shook his head seriously. "I think if he'd ever spent even a short time in Utri-sharrumma's presence, Lord Talmi-tesshub would realize what an uncontrollable factor the pretender is, my lady. I think he'd be an extremely dangerous man on any throne."

"We must be sure the viceroy is aware, then." She pinned him with a significant look and gave a carnivorous smile that sat strangely upon her little pink mouth.

"Yes, indeed."

Sharryelli reached out and took his hand. "I think you should write up the official report on this event, Ili-milku. Make it clear to the viceroy how dangerous that awful boy is and how he must never be put on any throne. Don't you think?"

"With pleasure, my lady."

She squeezed his hand in confirmation. "Is... is there anything else I need to know, my friend?" Sharryelli turned her sweetest, most confidence-worthy smile upon him.

"Need to, my lady? Well..."

"Is Pu-haddu's secret something I ought to know?" She tilted her head confidingly.

Still, he was reluctant. He hadn't forgotten how she had betrayed his own confidences. "Oh, uh. Perhaps no one but she needs to know, I think. Let's just say that were it widely known, Utri-sharrumma's hand would be strengthened."

"But *you* know it, don't you? And the queen..."

Ili-milku knew Sharryelli hated not knowing things, especially when everyone else seemed to be informed of them. But the scribe said nothing.

Everything appeared to have turned out well. Ili-milku was home safe. Lady Pu-haddu was unharmed. Uncle Teshamanu seemed to have received his life back—the life of a man who had put vice behind him at last and regained his nobility. *But what about me?* Amaya asked herself dismally. *I'm still going to be shackled to a stranger just to bring prestige to the family.* Everyone's dreams were fulfilled except hers.

Unable to settle, she drifted out into the street in front of the queen's temporary apartments and stared at the remains of the palace. The entire residential wing had been razed to the ground. She remembered how happy it had made her to find herself and the twins safe there, under the protection of the queen, after Father's death. She had felt that nothing could touch them in Lady Ehli-nikkalu's orbit. But her father's assassination had only been the start of all the dark and terrifying things that had followed—that were still going on.

Holding up her skirts carefully, she made her way into what had once been the royal garden. Desolated, like the rest of her life. She heaved a huge sigh and tried to fight down the anger of betrayal.

"Be careful, my lady—things are unstable and might yet fall," said someone behind her.

She whirled, fearing that a henchman of the regent might have sneaked up on her. But it was only a youth about her own age. He was smiling, a frank and cheerful expression on his face.

"What are you doing on the grounds of the king's house?" she challenged him. He seemed too young to be a scribe.

"The same thing you are—looking around and thinking how lucky I am not to have died here during the earthquake."

She gave a cynical sniff. "I'm not sure that makes me lucky. I'd almost rather be dead than have to be sold into marriage with a stranger." *Oh, stop,* she told herself. *You sound like a spoiled child.* But it felt good to vent her frustration on this bystander whom she would never see again.

"Haven't your parents tried to pick someone who'll be nice to you?" He tilted his head in what seemed to be honest concern. He was a nice-looking young man, scarcely more than a boy, with a neat, short beard.

Amaya said coldly, "My parents are dead. The regent had my father killed. And now I'm supposed to marry one of her sons."

The youth looked sober, then a smile crinkled the corners of his eyes. "Oh no. They're a terrible bunch."

"That's truer than you know. The late king was genuinely awful to his queen. I'd really rather be dead than have a marriage like that. I've always dreamed of living happily together, like my parents, and raising a big family. My little brother and sister deserve something better than the life of orphans."

Now his seriousness seemed real. "Not everybody is like King Niqmaddu." He stared at her in a rather bold way. "I've seen you before, you know."

"Oh?" She rather doubted it, but maybe the youth held some position at the palace—a page, perhaps. There was an assurance in his manner that spoke of privilege. He was no artisan.

"Yes. At the trial of Lord Shipti-ba'al. You struck me as a very brave and intelligent woman"—he smiled again—"Lady Amaya."

Amaya stared at him. *Surely this stripling wasn't on the council?* It was true, she had been so bent on giving her testimony clearly that she'd had eyes for little else. She drew back, feeling almost violated that this man knew all about her and she knew nothing of him, not even his name. She asked, rather more aggressively than was polite, "Who are you?"

"Talmiyannu son of Ibi-ranu."

At first, Amaya couldn't absorb the seeming implication of this name. This was the man to whom she was supposed to be betrothed. The king's uncle. Sharryelli's younger son. Her cheeks burning with shame, Amaya clapped her hands over her mouth. "Oh, forgive me! I've been so rude, my lord." She fell to her knees before the prince, who laughed and motioned her to rise.

"I think you have justification for being angry." Talmiyannu extended a hand to help her up. "But most of us are married off to people we haven't chosen. That's just the way things are." He smiled, but it flickered a bit; it had to be uncomfortable for him, too, to be confronted unexpectedly with the woman provided for his wife. There should have been a chaperone, of course.

Amaya was surprised that she wasn't resentful of the youth. Despite his parentage, he seemed like a decent fellow. And after all—she felt a twinge of humiliation—he hadn't asked for her any more than she had asked for him. She didn't know what to say.

Talmiyannu helped her out. "My brother was a difficult person. I didn't like him much. So it doesn't surprise me that he was unkind to his wife." He looked at Amaya almost shyly. "I'm not at all like him. Or even like my mother. I'm not ambitious at all."

"What are you then?"

The prince laughed again. "I just want to lead a quiet life. Have a nice family. Go to sea and trade, like any merchant."

"So I'd never even see you if we were married?" Amaya asked with a dry smile. "You'd always be at sea?"

"Not always. If my wife were a wonderful woman and my children were wonderful children, then I might settle down and raise horses or something." He grinned. "There are all sorts of possibilities."

Amaya's cheeks grew hot again, but not from shame. She found the prince considerably more attractive than she had expected—a pleasant, unassuming boy. Not terribly tall, but well-built in a slim, adolescent way, with an honest, likable face. It wasn't too hard to imagine being married happily to such a man. She stopped herself. *He's Sharryelli's son. It could be that not a word out of his mouth is true.*

Flustered, she stammered, "Perhaps we shouldn't be here together talking without anyone around. I should go back to the queen's apartments."

"As you wish. It's been a pleasure, though. One doesn't always have this kind of chance." He smiled, looking embarrassed, and dropped his eyes. "I'm honored that your uncle has offered me such a beautiful and intelligent woman."

Her heart unaccountably hammering, Amaya bobbed a bow. *Don't be too quick to lay down your arms,* she told herself and, turning, walked quickly away. Sounding over and over in her thoughts were the words, *Things are unstable and might yet fall...*

It was several days before Ehli-nikkalu called for Teshamanu once more. Her life had been so disrupted by recent events that she had almost forgotten about the writing lessons. Even more than picking up the lessons, she found she wanted to see her secretary, to talk to him about the adventures they had shared. To congratulate him on the happy turn his life had finally taken.

But then, she realized, his status had changed. He was managing Sharryelli's properties now in the absence of Shipti-ba'al. Perhaps he would have no more time or inclination for a secretarial post. She was almost surprised when Shamumanu knocked on the door and announced the *maryannu*'s arrival.

Teshamanu entered and swept a deep bow. When he rose, the queen saw he was smiling. *He's a new man altogether.*

"I don't know if you want to go on with our lessons," she said, feeling unaccountably shy. "But it would please me to continue them until I'm recalled."

"Nothing could give me more pleasure, my lady. I owe you a great deal. You believed in me when I didn't even believe in myself."

"You were unfortunate, that's all. And Iwiri-muza was using you. You've more than paid for your mistakes." Ehli-nikkalu laid a hand on his arm. She wanted to tell him that Pu-haddu had said he was sweet, but it seemed more prudent not to let him know she was aware of the details of his degradation. Instead, she led the way to the big table and, pulling out a stool, prepared to take her seat. "I took the liberty of ordering some wax tablets, in case you wanted to go on."

Teshamanu said hesitantly, "My lady, I... I took your advice and had my vow lifted. I think the gods were not pleased by it. What I had considered piety was just cowardice on my part. Perhaps that's why my luck has turned."

It took the queen a moment to remember what vow he referred to, but then she felt an unreasonable joy that sent a burn to her cheeks. "That's wonderful, Teshamanu. Even if you break your betrothal to the regent's daughter, you'll want to get married to someone. Perhaps you can take the twins in when you have a household set up."

He seemed to have trouble drawing a breath and lowered his eyes. "Unfortunately, the woman I most admire is above me in station. Nothing will ever come of it."

"Oh, I don't know. If Sharryelli accepted you to marry her daughter, she considers you princess worthy. I can't imagine who would be above you." Ehli-nikkalu smiled, a teasing note in her voice. She felt more than a little disappointed that he had settled so soon on another lady. But it was inevitable. He had paid for his wife's death many times over and deserved to take up a normal life again.

Then she realized what he meant. Her heart seemed to rise up her throat like a bird taking off.

He stared at her, a strange intensity in his dark-eyed gaze, until she felt uncomfortable. Uncomfortable yet powerfully attracted. Hardly recognizing herself, she reached up and, without lowering her eyes, unpinned her cap and veil, permitting them to fall to the ground.

They stood staring at one another. Ehli-nikkalu gave her head a shake and let the long, thick mane of her hair fall around her shoulders.

Teshamanu sucked in his breath. "It's so beautiful," he murmured.

She said in a coquettish voice she hardly knew as hers, "I don't want to distract you from that woman you feel unworthy of."

"You are that woman, my lady. From the moment I met you. Always so kind, so courageous, so willing to take risks for others. So beautiful..." He took a step toward her, almost as if he were in a trance.

Her face was burning. She tried to keep her voice playful. "You must be joking. No one has ever accused me of being beautiful."

"Then, they've never looked at you," he said. He took a handful of her thick hair and let it fall from his fingers in a waterfall.

Ehli-nikkalu strode quickly to the door and barred it, then turned to face him again. He had followed her over and was standing only a cubit away, his breath hot on her face. "It's as you said—nothing can come of this, Teshamanu. My father will recall me soon." Her eyes drank in this closest view she had ever had of the man—his heavily lashed black eyes, the warmth of his proximity, the musky smell of a clean male body dressed in wool.

The scribe reached out with his one hand and set to untying the neck of her blouse with surprising dexterity. "Don't we deserve a moment of happiness, then? Something to remember the rest of our lives?"

*A*uthor Note: *Even though women have a surprising number of rights, Ugarit is a patriarchal society, and as her guardian, Teshamanu has complete control over who Amaya marries.*

Unless they're working class, with a trade, or princesses, who might look forward to sharing their husband's rule, women in the Bronze Age would see marriage and a family as the fulfillment of their dreams.

There's someone who believes that everyone is beautiful! And after she stops being so unhappy, Ehli-nikkalu's real nature, kind and generous, can shine.

Chapter 25

Amaya and the children appeared at the queen's door the follow-ing morning. Since it seemed that the threat to their safety had dissipated, they had spent the night at their own house, as they had done with increasing frequency since Shipti-ba'al had been sent to his foreign trade mission. Lady Ehli-nikkalu greeted them with a joy that could only be described as radiant.

"Amaya, my dear. And my favorite twins—or maybe second fa-vorite." Her lips pursed in a suppressed smile as she squatted and gave a kiss to Ba'aluya and Yanakh. "I've arranged for you to play with the king. He loves to be in your company—there are so few children his age at court."

"Look what I brought!" Yanakh drew from behind him a wheeled toy horse. "I bet he doesn't have one of these!"

Ehli-nikkalu laughed. "He's going to meet you in the courtyard. Why don't you run down to wait for him?"

She and Amaya exchanged a smile of fond amusement as the children clattered out the door and down the corridor. Once alone, the two women fell silent. Amaya wanted to tell the queen about her meeting in the garden but wasn't sure how to start. She didn't want to exaggerate her feelings. Surely, her attitude couldn't have changed overnight as dramatically as it seemed to have done. And yet there was that shy burn of her cheeks, the unaccountable desire to laugh for joy and dance around, to talk about Talmiyannu and describe his frank good looks to all comers.

They got out their spindles, and she wrapped a puffy rove of wool around the distaff. Outside, the noises from the worksite across the street resounded dully in the cold air.

Amaya struggled to concentrate on her work until, at last, she said with an effort at a casual tone, "I met Prince Talmiyannu yesterday."

Ehli-nikkalu looked up. Her long mouth was curled at the ends. "Oh? Did Sharryelli push him on you?"

Amaya would have preferred not to blush—she didn't think of herself as the blushing sort. "No. We met by accident in the palace garden—what's left of it. We had no chaperone."

"That sounds like Sharryelli's doing, all right."

"Oh, I think it was just accidental." She dropped her eyes momentarily while the queen watched her with intensity. "He's actually quite a nice person. Not like his brother at all." She was aware that these were Talmiyannu's own words, but the facts seemed to bear him out.

The queen continued to observe Amaya over her spindle, saying nothing, her greenish eyes wide, her mouth twitching with affectionate amusement.

"I don't think I would mind so much being married to him. I don't know how I'd ever meet anyone else unless by total coincidence."

"Do what you feel you should, my dear. No one will force you. Your uncle believes in love too. He doesn't want you to be miserable."

"He doesn't want to marry me anymore?"

Ehli-nikkalu laughed. "He never did. We just thought he might when he needed gold so badly, remember? Now his debts are no more, and he's comfortable, thanks to your testimony against Shipti-ba'al. Not to mention his new job managing the regent's properties, since Shipti-ba'al's in gilded exile at the trading mission in Mizri." She reached out and stroked the girl's hair affectionately. "Don't forget the message of the Katharat. They want you to be happy."

Yes, the pigeons, Amaya remembered, a happy warmth igniting in her heart. It seemed significant now. *Perhaps the goddesses were speaking to me after all.* She hardly dared to believe that this providential meeting was an answer to her prayers. If only she could set up a happy household and the twins wouldn't have to go to the ends of the kingdom, abandoning all their little friends here in the city. Perhaps she owed it to them to take the chance. She thought it wouldn't be too painful a sacrifice after all.

Lady Ehli-nikkalu watched her with a penetrating, benevolent gaze, her eyes sparkling. She asked in a tender tone, "Isn't it wonderful to be in love?"

Two weeks passed, and Ehli-nikkalu was sure she had never been happier. Busy with the rebuilding of the palace, Sharryelli left her alone. And everyone knew Ehli-nikkalu's days in Ugarit were numbered; she no longer mattered in the slightest. She wasn't even worth tormenting. Her writing lessons had once more become the centerpiece of her day, as—to their mutual pleasure—Teshamanu insisted on finding the time despite his new duties.

"Good morning, my lady," he said with a bow as he appeared at the door that morning. His expression was mild, happy in his rough, quiet way.

It was hard to believe anyone could change so much so quickly. *You never know what unpleasant people may be going through, what they're really like inside,* Ehli-nikkalu told herself, marveling. And she wondered what changes others saw in her.

"I'm ready to work," she said with a smile that she suspected was almost arch—she, the serious, censorious Great Lady, always standing on her rank.

They seated themselves side by side at the big table, and Teshamanu spread out the wax tablets he had brought for practice.

She began to copy the lines he had produced for her, and after a while, the secretary took her hand and guided it firmly. A thrill of warmth passed from his fingers to hers.

Laughing, she corrected his pronunciation of the Neshite words, pleased to bring something, too, to their banquet of shared learning.

Upon occasion, they would lay aside the lesson and learn something more important. She had been married for seven years and had never known how much joy a man and a woman could generate—what flames the fire stick and the bow could ignite. She felt she had become another person, and Teshamanu too. Better people, freed from so much of the mud that had weighed down their steps.

Do I still pity him, or is it something truer I feel? He was no longer a man who needed pity, she thought. Her first reaction to the scarred stump of his arm had been a cringe of real anguish to imagine what such a terrible injury must have felt like. But Teshamanu, like the soldier he had been, shrugged it off. Pain was part of the job. It was past. And so, she discovered that love can also be dyed with admiration.

Toward the end of the morning, just as Teshamanu was preparing to leave, the chamberlain announced the arrival of Amaya and the children. Although they occupied their own house these days, the girl came daily to serve, and the children had a regular appointment to play with the young king. Ba'aluya stayed with her sister and the queen, learning to spin and be a royal lady-in-waiting, while Yanakh accompanied Ammurapi to some of his lessons. Ehli-nikkalu was aware of how much advantage it would be to him when he grew up to have been a childhood companion of his sovereign.

Although she knew these weeks were only a hiatus, she never wanted them to end.

But at last, Sharryelli summoned Ehli-nikkalu to her residence. The regent sat at her table at the end of a long upstairs room with tall windows that looked out across the city wall. Away below lay the white cubes of the port and the sea, with its misty silver horizon.

"A letter from your father has arrived," Sharryelli said. She managed to control what had to be her relief under a glaze of businesslike regret. "No doubt you'll have received one too. He's ready to recall you."

At last, Ehli-nikkalu thought. But she realized it was only force of habit that made her react that way. What she really wanted to cry out was *Not now...* She just tipped her head in acquiescence, hoping it would cover her disappointment. "I am at his disposal."

"Well then, my dear. I guess that's it. We've already talked about the sale of your properties and the return of your dowry." The regent eyed her daughter-in-law up and down, as if waiting for some kind of reaction.

And indeed, once, Ehli-nikkalu would have taken this moment to blast Sharryelli with all the accusations that had festered in her heart for seven years. But she felt lightened, magnanimous. The limitations of her mother-in-law were so glaring to her that she could hardly be bothered to recall them. Sharryelli just wasn't particularly smart—even her malices were mediocre. Ehli-nikkalu said blandly, "Very well."

"The viceroy will be here shortly to accompany you to Hattusha." The regent caught her eye. "I suppose you'll be glad to go, won't you?"

"I suppose I will."

But will I? Ehli-nikkalu thought of all the people she would be sorry to leave behind. Their lives would go on, but without her. Amaya married—happily, the queen prayed—and the twins settled in a loving home. Ili-milku back to his work in the chancery with no more adventures but plenty of ideas for poems. Pu-haddu secure in her quiet role as mother of King Ammurapi. Teshamanu... *What does his future look like?* Married, too, unquestionably—a nice-looking man like that. Taking his place as the eldest member of a noble family on the council. Growing prosperous and staid. Content.

As she rode in her litter back to Yabninu's mansion, Ehli-nikkalu wondered what her own life was likely to become. Probably destined for a second loveless marriage to some vassal of wavering loyalty. At the age of thirty-five, with a reputation for barrenness, she wouldn't be much of a prize. She was a bit deflated by the time she entered her own chambers.

And there sat the letter from her father—or rather, his chancery. She eyed it, but she still couldn't read a real correspondence in a scribal hand. The familiar round seal impression showed it was official, and she knew what it contained. Therefore, she felt neither excitement nor dread, only a dull resignation. She turned the clay tablet over in her hand.

"Shamumanu, find my secretary, please," she called. "I want him as soon as he's free of his other duties." *How ironic. It will be Teshamanu who announces my departure—who sends me away, in a sense.*

She mustered a huge sigh and tried to picture her father, her grandmother, her brothers and sisters. She hadn't embraced them—or even seen them—in more than seven years. *Did they miss me as I missed them? And seven years after I've left here, will my friends miss me? Will I miss them?* She would. She knew she would. And the person she was now would bear their imprint on her heart like the imprint of a seal.

Teshamanu arrived, bowed, and took the seat she offered him. He had a *maryannu*'s courteous manners with a little of the rough honesty of a soldier. She liked that. Her father had the same unvarnished lack of pretension about him.

"Teshamanu, I think this is my recall. Could you read it to me, please?"

He looked stricken but recovered himself quickly and said with a sad smile, "If I destroy the letter, would that mean you hadn't been recalled?"

She leaned against him, suddenly struck with faintness. Her cheery self-control wobbled, and her eyes smarted. "Sharryelli has a copy too. We can't stop it—we've known that. This has just been a wonderful interlude."

He nodded, as if not trusting himself to speak, but then, because it had to be done, he cracked open the clay envelope of the letter and began to read it. "Tudhaliya, Great King, son of Hattushili, Great King and hero in Hattusha. To his daughter, the Great Lady Ehli-nikkalu in Ugarit. May our daughter know that since her marriage is ended, we have decided to call her back to our side. She will take her place as wife of the governor of Hakpish, our cousin Tanhuwatassha. He is ill, and her experience as the helpmeet of a ruler will be of value to him. It would also be ideal if she could provide him with an heir before he passes down the Great Way."

There was more, but Ehli-nikkalu scarcely heard it. She remembered Tanhuwatassha from those happy days in the royal nursery. He wasn't much older than herself, and now, it seemed, he was sick. Her heart contracted with pity.

Teshamanu noticed her distraction. "You know this person?"

She nodded. "We were children together, although never close. He's my father's cousin but nearer to my age. Always easygoing and funny. I'm sorry he's not well."

The secretary pressed his lips together and dropped his eyes. "He has at least one piece of good fortune."

"Every time I touch him, I'll pretend it's you," Ehli-nikkalu promised, her eyes devouring Teshamanu as if she could keep him with her inside as a memory.

He forced a smile.

A gloomy cloud of farewell hung over them for the rest of the morning. Despite the fact that the year was moving toward spring, some of the melancholy of autumn fogged the air, stirred the falling leaves of their happiness. Prophesied an absence they were both too mature to weep over—aloud.

The next day, Ehli-nikkalu woke up ill. Her stomach heaved as if she were on the deck of a ship; the very smell of food sent her retching. But later, she felt better and regretted having sent Teshamanu away without their lesson. Perhaps he would think she was weaning herself away from him. Amaya spun quietly in the vestibule with the handmaids until the queen called her in at the end of the morning.

"Are you all right, my lady?" she asked solicitously. "You look very pale."

"I feel much better now, Amaya. Thank you. It must have been something I ate. I'm hardly ever sick," she said with a pallid smile. She started to pick up her spindle and distaff but then thought better of it. "Let's take a look at my things and start to pack them. I don't know when the viceroy is coming, and I want to be ready to go." *No, I don't,* she realized. *I don't want to go at all.*

Amaya shot her a look wise beyond her years. "Of course, my lady." She rose and began to collect the rovings of wool that filled the royal spinning basket. Finally, she said quietly, "Do you really want to go? After all that's happened?"

Ehli-nikkalu faced her frankly. "No. No, I don't. Even though there's no place for me here anymore. I don't love my family any less. It's just that..." Embarrassed and unable to say what she wanted to, she told Amaya about her father's letter and her new duties. As she spoke, she gazed out the long window. In the cold, cloudless sky of a winter midday, the full moon hung, pale, its scarred and peeling face barely visible. "Lord Arma," the queen murmured, "is something wrong with me that I no longer want to go home?"

Amaya watched her. "You have friends here now."

"Yes." Ehli-nikkalu opened a jewel box listlessly. "Who knows what I'm going toward? Hakpish is a high, cold little city that doesn't have much except a great temple of the Storm God. At least I'll have important duties. A husband who's a decent man." *But not someone I love...*

"I think you'll be a wonderful wife to him. You're so compassionate."

"Love and pity are not the same thing," the queen said with a rueful smile.

The following morning, Ehli-nikkalu was sick again. *Surely, I didn't eat something bad again,* she thought, panting over her basin. She wanted to see Teshamanu, but it was only too clear that she wouldn't be able to follow her lessons today. And she didn't want him feeling sorry for her.

Why is that, when I want to feel everyone else's sorrow? She wiped her mouth and splashed some cold water on her cheeks. *Perhaps it's a kind of arrogance and not compassion at all. A sense that I'm better and filled with something they lack. If they were to reciprocate, it would mean I was the one who was lacking.* The thought brought a flush of humiliation to her face. Her mother-in-law had accused her of acting superior to everyone, and it seemed it was true after all. She had really believed that. That she could fix people's lives, could save the lost.

Suddenly, shame overwhelmed her, and tears burned in her eyes. She felt very precariously emotional, as if she could laugh just as easily as cry, but neither quite expressed what she felt. She was immensely relieved when Shamumanu announced at the door that Lady Puhaddu had come for a visit.

The king's mother appeared, her face luminous.

It takes so little to make her happy, Ehli-nikkalu thought tenderly. *Now that she's free of the terrible fear of Iwiri-muza and his secret, Puhaddu has everything she wants. No power—but she has her children. Someone to love.*

Pu-haddu glanced at the basin and said hesitantly, "Would you prefer me to go away, my lady? If you're not well..."

"No. I'm fine now. For the last few days, I seem to have had a touch of nausea. But it passes quickly."

Pu-haddu looked at her with a curious tilt of the head. "Is it... is it morning sickness, my lady? I don't suppose you could be..."

Suddenly, it hit Ehli-nikkalu with the force of a blow. Her hair rose on the back of her neck as the truth penetrated. *Haven't I watched my mother carry seven children? I'm pregnant!* Of course. She should have noticed the absence of her monthly courses, except so much had been happening that she hadn't even given it a thought.

Her instinct was to shout aloud in triumph, *There was nothing wrong with me all along!* Then she wanted to laugh in delight—she would be carrying this dear memento of her years in Ugarit among her friends. Such beloved friends. But finally, *What will they say at home? My husband has been dead for months. Even if they believe it's Niqmaddu's child, will they feel duty bound to send the little one back, property of his supposed father's dynasty?*

Pu-haddu watched the queen's face. As if she had read Ehli-nikkalu's mind, she said, "This only starts a month or two after the baby's conceived. It must be Niqmaddu's." She seized Ehli-nikkalu's hands. "After you waited so long! Our children will be brothers!"

With Ammurapi, though, not the younger ones, the queen thought uneasily. She knew, as Pu-haddu didn't, how long it had been since Niqmaddu had taken her to bed. But joy and a sense of vindication were gaining ground over her fears. She said, "I won't let them separate him from me. He'll grow up a Hittite prince, and no one will think of his father." *Except me. And I'll no longer be the poor barren woman everyone pities or holds in contempt.*

Amaya, too, had seen her mother bear other children, and she recognized quickly what the queen's solitary mornings were about. She was so happy for Ehli-nikkalu that she hardly knew what to say. "You see, my lady? The Katharat had a blessing for you too!" she cried, clasping Ehli-nikkalu's hands.

The queen blushed, which made her look almost girlish and pretty. "We'll offer something nice to them. Only I don't want Sharryelli to know, or she'll try to make my father send the child back. You and I will offer in secret."

"And Uncle?"

The queen's smile faded, and she took on a nearly frightened air. "No. Because he'll never see the little one. It would only break his heart to find out—another child he doesn't even know about, poor man."

Amaya stared at her, not sure what she meant. There was something more complex going on here than she could fathom. It was clear. The girl said shyly, not wanting to subtract from the queen's joyous news, "Lady Sharryelli wants Talmiyannu and me to marry right after the spring festival. The viceroy will be here. I'm so sad that you'll be gone."

"Oh, I won't be gone. We won't be able to get to Hattusha before the spring thaw, and Hakpish will be even more inaccessible." The queen beamed and took Amaya's face between her hands. "I wouldn't miss this for anything, my dear. You still feel it's the right thing to do?"

The girl nodded, her cheeks growing warm. "We've talked often, and I think he's a really good person. His mother has always left him alone because he wasn't the heir to the throne, and his father was his model. Everyone says King Ibi-ranu was a fine person and that Niqmaddu resented being compared to him all the time. But not Talmiyannu."

Lady Ehli-nikkalu laughed. "You've gotten all the palace gossip, I see. Well, I've never heard anything bad about your prince. As long as he appreciates how lucky he is to have you, you'll get on well."

Author Note: A widowed princess is too good an asset not to make use of! Hakpish is part of Hatti Land but administered by a governor who ranks as a king, so Ehli-nikkalu isn't demoted by the match.

No one would have admitted that sterility was the fault of anyone but the woman! But Ehli-nikkalu has the last laugh.

Chapter 26

The last weeks of winter passed imperceptibly into spring, the damp chill of the air growing mild and caressing. Ships set out upon the sea once more. Lambs frolicked in the pastures. The rains withdrew in silvery curtains across the water, and the fields were yet again strewn with flowers until the roadside shimmered with their warm perfume. Ehli-nikkalu told herself more than once, *It's good to be alive. It's good to be in love*—even though every day brought her closer to her departure.

Along with Amaya, the queen concentrated on the girl's upcoming wedding. Amaya had no mother. *Who else can prepare everything for her—the flowery wedding canopy, the beautiful garments, the sacrificial banquet that will draw the entire populace of the city into the festivities?* Sharryelli had her role to play, to be sure. It was her son, an uncle of the king, who was the groom. But Ehli-nikkalu made as many arrangements as she could immediately so she could present the regent with an accomplished fact. This day would not be a triumph for Sharryelli, she swore. Nor would Amaya's marriage put the girl under the regent's thumb.

Lord Talmi-tesshub, the viceroy, arrived from Karkemish the day before the spring equinox. He would preside at the wedding then accompany Ehli-nikkalu north overland, in style, with a great train of servants and luxurious possessions. In a matter of weeks, she would be home.

And now, the joyous crowds filled the royal plaza, where the ceremony would take place. It wasn't quite as lavish as her own nuptials, which had united Crown Prince Niqmaddu to the Great Lady of Hatti, but a son of the regent deserved a festive celebration.

The steps of the royal chapel on the north side of the plaza were decked with flowers, and the colorful raiment of the noble guests spilled down the staircase like a living flowerbed of bright wool and jewels. The marriage canopy was erected. Musicians had taken their place along the city wall. Crowds of commoners, eager to see the spectacle and share in the wedding banquet, packed the plaza, everyone glad to put winter behind them. Ehli-nikkalu, on the temple porch, could see from her tall vantage point the even taller head of the viceroy. Once, the sight of one of her people would have filled her with contentment. Now...

The ceremony was nearly over. Talmiyannu had pinned the veil of a married woman on Amaya's cap, and Amaya, facing Ehli-nikkalu, was all but shining with happiness. The musicians struck up a joyous hymn to the seven daughters of the New Moon, and the queen dabbed surreptitiously at her nose. Suddenly, above the heads of the royal family standing before her on the porch, she glimpsed in the crowd below a thin, pretty woman who struck her as vaguely familiar, although she couldn't place the person. A thrill of unease fluttered in Ehli-nikkalu's stomach. *Who is that? I know her face.*

To the triumphant strains of fanfare, the newly married couple proceeded down the steps, and the royal family—Ehli-nikkalu included—and eminent guests fell in behind them. Teshamanu, as the guardian of the bride, walked at the queen's elbow. For these, the marriage feast would be held in one of the banquet halls of the palace that had been rebuilt.

The populace at large, laughing and talking, made their way to the gate into the city, where sweets and grain and the roasted meat that had been sanctified to the gods were available to share. Ehli-nikkalu's gaze drifted in curiosity toward the press at the food distribution tables. *I'm pleased to see so many people taking advantage of the food,* she told herself with a swell of self-satisfaction. She had paid for this public treat, cutting in before Sharryelli could take over the gesture.

As if he had overheard her thoughts, Teshamanu said under his breath, "The people will be sorry to see you leave, my lady."

But now that her attention was on the food distribution, Ehli-nikkalu noticed something. Despite the protestations of the busy butchers, several people seemed to have taken whole joints of meat, leaving their neighbors to object indignantly. A little boy was crying after even the small slice in his hands was snatched away.

"Look at those selfish pigs. We can't let that go on." Breaking out of the procession and forcing her way through the crush, she waded toward the congestion. Those who had snagged the meat melted into the crowd and disappeared before she could assail them, but others hovered around the tables as if watching for a chance.

"You! Stop!" She waved her arms at the harassed butchers. "Make those people share the meat. No one is supposed to get a whole animal." This belonged to her, after all, and her face was flushed with anger. *Who do these people think they are?*

A veiled woman scuttled past her, her bundled skirt full of raisin buns and sweetmeats. Ehli-nikkalu snatched at her arm, outraged, and the woman turned. It was the person the queen had seen a short while before; her thin, strikingly pretty face and amber eyes were unmistakable. She stared piercingly at Ehli-nikkalu with a vulpine smile, and all at once, the queen gasped.

"Utri-sharrumma! Stop him! Stop him, soldiers!" Ehli-nikkalu yelled. She grabbed at the little man's arm and tried to drag him back, but with surprising strength, he wrenched free and evaporated into the press around him.

Teshamanu, whose broader body had been caught in the crowd, finally appeared at the queen's side. "What is it?"

"The pretender—he's here! Gods forbid he's come for Amaya!"

Soldiers who appeared among the crowd found their way hampered by the clustered bodies that surrounded them. Indeed, Ehli-nikkalu would have sworn that the uniformed men made little effort to respond to her.

"They're all Umman-manda!" she cried in desperate realization. "Teshamanu, all those people robbing the tables are Utri-sharrumma's followers. Oh, why didn't I report the rebel guards before so they could be replaced?"

Teshamanu said nothing, but like a warhorse eager for battle, he forced his way into the crowd in the direction of Ehli-nikkalu's pointing finger. Almost immediately, he disappeared, and the queen was left combing the crowd with anxious eyes.

For a moment, she stood there, frozen, taller than almost all of the mob but helpless and surrounded by enemies. Fear stopped her mouth. The crowd had lost its jollity, and everyone seemed to turn upon her with hostile, rapacious expressions. Her heart was pounding. *Dear gods, grant that Amaya is safe—and the little king. Surely these people won't try to force their way into the palace.* Yet, of course, the sturdy walls that might have discouraged all but the hardiest were lying, in part, in ruin. *He's going to make his bid for the throne!*

She was alone in a hostile mob. This was where her meddling had gotten her. "Oh, Teshamanu, where are you?" she moaned under her breath. She put a hand over her belly, as if to protect the small life within her.

Ehli-nikkalu began to fight her way toward the palace porch. She could see the guard box beside the gate completely empty, and her heart sank. If only she could get word to the viceroy and his loyal men inside. But it was like trying to swim against a powerful current. No one had broken out arms, yet the crowd itself was an inexorable force that swept her farther and farther from the porch. "Teshamanu!" she cried, knowing he couldn't hear her from wherever he was.

And now some of the Umman-manda had wrested the butchers' bloody knives from their hands and brandished them aloft in triumph. Innocent citizens screamed and tried to flee with their families, only to be blocked, as the queen was, by the inertia of the mob itself. Someone pulled off her veil, almost falling over her in their flight, dragging her down. She cried out in terror as bodies around her stumbled on top.

I'll be knocked to the ground and crushed. The baby… The blood beat in her temples. "Teshamanu!"

Suddenly, the congestion of the mob seemed to release, and the Umman-manda began to suck away like the outflow of the tide.

Where are they going? Ehli-nikkalu couldn't have said. *Into the city proper? Out the royal gate into the road to the port?*

A shrill command of pipes sounded from the direction of the palace, and shouts and heavy footsteps revealed the approach of the viceroy's troops from within, along with a detachment of the loyal local soldiers. The panic-stricken people tried to reunite their families then grasped at their food—what little of it the Umman-manda had spared—and scuttled for the exits.

Gasping, Ehli-nikkalu dragged herself up the porch steps. Ili-milku burst from the doorway, his eyes popping, the viceroy at his heels. "What happened, my lady? When you didn't show up at the banquet, we didn't know what to think."

Talmi-tesshub looked grave. "My guards said there was a riot. Are you all right, my lady?"

"It was the Umman-manda. They were taking all the food, so I went over there to protest. At first, I didn't know what was happening, then I saw Utri-sharrumma—"

"What? Right here in the royal plaza during a public ceremony?" The viceroy's long jaw dropped in disbelief.

Ili-milku gave a simultaneous squawk of incredulity.

Giddy with relief, the queen began to laugh. "I kept yelling, 'Stop him!' but he was dressed as a woman. I'm sure no one knew who I was talking about."

"So, he got away again?" the viceroy asked.

"I'm almost sure he did. Teshamanu ran after him, but chances aren't good he could have found him in that crowd." *I just hope Teshamanu's safe.* Ehli-nikkalu recomposed herself with effort. She patted her head and realized she had no veil. No matter; it was no moment for proprieties.

"This must stop," the viceroy said grimly, staring out across the emptying plaza. His fists at his sides were clenched with resolve. "If the local government can't control these people, then I'll have to step in. But it must stop."

"Some of the guards were part of them. They didn't even try to intervene," she said.

Talmi-tesshub's lip curled with disgust.

Ili-milku took the queen respectfully by the elbow and said to the viceroy, "My lord, perhaps we should return to the banquet room. The young couple deserves not to have their feast spoiled."

Talmi-tesshub spun on his heel and made his way inside the great doors, Ehli-nikkalu and the chief scribe trailing. They exchanged a glance.

As they passed through the empty, darkened throne room, Sharryelli came hurtling toward them, wringing her hands. "Someone said the Umman-manda were here," she cried in distress. "Those wretches! This must stop."

The viceroy drilled her with a meaningful look. He was a tall, lean, formidable-looking man who reduced the regent to the proportions of a plump child. "It must indeed."

"Will Lady Ehli-nikkalu's party be safe on the road tomorrow?" Ili-milku asked under his breath.

"At least as safe as she would be within the walls of the city," Talmi-tesshub said dryly.

Ehli-nikkalu couldn't repress a thrill of satisfaction at the veiled rebuke of Sharryelli.

While the viceroy made his way outside to supervise his soldiers, everyone else drifted back to the banquet hall. Here and there, faces were raised in curiosity. Ehli-nikkalu saw the eyes of Ili-milku fixed on her in concern, and beside his mother, King Ammurapi stared, feet swinging.

Amaya sat beside the couch of her new husband, a little goddess wreathed in flowers. As the queen slipped into her own place, the girl caught Ehli-nikkalu's gaze and leaned closer to her. Her eyes asked the question she was too discreet to put into words in public.

"Our little friend is back," Ehli-nikkalu whispered.

Amaya's jaw dropped. "Here? With the viceroy present? Was that awful man purposely disrupting my wedding, do you think?"

Ehli-nikkalu twitched a shoulder in an unobtrusive shrug and forced herself to eat the mashed and seasoned chickpeas the servant left at her table, trying not to be self-conscious about her bare head. "I'll tell you about it later." She had a terrible suspicion Utri-sharrumma had had more in mind than raiding the sacrificial meat. This beginning of a new season would have made a symbolic moment for him to try to reclaim the throne—and perhaps the bride with whom he seemed so obsessed.

A brief space of time passed before a soldier of the viceroy slipped into the hall and leaned down to whisper to the regent. Sharryelli sprang from her seat and rushed excitedly from the room, leaving the guests looking back and forth in confusion.

A moment later, the man approached Ili-milku. "My lord, Lord Talmi-tesshub requires your presence outside, if you please," he said under his breath.

Maybe, at last, I'll find out what's going on, he thought. The chief scribe slid out from behind the small table and scurried off toward the doorway of the palace, dimly conscious of Lady Ehli-nikkalu in his wake.

They burst out onto the porch, with its cherubim columns. Overhead, the afternoon sun was beaming down from the pristine blue sky upon a royal court that was mostly cleared of occupants. Only a few slaves bent over their brooms, tidying up the debris. A ring of the viceroy's soldiers surrounded the entrance to the guardhouse beside the gate into the outer city, which was now shut.

"Where do we go?" Ili-milku asked uneasily.

At that moment, the viceroy stepped from the guardhouse and, seeing the queen approaching, held up a hand. The two of them hastened their steps. Ili-milku grew more and more nervous. Talmi-tesshub's face told him nothing. Sharryelli, too, peeked out, and the door was shut from within behind her. She looked anxious and relieved at the same time.

"My lady, my lord, we need you to identify the prisoner," the viceroy said. He led them into the guardhouse.

The small room was filled with people. Teshamanu, bruised and disheveled but looking unhurt, stood to one side, his thumb hooked in his sash. He caught Ehli-nikkalu's eye and grinned. Within a circle of guardsmen, a woman sat on the floor, her torn-off veil revealing wild hair cropped to the shoulder in masculine style. Although her mouth was dripping blood and her wrists were bound, she stared up in amusement at the newcomers, amber eyes glittering.

"Is that Prince Utri-sharrumma?" the viceroy asked. "Teshamanu wasn't completely sure."

Ili-milku nodded. He would have known those mad eyes any-where.

"It certainly is, my lord, despite his disguise." Ehli-nikkalu looked the pretender up and down, and he smiled his cheerful, mocking smile, somewhat marred by a bloody gap in the middle. "You've lost a tooth," she said.

The viceroy snorted. "That will just make his head lighter when it rolls from his body."

"Ooh, they're going to execute me? That seems a little exalted for a man who is only trying to regain his stolen kingdom." The pre-tender seemed as delighted as if he had been promised a reward.

"You're not being arrested for that, since nothing you did here today was openly seditious," Talmi-tesshub said with a curl of the lip. "In fact, I was seriously considering your candidacy. But as leader of the Umman-manda, even beheading is too good for you."

"What makes you think I'm the leader of the Umman-manda?" Utri-sharrumma asked in a genuinely curious voice.

"Why, you told me so yourself," Ehli-nikkalu said, smiling in tri-umph. "I heard you with my own ears."

But the pretender fixed his foxy eyes on her, round with pretend innocence. "Were there any witnesses to that so-called confession, cousin? Because, otherwise, it seems to be your word against mine."

"My lord?" Talmi-tesshub turned to the scribe. "Did he ever say anything to you when you were his prisoner?"

"Er, no," Ili-milku had to admit. "I couldn't even swear from my own experience alone that he had anything to do with them. It was Iwiri-muza who was his confederate."

Ehli-nikkalu's cheeks flamed, and she drew herself up to her full height. "Is my word not good enough? I am a princess of Hatti Land."

"And I," Utri-sharrumma said with his daft smile, "am a prince of Hatti Land."

An uncomfortable silence fell upon the little crowd. Sharryelli gaped at the viceroy as if to say, *But you promised me*, while he knit his brows and looked troubled. Ili-milku and Teshamanu exchanged an anxious stare, then the chief scribe shrugged regretfully at the queen.

At last, Utri-sharrumma let out a wild, cackling laugh. "Oh, look! As a male, I outrank you! Isn't that fun?"

Ehli-nikkalu glared from face to face as if she could hardly believe her ears. She must have been furious that they weren't going to accept her word against this madman's just because she was a woman. "Then why was Amaya's word taken before that of Shipti-ba'al? He denied the crime she accused him of too," she said in a trembling voice.

The viceroy let a sigh out through his nose. "He wasn't a prince of Hatti. I'm on my way to Hattusha in the morning. I'll ask Our Sun for a ruling. In the meantime, this man is to be held here under strict watch. But give him the comforts of a guest." Talmi-tesshub turned and departed the small room, no doubt relieved to be out of the queen's accusing sight. The others were left staring at one another.

"Ili-milku," the prisoner said, patting his bloody lips, "I have a line in my latest poem I'd like you to listen to."

The next morning Ehli-nikkalu awoke far too early, but finding she couldn't fall back asleep, she eventually rose and dressed without waking any servants. She slid from Yabni-shapshu's mansion into the street. It was still chilly, and she wrapped herself in her shawl. The sky was barely light, a pearly, colorless mist softened the white-washed buildings around her, and her soft shoes scuffed quietly on the paving stones.

In a few hours, I'll be gone. In a few weeks, I'll be home. Such a thought seemed unreal. Perhaps everything seemed unreal at this moment neither day nor night. Somehow, her fury over the injustice of Utri-sharrumma's situation had become remote. Teshamanu had risked his life to capture the man... and then this. The pretender would probably be turned loose. *Father is famous for his clemency.* And for once, that didn't elicit her admiration. But it would be someone else's problem.

She wandered toward the city wall, which was still intact here, and climbed the stairs to the ramparts. A pair of soldiers making their rounds turned to identify her then let her lean against the parapet overlooking the road to the port. On the road below, the barbican that guarded the royal gate bristled with watchful troops, and as she observed, they extinguished their torches before the rising sun. Even so was a chapter of her life being extinguished. She thought of Teshamanu and that she would never see him again. *He risked his life for me yesterday.*

She turned back, her heart heavy, and who should be approaching but Teshamanu and Ili-milku, their heads together in conversation. They looked up and saw her and dropped in deep bows.

"We'll miss you, my lady," the chief scribe said with a melancholy smile. "Things will be dull."

"You mean because no one will be causing problems with her attempts to make things right?" she said, her voice sharp with self-blame. "If I had reported the disloyal guards as soon as we came home the first time, this never would have happened. Amaya's beautiful wedding wouldn't have been spoiled."

Teshamanu assured her, "Amaya's wedding wasn't spoiled, my lady. She'll never forget that day." His gaze lingered on Ehli-nikkalu's.

She tried hungrily to memorize his face—its dark, fringed eyes, the crescent nose, and strong cheekbones—and perhaps he was doing the same with her. *I love you,* she thought. *That's what this spear-*

point is in my heart. I love you, and I have to say goodbye forever. So much for the honor of being a princess of Hatti. It just means I get traded around to reward kings and can't be with the one I want.

Ili-milku shot a sideways glance at his colleague, and Ehli-nikkalu wondered what he knew. "We'll be going, my lady. I'm sure you have many things to see to before you set off. I understand Lord Talmi-tesshub wants to leave as soon as the sun is fully up." The chief scribe smiled at her kindly.

"You've been a real friend, Ili-milku. I put your life in danger, and you never blamed me." Her voice had grown wobbly. "I endangered your life, too, Teshamanu. Forgive me, both of you."

Then, to her utter amazement, Teshamanu put his arm around her waist, drew her to him, and kissed her on the mouth. She stood there, pressed against the warmth of his chest, her own arms stealing around his back as if she could anchor herself to him. When she caught her breath, they stepped apart, and she felt the tears trickling down her cheeks. Ili-milku stood watching with a benevolent and knowing expression.

"Goodbye, my lady." Teshamanu lowered his eyes, suddenly afflicted with shyness. "I wish you happiness."

She nodded, speechless, throbbing, and the two men made their way down the staircase. Her eyes lingered with longing on Teshamanu's broad, erect back.

From the royal plaza below sounded a blare of trumpets. A man called, "Form up!" and grooms began to lead horses and donkeys in from the stable outside the city gate. Slow oxcarts creaked in from the neighboring streets, and servants appeared as if by magic, piling the carts and pack animals with baggage and supplies for a long journey for many people.

By the time the sun had broken its shadows over the palace roof, the party was ready. The viceroy had gone up and down the procession to be sure everyone was present. Then, just as Ehli-nikkalu was preparing to climb into her carriage, Amaya came running, the twins at her side.

The children were waving and yelling, "Don't leave yet! We haven't said goodbye!"

The queen turned back and crouched to take them in her arms. "I don't want to leave you, sweet children. Promise me you'll live happy lives. Your sister will take care of you."

"We have something to give you," Yanakh said, bashful for once.

"Nobody else in Hattusha will have one," Ba'aluya informed her earnestly.

The little boy drew from behind his back the worn and soiled toy horse on wheels he so loved to play with and thrust it into the queen's hands. "We want you to be happy too," he mumbled.

Ehli-nikkalu was blinded by a cataract of tears, and she clung to the children for a moment, her face buried in the little girl's soft neck. "It will make me happy. It will!"

At last, she looked up at Amaya with swimming eyes. "And you, my dear sister. I pray the Katharat and the Hutellura will make you the happiest of all. Thank you for everything."

Amaya threw her arms around the queen. "Oh no, my lady. I'm the one who has to thank you. You treated us like members of your family. We'll never forget your kindness. Don't forget us either."

"Never, never." Ehli-nikkalu was beyond speech now, mucus running down her lip unwiped. "You've taught me so much..."

"Everybody, mount up," came the order from down the line.

Ehli-nikkalu pulled herself up into the carriage while Rab-ilu's children stepped back. The royal plaza was filled with the pleasurable tension of departure—the jingling of harnesses, the clopping hooves of restive animals, shouted commands. A sense of change was in the air—a new season. A new life.

On the porch of the palace, between the *karubuma* columns, stood Sharryelli, waggling her fingers in a half-hearted gesture of Godspeed.

I'll wager she's relieved.

Pu-haddu and the little king were beside her, waving wildly. Courtiers and officials packed the space to give the Great Lady of Hatti an appropriate send-off, and Ehli-nikkalu thought she saw Ili-milku and Teshamanu among the scribes.

She laid a hand on her belly, on the living souvenir within. *Someone to love.*

"Goodbye," she called. "Goodbye. Goodbye."

*A*uthor Note: *Utri-sharrumma takes advantage of any breach of security to feed his followers. It won't surprise you to know that people like the Umman actually end up bringing down the kingdoms of the Late Bronze Age.*

Being a blood relation of the Great King of Hatti (his nephew) gives Utri-sharrumma an almost insurmountable status. No plain old torture and death for a prince of the blood.

And so Ehli-nikkalu's years in Ugarit come to an end. She does, in fact, go to Hakpish to marry Tanhuwatassha, but we don't know if she is happy there. I like to think she is.

Acknowledgments

The author gratefully acknowledges all those who have helped her in the production of this book.

To the wonderful women of my writers' group, for their critique and encouragement, my thanks.

To Lynn McNamee and her editorial team at Red Adept, profound gratitude—a book is no better than its editors.

To the flexible and talented gang at Streetlight Graphics, my kudos for the cover.

And most of all, to my husband, Ippokratis, who put up with the months of fixation it takes to write a novel, many, many thanks.

About the Author

N.L. Holmes is the pen name of a professional archaeologist who received her doctorate from Bryn Mawr College. She has excavated in Greece and in Israel and taught ancient history and humanities at the university level for many years. She has always had a passion for books, and in childhood, she and her cousin (also an author today) used to write stories for fun. Married, with a grown son and three cats, she splits her time between Florida and northern France, where she likes to weave, garden, play the violin... and, of course, read.

Read more at https://www.nlholmes.com/.

About the Publisher

Dear Reader,

We hope you enjoyed this book. Please consider leaving a review on your favorite book site.

Visit https://RedAdeptPublishing.com to see our entire catalogue.

Check out our app for short stories, articles, and interviews. You'll also be notified of future releases and special sales.